Tinker's Plague

TO TIM
NO STARSHIPS OR DESERT
WORLDS BUT FUN NONE
THE LESS

Tinker's Plague

Stephen B. Pearl

Draumr Publishing, LLC
Maryland

Tinker's Plague

Cover art by Alayna Lemmer.

ISBN: 978-1-933157-30-6
PUBLISHED BY DRAUMR PUBLISHING, LLC
www.draumrpublishing.com
Columbia, Maryland

Printed in the United States of America

Dedication

I want to dedicate this book first to my wife, Joy, without whose love and support it would never have come into being. You are my muse and my beloved. Without you there would be no water to drink or air to breathe, no colours in a world gone grey. You are the philosopher's stone that takes the lead of my existence and transmutes it into the gold of life. Simply said, I love you.

I would also like to honour my late father, Vernon W. Pearl, who taught me a simple truth that pervades this book. If a man has done it, then a man can do it! Knowledge and skill are power there for the taking. Open your mind and reach out your hand.

Acknowledgments

Many people have helped refine my writing, from teachers in creative writing classes to people I eaves dropped on in coffee shops to try and get a sense of character voice. I thank you all, but especially I wish to thank the following:

Fran Wobbler, your critique and expertise in pathology and horse care were invaluable.

Kim Ophine and Mark Aldiss from my face to face writers' group, your input on all my works has made them stronger and shaped the writer I've become.

Andrew Burt and all the members of the Critters on-line writers' group who told me where I was going wrong so often, it penetrated my rather thick scull and necessary changes were made.

Gisela Sherman, your class opened my eyes to where I was going wrong.

Melodie Campbell, whose class let me see that my writing, while rough, had potential and helped me learn to polish the work.

Finally, a special thanks to the town of Eden Mills. Your beauty and old-world charm touched my heart, and your dedication to the principal of a zero-carbon footprint has earned my respect.

Chapter One

Knife Healing

THE BOY SPRINTED along the crumbling asphalt road, his twisted left arm flailing in his haste. He scrambled over a wooden gate and ran to an ancient van sitting in a field. A tower of interlocking pipes topped with a windmill rose from the van's back corner. Thin-film solar panels covered its roof and sides. Gasping, the boy wailed, "*Tinker!*"

The van's backdoor opened to reveal a man dressed in light, hemp clothing. His blond hair peeked out from under a wide-brimmed hat.

"What is it?" he asked, donning a pair of mirrored sunglasses.

The boy tried to explain, but all that came past his cleft palate was a babble.

"Slow down. I can't understand you," said the tinker. Stepping from the van, he touched the boy's shoulder. "Take some deep breaths and try again."

Trembling, the boy obeyed.

"It's me maw, she's a dyin'. Meb says she needs a doctor, like in Gridtown, but we ain't got none. Youse a tinker, Meb says maybe youse can 'elp. Da says 'e'll pay. Please, Tinker, save me maw."

"Meb, the midwife from the village sent you?"

"Yeah."

"You're Greg Thomson's boy. I remember you from last year."

"Yeah. Please, Tinker, youse gotta 'elps me maw."

"Is your mother having a baby?"

"Yeah. Meb ses it's what's killin' 'er."

"Damn it, I told Thomson to stop having kids. All right, run to the James' place. Have one of them hitch my team and bring my wagon to your house. I'll grab my med kit and go straight there."

"Thank youse, Tinker, thank youse." The child sprinted toward the main road.

"Damn Thomson! How many monsters will it take for him to accept the obvious?" The tinker entered the van emerging seconds later with a pack on his back and a laptop computer in his hand.

Could be a malpresentation, or an umbilical tangle. Probably a foetal malformation knowing Thomson's seed, he thought as he started down the road.

Five minutes later he approached the farmhouse of the Thomson clan. Its worn, vinyl siding had torn from the walls in many places, exposing the styrofoam beneath. Boarded-over windows made its two stories seem taller. The outbuildings looked ready to collapse. Despite the warm, spring day, smoke flowed from the chimney.

"Tinker," called a well-shaped girl with delicate features standing on the porch. She wore a homespun shirt, leggings and leather sandals.

"Where's Mrs. Thomson?" asked the tinker.

"I'll take you." The girl led the way into the house. Dim light entered around the boards covering the smashed windows, highlighting years of filth and neglect. Deformed children stared at the tinker as he passed them.

"I'm Meb's granddaughter, Carla. Thanks for coming. Grandma said Mrs. Thomson's in a bad way. She said it's a malpresentation, but she can't find an arm or leg to turn the baby." The girl pulled a strand of her long, ebony hair away from her dark-blue eyes.

"I'll do what I can. By the way, I'm Brad." He removed his sunglasses to reveal piercing, blue eyes.

Carla led the way up a creaky staircase to a room containing a narrow bed and a birthing stool. A woman, with grey-streaked, black hair and a distended belly, lay naked on the bed. Her body was covered with bruises. She screamed, displaying that she was missing several teeth. A handsome, grey-haired woman, dressed in a cream smock, massaged the pregnant woman's abdomen and spoke soothingly. A fat man, in a tattered suit, sat on a stool in the corner. He chewed on the end of an unlit pipe and scowled.

"Grandmother, the tinker's here," said Carla.

"Brad, thank all the Goddesses you came. Damn lucky I spotted your windmill on my way here. I'm in over my head," said the grey-haired woman.

"Carla told me. Let me have a look." Brad set his laptop on the floor and removed his pack.

Mr. Thomson rose from his stool and moved to stand in front of the tinker. His harsh features reflected hatred and distrust. Brad noted the discolouration spreading over the shorter man's bald scalp.

"I's don't trust youse, Tinker," snarled Thomson. "Youse save me Emily and I'll pay. Youse don't and I's don't. And no funny business."

"Get out of my way. This wouldn't be happening if you had half a brain." Brad pushed past the shorter man. "Okay, Emily, I'm going to check some things."

"It hurts, it hurts. *No!*" She screamed, as a contraction ripped across her belly.

"Meb, my stethoscope please. Thomson, rip the wood off the window, so I can see what I'm doing." Brad gestured to a sheet of plywood nailed to the wall.

Muttering, Thomson complied.

Minutes later the examination was complete. Brad returned his portable sonogram to his pack and prepared a shot.

"This will knock her out and stop the labour. The foetus is already dead."

"Youse got to save me child, Tinker," snapped Mr. Thomson.

"It's dead. I doubt that it was ever really alive. It looks like a lump of flesh, more tumour than child. I told you, Thomson, your seed is poisoned. The water from your well is a mess."

"Tinker lies. Water's water, youse drinks it. All youse tinkers wants is to sell them phoney stills. I'll not—"

Thomson's tirade was cut short by his wife's scream. Brad pressed a needle into the woman's vein. Seconds later she was unconscious.

"Thomson, bring in a table. The only way to save her is to remove the growth."

"She'll still be a woman when youse done, won'ts she?"

"If by that asinine statement you mean, will she be able to have children? No!"

"Youse lie, Tinker. 'ealers cleans out growths and women 'ave babies. I's knows a woman from Brookville 'ad it done. Alls youse want is to take away me manhood. Make it so's I's can't 'ave no more children. Youse won't."

"Listen to me, Thomson. Maybe a healer could leave her womb strong enough that she could deliver normally next time. I'm not a healer, I'm a tinker. It's going to push what I know to the limit to save her life. Get me that table, or your wife is as good as dead. As soon as that sedative wears off, she'll start pushing again. It won't take her long to burst her uterus."

"'Er whats?" demanded Thomson.

"The sack the baby's in," supplied Meb.

"The growth's in," corrected Brad.

"I'll get youse table," snarled Thomson as he stamped from the room.

"What are her chances?" asked Meb.

Brad pulled a data cube from his med kit and inserted it into his laptop. "With a healer, ninety-nine to one she'd live. With me, maybe fifty-fifty. If I'd taken an extra surgical elective at the Academy, she'd be better off. Get some blocks and ropes, so we can elevate the table's foot. Boil some towels, and see if there's a clean sheet in this place. Also, check that my wagon's arrived. I'll need a power cable from it for my instruments."

"I'll have Carla throw it to me." Meb left the room. Brad pressed several keys on his computer and began reviewing texts on surgical technique.

Fifteen minutes later Meb returned and, leaning out the window, caught an electrical cord and pulled it into the room. Shortly after that Thomson entered, carrying one end of a battered table. Carla carried the other.

"The towels are boiling, and Jeremy is bringing up a clean sheet," announced Meb.

"Good. The blocks and ropes?" asked Brad.

"I'll fetch them." Carla ran from the room.

"Thomson, you're with me. I need a pack mule." Brad snatched up his laptop and left the room.

Thomson followed, stopping at the door to Brad's wagon. A heavyset, older man, dressed in homespun, wearing a broad-brimmed hat and dark sunglasses, waited by the battered van.

"Hello, Tinker, Greg. How's she doing?"

"Not well, Mr. James." Brad scanned the pasture where his four mares grazed.

"I locked down your windmill before moving her and loosed your team while I was waiting. Do you need anything else?"

"Not that I can think of. Thanks for bringing my wagon, but for now you'll have to forgive me." Brad climbed into his van.

"Certainly." Mr. James started toward the road.

Brad emerged carrying a toaster oven, spotlight, electric razor and portable respirator. "Take these to your wife's room. Tell Meb to prep the gear. I'll be up in a minute."

With a grunt Thomson moved to obey.

Reopening his laptop, Brad sat on his rear bumper and continued to review his data cube. When he returned to the impromptu operating room his surgical tools were in the toaster oven, and Meb was shaving Emily.

"Meb, you are a wonder." Brad lifted the unconscious woman onto the table and secured her in place with the ropes.

"Do you think she'll come to?"

"No, but once she's open, we'll have to tilt up the table. It will make her guts fall up out of the way. Tell Thomson to put a rag over his ugly mug and get in here. We'll need Carla to slide the blocks in place when he lifts the table."

"I'll tell them."

"Good. I'll intubate her and set up the respirator while you do that. Last thing I need is her puking into her lungs."

"I wish I knew how to intubate. Who would have thought a tube down the throat could save so many lives?"

Minutes later Meb returned with Thomson and Carla.

"Youse ready to do somethin' now, Tinker?" snarled Thomson.

"Once you've tied a cloth over your mouth. There's no point in saving her with an operation to have her die of an infection."

Thomson snorted but tied a damp, clean handkerchief over his mouth and nose.

"Meb, scrub with me. You're my sterile nurse.

"Carla, you're my grunge nurse. That means you deal with any dirty stuff. Clear?"

"Clear."

They scrubbed. Meb moved to stand between the instruments in the toaster oven and Brad.

"Here we go," said Brad. "Bloodless scalpel."

Meb passed him the end of the fibre optic tube. Setting it against Emily's abdomen he pressed its button. A flicker of laser light pierced the flesh, which peeled back to reveal the fat beneath. Brad extended the cut to just above the mons Veneris.

He cut through other layers of flesh, dragging them aside with retractors.

"Carla, shine the light into the wound. Meb, a regular scalpel. I don't want to risk burning the intestines when I open the peritoneum." The knife cut clean, and the uterus bulged up from the incision.

"Taweret! It's huge," swore Meb.

"Worse than that. It has to come out."

"What? Why?" demanded Thomson.

"Those white things piercing the muscle wall. They're claws. The foetus is a mutation. I can't separate it from the surrounding tissue. Meb, I'll need four clamps to seal the uterine arteries.

"Thomson, lift the foot of the table."

"Youse can'ts take 'er... 'er... the sack baby grows in!" snarled Thomson.

"I can and will. I pray the creature in there didn't do any more damage than I can see. Now lift this damn table!"

Teeth gritted, Thomson obeyed while Carla placed the blocks.

"Carla, wipe my brow. I'm sweating like a pig." With hands held steady by an act of will, Brad clamped the uterine arteries and separated them with the bloodless scalpel, cauterizing the wound. Two more cuts and the fallopian tubes separated. Drawing the bloated uterus to one side, he cut its connection to the bladder then the cervix and lifted it out.

"That has it." Brad glanced around the room. Thomson leaned against the wall, white as a sheet. "Get out of here Thomson, before you faint!"

Silently the farmer shuffled from the room.

"I have to close now. Curved needle, with the white thread. That's the one the body will absorb."

"Good work." Meb passed him the needle.

"I'll believe that when she's back on her feet."

When the operation was over, they returned Emily to the bed and removed the intubation tube.

"She'll probably sleep for a few more hours, but she mustn't get up for at least a week," explained Brad as they moved his equipment into the hall. "Can you get one of her kids to watch her until she wakes up?"

"I'll see to it. I tossed your power cable out the window."

"Thanks, Meb. Did you save the uterus?"

"Yes. Are you going to do what I think you're going to do?"

"Probably."

"I want to be there."

"What are you two talking about?" asked Carla.

"I've been after Thomson for years to stop fathering children. His seed is polluted."

"He tries to spread it around enough. He's been after me since I turned thirteen."

"I can't fault his taste," remarked Brad.

Carla blushed.

"Now, Brad. Carla is my granddaughter. Have the decency to seduce her behind my back," interrupted Meb.

"Grandmother!" Carla's blush deepened.

"Tell me, Meb, are all the women of your line beautiful, or

does it skip a generation?"

"Brad, if I were twenty-years younger." Meb grew serious. "We should confront Thomson. I worry about his oldest girl, she's just entering puberty, and with Emily infertile..."

"He's that twisted?"

"Yes he is! Nick wanted the town council to take his children from him, but we don't think anything has happened yet. Even if he fathered a child on his daughter, how could we prove it without gene testing?"

"If we can scare Thomson off long enough, he won't get the chance."

"What do you mean?" asked Carla

"That rash on his scalp. Skin cancer. Not breeding wasn't the only advice he refused to listen to. He doesn't wear a hat in the sun, and he refuses to get a still to clean his water."

"I saw it to. My guess is in six months, Emily will finally have a proper chance to heal." Meb shook her head.

Brad stared at the floor. "I noticed the bruises. Men like Greg make me embarrassed for my gender."

Meb looked at Carla as she spoke. "Fortunately, they are the exception, and women can be every bit as bad."

Carla rolled her eyes.

Brad shrugged. "Carla, if you would move my gear to my wagon, your grandmother and have an unpleasant task to perform."

Chapter Two

The Inn

MEB LED BRAD down the stairs and into the dining room. The dirty, drywall was holed in several places, and the smells of cabbage and urine lingered in the air. Thomson sat at a table made from planks supported by crates.

"We brought you something to look at," said Brad.

"Don'ts want to see it," snarled Thomson.

"Who cares?" Brad set the uterus on the table.

"It is your child. Don't you want to know if it was a boy or a girl?" asked Meb.

"Youse done youse work. Leaves my 'ouse," demanded Thomson.

"You haven't paid me yet," said Brad. Opening a clipped scabbard, on his belt, he pulled out a utility knife and sliced the uterus, revealing the corpse.

"Look Mr. Thomson," ordered Meb.

"Yes. Look at your son, Thomson. I told you, your seed is poison. Now you see its results, again! Stop breeding. Look at the abomination that almost killed your wife."

Thomson's eyes focussed on the twisted corpse. The arms and legs were stumps, ending in long, curved claws, while the skin was scaly. The face was a mass of flesh, save for the mouth, which was thrown open in silent torment.

"No. Takes it away. It's 'er fault. If she weren't such a sinful woman, we's wouldn't be cursed like this."

"It has nothing to do with sin or virtue. It's the water you drink, the food you eat, the air you breathe. Thomson, your parents came from a Gridtown. They must have told you Gridtowners treat their water. We Novo Gaians do the same thing," said Brad.

"No, no, no. Tinker, lies! Gets out. I won't pays youse. Youse failed. Emily ain't no woman no more."

"You'll pay me! You can't afford to be red Teed," observed Brad.

"Youse wouldn't?"

"You will pay me, or no one but a Gridtowner will ever trade with you again."

Thomson shifted uncomfortably in his chair, the corpse on the table forgotten. With a grunt he stood.

"Come on. I's 'ave somit youse want."

"I'll go see how Carla's doing," said Meb.

"Could you repack my wagon and hitch my team? I'll give you a lift back to town once I'm paid," said Brad.

"Of course."

Brad followed Thomson into the yard. Piles of manure covered half of the weed-infested grass.

"Bloody waste. A methane composter and your cattle would heat your house and water for you Thomson."

"Shut up, Tinker! We Thomsons are decent folk. I'll not 'ave any of youse tinker filth on my farm." Thomson led the way to a rickety barn and pulled open its door. The inside was stuffy, and the smell of animals permeated the air.

"It's over 'ere," he said, pulling back a tarp in the corner.

Brad inhaled sharply. A jumble of laser disks, a pair of computers, complete with screens, printers and scanners, three televisions, a stereo and an assortment of other electronics formed a pile on the floor. "There's enough here to pay for solar panels, windmills, water purifiers!"

"I's don't trade with tinkers, and my daddy told me never to trade anything but cattle with Gridtowners. Said they'd take me if

I's tried. 'ow much?"

"If it works, one computer system."

"'Alf a system."

"One system. That's my price, and it's fair!"

Thomson glared at Brad, his beady, brown eyes gauging the tinker. "One system, takes it and go." He stomped from the barn.

Minutes later Brad stood by his wagon connecting the last bus feed and plugging the system into his A.C. power inverter. He threw the activation switch. The flat screen fought its way to life then a cursor appeared.

"Is that good?" asked Meb.

"The memory was scrambled." Brad inserted a data cube. A minute later the screen filled with stats, followed by 'system okay.'

"It's alive," cried Brad. Carla laughed.

"Well Dr. Frankenstein, you said something about a lift into town," remarked Meb.

"Of course." Brad opened the back door of his wagon and motioned for the women to enter. He followed them, after loading the computer.

Just past the door was a toilet stall beyond which was a table flanked by bench-seats. Past that, on one side, was a built-in desk and chair, with a flat screen above the desktop. A video player recorder hung above the screen. Opposite the desk was a small fridge, topped by a sink and a two-burner stove. A toaster oven was clipped to the ceiling above the sink. A walkway, flanked by floor to ceiling cupboards, led to the driver's section of the van. A bench-seat, with the middle of its back cut away, spanned the vehicle's width. The windscreen had been replaced with shutters, which stood open. A set of reins dangled in place of the steering wheel. The dash was a mass of switches and gauges.

"It's amazing," breathed Carla.

"We could have used the side doors, Brad. I'm getting too old to stoop over and shuffle through your wagon, so you can impress my granddaughter," scolded Meb.

"Sorry, Meb." Brad grinned.

Carla sat in the middle of the bench-seat; Brad let his fingers trail over her shoulders as he passed her.

"That operation killed my battery's charge. I'll have to eat at the inn tonight," he said, checking a gauge on the dashboard.

"Here it comes," said Meb.

"What?" asked Carla.

"My girl, there are a few things that never change. Water is wet, the sun will rise, and tinkers hate cooking! Our good tinker is fishing for a dinner invitation. Sorry, I'll be eating at the inn myself."

"Meb, you wound me. I was about to ask if you two would join me," objected Brad. He started his team moving.

"I will," said Carla.

"Your mother's expecting you home before sunset. You'll barely make it as it is. I'll keep Brad company for you."

"But Grandmother."

"You can see him tomorrow. How long will you be staying this trip, Brad?"

"Well, I have to install two more solar strips and another battery pack at the inn, set up a basic system at the James' place, install a solar still at the Sungs'. Then there's the incidentals, and the clinic tomorrow if John can spare Billy to spread the word. Anything I should keep an eye out for during that?"

"Not really. Cancer's down, now that the stills are catching on," said Meb.

"Can I help with the clinic? I want to be a healer," said Carla.

"I don't have a problem with that." Brad laid his hand on her knee. Carla blushed and smiled.

"Better not let Michelle catch you acting like that," observed Meb.

"Michelle doesn't own me. And since when did you care what she thought?" countered Carla.

Meb smirked.

Brad stared at the women, shrugged then looked out the window. The road was flanked by second-growth forest that was occasionally cut back to reveal farmsteads. Slowly the scenery changed as boxlike, twenty-first-century houses took the place of the trees. Here the potholes had been filled with broken brick.

"Always amazes me how many people lived in Dark Lands' towns before the collapse," observed Brad.

"Are Bright Lands' towns different?" asked Carla.

"I can only speak to Novo Gaian towns. I've never visited the United Grid Regions. I tried to one summer. I wanted to see the Niagara cliffs, where the falls were before they diverted all the water to power generation, but they wouldn't give me a visitor's Visa."

"Okay then, are Novo Gaian towns different?" An exasperated expression crossed Carla's face.

Brad smiled. "Yes. We've reshaped our towns to respect nature and use the sun and wind for power.

"It's a point of pride with us that while the United Grid Regions own all the large, hydroelectric plants, we support a population equal to theirs using our smaller facilities.

"By the by, where do you live?" They were approaching a fork in the road.

"Drop me here, my house is just around the corner."

"As you wish." Brad reined the horses to a stop.

Meb opened the door beside her and climbed from the van, letting Carla exit.

"See you tomorrow, Carla. I'll do the clinic at your Grandmother's, if it's okay with you, Meb?"

"Of course it is. We do it there every year. Is about ten o'clock good?" Meb re-entered the van.

"Sure."

"I'll see you tomorrow, Brad. Bye grandma." Carla blew a kiss toward the wagon.

"Who do you think she meant that for?" asked Brad, as his team resumed their slow progress.

"Probably you; I'm glad to see it."

"Problems?"

"She's been stepping out with this girl from down the street, Michelle. I don't like it!"

Brad lifted an eyebrow. "Speaking as a man, it is a pity that a lass as pretty as Carla prefers women, but it's her choice."

"I know that! I wouldn't mind except she's so young. She doesn't really know what she likes, but you know small towns. Get marked as liking women; the boys stop trying. It becomes a self-fulfilling prophecy. Besides, Michelle isn't the right life mate for Carla."

"Oh?"

"You saw her today. Carla's smart! Michelle's not as bright as some. She'll be fine working a farm or waiting tables, but Carla can do better. She wants to be a healer, and she could do it. She's read all my old medical books and she remembers."

"That's good. There'll be someone to take your place when you retire."

Meb grinned. "She can do better than that. I want to send her to the Novo Gaian academy."

Brad whistled. "Wish I could help, but the cost of training a Dark Lander!"

"I can afford it. I think? Keep some time open after the clinic."

Brad smiled. "You found a cache?"

"Tomorrow. My biggest concern is getting her to the academy."

"Meb. Meb. Meb. I'll take Carla. You should know all you have to do is ask. Shorting, I'll even let her do the high school equivalency exam on my computer, free. Don't spread it around. I don't like people to think I play favourites."

"Everyone will just think you're having your wicked way with Carla. Probably be right, if you're half the lech I think you are. Do her good to walk the right side of the street."

Brad coughed, blushed then exclaimed, "We're here!" He stopped the horses at the side of the road. In front of them was a pair of two story houses, joined at the second floor by a covered walkway. The south face of the structure was mostly glass, and the metal roof sported a collection of thin-film, solar panels glued to its surface. A solar still rose the height of the central causeway. A woman scurried between a methane oven and table, beneath the walkway, carrying plates of food.

"I remember this place before you tinkers showed up. Ugly! Eddie sure made a change here. Facing those shacks with stone makes them look like fairytale towers."

"Standard procedure. Get the common-house to advertise what you can do. Besides, Eden Mills is such a pretty place; it should be preserved. The mill is its wealth, but the buildings are its spirit."

Brad indicated the fieldstone mill then expanded the gesture to encompass the main street. The well-spaced, stone and wood shops occupied an island made by the river and the millstream. The river valley rose on both sides, and a pair of bridges supported the street. Past the mill the road turned sharply left, paralleling the river, until it climbed onto the flat land above. A set of stocks stood empty in front of the general store.

"It is pretty, once you get past the twenty-first-century dross," agreed Meb.

They walked to the sliding, glass door that formed the inn's entrance. It stood open, and voices spilled onto the street.

The common-room filled the south side of the main floor and was littered with wooden tables. A bar counter stood beside a masonry fireplace at the back of the room, with a kitchen visible behind it. A tall, slender man, dressed in a blue shirt, slacks and an apron, leaned against the bar. Two sets of stairs, one above the other, lined the wall of the common-room opposite the bar. A heavy, wooden door stood closed on the wall behind the stairs.

"Just my luck. I hate crowds." Brad took a deep breath bracing himself.

"Tinker," called the man in the apron who moved to greet Brad.

"Hi John, got some food for a pair of weary folk?"

"Well, I'll tell you. I wish you'd come yesterday. I'm full up; inn and bar. Had a group came down the Eramosa river from Ospringe. By the by, Meb. That salve you gave Milly for her leg is a wonder." John wiped sweat from his bald pate with a handkerchief.

"That's good. All we need is a bite. Can't you squeeze us in?" asked Meb.

"Tell you what. I've got a couple of tables left in the viewing room. I'll set you up there, no extra charge."

"Thanks. Could you send your boy to see to my horses? Put everything on my tab." Brad started up the stairs.

"Not a problem." Raising his voice so everyone in the bar could hear, John added, "Tinkers always pay what they owe."

The stairway ended in a room similar to the one below, save that the hearth was only a chimney. A flat-screen television, one metre across, hung on the west wall. A pre-collapse program filled the screen. All the tables near the front of the room were crowded with mesmerized viewers.

"Hard to believe the ancestors accomplished so much watching that thing all the time," observed Meb, as they took seats at a table at the back of the room.

"People's opiate. The novelty wears off. I'd guess most of these folk have never seen a working television before."

"That's not a bad thing. Milly's meat pies are still the best thing on the menu. Stay away from the goldenrod wine. I keep hoping John will run it through his still. The only thing it's good for is lamp fuel."

"Nice to know my efforts are appreciated. I sold him that still."

"I know. You should have heard the Gridtown traders curse when people stopped buying flashlights. That reminds me, I need a new wick for my alcohol lantern."

"For you, Meb, at cost..."

"Sure. Come to my inn and don't say hello. All I'm good for is cooking the food and scrubbing the pots," interrupted a plump, middle-aged woman. Her dark hair was pulled into a bun, and she wore a cotton dress and greasy apron.

"Please, Milly, will you ever forgive me," pleaded Brad in mock distress.

"You watch this one, Meb. Best keep him away from that granddaughter of yours. His seed may be clean, but he's a charmer."

"The novelty wears off," quipped Meb.

"Milly love, I've three tables waiting on dinner, and I think something's burning," called John from the foot of the stairs.

"Dear man, good husband, fair brewer, horrible cook. I have to go. I sent Billy to fetch Vicky. Her baby was born three months ago, and he's just perfect. Figured you'd like to see him."

"Thanks," said Brad, to the woman's retreating back.

"They don't understand," said Meb, in reply to the look on his face.

The food arrived and was eaten, leaving Brad to lean back with a clay tankard of cider, while Meb sipped at a dark ale. The program on the television changed. Brad's ears perked as the introduction music played. A voice-over began.

"The collapse, a time of darkness and despair. The thronging masses, glutted on energy pulled from the earth, could find no more. Warring nations decimated the land as they fought over the remaining scraps. Unthinking mobs rioted as the rising seas drove refugees into the inland cities over burdening them. Droughts, brought on by the changing climate decimated the crops, spreading starvation throughout the land. Plagues raced through the populace. The environment itself teetered on the edge of collapse, as global warming and toxic waste fouled all they touched. Into this world came a new type of hero. A new type of champion. This was the world of the *Collapse Police*."

The music continued as scenes of uniformed men and women shooting menacing-looking thugs paraded across the screen.

"New show?" asked Meb.

"I've read about it. It's a Gridtown production. Propaganda."

"I've never understood why plagues became such a problem."

"The ancients used a lot of energy to clean their water. When the generators stopped turning, people still had to drink. The pollution was unbelievable. My grandfather was in his teens. He remembers drawing water from a river with bodies floating down it."

"Birr. It's hard to believe that's still living memory," observed Meb.

A plump, red-haired woman, carrying a baby, climbed the stairs. A heavily-muscled man with Nordic features followed her. They were both dressed in hemp clothing.

"Vicky, Nick," greeted Brad.

"Hello, Brad." The woman spoke in a light alto, with a touch of come hither.

"Hi, Brad." Nick fingered a tin badge pinned at his collar.

"I think I should go now," observed Meb.

"But," began Brad as she stood.

"It's late, and we have the clinic tomorrow." She descended the stairs.

"I thought you might like to see Jarod," said Vicky.

"You and Nick have a fine looking son," remarked Brad, emphasizing the Nick.

"Yes we do," agreed Nick, a trace of anger in his voice.

"What can I do for you?"

"Oh nothing. I just thought that since Jarod came from your seed you should see him. I mean, real men do like to see their offspring," remarked Vicky.

"He's got no claim on me. Cute kid, but I just gave the seed. Nick is his father."

"Father of monsters you mean."

Brad inhaled deeply before speaking.

"Vicky, Nick's seed is poisoned. Your miscarriages and those tests I had done for him proved that. You both told me you wanted a child, so I gave you my seed. Stop beating Nick up over it, or you'll lose him. He's a good man. He doesn't deserve to be punished for something that isn't his fault. The only tie, Jarod was it?"

"Yes."

"The only tie Jarod has to me is that medical file I left with you. In another seven years I'll finish my term on this route, after that he'll probably never see me again. Nick is his father.

"It was good seeing you both, but I have to be going. Busy day tomorrow." Brad stood and moved to the stair.

"Thank you, Tinker." Nick slipped a comforting arm over the shoulders of his subdued wife.

Chapter Three

Clinic

BRAD LEFT THE inn and sadly whispered an apprentice's teaching rhyme.

"Tinker seed is clean seed.
In poisoned land now take thee heed.
Father to many, parent to none.
Heed this wisdom, tinker run.
Let not your heart to child go.
For family ties are traveller's foe."

Down the street he saw a house where electric lights glittered as behind him the sound of a pre-collapse song wafted through the open window of the inn's music room.

"Get over it, Brad," he grumbled. In his wagon, he lowered the table between the bench-seats to form a bed.

The next morning Brad rolled over and groaned, but the pounding didn't disappear. Opening his eyes, he saw light through the curtains at the foot of his bed.

"All right, all right. I'm coming," he snapped. After pulling on his pants he unclipped the strap on his belt holster and opened the door a crack. A boy of twelve stood holding a tray in one hand. A hat covered his head, and mirror sunglasses protected his eyes.

His blue shirt and slacks were clean but patched.

"Billy, did your mother send you?" Brad re-clipped his holster strap.

"She told me to wake you at eight-thirty. I figured you'd want some breakfast."

"Good as wattage. Milly's the best cook on my route. How are my team?"

"I groomed them, Tinker, and gave them a good feed of oats."

"You did well by them. Could you fetch two of them here, and when you get a minute take the others to the visitors' field?"

"Sure, Tinker. I heard you were doing a clinic today. My cat needs his booster."

"We'll consider it your tip."

Half an hour later, Brad sat in the driver's seat of his van the horses waiting at the rein. Glancing at the chronometer in his dash he muttered sarcastically "Nine-twenty, better call mother."

He activated the short wave in his dashboard and tuned to the official frequency. Pressing the mic's button, he spoke.

"Tinker, Tinker, Tinker, Check in, Check in, Check in. Over."

The radio crackled to life.

"Home, Home, Home. We read you tinker, proceed with Ident. Over."

With a disgusted look Brad replied. "B zero, R nine, A twenty, D two, L two, Y one, I zero, R four, V one, I zero, N seven, G PC. Over."

"Ident confirmed. How's it hanging, 'Bradly'? Over."

"Slightly to the right, 'Edward'. I'm still at Eden Mills. Meb tells me cancer's down. I'll be doing the clinic today. By the by, she says hello. Temperature's at twelve degrees C and rising, barometer's at one hundred and steady. Humidity's 60 percent. I see some light cirrus cloud in an otherwise blue sky. Ground breeze is from the south at ten klicks. Over."

"Got ya. Meteorology is predicting clear and cool for the next three days, with no chance of rain. Over."

"So I can expect it to pour. Damn those Japanese butterflies and their infernal flapping! Over."

"Watch the language, Brad. Over."

"Sorry home. Signing off. Over and out."

"Call in acknowledged. Say Hi to Meb for me. Home over and out."

Turning off the short wave Brad clucked to his horses and started along the street. Minutes later he crested the edge of the river valley and turned down a dirt track, stopping in front of an earth-shelter home with large, south-facing windows. A solar still ran up the southwest face of the structure, while a solar, hot-water pre-heater and several thin-film solar-electric panels formed a canopy over the windows. About twenty people sat on blankets in front of the structure. Exiting his van, he tied his horses to the hitching post.

"Once my gear's in Meb's examination room I'll get started." Brad passed his med kits to the helpful hands that besieged him.

"About time you arrived," snapped Meb from her doorway.

"Hi, Brad," called Carla from behind her grandmother. Brad led the people carrying his gear into Meb's examination room. In the corner was a birthing stool. An ancient massage table, re-upholstered in thick leather, occupied the centre of the room. A hot plate, kettle and pot were on a table in the corner, and shelves on the east wall were filled with books and sealed glass jars of herbs. A porcelain sink stood against the west wall.

"I'm not late, am I?" asked Brad.

"Not yet, but you left damn little time to get everything set up," said Meb.

"Don't need much time with two beautiful women helping me."

"Honestly, Brad!" Meb put the instruments to boil.

In minutes everything was arranged.

Brad, glanced at his watch. "Ten on the nose."

"Good, now maybe we can get started?" said Meb.

"Of course. Carla, you're my nurse. Meb, would you activate the outside speaker on my wagon. I tuned my radio to an entertainment station before I arrived. With the sun so bright, I can spare the watts to give folk a treat."

"And get half the town to come for a check up so they can listen. Tinker tricks."

"Marketing strategy. Besides, it's the only way some of them will come for a booster. Oh yes, could you ask one of them to unhitch my team. That is, if you don't mind them grazing?"

"Of course." Meb left. A moment later a bony woman with stringy, blonde hair entered. She was carrying a bolt of cloth, and her bloodshot, blue eyes had a pleading quality.

"That's Colleen McPherson," whispered Carla.

"Hello Colleen, what can I do for you?" Brad smiled winningly.

"I need your help, Tinker. It, well, I have... There was this Gridtown trader, and well... He seemed nice. He said he really loved me. We well... You know. And I haven't been right since. I always have to pee, and I'm puffy and sore down there."

"Get up on the table," said Brad. The examination commenced. Minutes later Brad was spreading a smear on an Agar plate and placing it in a small rectangular box.

"Will that cure me?" asked Colleen.

"No, this is just my incubator. You'll have to come back this evening for treatment. This is important, have you... lain... with anyone since the Gridtowner?"

"No. He said he loved me. That he'd marry me and take me back to Gridtown. He said he could get me a job sorting trash mined from their dump for recycling. That's the only reason why."

"You mustn't lay with anyone for at least two moons. Do you understand?"

"Yes, Tinker."

"Good. Is the cloth my payment?"

"If you'll take it." Colleen unrolled a length of the material and held it out for inspection. The cloth was a heavy, tight-woven wool, died a deep blue.

"That will pay for the examination and tests. I'll need another like it for the treatment, if you have what I think you have."

"That's a lot, Tinker. Feel this cloth, it's very good. The fuller said it was as fine as he'd ever seen."

Brad cocked an eyebrow and Colleen collapsed in on herself.

"I have another bolt in green."

"That will do. Bring it when you come back this evening."

Hours later Brad took stock of his payments. In addition to a small heap of Gridtown credits and a handful of Novo Gaian marks, there were seven bolts of cloth and an assortment of electrical gear. He picked up one of the plastic Gridtown credits. It looked like a poker chip, emblazoned with the leaping fish crest of the Muskoka-grid-region.

"You know something, Carla. I'm too nice. That cloth is shorting, bulky. Usually I wouldn't take it on the out leg of my route, but this is medical; I feel bad saying no."

"Which is why we all love the tinkers so." Meb entered the room wiping her hands on a cloth. "I screened out the nothing cases. I can treat a cold with feverfew and lemon toddies as well as you can. Nice cloth, they usually only give me half a bolt."

"Price of my extensive education."

"I'll take the green one off your hands for a silver mark, if you'll throw in the wick for my lantern."

"You'll bankrupt me, Meb, but for you..." Brad smiled as she passed him the silver, plastic oval, impressed with the image of a black bear.

"Carla, be a dear and clean up. I have something I want to show, Brad."

"Grandmother?"

"Tell you what, Carla. When you're done, put on your best dress. I'm treating you to dinner and a movie," offered Brad.

"Really? okay. See you later." Carla's voice dropped slightly and fire sparkling in her eyes.

"Where did she learn that?" Brad followed Meb from her house.

"What?"

"That look that can turn a man to jelly on the spot."

"Heredity." Meb struck a pose that melted years off her and added a seductive lilt to her voice.

"A family of evil women to torture this poor, innocent, young tinker. Are you sure you follow Taweret and not Ishtar?"

Meb laughed as she began walking. "Well, you're a tinker at least. Innocent, I'll believe when I go ice skating in July. How old are you?"

"Thirty-two."

Meb stopped walking and stared at Brad. "You don't look it."

"I know, it gets to be a pain sometimes. Would you like me to back off with Carla? She is young."

Meb shook her head and led Brad into the nearby woods. "No, fourteen years doesn't mean much these days, besides, you're not the type a girl marries. You're the type she plays with for a while then thinks back on with a smile for the rest of her life. Carla deserves that, there's plenty of time for a husband and children later."

Brad blushed and stared at the ground. "So, umm, about this treasure trove you're taking me to?"

Meb grinned. "Never be embarrassed about the truth. Honesty is what keeps you from becoming a cad."

"Okay. But about my question?"

"Of course. I found this last autumn. I was cutting across country and literally tripped over it."

Meb stopped at a crumbling, asphalt ramp opening into the ground.

"How big is the chamber this leads to?" Brad's voice was anxious.

"It holds two old-style cars, with room to walk around them. Why?" Meb's face reflected concern.

Brad released his breath. "No reason."

Pulling a flashlight from a pouch on his belt, he descended the ramp into a basement garage. A pair of cars filled the space. A tool cupboard stood in one corner and a battered stereo occupied another. Video display panels covered one wall. Cobwebs hung from the rafters.

"Meb, you're rich." Brad moved to inspect the nearest vehicle. It was a rust-encrusted station wagon. A glance at the dash revealed a full stereo system and a cellular phone.

Moving to the second vehicle he saw it was a sports car, equipped with all the niceties of the late twenty-first-century.

"This one's a real find. Ceramic-turbine engine, sat-nav. uplink, auto-drive sensors, data-cube-CD player, fax, on-board computer, cell phone, full GPS."

With the enthusiasm of a child on his birthday Brad moved to the tool cupboard.

"Sockets, screw drivers, something I don't recognize, but it must be worth a lot," he remarked.

"Is it enough for Carla's education?"

"The tools should cover most of her first year. I can unload the D.C. audio equipment in the Dark Lands, so the tax office doesn't have to know about it. CDs and data cubes aren't the perma-burn verity, so they'll have degraded; I should be able to reformat them. Cell phones have to go in, unless I meet a Gridtowner who'll buy under the table. Hmm." Brad fell silent.

"Meb, this will pay for three years, maybe three and a half. Dark Lands Healer Cert. is a six-year program. Now if Carla's grades are good, she can apply to the S.D.A. for a grant."

"S.D.A.?"

"Society for Dark Lands Assistance. You could finish up your house with this and live well the rest of your days."

"This town needs a proper healer. There isn't one for kilometres about, and Carla needs an education."

"Fine. I'll take the tools and sound equipment this year; the rest over the next two. You can probably get a silver mark for the metal from the smith."

Meb nodded. "Good, I'll tell Carla she's leaving with you when you finish here."

"I could detour and pick her up this fall."

"Not a chance. I don't want Michelle persuading her to stay. She's going with you when you leave for Arkell! Besides, she should see a bit of the world."

A grin split Brad's face. "Well, I'm glad that's settled."

When they returned to Meb's house the sun had almost set, and a group of seven people were waiting by the door.

"Colleen, you first," said Brad. Returning to the examination room, he prepared a microscope slide. Slipping it into his unit he turned on the light and stared through the eyepiece. Looking up he entered data into his laptop. Writing scrolled across the screen, detailing disease and suggested treatment.

"Okay, you need a shot and some pills. Remember, no fooling around for two moons, and be sure to take all the pills," said Brad.

"Yes, Tinker." The woman added another bolt of cloth to the pile on the floor.

The last patient was leaving when a holler echoed through the house.

"Brad, Grandmother just told me. The Novo Gaian academy. I'm going," breathed Carla, bursting into the room.

Chapter Four

The Road

A WEEK LATER Brad stared at the thin-film, solar panels on the inn, pondering a question.

"No John, I think you'll still fall short around December. If you were out of town, I'd suggest a windmill, but you don't want those blades turning in town. They make a bloody racket."

"Well then, you better bring me another panel next year. What about my battery pack?" John gazed at the steel-grey sky.

"You don't need any more batteries. You've got plenty of storage. What you need is input."

"As I'm sure you do. Come have a bite before you leave."

"Carla's meeting me at my wagon."

"I'm sure." John smirked. "She's a lass, she'll be late. You might as well have a bite while we settle your bill, and I pay for next year's panel."

"As you say."

John led the way into the inn. The door to the back room stood open, and the sound of violins spilled out.

"I love this piece." John retrieved a plate of mixed sandwiches. "Most of the day I have to play what the customers like, but in the morning it's my choice. The Boston Philharmonic performs the

Four Seasons. Beautiful!"

"I could add some tracks to your music cube in lieu of my bill."

"Brad, you know I'm always up to a good barter, but Milly put her foot down. No music. It just doesn't bring in the customers the way it used to."

"How about a video?"

"CD or cube?"

"CD, it's not a perma-burn, but it should be more durable than a cube. I picked up a video cache of perma-burns last year and spent the winter making copies. The video's a Schwarzenegger."

"Do I have it? Has it been on the air lately?"

"Gridtowns won't play it, it's about a rebellion. I checked the long-term schedule for the Kimberley station in Novo Gaia. It's not scheduled within the next two years. The show's called Total Recall, classic Arnold."

"I'll make twice your tab the first Saturday I play it. You have a deal, Tinker. Oh yes, and here." John pressed a small pouch into Brad's hand. Opening it, Brad counted two gold and three silver Novo Gaian marks.

"That's the panel all right. Remember the price from last year?"

"And the year before. I like electricity, but I'm beginning to think I'm building the system for Billy."

Brad smiled and took a sandwich. Minutes later they arrived at the visitors' field to find Carla and a slender girl with short, blonde hair hitching Brad's team.

"You're late," said Carla.

"I took some bad advice." Brad retrieved a CD from his van and passed it to John.

"You won't go selling other copies of this to Frank in Arkell, will you? I get a lot of business from there," said John.

"You have the only copy I'll sell for the next three towns," assured Brad.

"Good. See you next year." John eyed his prize then left with a wave of his hand.

"Brad, this is Michelle," said Carla, as Brad inspected the hitch that held a gutted truck to his van. Satisfied that his cargo trailer was secure, he turned to the blonde girl.

"Hello."

"You bastard! You're taking her away from me." Michelle's open palm connected with Brad's cheek.

"Michelle!" gasped Carla.

Brad's face reddened as he ground his teeth. Walking away he started checking his tack.

"He is. He deserved it!"

"Michelle. I'm going to school to be a healer. This is important to me," said Carla.

"I'm losing you. Don't go. Stay with me. We can have a life together. Remember all the things we talked about."

Carla looked from Michelle to Brad. "I have to do this. If you loved me, you'd understand. I can be a healer. A real healer!"

"Your bitch grandmother did this. She hates me!"

Carla looked at the ground.

"We have to go," Brad said evenly, moving to enter his van.

"I have to go, Michelle." Carla took the sobbing girl into her arms. They kissed then Carla turned and picked up her bag.

"Don't go!" sobbed Michelle, grasping Carla's arm.

"Stay here, and if you love me, don't try and follow the wagon. It's hard enough saying goodbye." Carla climbed into the van.

Brad clucked and the team began their slow progress. In his rear-view mirror he saw Michelle, tears running over her face, her hands balled into fists. Carla stared out the window looking thoughtful.

Nearly an hour passed before he broke the silence.

"Carla, I hate to bother you. I know you're upset, but I'd appreciate it, if you'd fake a smile when we reach Arkell. You look upset. People might think the worst."

Carla looked at him and smiled. "More thoughtful really. Don't tell my grandmother, but this is kind of a relief."

"Oh." Brad examined Carla's face.

"I've been thinking of breaking up with Michelle for a while. I just didn't know how to tell her. When we were younger it was fun and new, but lately... I hate to say it, but Michelle isn't all that bright. We ran out of things to talk about, and... Well, I've been wondering what it might be like with a man. I mean... I don't want to make a choice and wonder the rest of my life if it was the right one. To be honest, lately I've stayed with Michelle as much because my grandmother didn't want me to as anything. I mean, I love my grandmother, but..."

"She's a bit like a force of nature. Her way or no way."

Carla chuckled. "Right. So why are you concerned that they might think the worse of you in Arkell?"

"You've never been to Arkell, have you?" Brad became serious.

"No, I wanted to go, but mother said I shouldn't. I went to Rockwood once."

"We'll be in Arkell in a few minutes, and you'll see why your mother didn't want you to go."

"I've heard Arkellians talking about tinkers. Why do they say those things?"

Brad shrugged. "The Gridtowners deal with them more than they do with Eden Mills. Gridtown traders prefer to buy grain instead of flour. They take it back and grind it in Gridtown. That way they increase their profit by devaluing Dark Lands' labour."

"But the mill is always busy during harvest?"

"Grinding the grain that's used locally."

"Why do Gridtowners hate Novo Gaians?"

Brad sighed and drummed his fingers on the seat. "It goes back before the collapse. In 2067 the nuke plants went up, adding the last stroke to the C zone. After that the electricity company went bankrupt and had to auction off its plants to pay the lawsuits. The larger plants were bought by multinationals, but a bunch of the smaller ones were purchased by a coalition of environmental groups and earth-first religions.

"As time passed, the earth-first plants encouraged people to use wind and solar. They undercut the fuel driven plants in price to keep their market.

"The business run plants kept gouging for maximum, short-term profits. People who shared an environmental idealism gathered around the earth-first plants. When the collapse happened, the country of Ontario broke up. We Novo Gaians decided to try new ways of doing things. We attempt to stretch the limited power resource as far as we can, taking a long view of payback.

"The major shareholders of the large hydroelectric plants declared themselves rulers of the areas covered by the utility grid that they could maintain. The regular military units agreed to support them in exchange for living accommodations.

"That's where the Gridtowns came from. Novo Gaia might have been taken over in those early days, but we started bringing in militia units with a deal like the shareholders were offering the regs. They taught us how to defend ourselves. To this day, every Novo Gaian between eighteen and forty is a reservist in the militia. Mostly you just have to put in one hundred hours training each year. Last year I learned how to drive a tank. It was fun, I got to turn some scrap cars into pancakes before they went for recycling." Brad smiled.

Carla shook her head indulgently. "How do you know so much?"

"Shorting! What I just told you is grade school history back home."

Carla stared at her feet. "I guess we Dark Landers seem pretty ignorant to you."

"Not your fault there wasn't enough power to keep your towns electrified. I respect people who make the best out of what they have. In my book, the Dark has more than its share of geniuses."

"I hope I can pass the exam to get into the academy."

Reaching over Brad squeezed her hand. "You can read, write, and do basic math. You'll pass, don't worry. Would you make us a pot of tea, please? There's a jar of camomile in the cupboard."

With a nod Carla moved to the kitchenette.

"You tinkers are so rich." She turned on the burner.

"I wish. I only paid off my wagon last year. Now I have all this cargo on loan. Maybe next year I'll be able to restock without mortgaging my behind, but that depends on how good this year is."

Carla stared at him quizzically, shrugged and made the tea.

The forest at the roadside gave way to rows of boxy houses. The few people they saw stared at the tinker's wagon in fear. A mother dragged a pair of dirty-faced children inside.

"What are your contracts here?" asked Carla.

"The clinic and vet rounds, but they won't take more than half a day, and I have to install two solar stills. Shouldn't take more than two days."

"Maybe I should walk home and see Michelle. Try and sort things out. She was awfully upset."

Brad shook his head. "Take my advice, don't! One thing tinkers know about is partings. Quick, clean, and no looking back is best. You shouldn't poke at an open wound if you want it to heal. Besides, I'll need your help with my work. Did you think you were riding for free?"

"I wasn't sure."

Before long, they reached a collection of rickety storefronts and a large, ugly building with a sign depicting a foaming mug. The smell of animal dung rose from piles at the street edge. An overweight woman with brown hair dressed in a short skirt and bodice stood on the corner. As Brad reined to a stop she approached.

"Hello, Tinker. Road made you lonely yet?" She leaned through the driver's window. Then she saw Carla. "Guess not. Don't get your hopes too high on this one. She's as much a man as you are." The woman stalked back to her corner.

"What was that?" asked Carla.

"Jealousy. Nancy tries to get me to recharge her flashlights each year. She wants to barter, and I won't."

"I know her, she came to see grandmother last year. Michelle was visiting."

"I can guess the rest. Let's speak to the innkeep. Frank's a good customer for recharge, and he might want some music tracks for his cube."

Leaving his wagon, Brad moved to the inn's door. Its small, north-facing windows gave it a cramped appearance. Opening the door released a blast of stale air, crowded with the smells of grease, dirty bodies and tobacco.

"Stay close. This place isn't like John's." Brad led the way into the common-room. Battered tables crowded the floor, and a fire burnt in a smoky fireplace on the outside wall. A pig occupied a spit over the flames. Pillars replaced the load-bearing walls, and battery-operated lanterns hung from the ceiling. The only light came from the grubby windows. A ghetto blaster sat on the bar in the back corner. A muscular man, with a crushed nose and curly, red hair, wearing dirty leather, stood behind the bar. Several rough-looking men sat at a table playing cards.

"Frank," called Brad.

The man behind the bar eyed Brad in an unfriendly way. "You're here now, eh. Heard you were at Eden Mills. How's John, the business stealin' son of a bitch?"

"He's fine. Could you draw us a couple of cider?" Brad led Carla to a table that afforded him a view of the room and both doors. The barkeep arrived, holding a pair of mugs filled with a dirty looking brew.

"A copper credit or four copper marks, take your pick."

"The trading is two marks for a credit nowadays," observed Brad.

"My place, my rules, and no tabs for the likes of you. Though if the girly here wants to discuss a trade?"

Brad placed a copper credit on the table then spoke. "She's mine, Frank! Think of Blair if you need to be reminded about what that means."

"Shit!" whispered Frank as a pallor spread across his face. Snatching up the credit, he left the table.

"Who's Blair and what happened?" asked Carla.

"I caught him trying to steal from me last year."

"What did you do?"

"What I had to."

Carla lifted her mug, took a sip and grimaced. "This is awful. How does he stay in business?"

"He's an outlet for Gridtown liquors."

They talked for a time before the innkeep returned to their table.

"I just gave my stuff a count. I have thirteen lanterns and three blasters as need recharge. I'll give you twenty copper marks for them."

"Twenty-one copper credits or two silver." Brad swirled the cider in his mug.

"That's too much."

"Same as last year."

"You're a thief! Your charges aren't worth their price."

"Maybe, but it's the Gridders who put superfluous resistors in their stuff, so that most folk can't get the voltage right to recharge a unit. Now if you bought some decent batteries..."

"From you. Every year the same thing. I have a business to run. I can't waste my money on tinker toys. Sell your trash to those fools in Eden Mills."

"At least in Eden Mills we have enough sense to know it's better to make your own power than rely on Gridtown traders," snapped Carla, anger touching her eyes.

"Carla, please." Brad came to his feet. "From that I take it you're not interested in the pre-collapse cube, CD, AM-FM I can rig for you? With a solar panel and battery pack it would give you music for years. But if you'd rather buy battery boom boxes from the Gridtowners..."

"Pre-collapse. How much?"

"Two gold, five silver marks for the panel and charge controller, one gold for the battery. I'll give you a break on the unit. Regular two gold ten silver, I'll let you have it for two gold, and I trade two for one."

"Five and a half gold credits. Tinker, you're an asshole, if you think I'll pay that much."

"How many blasters do you go through in a year? Five, six, more? That's easily over a gold a year. Do the math."

The innkeep glanced at the empty tables about the room.

"Five gold, five silver. You'll install it this year, none of your future contract shit?"

"I'll install it today. It's still early enough. You'll have music by tonight. Tell you what. As a bonus, I'll bring up your lanterns for a silver and having one of your men spread the word about the clinic tomorrow."

Frank sniffed through his crushed nose. "I have just the messenger to let the folk know what you tinkers are about." Rising his voice, he bellowed, "Blair." A minute passed before a tall man, with a hook where his left hand should have been, descended the stairs. His short, blond hair accentuated a black Tee burned into his forehead. Upon seeing Brad the man cowered against the wall.

"I ain't done nothin', 'onest," he pleaded.

"Got a job for you, asshole. Tinker here wants folk told he'll be having a clinic in the visitors' field tomorrow. Those as are stupid enough to trust him, can go get their bodies wrecked."

"Sure thing, Frank." Blair edged toward the door.

"Well then, show me your credits and we'll get started," said Brad. Carla glared at him in silent accusation.

The sun was setting when Brad descended the ladder from the roof and recoiled the power cable onto its spool at his wagon's side.

"That should do it," he said to Carla, who stood waiting.

"I'll tell Frank," she said flatly and disappeared into the inn. The sound of a screaming guitar blasted onto the street.

"It works," screamed Frank from the doorway.

"My money," shouted Brad.

With a resigned shrug Frank moved to Brad's side. "Five, was it?"

"And a half."

With a grimace Frank withdrew a money pouch, counted out the credits then passed them to Brad.

"If this were fall I'd never have gone for it, but I'm still stocked on liquor from last year. You've pretty much cleaned me out."

"You'll make it back."

"You want a room for the night?"

"No. I sleep better in my own bed."

"That bit of fluff you have with you is a nice enough piece I wouldn't want to sleep. How is she?"

"None of your concern." Brad turned on his heel and joined Carla in the wagon.

"On to the visitors' field. One of Frank's meals is about all I can handle per trip," remarked Brad.

Carla stared out the window.

"You've hardly said twelve words to me all afternoon."

"How could you? That poor man!"

"He tried to steal from me." Brad started his team moving.

"But to cripple him and burn a T into his forehead."

"It was Frank who did the hand. He caught Blair steeling liquor. Although, under traders' laws I could have taken his other one when I caught him in my wagon. All things considered, I was pretty merciful when I left it with a whipping and black Teeing him."

"You whipped him as well? You call that mercy?"

"Carla, what would happen if I let him go?"

"Well, I don't know. There had to be something else you could have done."

"True. I could have killed him, blinded him, cut out his tongue—"

"*Stop!* That's not what I meant, and you know it."

"That's traders' law. If you don't like it, give me some options. If this were the Mills, I'd have hauled him in front of the council, and they'd have punished him. As it was, I went to Frank, who's the closest thing Arkell has to a leader; he wouldn't do anything. He said if I wasn't man enough to look after my own problems, I shouldn't whine to him. I can't afford to let an affront go unpunished. If word gets around that tinkers are weak, it's trouble. Tinkers travel, usually alone. The only protection we have is the knowledge that to harm a tinker is to suffer dire consequences. Do you remember the story of Argyle?"

"They killed a tinker, so Novo Gaia destroyed them."

"To be accurate, we killed the town leaders, who ordered the murder, and C zoned the lynch mob. Then we took the orphans back to Novo Gaia. They were thinking of black Teeing the town, so no trader would deal with them. The murdered tinker's family intervened, saying we shouldn't deny the people medical aid. So we only red Teed them for five years. We didn't do that for revenge. It was an example. Novo Gaia will help anyone willing to help themselves, but we're nobody's doormat."

"How did Teeing get started?"

"In the Dark each town is its own little country. There's no central authority. We found in the early days of the tinker program we needed a way of punishing those who hurt us that could be enforced across borders. Thus the Teeing. Travelling merchants agreed to honour it because it helps protect them as much as us."

Depressing the clutch, Brad pressed his gearshift into first. The wagon slowed and the floorboards vibrated.

"What did you do?" asked Carla.

"Charging Frank's batteries took a lot out of my system. I have a generator hooked to the rear wheels. It converts their turning to power. I try not to use it unless I'm going down hill, it puts extra strain on the team."

"Brad... Have you ever killed someone?"

"Yes."

"Why?"

"She was trying to kill me. I woke up and she had a gun to my head. She was beautiful, but I've since learned she was probably a Gridtown agent.

"Carla. Eden Mills is a very civilised place. It wasn't hit as hard by the collapse as most areas. Most of the Dark Lands are populated by exiles. A lot of them were thrown out of Gridtowns for being unemployed, but not all."

Chapter Five

The Candler

IN MINUTES A pasture, reclaimed from the twenty-first-century-urban sprawl, came into view. A brick fence surrounded it, and a decrepit building had been left standing in one corner to act as a barn. A rusty, steel barrel, cut in half and supported by a frame of two by fours, stood by the structure and served as a water trough. A battered station wagon topped by peel and stick solar panels rested by the barn. A Clydesdale gelding nickered at Brad's team.

"Another trader," remarked Brad.

"Won't the horses fight?" asked Carla.

"Probably not. My girls are use to strangers."

Reaching the field's gate Carla opened it, while Brad brought the horses through, parking his van as far from the station wagon as possible.

"Let's see who our neighbour is," he said.

"I think I recognize that wagon. It belongs to the candler that comes to Eden Mills each year."

"Well, it's a candler's all right," said Brad, as they drew nearer. The boiling caldron in a ring of flowers that formed the crest of that profession was painted on the driver's side door. Looking closer Brad found a small star hidden in a rose petal.

Profanity exploded from the other side of the barn.

"Stay here." Gripping his semi-automatic pistol Brad moved towards the sound. Turning the corner, he saw a short, plump man dressed in patched, but clean, hemp clothing, swearing at a solar still.

"Problem?" asked Brad.

The man snapped around, his hand slipping to a holster on his belt. His eyes took in Brad then he relaxed.

"You have the look of a tinker. I'll tell you, after the day I've had, I'm about ready to fall on my sword," said the small man in a pleasant alto.

"I know what you mean. If it wasn't for the love and trust of my friends, sometimes I just couldn't cope," replied Brad.

The smaller man beamed. "Haven't spoken to another Novo Gaian... trader in nearly a year." He held out his hand. "Me name's Dan, Dan Timothy, candler, soap maker, extraordinaire!"

"Brad, and this is my friend Carla." He gestured to the girl who stepped out from around the edge of the building.

"Carla, Meb's granddaughter." Dan beamed.

"You know me?" Carla's voice was unsure.

"Sure. If you do business in the Mills, it pays to know Meb and her folk. Travelling with a tinker now. None of me business mind you, but it's a good choice.

"And you, Brad, must be the one who sold John that still. I've a bone to pick with you. I hardly sold a candle in the Mills last year, doubt I will this year either." Dan's smile removed the sting from the words.

"Sorry," remarked Brad.

"Not to worry. I made it up in soap, and I can always stretch deeper into the Dark.

"If you want water, we're all S.O.L. Somebody doesn't have the sense to refill the reservoir. I just pumped it full, but the sun's setting."

"Arkell! This town. Let me check the system to see that no one damaged it." Brad began inspecting the unit.

The still consisted of a hand pump connected to a black steel drum set behind a sheet of glass. Reflective panels directed sunlight onto the drum, from which a length of black pipe rose above the barn. A float opened a vent at the top of the pipe, allowing the first few litres of the water to escape. When the vent closed the humid air flowed along another pipe to the north side of the building, where it condensed into a barrel on the second floor. When the float neared the tank's bottom, it opened a valve, dumping the remaining water. A pipe led from the condensing tank, to just above the horse trough.

"System's okay," announced Brad, after scrambling around it for several minutes.

"I figured it would be. I don't mind them drinking the clean, but I wish they'd refill the cistern afterwards. When you tinkers going to rig a solar pump to refill this unit anyways?" Dan leaned against the barn like he owned it.

"Probably when we don't have to anymore." Brad grinned. "I've enough water for us and the horses on board. Last year's tests showed the well good enough for washing in; we should do okay."

"That's a relief."

They moved Brad's wagon to the side of the barn and saw to his team, leaving the horses to graze.

"I'm tempted to buy some oats to help me horse along." Dan looked over the much-abused grass of the field.

"I know what you mean. I think someone's been pasturing sheep here again." Brad collected off-cut two-by-fours from a wood box by the barn and began preparing a fire pit.

"That's just not done. This is the visitors' field," objected Carla.

"A lot of things get done as are just aren't done, me girl," observed Dan.

Brad nodded then asked "Where you out from?"

"Guelph, outskirts, along the old seven."

"Heading that way in a day or two. What's happening? Did you see anything interesting? I hear they've been practising with a new toy." Brad struck a match and held it to the kindling.

Dan's voice was grave. "I heard tell of the toy. Folk say someone found it under the rubble of an old building. Never saw it though."

"Are you two talking about that old, armoured vehicle they

dug up last year?" Carla sounded exasperated.

"You've seen it?" Brad's voice held interest.

"Duh, everyone saw it." Carla rolled her eyes. "Didn't anyone tell you? They took it on a joy ride to show off for all the local towns. I can't guess where they got the fuel. It's a big ugly thing, but I'll bet no ones going to try raiding Guelph for a while."

Brad stared at Carla for a long moment then finally said, "The fuel is the problem." he turned to Dan. "Anything else I should know about?"

Dan pursed his lips in thought. "I think you'll make a credit or two. There's a flu or something. Started showing up just as I was leaving. Have to tell you, I was glad to get out of there. Can't afford to be sick, too much work to do. I've got at least two weeks here before I move on."

"Could it be--?"

Dan cut him off. "You'd know better then me, but as I remember it, the symptoms don't match. I figure it's just a flu. How are things in the Mills?"

Brad seemed to relax. "Stay away from the goldenrod wine. Other than that, good."

"There's a lot more than that going on," objected Carla.

"Oh?" Dan smirked knowingly. Brad left to get food from his wagon.

"Peter and Francine had another baby. It's a girl. The Brookfields bought a new calf. Will at the general store bought some books from a traveller and is renting them. They're all about pre-collapse lovers. Some of them are very good and..." Carla paused hearing her own words.

"Don't worry about it, girly. Those are important things back in the Mills, but travellers look at other news."

Carla hung her head and blushed. "I guess my world is pretty small."

"Nothing wrong with that, so long as you remember your world's part of a bigger one. Was a time I cared a lot about the new type of candy at the general store, before I left home and was trained for me craft." Dan tossed a piece of wood on the fire then leaned back and watched the stars appear overhead.

"Where did you grow up?"

"Little place called Janetville, just a few klicks outside the Otonabee province of Novo Gaia."

"You're not Novo Gaian?"

"Not hardly. A tinker recommended me for the basic skills training program. Spent two years learning me trade, and a few other things then they kitted me out and sent me to wander. Checked in once a year 'till I paid off me cart and loans. Haven't been back since."

"I'm going to the academy to be trained as a healer."

"Now that's a full degree. I'll be glad to see it. As good as Meb is, sometimes a fellow needs more than a root or a berry." Dan's blue eyes sparkled.

Brad returned and soon they were all roasting sausages on spits.

"I'm all in," said Brad as the evening drew on.

"Yup, got a busy day tomorrow. Many a good wife wants a light," agreed Dan, with a leer. Rising, he went to his wagon.

"Ah, Brad. There's something I have to ask you," opened Carla.

Brad smiled wickedly and ran his fingers across her shoulders. "Yes?"

"Brad, I mean...?"

"There's an extra blanket and pillow in the cupboard, and the front bench-seat is quite comfortable," he remarked in seductive tones then laughed.

"What's so funny?"

"Your face. Carla, I wouldn't throw you out of my bed, but it's your choice. You're paying for your passage by helping me with the work. The other, I don't pay for with credit or barter."

"Pretty sure of yourself!"

"One of my better traits. Now let's turn in."

The next day a small crowd of people had gathered in the visitors' field. Brad stood beside a petite, dark-haired child that squinted at a chart on the side of his van.

"Triangle, square, squiggle, circle," she said.

A heavyset, twenty-something woman, wearing a simple, grey dress and a broad-brimmed hat, stood beside Brad, shaking her head. "You see what I mean, Tinker. Blind as a bat! How can she spin when she sees so little? She's useless. Gridtown doctor said there was an operation that would let her see, but it costs more then she's worth. If she was a few years older she could earn her keep on her back, but I can't wait for that. I paid her maw good credits for this one. Look what I've got for it."

Brad turned a cold eye on the woman then returned his attention to the child. "Monique, I want you to try something on."

"What is it?"

Brad pulled a device that looked like a hat with connected glasses from under the hood of his van and placed it on Monique's head. "Tell me what you see now?" He slipped a set of lenses into the eye rims.

"Circle, square, squiggle, and it looks like a duck." The little girl smiled.

Brad changed the lenses several times before collecting a set of simple frames from his wagon. Searching through another box he produced a pair of thick numbered lenses and inserted them into the frames.

"Try these on." He passed the glasses to Monique.

"It's clear, Tinker. I can see everything."

"That will be four silver, Amanda." Brad faced the heavyset woman.

"It's more than she's worth. She won't spin enough to cover that in a year." Amanda grabbed Monique's arm and made to walk off.

Brad grabbed Amanda's pudgy arm. "That's the price, and it's fair. Think of the child. Being able to see could change her life."

"I need a spinner! She'll just be another cheap whore, like her mother. Probably catch something and die before she's thirty." Amanda shook off Brad's hand.

"You are a cold bitch! Three silver and she works for me anytime I'm in town until she's old enough to tell you to screw off!"

Amanda eyed Brad then pulled the credits from the leather purse she wore and slammed them into his palm.

"Just see to it she isn't walking too funny when you return her. She's a little young for that type of work." Amanda stalked off.

"Monique, you're going to work for me when I'm in town from

now on. Carla, there's a scoop in the trailer. Get it for Monique, please. Have her collect the manure in the visitor field and put it in the barn's methane composter."

"Sure, Brad." Carla stood at the corner of the wagon, her cheeks flushed and fists clenched, staring at Amanda's retreating back. "Come on, honey. I'll show you where everything is," she added, moving to the little girl's side.

"That woman is a monster!" observed a slender man with a prominent nose. "I'm Jack, Jack Horner. Not to be confused with Corner, though I am a baker."

"Hello Jack, I'm Brad, what can I do for you?"

"Well, Brad. I'm new to the Dark. Fresh out of Niagara Grid Region. Heard a lot of things about you tinkers. Most of it bad, but I always say a man should find out for himself. Been standing back watching. Just wanted to ask. What you're gonna do to that little girl?"

Brad shrugged. "Not what Amanda thinks; I'll use her for odd jobs, running errands. Over the next few years she'll work off the price of her glasses."

"All I needed to know. I need a shot. I'm told there are some things out here that are pretty deadly." Jack smiled revealing even, white teeth.

"Standard inoculation series costs six silver. I will barter though." Brad set his optical tools to one side.

"Thought you might." Jack pulled a ghetto blaster out of his bag.

Brad inspected the unit. "Hmm. Gridtown manufacture. You'd do better waiting for the Gridtown traders this fall. They do a return deposit for items with dead batteries."

"Don't want to wait. No telling what I could catch."

"Good way of looking at things. I'll trade even for the shot if you're willing."

"Wattage. I used to get the banned channels. I had a pre-collapse T.V. back home. I can see that show Tinker's Road wasn't just propaganda." Jack rolled up his sleeve.

"What station did you get it on?"

"Why?"

"Just curious. I might get a route in the Niagara area when I finish this one, and I like to keep up with my shows."

"Five."

A wintery smile touched Brad's lips as he left to retrieve the serum from his refrigerator.

The morning passed quickly then Brad and Carla spent the afternoon installing the stills, returning to the visitors' field after sunset.

"Brad?" Carla prepared a stir-fry on his stove.

"What?" He closed the book he was reading and shifted on the bench-seat by his table to face her.

"How much would it cost to buy Monique and set her free?"

"Maybe a gold to buy her and get someone to look after her until she's old enough to care for herself."

"What's my share of the stereo you sold to the inn?"

"Don't even think about it! That money is for your education."

"But Monique doesn't deserve to be bought and sold. She's just a little girl." Carla's face became an earnest mask.

"I know." Brad gazed at the table and his voice took on an angry edge. "Amanda has a dozen others just like her. And there are six people in the child trade on my route alone. There are over four hundred tinker routes. Do the math. You can't help them all. All you can do is become the best healer you can be. Bring a service this area needs into it. In the future, Novo Gaia will stop the Amandas of the world, but for now all we can do is watch the Moniques suffer."

"How will Novo Gaia stop them?"

Brad bit his lip and fell silent as Carla looked at him suspiciously before returning her attention to the stir-fry.

She awoke the next morning to a hissing sound. Sitting up on the front seat, she looked at the back of the wagon.

"Brad, your pot's boiling dry," she warned.

Brad looked up from his computer.

"I know. I'm doing a fractional distillation of the well water."

"Why?"

Brad shrugged. "The academy's hydrology department will store my van through the winter for free if I send them test results on all the communal wells on my route."

"Oh. What's it like?"

"Petroleum distillates, e-coli bacteria, metallic salts, a variety of trace elements too numerous to mention."

"Yech."

"Our inheritance. You have to love our ancestors. At least it's washed out of the surface layer, or it would be in everything we ate."

"Are we going today?" Carla knuckled sleep from her eyes.

"Yup."

Turning off the burner, Brad left the wagon and stood outside in the cool, spring morning. After stretching, he refilled his water tanks from the solar still and pulled a thin hose from a spool on the roof of his cart.

"What's that?" Carla sat on the van's bumper, pulling on her boots.

"Methane for the stove. Eddie installed a composter and gas sterilizer in the barn when this was his route."

"John has something like that at the inn."

"Yeah, it feeds off his toilets and stable. He even hires kids to shovel up the street every morning. That's why Eden Mills is so clean."

"That's such a shitty job."

Brad shook with a loud guffaw.

"Now, so we don't annoy Dan, you refill the still while I hitch the team. Then you can cook us breakfast," he suggested.

"Tinkers hate to cook!" Carla moved to follow his instructions.

She returned to find Brad at his radio.

"Tinker, tinker, tinker. Check in, check in, check in. Over."

"Home, home, home. We read you tinker, proceed with I-dent."

Brad snorted disgustedly then spoke. "B zero, R nine, A one, D five, L zero, Y one, I zero, R five, V one, I zero, N seven, G PC."

"I-dent in range, adjust one unit negative."

"Understood, Eddie. Leaving Arkell today. I'll be in Guelph in a couple of hours. I think there may be some spy activity here. A Gridtown exile named Jack. He seems too good to be true.

Checked him on our frequencies. He said he was picking up the French River signal in the Niagara Grid Region. Over."

"Understood. As long as our friends listening in know that we know that they know. Over."

Brad smirked. "The silly games we play. Over"

"Have you uncovered any interesting antiques this trip? Over."

"Carla tells me she saw one last winter, but she doesn't know where it is now. Over."

"Keep looking, some antiques can really glow. Over."

"Don't I know it. Over."

"I'm standing by for weather and well information. Over."

Moments later Brad turned off the radio. Carla passed him a bowl of oatmeal as he started his team moving. She took a seat beside him.

Chapter Six

Plague Plague

Ugly houses with weed-choked lawns crowded the roadside leading to the ancient city.

"Brad, I noticed something," opened Carla.

"Did it interest you?" Brad grinned and laid his hand on her knee.

"Brad." Carla blushed.

"What was it?"

"Your call ident. It keeps changing."

"Yup. If it stayed the same, anyone could listen in then pretend to be me."

"How do you know what it is then?"

"It's a tinker secret." Brad winked.

"You can tell me."

"Then it wouldn't be a secret, now would it?"

The discussion continued until a young man, in hemp clothing, mounted on a plough horse galloped towards them. His dark-skinned face was sweat drenched while his wiry, black hair was in need of a wash. Brad reined the horses to a stop. The rider pulled his mount up by the van's door. His deep, brown eyes held both pleading and panic.

"What is it?" asked Brad.

"Tinker, we just heard you were in Arkell. There's a sickness. We need help!"

"What kind of sickness?"

"I've never seen nothing like it. Trina's Gridtown pills don't work on it."

"Trina?" asked Carla.

"The local healer, if you can call her that. Gridtown traders sell her a mix of broad spectrum antibiotics, and she treats them like candy," explained Brad.

"We need your help," repeated the man, his classic African features drawn into a pleading expression.

"I'll give it a look. Guide us to the closest sick house."

"We've put all the sickins together in the village hall. We're using the cots from the summer fair. It's the only way Trina could keep track of them all."

"That's convenient." Brad paused in thought. "Are the victims neighbours?"

"No, Tinker, they're from all over town."

"That's something at least. By the way, what's your name?"

"Ingram."

"Let's get going." Brad snapped his reins starting his team forward.

"Do you think this is anything to worry about?" Carla fidgeted nervously.

Brad drummed his fingers on his dashboard. "I hope not. Trina's an ignorant woman with delusions of grandeur. It might be viral, or an antibiotic resistant bacteria, or... Can you take the reins while I get some things together?"

"Of course."

"Thanks. I'd like you to take one of these." Brad pulled a package of iodine tablets from the glove compartment.

"Why?" Carla looked suspicious.

"It's just a precaution. It's probably nothing, but the pill won't do you any harm."

Carla looked at Brad as wheels seamed to turn in her head. "I may not be educated, but I can read, and I'm not stupid. I pray to every god and goddess there ever was you're wrong about that tank." Carla took the iodine pill.

"Me to. I'll have to remember not to underestimate you. You figured that out with very few clues." Brad moved to the back of the wagon.

Carla smirked. "I've lived all my life in the dark. Pretty stupid of me if I didn't worry about radiation from old tech."

Half an hour later Carla pulled the horses to a stop in the middle of the town square. A collection of dirty, brick buildings, with signs depicting crafts, lined the broad, central street. On her right was a large, flat-roofed structure that in a previous century would have been a plaza. Most of its front had been sealed with scrounged bricks, and chimneys sprouted from its roof.

"This is it," called Ingram.

Brad moved from his van, carrying his medical kit.

"Carla, you're with me. Ingram, could you see to the horses and unhitch my trailer. Keep two of my horses on the hitch and take the rest to the livery, please. After that, if you could keep folk away from my wagon, I'd appreciate it."

"Sure," said Ingram.

Carla stepped onto the cracked asphalt street and ran to follow Brad, who strode to the plywood-covered door of the village hall.

Opening the door released a blast of stale air, crowded with the odours of feces, vomit and illness.

"That's disgusting!" exclaimed Carla.

"Here, use this." Brad pulled a tube from his pocket.

Carla took the tube and opened it. A cream with a heavy odour of mint almost drowned out the other stenches. She rubbed it under her nose and followed him into the building.

In the dim light, which leaked through the remaining windows, they could see twelve cots. Each was piled with blankets and held a victim of the illness. A skeletal woman, of about forty, moved between the beds with a glass in one hand and a bottle in the other. She stopped at each patient and pushed a pill into their mouth, followed by a sip from the glass.

"Trina," called Brad.

"Tinker," said the woman coldly.

"What have you got here?"

"They're sick. What does it look like? I don't think any of

them will live." Trina sniffed.

"What are the symptoms?"

"None of the pills work. I even tried cutting their hair to let the bad out, but they just don't get better."

"I'll take a look at them."

"They're my patients. You're no doctor; you're not going to touch them!" Trina's pinched features pulled into a scowl.

"Watch me!" Brad moved to the closest bed.

The patient was a middle-aged woman with dark hair and sunken, brown eyes. She breathed in ragged gasps and sweat soaked her blankets. Placing his electronic thermometer in her ear, Brad took the reading.

"Forty!" With angry gestures he pulled away the pile of blankets.

"What are you doing? She'll catch a chill." Trina grabbed Brad's arm trying to stop him.

"She's burning up. This woman needs cold baths not blankets, you idiot." Brad pulled the thick pillow from under the woman's head and hurled it into Trina who instinctively clutched it. Retrieving a blanket he rolled it and placed it under the patient's neck, so it tilted her chin up. Immediately, her breathing quieted.

"Carla, take my thermometer. Check the other patients. Anyone over thirty-seven degrees, strip the bed. Hyper-extend the neck of all unconscious patients."

"This is my clinic," objected Trina.

"You almost killed these people, you..." Brad clamped down on his anger and turned back to his patient, noting her symptoms.

"I'll get the village elders; they'll throw you out of here. You'll never trade in Guelph again," screamed Trina.

"Shut up! It's hard enough to get a blood pressure when it's this low." Brad inflated the cuff. A moment later he moved to the next cot.

"Acute dehydration. Have you been giving them water?" he asked, when he finished at the last bed.

"They can't keep it down. They can't keep anything down, not even the pills that would make them better." Trina took on a haughty demeanour.

"Shit! okay, first things first." Moving to his laptop, which sat on a table in the room's centre, he inserted a cube and entered the symptoms. Minutes later the screen flashed "Unknown."

"Has anyone died yet?" he asked.

"Old man Sung, but he was weak to start with." Trina stood behind Brad, her arms crossed beneath her slight breasts. The sweat-stained dress she wore had many patches.

"When in doubt, symptoms shout," muttered Brad, who moved to his kit. "Carla, how are their temperatures?"

"Still high, but a little lower since we took off the blankets. Their breathing's easier, except for the case in the last bed."

"Good. I want to try bringing their fluids up. We'll set up some I.V.s. I want to keep the solution consistent for each patient. We'll set up one lactated ringers, one normal saline, one saline, and a D5W. Trina, I need you to point out four cases that arrived at about the same time."

"Why should I help you? You have been nothing but rude to me."

"If this is contagious, you could get it next. That's why you should help me, because if we can figure out how to help these people now, maybe I'll be able to save you when you catch it!"

"I take my pills, one a day. I can't get sick, they kill the germs."

Brad rolled his eyes. "They're not working for these people, are they? They don't work on this 'germ'."

A moment passed before Trina spoke.

"Mary in the third cot, Victor in the fifth one, Henrietta in the sixth, she's his wife, and Mitchell on the end. They all came in yesterday."

"Good." Brad moved to the side of the first cot. "We'll need something to hang the bags on."

"Real doctors have a proper stand, but you wouldn't know that since you're just a tinker. There are some torch stands from the summer festival in the back room. I'll get them," said Trina.

Tying off the arm, Brad waited for a vein to rise. Slowly, slowly the purple cord bulged against the skin.

"I hate needles," he remarked to Carla, who stood behind him.

"Strange thing for a tinker," she observed.

"I like mechanics, that's why I'm a tinker. Medical is not my strongest skill. Carla, I think we may have trouble. Try and find out from Trina who the first victim was. If this is the flu Dan told us about, it's spreading fast."

"Right." Carla moved to help Trina bring the stands while Brad pushed the needle home.

He'd just started the last I.V. when Carla rejoined him.

"She said it was Yackaharo. The second bed from the end."

"Figures, he's one of the worst cases." Brad moved to Yackaharo's bedside. The naked man before him was nothing but dry, brittle skin stretch over bone. A dribble of liquid feces stained his cot, and his brown eyes were sunken with dehydration. His black hair was matted with sweat.

"Yackaharo." Brad gently shook the man.

A faint groan escaped his lips.

"Yackaharo, this is a tinker. Can you speak?"

"T…t…t…h…h…h…inker?" breathed the man.

"Yes, I need to speak to you."

"Y…y…you save. I pay. Rich, so rich." Yackaharo fell into a fit of coughing.

"Do you know where you might have gotten sick?" Brad fought to keep his voice soothing.

"Rich, so rich. Wendell show yoooo." The last word escaped as a death rattle.

Carla stared at the corpse. "He's gone," she said. It was an affirmation, not a question.

Brad took the victim's pulse and nodded.

"You didn't do much good, did you?" snapped Trina, coming up behind them.

"Who's Wendell?" Carla turned to face the other woman.

"Him. Yacky here was a bit of a funny boy. Would have liked your tinker there over either of us, if you get what I mean? Wendell was his, tail-gunner."

"I'll go talk to him. It will be a while before the I.V.s have any effect. Maybe he can tell me something."

"Silly waste of time. Give them a pill, or a shot, or something. Not much of a healer, is he?" Trina looked to Carla for confirmation.

"My grandmother always takes a history. You can't heal without one." Carla met Trina's gaze.

"Who's your grandmother?"

"Meb."

"That old witch from Eden Mills, with her nuts and berries." Trina laughed.

Carla began to bristle; Brad's voice cut in like ice.

"Yes. Meb is a witch, in the best sense of the word. Master herbalist, midwife, practical psychologist. Have a mind to what you say, Trina. I like Meb!"

The whites showed around the skinny woman's eyes as she slunk away.

"She is a fool," growled Carla.

"Yes! I dare say you know more about healing from your reading and working with Meb than she ever will, but she knows the townsfolk. Try to stay out of her way. Keep an eye on the patients, and check their vitals every hour."

"Sure, Brad. What should we do with the body?"

"Burn it and the cot."

"Right."

Brad turned and left the building. Ingram was waiting beside the horses.

"How are they?" he asked.

"It's bad. Old man Sung and Yackaharo have died." Brad stroked one of his mares' flanks.

"Shit, poor Yacky." Ingram stared at the ground. "I was at his wedding. He and Wendell were stripping down a couple of blocks on Watson Road. They were going to farm it."

"I need to talk to Wendell."

Ingram looked up. "I'll guide you."

Entering the van, the two men started back the way Brad had come.

"The other victims, did any of them have something to do with Yackaharo or Wendell in a bedroom, sort of way?" Brad stared out the front window as he mentally ticked off possibilities.

Ingram shook his head. "Not a chance. Both Yacky and Wendy were straight shooters. They were so into each other it was embarrassing."

Minutes later they reached a twenty-first-century house with a large, southern exposure. The houses beside it had been dismantled and their materials stacked neatly for reuse. Going to the door, Brad knocked. Several minutes passed before a slender man of about twenty-five appeared. His blond hair fell limply around an angular face and dark circles stood out under his blue eyes. He was dressed in a wrap-around robe.

"Yes?" he asked then looking past Brad he said "Hi, Ingram."

"Wendy, we have bad news," opened Ingram.

"No, no." Wendell shuddered and tears sprang to his eyes.

Brad caught Wendell as he collapsed. "Help me get him inside."

Soon Brad sat across a battered coffee table from Wendell in what had once been an expensive parlour. The tattered furniture was draped in material, and the worst of the holes in the walls had been patched.

"We were going to have a farm. Grow wheat and have a tram and horses. My sister already told us she'd carry Yacky's child when we were ready."

"I'm sorry, but I need your help. Can you think of any place Yackaharo might have caught the disease?"

"The cache. I said we should wait for you, Tinker, but Yacky wanted to see what was inside."

"Inside?"

"A week ago, we found a concrete bunker in our field. The ground was empty, that's why we chose this place. We could get a small crop to see us through while we cleared the land. It was just under the surface. The door had been covered with cement, but it had mostly crumbled. We hit it while we were ploughing. When we cleared away the dirt we found a steel door. I said we should wait, but Yacky said we had to check it out. He can be so stubborn. Baha'u'llah, help me, he's gone."

"Can you show me this place?"

Wendell nodded.

Minutes later the three men made their way across a field of barley.

"It's right here. It's really big inside, with all sorts of computers and glass vials," explained Wendell.

Brad moved to the opening. It loomed before him like the jaws of a hungry beast, ready to devour them all. A broken seal, lying by the hatch, caught his attention. He picked it up. Three crescents pierced the sides of a triangle on a field of orange.

"*Shit!*" With the speed only adrenaline can give, he ran to his van, dove onto the seat and grabbed his short wave. Drawing a breath to steady himself, he turned to the frequency every tinker prays they won't ever have to use and spoke.

"Tinker, Tinker, Tinker, Guelph, Guelph, Guelph, plague. Plague. Plague!"

Chapter Seven

Politics

EDDIE SAT AT his station in the tinker facility, scratching the stump of his left arm. A limb about the size of a two-year-old's grew from its centre. He flexed the infantile hand and watched it make a fist.

"Five more years and you go through puberty. Probably have an uncontrollable urge to grab girls in the back of cars," he muttered at the growth. A smile split his weathered, Amerindian features.

A red light flashed, and a sharp beep riveted his attention to the radio equipment on the desk in front of him.

"Tinker, Tinker, Tinker, Guelph, Guelph, Guelph, Plague. Plague. Plague!" echoed the speaker.

Grabbing the mic in his good hand, Eddie took a breath that filled his solidly-built body and depressed the key.

"Go ahead with priority ident tinker."

"Eddie, it's Brad. Cut the crap. I'm in trouble!"

"Identify Brad."

"Shorting! B one, R five, A two, D seven, L zero, Y one, I zero, R five, V one, I zero, N seven, G PC. Satisfied?"

"You called a plague, activating tape." Eddie set the mic down and pressed a button on his console. He pushed a lock of medium-length, black hair away from his brown eyes before continuing. "What's the story?"

"I need some top notch germ dogs. A couple of farmers stumbled across an old biohazard facility. They decided to take a peek. This happened about a week ago. There are twelve people down with the disease and two dead. Symptoms are fever, diaphoresis, vomiting, diarrhea. Low, blood pressure, and tachycardia. These people are dying of hypovolemic shock. The bodies look like they've been mummified. There's no match on my database. I don't know the contagion vectors yet, but it seems to be readily communicable. I suggest you call out the militia, and set up a quarantine until we get this figured out. You better cut off Arkell as well. A candler went there from here when things were just starting. The man's name is Dan Timothy. He's a real star, you can trust him. Over."

"Received. I'll put a call through to Dr. Frankel in Nipissin. He's the best contagious disease man in Novo Gaia. I'll talk to the Minister about the militia quarantine. Over."

"Get our friends from the Grid in on this. Bugs don't respect lines on a map. I don't know if this is zoonotic. One busy chipmunk and we could all be fouling our drawers. Over."

"I'll speak to the Minister. Monitor this frequency. Anything more to report? Over."

"Tell my parents I love them. Over and out."

"Home, out." Eddie swivelled his chair and hit the speed dial on the vid phone occupying the corner of his desk. Turning, he activated a computer and brought up a file. Awkward from the use of one hand, he began filling in a computerized form. The line picked up.

"Ministry of Dark Lands Affairs. Can I help you?" asked a pretty, blonde woman who appeared on the phone screen.

"This is Edward Baily, Eugenia Falls, Tinker facility. I need to speak with the Minister."

"The Minister is in a meeting and cannot be disturbed. Would you like to make an appointment?"

Eddie gritted his teeth and spoke softly.

"Tell Francis I need him now. This is a priority call."

"I'm sorry, sir, but..."

"Shorting! So much for discretion. Crap cut, A A A, Authorization, Major Edward Baily! Now, Miss, put me through. The reporter monitoring the line is probably already heading towards Francis's office, and it would be nice if he knew what was going on!"

"I'll get him immediately, sir."

The line went silent then was picked up. A man with thick, grey hair and a scar on his cheek appeared. His deep rumbling voice issued from the speaker.

"This had better be important. Calling a crap cut on a Minister's line. You know press has free monitoring of all government communications."

"Blame your secretary, Francis! I hope her legs are worth the aggravation. Get down here, fast! One of my tinkers has called in a plague."

"Is it serious? I mean, it's not just a case of the sniffles is it?"

"Damn it, I know this man. He took over the Guelph route when I moved on. He's no alarmist; he's asked that we coordinate with the Gridtowners."

"I see! If I hurry, I can catch the last mag-lev. I'll just have to spend the night in Eugenia falls. Meet me at the station."

"I need the okay to call in a biohazard team."

"This is a Dark Lands matter. Let's not be hasty. I'll authorize any consultations you need. Draw up a quarantine plan, but don't send anyone into the area without my say so."

"But, Francis...?"

"We'll discuss this when I arrive. The mag-lev is leaving in an hour. Be at the station in two."

The line went dead. Eddie swore under his breath.

Turning back to his computer, he attached an address and explanatory note to the form he'd filled in and e-mailed it before dialling a new number.

"Dr. Frankel, please," he said as soon as the line was picked up.

"Speaking." A screen block displayed a Renoir on Eddie's unit.

"Doctor, I represent the tinker's guild. I just e-mailed you a priority message regarding a plague we have discovered in the Dark Lands. I am authorized to approve your consultation fee."

"I'll call my team together. When and where do we roll out from?"

"At the moment, we're not sending in any more people. We're going to quarantine and give our field man radio support."

"That is outrageous! I know you tinkers are competent, but a biohazard is beyond anything you're trained for."

"We all have our orders. Please review the material I sent you, and look for matches in the database."

"Yes, and good luck to your man. He will need it!"

The line went dead as Eddie pushed back from the desk. The four-meter square confines of the radio room seemed cramped to him. Through the lone window, blue sky beckoned. Grabbing a dark-green jacket, he'd draped over his chair, he opened the door opposite the radio equipment.

"Beth, take my duty, something's come up. Especially watch the emergency frequency. I'm taking the portable. If anything comes in from a tinker named Bradly Irving, relay it to me immediately. okay?"

"Sure thing," agreed a pretty, slender woman with brown hair, who sat at a computer in the large outer office.

Eddie grabbed a cellular phone and laptop computer from a shelf by the door and left the building. The sun slanted onto the row of windows behind him. He heard the steady thunk, thunk, thunk, of the windmill blades in the backyard of the modified condominium that formed this tinker centre. The street before him was an unbroken strip of asphalt, and the houses on its far side had been removed to maximize solar gains on the south facing structures. Photovoltaic shingles covered the roofs behind him and several more windmills turned in the breeze. The corner houses had been removed, creating lots, the back of which were parkland, while the front was a small covered parking area. The roof over the cars was made from solar panels. Five small, identical vehicles sat in the closest lot.

At least there's always cars here at this hour, thought Eddie. Moving to the closest car he disconnected the recharge cable, which recoiled into a parking-meter like device. Climbing into the boxy vehicle, he adjusted the seat then pulled a plastic card from his wallet and swiped it down an electric reader. Pressing his thumb against a scan plate he activated the car. The slight whine of an electric motor accompanied his backing onto the street. Reversing the motor, he headed toward the train station.

The industrial sector gave way to Flesherton suburbs. The houses were well spaced, and the east-west streets were partially stripped of houses, allowing those that remained to benefit from the sun's light. All roofs were photovoltaic.

Eddie drove on, leaving the town behind. Farms covered about half the land, while second-growth forest filled the rest. Pressing the accelerator to the floor, the car maxed out at fifty kilometres an hour. Five minutes later he pulled into the train station.

The depot was buried on all but its south face, which formed a wall of glass. Light tubes pierced the earthen mound while a solar canopy formed a strip over the front glass. A windmill turned at the top of the mound. Two sets of tracks led away from the station. One was a standard freight gauge, the other a strip of magnetic rail, which vanished under a mound of earth.

Eddie pulled into a parking space by the main doors. Standing, he connected a charge line from a wall stand to the vehicle. Habit made him check that the car's meter had stopped running before he walked to the station.

Inside the depot was a long, narrow room. Wash and maintenance rooms were along its back. Kiosks selling literature disks, snacks and souvenirs formed islands in the centre of the main area. The boarding platform was reached by a split in the back wall.

Taking a seat on a bench, Eddie brought a map of the Guelph area up on the laptop and began planning the quarantine. About an hour later a hum reverberated through the station then the streamlined shape of the magnetic-levitation train's link shuttle appeared on the platform. Its nose and sides showed where bondo had been used to patch the wear of over a century's service.

Eddie met Francis with a grave expression.

"Minister. I've mapped out a basic quarantine plan and included the Gridtowners."

"Good, I've been on the phone with the diplomatic Minister.

Bloody ass! He didn't want to alarm the Gridtowners without just cause." Francis rubbed the back of his thick neck with a calloused hand.

"He is telling them, isn't he?" Eddie looked worried.

Francis straightened the lapels of his suit over his overweight frame. "He'll tell them. As soon as he heard that the media knew about it, he became very cooperative. No secrets may be a political pain, but it has its advantages as well."

"The media?"

"They've agreed to sit on the story until we can give them full details. We were lucky it was the Crier's day to monitor the line. If it had been the Speculator, we'd be shorted." Francis ran his fingers through his hair.

"We should head back to the tinker centre. This isn't the place to discuss this."

"You're right."

The two men left the building, taking the first car they came to.

"You said you'd drawn up a preliminary plan for the quarantine?" opened Francis.

"Yes, on the laptop. I'd pass it to you, but..." Eddie waved his infantile left arm causing his sleeve to flap.

"Got it." The Minister picked up the battered computer and scanned Eddie's notes. "Guelph is more trouble than it's worth. First they find that shorted, rolling, radiation hazard, now this! Do you really need this many people?"

"Yes, is that a problem?"

"The private sector isn't going to like having the militia mobilized. The height of the production year's coming up."

"It's not that bad. I'll only need a lieutenant to command each unit, the rest can be non coms."

"So?"

"Francis, you may have been named after a mule, but you don't have to think like one. Even though you are a politician. The lieutenants are the only degree people we'll be taking off the job. Non coms are general labour. All that will happen is the sorting at the dumps will slow down when people leave them to fill the private sector jobs."

"Probably true. I was thinking of Colonel Ramses as C.O."

"Ramses is an overblown, self-important idiot. He doesn't know squat about the Dark Lands. I should command the mission."

"Eddie, your arm, is that a good idea?"

Eddie snorted. "My H.Q. will be Eden Mills, they're tinker friendly. I know the area and the village leaders. It was my route for ten years. I don't want some self-important twit fouling up all the time and effort I put into PR."

"Fine. I'm activating your commission, Major. Don't make me regret it."

"Yes, Minister. Two more things. I want each assigned trooper granted two silver marks a week bonus, conditional on them spending it in town, on goods made by the locals."

"Why?"

"Troops can get rowdy. Generosity buys tolerance. I also want that biohazard team."

Frances shook his head. "There I draw the line. I will not be known as the Minister who sent Novo Gaian citizens into a plague zone for the sake of a bunch of Dark Landers."

"But..."

"No, damn it! I'm going to be roasted over the cost of this as it stands. The only justification is keeping our voters safe. Plagues may not see lines on a map; I have to. Your man's on his own. Anything we can do from a distance, we'll do. Even airdrops of supplies. Be sure and take one of the ultralights with you."

"What, no F-50 jet fighters?" Eddie's tone was sarcastic.

Frances ignored the sarcasm. "Why kill a fly with a sledge hammer? An ultralight will do for airdrops and surveillance. Besides, you can launch it from a field if you have to."

They pulled into the parking station by the tinker facility.

"I'll leave the details to you, just try and keep the costs down." Francis climbed from the car.

"The Gridtowners. What can I expect from them?"

"Diplomacy says they'll commit sixty troops. You can liaison with their commander, a General McPherson, as to their placement."

"Who takes precedence of command?" Eddie reconnected the

charger.

"Our man is the one on the scene. You place the general's troops and leave him to see to them, but you have choice of placement." Francis started walking away from the tinker facility.

"Good. Where are you going?"

Frances grinned. "It's your operation, Major, you don't need me. If you do, I'll be in the Pink Pussycat until tomorrow morning's mag-lev. Don't tell my wife."

Eddie stared at the minister's back, shook his head and muttered "Politicians!"

Chapter Eight

Alone Against The Dark

BRAD SAT IN his wagon, allowing the adrenaline to purge from his system.

Ingram gazed through the open window. "Tinker, what is it?"

"Trouble. That seal was a biohazard warning. That cache must have been a disease, research facility. They'd have had a range of diseases there. The sickness could be almost anything, from almost anywhere. Ground out! It could even be man-made."

"Shit! Is there anything you can do?"

"I called my base. They're trying to arrange for some help."

"Tinker?" asked a pleading voice from behind Ingram.

Brad shifted to look at Wendell. "What?"

"Am I going to die?" The grieving man shifted about nervously.

"I don't know. I'll need a list of everyone you and Yackaharo came into contact with since you found the cache."

"That's almost everyone. We had a town meeting the day Yacky got sick." Ingram stared at his feet.

Brad sighed. "Better and better. First things first. I'm going back to the clinic to see if the treatment is helping. Wendell, I need you to collect anything you brought out of the cache, and bring it to me. Ingram, you're with me, if you're willing? I need someone to look after my team, run errands, all the little B.S. things I won't have time for."

"I'm your man, Tinker. If I can help, I will."

"Good, then climb aboard."

Brad spent the journey back to the converted plaza in thought. When he entered the clinic, the smell had lessened, due to the newly opened windows, and the stifling heat was gone.

Carla met him at the door. "Two more have died, and seven arrived while you were gone. I put the new ones on the cots at the end of the row. They're just like the others, but not as bad. I've recorded their vitals."

"It's spreading fast. You did the right thing." Brad scanned the room as a chill went up his spine.

"I gave them all pills. If they keep them down it should help." Trina approached from the side.

"I wrote down a description of the capsules and made sure she used only one type on each patient," explained Carla.

"Good work, both of you. Now put these on, and keep them on whenever you deal with anyone who's infected." Brad held out two boxes; one held latex gloves, the other paper facemasks.

"What is this?" demanded Trina.

"Quarantine procedures. I wish I could do better, but I can't. We may already be infected. These may not be enough to stop the bug, but it's better than nothing."

"Brad, what are we dealing with here?" Carla accepted a pair of gloves and a mask.

"Yackaharo stumbled across an ancient, bio-research facility and brought something out of it. I don't know what."

"My pills protect me." Trina's voice lacked conviction.

"Not against what's in that facility. I haven't gone into it, but we were briefed on them when we studied artefact retrieval. Basically, 'unless you want to die, stay clear' was the message. I've put a call in for a biohazard team. I hope they arrive soon." Brad pulled on a mask and gloves then moved to the closest of the patients with an I.V. He spent the next hour checking patients, stopping as darkness covered the western windows.

"I'm giving up on the saline solution," he said, as he stood beside one unconscious, desiccated figure.

"Why?" Carla paused in her sponging down of a slender Asian looking woman.

"It's doing more harm than good. A saline solution draws water out of the tissues into the blood stream, so the heart has something to pump. With this disease the tissues don't have any water to give up. All it's doing is throwing off the body's chemical balance. The normal saline is okay. Its salt content is the same as blood's, so it's at least adding fluid to that poor bugger. The Lactated Ringers seems to be doing the most good. Have you noticed that that patient's skin has a bit of elasticity? The Ringers is helping restore the electrolyte balance."

"How about the D5W?"

"Keep it up. It can't hurt. Besides—"

"Tinker, your radio is talking. Someone named Eddie wants you," called Ingram from the doorway.

"I'm coming!" Minutes later with the call signs exchanged Brad sat in his van.

"Do you want the good news or the bad news first? Over," came the voice from the speaker.

Brad stared out his window at the drizzle that matched his mood. "Give me the bad. It might as well join the parade. Over."

"The Minister refuses to send anyone in to help you. You're on your own. Over."

Brad slumped in his seat and rubbed at his grainy eyes. Depressing the button on his mic, he spoke. "You said there was good news. Please tell me. If I don't hear something positive, I might just jump off a cliff! Over."

"The quarantine has been agreed to. Novo Gaian militia and Gridtown regulars will have the Guelph area cordoned off by tomorrow evening. Also, I've been given an open purse on this. Anything you need that doesn't involve someone entering the quarantine zone is yours. This includes airdrops and consultations. I spoke to Dr. Frankel. He's joining me in Eden Mills. Over."

"Back on the old route, eh? How you mobilizing the troops? Over."

"Transport trucks are being prepped. Why? Over."

"It's no extra for the call. Would you pull my contract orders for next year and drop off the materials I'll need in the Eden Mills visitor's barn? Over."

"Tinker, you're amazing. In a plague zone and you're thinking of next year's profits. Over."

"Have to make a living, if I survive this. Over."

"I'll do what I can without delaying departure. As well, I must inform you that your reserve commission has been activated, Lieutenant. Over."

"At least I'll get paid, sir. Thank you, Major. Look, Eddie, I really need that biohazard team! Over."

"The Minister of Dark Land Affairs is a mollusc; slimy with no backbone. Over."

"Understood. I'll need an airdrop. Lactated Ringers and D5W. I'll also need a pair of biohazard suits, best you can get. I want to take a look in that facility. Maybe I can find a clue there. Did the records search turn up anything? Over."

"On the exotics, dozens of possibilities and more coming in from Gridtown. We need more information to narrow it down. We don't even have a record of that facility yet. Of course anything pre-collapse is spotty, so we'll keep trying. Over."

"Understood. Over and out."

"Good luck. Over and out."

Brad sat in his van, allowing the evening's darkness to envelop him. It seemed a fitting allegory to the fear that clutched his heart. Opening the glove compartment, he pulled out a small photo album and opened it. The first picture was of a middle-aged couple they stood with Brad to one side and an attractive blonde woman to the other. A large, tabby cat strained against a leash in front of them.

"A father shouldn't have to bury his son." Brad closed the album, collected his incubator and exited his van. Grabbing his power cable, he yelled, "Ingram!"

"Tinker?" The man appeared from under the eaves of a nearby house.

"First, where is my team?"

"They're in the visitors' field. I figured there wasn't any point in keeping them here. I borrowed a riding horse for you. It's in the inn's stable." He pointed to a decrepit-looking building with a one-car garage across the street.

"Good. Secondly, get some wood or something to keep my extension cord off the ground. If you can manage it, set up my windmill then get some sleep. Use my van, so you're close. Tomorrow is going to be one shorting day."

Dragging the power cable into the clinic, Brad cleared a space on a table and set up the incubator.

"Carla, we need to make a culture. I'm hoping this thing's a bacteria. If it's a virus, we're screwed. Second, I'm hoping it's in the blood. If it isn't, I don't know where to look for it."

"What's a culture?" Trina left a woman who was groaning in agony.

"I'm going to try and grow the germs causing the disease. If I succeed, I'll be able to see them in my microscope and tell the doctors on the radio what they look like."

Carla looked at Brad in astonishment. A glance from him stilled her questions.

"Real doctors are going to help us?" said Trina, in a tone of fanatic devotion.

"Yes. They're taking all the information I send them and looking for a treatment." Brad forced a false confidence into his voice.

The door flew open, and a tall man rushed into the room. A child of about twelve was cradled in his arms. Brad moved to the man's side. The newcomer looked down at him with pleading in his blue eyes.

"Please, Tinker. Youse got to save her!"

"Get her to a cot." Brad led the way to the end of the row of patients and began examining the child. Her almond-shaped, brown eyes snapped open as he took her temperature.

"Daddy," she wailed.

"I's here, honey," comforted the man. Kneeling beside her, he ran his hand through her sweat-soaked, black hair.

"She's only in the first stage. Her temperature's up, but it's not that bad, and she's only slightly dehydrated," said Brad. Moving to his supplies, he pulled out the last bag of Lactated Ringers. After a moment's thought he pulled out a bag of D5W as well then returned to the child.

"I want to start two I.V.s and sedate her, so she doesn't panic," he explained.

"Anythin', Tinker. Just save 'er." The man's Germanic features reflecting fear and concern.

The child's veins rose, and Brad pushed his needles home. The sedative took and she nodded off.

"That's it for the moment," he said.

"Will she live?" asked the distraught father.

"I don't know. We don't have a cure. Even the I.V.s are a guess. When did she start showing symptoms, Mr.?"

"Aberdon, Mark. She took ill after lunch. Brought up everythin' she ate. I thought it weren't nothing till after supper, when she did the same then passed out. Would have fallen right in the outhouse, if I hadn't pulled 'er back. Been hearing about this sickness. Kept clear of other folk these last three days. Guess it weren't enough." Marks face was pale with worry.

"Were you at the town meeting?"

"Sure if we weren't. Rose, that's me daughter, she wanted to see the other girls as would be there. It's been hard on 'er since 'er mother ran off with that travelling cooper." Mark made as if to spit but stopped himself.

"Brad, maybe we should try her on barley soup. Grandmother swears by it. People who can't keep anything else down can manage it," suggested Carla.

"I don't know. I'm no herbalist, but even a drop of water is too much for these people."

"Won't know unless we try. She's the least advanced case we've seen. Maybe if we catch things early enough?"

"Go ahead. It probably won't hurt."

"I'll mix some caraway into it, that settles the bowel too."

"You've been looking through my wagon's cupboard." Brad grinned.

"Cook's prerogative." Carla moved towards the door.

"Tinker, Patrick just stopped breathing!" yelled Trina from the far end of the room.

"No," whispered Mark, who sank to the ground and held his daughter's hand.

Brad left the child and moved to one of the other cases.

Nearly an hour later Carla moved to Brad's side. "What did you mean you'd be talking with doctors? Aren't they sending in a team?"

He placed a tourniquet around the patient's arm. The man opened his brown eyes, worked his mouth around a swollen tongue then fell unconscious again.

"Novo Gaia is refusing to send anyone into the plague zone. They'll help us with supplies, quarantine the area, and give us radio support, but that's all," said Brad.

"I thought Novo Gaia cared about the Dark Lands."

"Doing a damn sight more than Gridtown, aren't we?"

Carla looked at him, hurt and anger marring her features.

"All I meant was, we Dark Landers always get left in the crunch."

"What do you mean, 'we Dark Landers'?" Brad prepared agar plates to receive the blood sample.

Carla stared at him then looked at the floor. "Open mouth, insert foot. Sorry Brad. It's easy to forget you're Novo Gaian."

"Apology accepted. If it's any consolation, if I survive to the next election, the Minister of Dark Land Affairs has lost my votes." Brad inserted a needle into the patient's vein and withdrew a half vial of blood. Smearing the blood onto the agar plates he closed their lids.

"Put that in my incubator, would you? Be sure the plates are upside down."

"Will do."

Carla rose with the plates in hand as the door opened.

"Tinker, you gotta help me. It's my mum, she has it." Ingram carried a slender, dark-skinned, middle-aged woman to the empty cot closest to the door.

Chapter Nine

Troop Movements

"LISTEN UP, TROOPS. I expect good behaviour. Show the colours, and make Novo Gaia proud. And for Gods' sake, don't get anyone pregnant! Remember we're going into the Dark Lands. A lot of the folk aren't on birth control, so if you play, make damn sure you are." Eddie stood at the front of a train car, with a large map of the Guelph area behind him. Symbols depicting three Gridtown and five Novo Gaian units blocked all the roads in and out of Guelph.

"Sir, what can we expect? I mean, is it as bad as they say in the Dark Lands?" asked a young man with brown hair and a bushy moustache.

Eddie leaned against the front row of seats. His camouflage slacks and shirt rumpled, displaying a cut meant for comfort over appearance.

"If you mean, is it like Gridtown T.V. shows with gangs of bloodthirsty thugs behind every tree and plague in every stream? No! If you mean, is it mostly pre-electric, with a dodgy water supply and a lot of subsistence labour? That's true. The companies bivouacking in Eden Mills will have an easy time of it. The rest of you, look at it like an extended camping trip. If you want an idea of what it's really like, think of the Tinker's Road series."

A murmur passed among the troops at this.

"Sir. I heard Dark Lands men can be, well, insistent," said a large-busted, black-haired woman.

"Don't worry about it, sergeant. If they come on too strong, make them sing soprano. One thing to remember about the Dark Lands, it's schoolyard rules. Never throw the first punch, but by the Gods throw the last.

"We'll be at Cookstown station in three minutes. Your lieutenants will brief you on the specifics en-route to your postings. Don't be heroes, don't be jerks, and everything will be okay."

Eddie took his seat and closed his eyes, visualizing Eden Mills and mentally placing his equipment. The whisper of the train's passage changed as it slowed then stopped. The doors opened, and his troops spilled into the central aisle, pulling duffles from the overhead racks. Crossing the infantile fingers of his left hand beneath the sleeve of his uniform, Eddie stood.

"I'll carry your bag, sir," offered a slender, young woman with blonde hair held in a braid.

"No need. Lieutenant?"

"Newicky, Barbara Newicky. I pulled duty as your aide, sir."

"So you're the short straw." Eddie hauled his duffle onto his shoulder.

"Guess so, sir."

They stepped from the train onto a cargo platform. A line of twenty-first-century tractor-trailers were backed against the loading bay.

Eddie smiled as the trucks brought back pleasant memories. "Okay, Lieutenant Newicky, let's get going. Our squad's in the alcohol fuelled truck with the aircraft strapped to its roof. The methane powered trucks are for the other posts."

They walked to the vehicle, which in addition to the plane and passenger extension, had a battered van on its flat bed. Behind the van were boxes of equipment.

"A tinker van?" Barbara noted the power drill underneath a flaming sun crest on the van's side. The drill's cord looped up into the sun; everything was on a field of sky blue.

"Mine. I wasn't expecting to be able to use it for a few more years, but it's the best portable H.Q. you could ask for."

"You're a tinker?"

"Before I got hurt. Why?"

"I just started feeling a whole lot better about this mission."

"Good. You handle the briefing. I'll sit up front with the driver."

Minutes later the rest of the troop had been checked off on the roster and taken seats in the passenger extension. With a whine of fuel-cell, powered turbines, the trucks pulled out along a stretch of Highway 89 that paralleled the Novo Gaian rail. In minutes Eddie's truck pulled to a stop at a tollgate.

"Toll," demanded a middle-aged attendant with rotting teeth. He was dressed in a stiff looking uniform, and his grey hair was cut short.

"We're on a joint mission with the Niagara Grid Region regulars," explained Eddie.

"Toll," demanded the attendant.

"We were assured passage."

"We maintain the highways. You Novo Gaians just leach off us. Now you want to drive them for free. If you don't like the roads, you can always ride your toy trains, or aren't they up to the job?"

"Sir, just pay him," suggested the driver, an overweight, middle-aged man. His features were almost hidden by the Stetson and mirrored sunglasses he wore.

Eddie fished a silver mark from his pouch and passed it to the Gridtowner.

"That's better. Now you may proceed to customs, so we can be sure you're not bringing contraband onto United Grid Region's soil," said the attendant.

"The roads are not Grid regions' soil, for purposes of customs and visas, and you know it," objected Eddie.

"Maybe if I had some assurance of your honesty, we could forgo customs." The attendant pulled a credit chip from his pocket and rubbed it suggestively between thumb and forefinger.

"I've had enough of this crap!" Eddie picked up the truck's handset.

"This is Major Baily to convoy. We are rolling through. Repeat, we are rolling through. Anyone attempting to stop you is to be dealt with. Use whatever force necessary! Over." Eddie slammed the mic onto its clip.

"Open the gate or lose it," Eddie snapped at the attendant then turning to his driver he barked "Forward."

The truck rammed the wooden dividing bar, hurling it into the highway beyond. The attendant stared open mouthed as the convoy rolled by him, horns blaring.

As the trucks hurtled down the maintained highway, Eddie burnt up the airwaves. The result was that no other tollbooths stopped them before they turned onto the shattered asphalt of the old Highway Fifteen. Here they slowed as the vehicles going to Eden Mills bumped over the broken pavement, receiving astonished stares from the locals. The sun was passing its zenith when Eden Mills came into view.

"Stop by the visitor field, that one to the right with the panelled house in the corner," ordered Eddie.

The trucks stopped just short of the gate in the stone fence enclosing the area. The field was empty, but before Eddie had climbed from the cab a crowd of curious townsfolk were rounding the bend in the road.

"Early for trade aren't you Gridtowner?" called John, the innkeeper, as he strode towards them. Seeing Eddie he stopped and his jaw fell.

"Hello John, good to see you." Eddie walked to the other man.

"Eddie. What in the name of Bacchus is goin' on?" There was fear in the innkeeper's voice.

"Trouble, John. We're with the Novo Gaian militia."

A collective gasp ran through the crowd, and many began searching for a route of escape.

"Brad left here in fine shape. He even took Meb's granddaughter, Carla, with him. You know us, Tinker. No argument with Bright Landers. Shorting, I even ordered a new panel for next year."

Eddie raised his voice, so the crowd could hear him. "We've come to protect you. Brad told us about some trouble hereabouts and asked if we could help. I like Eden Mills and figured it would be a good time for a friendly visit."

Suspicious glances still leapt from the crowd to the men and women climbing from the flat beds, but a relieved murmur passed among the locals.

"John, you still chief councillor?" Eddie spoke for John's ears alone.

"Long as I supply the drinks at the council meetings I am."

"Could you call a town meeting? People should know why we're here. Besides, it's your town, if you tell us to leave, we'll leave."

John visibly relaxed. "Can't ask fairer than that. I'll send Billy to fetch Meb and Nick. The town council should be able to hear your case in an hour or two. While you're waiting, send your people round my inn." he smiled. "Still the best public kitchen in town."

"It's the only public kitchen in town." Eddie smiled and slapped John on the arm so the crowd could see. "but as long as Milly's doing the cooking, they won't do badly by you."

John nodded. "It's good to see you. Brad's a fine man, but old friends are best friends, as they say."

Eddie nodded then turned to the ordering of his troop. "Who grew up on a farm?"

Three hands were raised.

"Good. You three check the methane composter in the visitor's barn, see that it's fully charged. Lieutenant Newicky, take two of the squad and start off loading the boxes marked with a T. They're to go into the locked storage room in the barn. There's a key in my wagon's dash. The rest of my squad are going to help me assemble the ultralight. Lieutenant Carshay, take your truck to the highway seven checkpoint and establish a perimeter. Return here after you've set up your troops."

"Yes sir," replied a man in his early twenties with strong, Nordic features and blond hair.

"Now to work." Eddie joined the team by the ultralight.

Chapter Ten

Airdrop

Brad rubbed his eyes and turned off the electric light as the morning sun pierced the clinic's few remaining windows.

"The I.V.s are running low." Carla stood beside him where he sat at a table in front of his laptop.

"Send Ingram to the visitors' field. Tell him to bring water from the still. We'll boil it and add salt. At least we can approximate normal saline."

"You look like what the cow left behind. You should get some sleep."

"No time." Brad pulled a bottle of pills from his med kit and popped one into his mouth.

"Amphetamines?" Carla's voice was disapproving.

Brad shrugged. "We don't have coffee like in the old movies. I normally wouldn't, but since my courageous government appointed me instant contagion expert, I don't have much choice."

"I'll go speak to Ingram."

"Good. When he's gone, you get some sleep." Brad patted her hand.

"I'm okay."

"No, you're not. You're going on twenty-four hours. I'll need you later, and I'll need you alert. Besides, someone has to stay by the radio."

Brad snapped on a pair of gloves, moved to the incubator and withdrew an agar plate. Preparing a slide took only minutes; then he was staring down the barrel of his microscope. Pulling away, he blinked hard then returned to his viewing.

"Not a damn bloody thing," he muttered.

"Maybe you didn't follow the doctor's instructions." Trina approached from the far end of the room.

"I've prepared smears before. It's not in their blood, or it's a virus."

"Is that why my pills didn't work?"

"Yes. Disease organisms come in several types. The most common are bacteria and viruses. Antibiotics work against bacteria, but have no effect on viruses."

"What works against viruses?"

"Not much. Sometimes you can make a serum from the blood of survivors, but it's specific to that virus. Best we can do is try to support the victims, give their bodies time to discover how to fight the virus."

Brad moved to Rose's bedside and stared down at the child. Her skin was turning deathly white and sweat soaked her. Despite the constant I.V.s, dehydration was apparent. Her father slept on the floor beside her.

"She kept down that barley soup. Strange that it could do what my pills couldn't," observed Trina.

"If it works, use it. The credo of Novo Gaian medicine. Carla wants to try boiling some huckleberries in the water we use to make the soup. She says it might help with the fever and diarrhea. She's been right so far. I figure we should try it. That reminds me. We're going to need more help here. Can you think of anyone willing to lend a hand?"

Trina bit her lip as she thought. "Other than Mark here? No! Folk remember the coughing sickness of 102. They've all locked themselves away on their farms."

"Damn, that means we could have cases out there we know nothing about. We'll also need more barley and caraway. Do you know where we can get them?"

"I can help with that," interrupted a weary voice from the doorway.

"Wendell?" Brad squinted into the light.

"I brought the stuff from the cache. Ingram told me you burnt Yacky." Wendell stepped into the dim room he was carrying a pair of sacks.

"We couldn't risk letting his body spread the infection." Brad moved to the new arrival's side.

Wendell nodded once. His face was drawn, and he moved sluggishly. "My mum use to collect caraway. She took me with her. I'll go gathering. There are a few sacks of barley left in my barn you can have. Is it the cure?"

"They can keep it down; that helps."

Wendell turned and left the building.

"Well maybe some good will come of this. Now that boy can find a nice girl and have a normal life," said Trina.

Brad glanced at her, shook his head, and returned to Rose.

"The I.V.s almost through," he observed.

"We only have one bag of the ones you said might help left."

"I know. We'll use it on the child. We started her treatment earliest, so she probably has the best chance."

When the I.V. was replenished Brad moved among the patients, taking vital signs, trying to chart the disease's progress. He had just dragged a body into the storeroom that was serving as a morgue when Ingram arrived carrying two large clay jugs of water.

"This is all there was, Tinker. Someone must have drained the system. The rain refilled it, but it'll be a while afore the water goes through."

"It will be enough. I'll need you to fetch more later though." Brad moved to help with the jugs. In minutes the water was boiling in a set of pre-collapse, stainless-steel pots. The heat from the wood stove, mingled with the stuffiness of the room, made the odours seem stronger.

"We have to add just the right amount of salt." Brad filled a measuring spoon and dumped the crystals into the water. "Let that boil for twenty minutes, no less!" he told Trina. "Ingram, in my trailer, at the back, there are cases of mason jars."

"What?"

"Canning jars. Like they use for jams."

"Oh, okay, I'll fetch them in."

Brad opened the oven door on the wood stove and pulled a basting thermometer out with a rag.

When the mason jars arrived they went into the oven, and, half an hour later, were being filled with the steaming saline solution.

"This should last us a while." Trina set the jars to one side.

"I hope it will last us long enough. As soon as this is cooled, I want to set up I.V.s on as many cases as we have needles for. Do the most recent ones first. And set another pot of water to boil. I'm running out of equipment. I need to sterilize needles for reuse."

"Gridtown doctors never use the same needle twice."

"Gridtown doctors don't have to. How much stuff do you think I can fit in a tinker wagon?"

The sun was passing noon when Carla entered the clinic. Mason jars with I.V. tubing looping into them occupied stands by half the beds. Brad was once again in front of his computer.

"Carla, come here. I found something interesting on Rose."

"Is it good?" she rushed to his side trying not to look at the vacant spaces where cots had been before she slept.

"I don't know, but it's one more thing to tell the germ dogs in their nice, safe kennel."

"About that. Eddie wants you on the radio."

Brad left the building. The shock of fresh air was like diving into cold water. Moving to his van, he settled and scanned his dash.

Shorting, my charge is in the toilet! He thought as he picked up the radio and gave his call sign.

"Brad, we're at Eden Mills, and the plane's ready for take off. Where do you want the airdrop? Over," asked Eddie's voice.

"Hallelujah! I've been using home made normal saline all morning. There's an old school about two blocks from the town hall. It had a huge field they've put to the plough. Can you find it on the old maps? Over."

"Negative. Nothing like that near Guelph City Hall. Over."

"Not the old City Hall, the northeast, Guelph suburb's town hall. The old converted plaza. Over."

"They're still using that thing? The place is an energy eater. I know the school you're talking about. Hold on while I speak with my pilot. Over."

The radio went dead. Brad listened to the slow whump, whump, whump, of his windmill blades.

"Brad, the pilot says she can drop the stuff in that field. I.V.s, contagion suits. She'll be there in about an hour. Over."

"Marvellous, now I'm only underqualified, not underqualified and ill equipped. Over."

"You're beginning to sound like a locked up program. Dr. Frankel wants a word with you. Over."

Eddie's voice was replaced by the more resonant tones of the medical doctor.

"Dr. Irving, I have been trying to narrow the field of possible disease vectors. Frankly, I need more information. Is there anything more you can tell me? Over."

"We had a little girl brought in in the first stage of the disease. I started I.V. therapy. She's kept down some barley soup. I noticed this morning that her lymph glands were swollen. That seems to be happening in about a quarter of the cases. Also, I took a blood culture and found nothing. Over."

"What is the white cell count? Over."

"Hard to take. I sat up half the night staring and counting. My eyes hurt. It's around 30,000. Over."

"Thirty thousand! Are you sure? You didn't double count did you? Over."

"I'm not a complete git. I checked it twice. Over."

"My apologies. Things sound worse than I had imagined. I am sending vital signs monitors and a telemetry transmitter along with the drop. How many do you need? Over."

"Doc, I only have my wagon to supply juice to run this show. I can't power up a whole I.C.U. Over."

"Very well. I will only send six monitor rings and one telemeter. You should place them on your newest patients, so I can monitor the disease's progress from here. Over."

"Can do, Doc, but if it becomes a choice of dropping the telemeter or losing the lights, the telemeter goes. Over."

"Very well. Also, I need you to do something that I know you will not like. Over."

"Doc, I haven't slept in two days. I'm not up to guessing games. Over."

"I need an autopsy and a set of organ samples. I have permission from the Minister to bring them out and examine them in my portable Lab. Over."

"An autopsy? With knives that can cut through gloves and flesh? Doc, people are dying here! I may already have been exposed, but I'd rather not improve my chances of catching this! Over."

"I require the samples. If you are careful, you should be safe enough. Over."

"Look, let me check out the facility first, who knows what we'll find. Over."

"Lieutenant, the Minister authorized this action himself. Over."

"Then let that fat-assed idiot come in here and do it himself! If, and only if, the search of the facility doesn't turn up an answer, will I risk cutting into an infected corpse. Over!"

"Brad, language! Over," interjected Eddie's voice.

"I'm up to my ass in dead bodies, with crap all for help, and you expect me to care about using some fucking four letter words on the radio. Tell the good Minister that the next time he tries to strong arm me into doing something asinine, I'll leave the quarantine zone and give him a great big kiss! Over!"

Static filled the airwaves then the radio came back to life with the doctor's voice.

"Of course, you are right, Tinker. It is easy to forget you do not have a proper team to back you up. Preserving your well-being must be a priority. Please, if your inspection of the facility fails to find an agent, consider my request. Over."

"That's all I ask, Doc. If there's nothing else, I have to sign off. Over." Brad wearily rubbed his own shoulders.

"That Dan Timothy you mentioned in Arkell? Over," continued Eddie's voice.

"A stellar gentleman, a real star. Over."

"If you hear from him in there, tell him hello from my mother. She knew him during his school days. Over."

"Will do. Over and out."

"Thanks. Over and out."

Brad stared at his console for several seconds, swore and climbed from the wagon.

"What did they say?" Ingram leaned against the van.

"They're sending us a package. It should be arriving in the old schoolyard in about an hour. Before it gets here I need your help. My batteries are almost dead. Running lights and everything in the clinic is killing them."

"What can we do?"

"Glad you asked." Brad moved to the hood of his van and pulled it open, revealing four deep-cycle, twelve-volt batteries. He started checking their water levels. Half an hour later he was connecting the wires on three thin-film solar panels he'd unrolled onto an old piece of sheet metal without stripping off their backings. He set this on the crumbling sidewalk in front of the clinic.

"Remember how it's done?" he asked.

"I think so, Tinker," replied Ingram.

"Good. I'll link these three to my system then I want you to set up six more just like we did. Keep them angled about like these ones. Damn, my customers are going to be pissed. I used their purchases. I'll just sell it as a field trial. Shit, maybe bump the price a copper or two to impress them."

Brad ran cable from his battery pack to the new solar panels and connected the system before entering the clinic.

"Mark, I need your help." Brad laid a hand on the bereaved man's shoulder.

"Will it help Rose?"

"Probably. They're dropping some equipment for me in that field by the old school. I need help dragging it here."

Mark rose, kissed his daughter's brow and followed Brad from the building.

"Hold on a moment." Brad pulled a pair of flares from his truck.

"This sickness is a right bugger. It makes it so there's no dignity in living," said Mark, as they walked down the street.

"I know. It's almost like it was meant to humiliate its victims before killing them."

"My Rose, she woke up earlier and was crying 'cause she loosed 'er bowel. It's not fair that a sweet child like 'er should be shamed like that."

Brad nodded. "Disease is never fair."

Turning a corner they saw the field. The old school was little more than a pile of bricks and broken glass, while the yard was covered in rye grass. The asphalt, playing surface around the building had long since been mined for recycling.

"It shouldn't be long." Brad strode to the middle of the field and lit the first of his flares. It sent a streamer of red smoke into the air.

He was turning around when the soil exploded by his feet. Throwing himself to the ground, he groped for the pistol at his side.

"Get off me land, youse plague-riddled son's of bitches. Youse won't infect me or mine." Screamed a voice from the edge of the field.

"Paterson, get back in your damn house. There's an aireo plane coming that's gonna drop medicine in this here field. Once we take it, you won't see us for dust," yelled Mark.

"Not a chance. Youse won't poison me crops or me family. Now be off, or I'll shoot youse dead. I swear it."

A new sound intruded on Brad's awareness. A drone like a dragonfly, only a thousand times louder. The sound grew nearer as the men argued.

"Paterson you ass, Rose needs this medicine. Get back in your house."

"Rose is suffering from her mother's sins. We're all suffering for our sins. I'll not have youse plague bearers pollutin' me land. Now get off."

The sound grew as Brad crawled toward Paterson. Finally it reached a volume where it pierced the crazed farmer's fervour. He turned to gaze skyward. Leaping to his feet, Brad rushed the farmer.

Paterson glanced toward Brad and tried to bring his gun to bear. Brad tackled his foe, forcing the man to the ground as they grappled for the rifle.

Enraged Paterson swung the butt of his gun, catching Brad

under the chin. Brad's vision clouded red as long hours of training took over. He grasped the gun barrel in one hand and drove the other against Paterson's throat, pushing his thumb and fingers against the farmer's carotid arteries.

Paterson struggled vainly as his blood-starved brain grew dim then he passed out.

"Tinker, he's out." Brad heard Mark's voice calling him back to sanity.

"Mark." Brad released his hold on the farmer. He shook his head to clear it then stood.

"You okay?"

"My jaw's in one piece, barely. I'll have a nasty bruise." Kneeling Brad felt for Paterson's pulse. "He should be okay as well. Good thing you stopped me." Brad arranged the man on his side, so the drool spilt from his mouth onto the ground then pulled the firing pin from the rifle and pocketed it. "Shorting, I hate this kind of crap. My headache will only be a hair less than his."

Just then the camouflage-patterned wings of the ultralight came into view. The pilot sat in an open cockpit, made of linked pipes, and the plane's broad wingspan stretched above her on both sides. A single back facing propeller whirred, and a large sphere was attached to the undercarriage. The pilot waved, making a low pass. Brad waved back and moved to the field's edge. Mark stared skyward in awed silence.

The pilot made another pass, dropping the sphere. It struck the rye field like a bowling ball, tumbling end for end, leaving a trail of destruction in its wake. It finally rolled to a stop. The plane wiggled its wings then flew off to the west.

"A flying person. I read about it in old books, but to see it," breathed Mark.

A crowd of people were beginning to collect at the field's edge, all with their eyes riveted to the sky.

"Let's go." Brad rubbed his jaw. The layer of padding on the drop sphere's outside was torn in places, but had kept its hard inner shell from cracking. Brad found the clasp and opened it. Inside were four backpacks filled with I.V. solution, and, in a cushioned package in the centre, the biohazard suits. Their orange material seemed to glow in the daylight, and the air tanks in their additional foam covering showed full.

"Lucky they didn't blow the whole bloody, grounded thing, dropping full cylinders. Would have thought Eddie had the sense to send a compressor and empty tanks. Oh well." Brad shouldered a pack. By now several members of the crowd were approaching.

"Tinker," called Mark. The crowd around them was slowly inching in.

"I'm the tinker from the clinic. I need help getting this equipment there," called Brad.

The advancing group paused then all but two retreated.

"We'll carry the stuff to the clinic's door, but no further," yelled the pair that remained. They were a middle-aged couple of Asian descent, dressed in simple clothing and wearing broad-brimmed hats.

"Thank you, Mr. and Mrs. Lee. Both from Rosie and me self," hollered Mark.

"Yes, thank you," added Brad. A sound drew his attention and he turned. Paterson stood unsteadily and pointed the disabled gun at them. He shook his head, stared mutely at the rifle then stumbled away.

"At least that's done." Brad started toward the clinic.

"Are there many flying machines in Novo Gaia?" asked Mark, as they walked.

"A few. They're useful for search and rescue and getting to remote areas."

"Wonderful thing that. People who can fly. Rose would love it."

Brad smiled. "Tell you what, when she gets better, I'll talk to the pilot. Maybe she can go up in it."

"Do you think she'll get better, Tinker?"

"I don't know. She's not as sick as the others, but that might be because the I.V. delays the dehydration."

"That was some scrap you and Paterson had back there. I heard about tinkers being tough in a fight, but I ain't never seen nothin' like that before. You put his lights out without throwing a punch."

Brad looked at the ground. "Necessary skills if you travel much in the Dark. Combat arms is part of every tinker's training."

"They teach you how to fight?"

"No. They teach us how to kill. There's a big difference. Paterson is one lucky bastard. The move I used is one of the few that can be pulled up short. You saved his life when you called me off."

Mark stared at Brad in disbelief. "No. You're kidding me."

"You're a hero, Mark. Whether anyone knows it or not."

Mark smiled for the first time in two days. The action transformed his face, smoothing away many lines of care and worry. Then it passed.

Chapter Eleven

Ace In The Hole

THE BUZZING SOUND grew louder, drawing the populace of Arkell from their homes. The pilot manoeuvred the ultralight in a circle around the settlement.

Dan traced his hand along the spine of the woman beside him. She rolled to look at him, with lusty, hazel eyes. Her well-rounded body beckoned, and her long, grey-streaked, brown hair, fell across the bed.

"My husband won't be back for at least a hour, and you've made us so many candles. I think you should 'ave another bonus," she said.

Dan smiled and moved to kiss her, but the sound passing over the house distracted him.

"What the shorting is that?" he muttered.

"Does it matter?" asked the woman.

Dan searched his memory for a name before replying.

"Dinah, me sweet, you are enough to make a man forget the world, but I remember that sound from somewhere. It bothers me."

The sound returned and recognition dawned.

"It's an aircraft. Shorting, someone has an aeroplane flying around out there."

"A what?" asked Dinah, her mood now broken.

Dan leapt from the bed and started pulling on his clothes. A veteran of many close calls, he was dressed in seconds and out the back door. He paused by his bubbling caldron, disconnected an automatic mixing device, and made great show of stirring the soap while he waited. The ultralight flew past, trailing a streamer of red cloth.

"What is it, Dan? Who sent a flying machine?" Dinah had pulled on a homespun dress and stood beside him.

"I don't know, me girl, but I know how to find out. Douse the fire for me, would you love? The soap's done." Dan sprinted to his wagon, which was parked on the street, and pulled a flare from under its hood. Moving to a stretch of ground where several houses had been dismantled for materials, he lit the flare.

The plane made another pass, dropping a small sphere. Dan ran after it. Reaching the sphere, he turned to wave at the pilot. She waggled her wings in reply and flew off to the northeast. Undoing the latch on the container, he opened it revealing a portable, two-way radio.

"Now what could those boys be up to?" he grumbled while activating the unit. A note instructed him to tune to a frequency.

"This is Dan Timothy, Candler, graduate of the Novo Gaian Dark Lands skills academy. Who's listening?"

"Corporal Timothy, this is Major Edward Baily. Time to knock the rust off your sword. We're reactivating you. Over."

Dan stared at the speaker, dumbfounded, before replying.

"That's just great. You've got to love the trust the Novo Gaian militia has in their people. Been out here twenty years and not a worry I may have turned bad. What's the story that you want an old candler back in the army? ... Oh yes, Over."

"Are you alone? Over."

"I will be. Give me five minutes to get away from the locals. I hear them coming. Over."

Dan resealed the radio in the drop sphere and, picking it up, ran behind a nearby pile of rubble. The flare continued to belch smoke, which was attracting the townspeople now that the plane had gone. Creeping from the rubble, he moved to an abandoned building then slipped away. Five minutes later he reopened the sphere and picked up the radio.

"Major Baily, Corporal Timothy to Major Baily, come in. Over."

"We read you Corporal. Are you safe to speak? Over."

"Safe as in my mother's arms. Now why did you interrupt my... soap making? Over."

"That sickness you saw in Guelph. It's a plague! Your area is quarantined. So far the locals don't know, but that won't last. We need you to be our eyes and ears. If you can arrange it so folk stay clear of Guelph, it would be for the best. Keep a low profile. Your eyes are more important than heroics. Over."

"There was a tinker, nice chap name of Brad, heading to Guelph. Had a lass, name of Carla, with him. Did you know about them? Over."

"Brad told us about the plague. We'll be monitoring this frequency, relay anything you hear to us. The doctor will fill you in on the symptoms to watch for. Over."

"Understood, Major. I'm your eyes and ears in Arkell. My mother told me there'd be days like this! Over."

When the doctor had finished describing the symptoms, Dan hid the radio in his station wagon and returned to his soap making.

An hour later Ward, Dinah's husband, burst into his backyard. He was huge, with muscles that bulged from his shirt like iron and a face that showed the effects of many brawls. "Candler, youse done?"

"Yup, won't be stinking up your yard any more this year." Dan cut the soap into bars and stacked them at the side of the table he worked on.

"Glad o' that. Join us for dinner. 'Tween youse and me, I'd appreciate it. Dinah's always easier when youse about. Seems like 'avin' fresh soap for a wash sooths 'er mood."

Dan smiled at the larger man. "Thank you, Ward, dinner sounds marvellous. One thing you miss on the road is good home cooking."

Chapter Twelve

Town Council

EDDIE STOOD IN the small, upstairs room of the inn that served as a council hall. A battered, formica table, with rusty chrome legs, filled the centre of the room. Four sturdy, wooden chairs sat around it. Evening light leaked in through the small, north-facing window. John, the innkeep, sat at the table with Nick, who fidgeted with the badge at his collar as he nursed a tankard of ale.

"Where is she?" demanded Eddie, for the seventh time.

"She'll be around. Babies come at their own pace. Billy said she was almost through. Relax, you have your troops in place, and that aeroplane is buzzing around up there. Read about things like that, but you don't expect to see them," replied John.

"Have a drink, Tinker. It will do you good," suggested Nick.

The door opened, revealing Meb. Blood was spattered on her dress, and her sleeve cuffs were damp.

"What in the name of Taweret happened to you?" She glared at Eddie's empty shirtsleeve.

"Second year out on my new route. I was coming down a ladder from an installation when a cougar jumped me. It sank its teeth into my arm before I could do anything."

"It bit off your arm and didn't kill you?" Nick sounded

impressed.

"Not exactly. If it had been my right arm, I would have been in trouble. I wear my gun on my right side. If you come by my wagon, I can show you a beautiful cougar-skin rug."

"Tinkers! You're all boys who never grow up. You lost an arm, Eddie," snapped Meb.

Smiling, Eddie rolled up his sleeve and waved to her with the infantile left arm. "Take a few more years for it to grow in, but it's doing well."

Meb stared speechlessly at the appendage and stretched out a hand to touch it then she turned to John. "Do you see why we need a real healer here? Think what this could have meant for your father."

John coughed then spoke. "That's a different matter. For now, Eddie isn't here as a tinker, but as a Major in the Novo Gaian reserve. Eddie, maybe you should fill us in."

"There's a plague in Guelph. It may have spread to Arkell. We're here to enforce a quarantine."

"A plague in Guelph! How do you know about it?" demanded Meb.

"Brad radioed it in."

Meb leaned heavily against the table as John leapt to place a chair behind her.

"I sent her into a plague zone. Taweret help me, what have I done?" Meb sank into the seat.

"Steady, Meb, Carla's fine. I spoke to Brad. She's helping him in the clinic. I promise to keep you posted." Eddie placed a hand on the old midwife's shoulder.

"All right, Tin... Major, what do you want from us?" Nick voice was all business, but fear could be seen in how he clutched his tankard.

"Let my people stay at the inn and respect the quarantine. We'll pay full marks for anything we use. I think you'll find my squad's a good lot. As well, an official request from you for our protection would go a long way to legitimizing our presence."

"Rot. If givin' me trade is all you want to do, I can live with that." John smiled but his voice held tension.

"Can I join the team going to Guelph? You know I'm a good

practical nurse," demanded Meb.

"That would break quarantine. No one's going in or coming out. My squad has orders to shoot to kill if necessary. I'm sorry, but we can't let this thing spread." Eddie moved so he faced all three councillors.

"No one going in? You're not sending in doctors? You're leaving it up to Brad. *My granddaughter's in there!*" Meb slammed her hand down on the table.

"Brad's a good man. He'll—"

"I know he's a good man. But he's a tinker, not a medical doctor! He can't possibly know how to handle a plague!"

"Calm down, Meb. Screaming won't make it any better." John focussed on Eddie. "Now, Major, surely you're doin' more than just surrounding Guelph and letting the disease run its course. I'd expect that of Gridtown, not Novo Gaia."

Eddie looked at the floor. "We're giving Brad full radio and equipment support. Everything short of sending people into the plague zone."

"See, Meb. You can always count on the tinkers. I bet Brad is wishin' they'd leave him alone, so he could get on with it." John forced false confidence into his voice.

Meb turned a cold eye on him that shifted to Eddie. "Why won't you send in real help?"

"Meb, this isn't like when I was here as a tinker. Then I was a law unto myself. Now I have to kiss the ass of the Minister of Dark Land Affairs. He was a tinker, about twenty years ago. I think he's forgotten everything he ever knew about being a vertebrate."

Meb nodded at the rage in Eddie's voice.

"Being a what?" asked Nick.

"Having a backbone," explained Meb. "I cast my vote for offering Eddie's squad any help we can. I also think we should make an official request for their help."

"I agree," said John.

"I don't like having troops in the town. But so long as they behave, I can't see where we'll suffer from this. I want to know, will this official request business cost us anything?" asked Nick.

"Not a copper. I just want the legitimacy of being invited in by local authority."

"Well then, since if what Eddie here says is true, and I've never known a tinker to lie, it needs to be done. I say let's help our old tinker out."

"Thank you." Eddie moved to the door.

"Stay for a drink?" offered John.

"Do your job." Meb rose to escort Eddie.

"Do you think there'll be trouble about the quarantine?" he asked as they descended the stairs to the inn's main floor.

"Some. We'll have to have a town meeting to ratify the decision. Greg Thomson can be counted on to make trouble."

Eddie paused to examine the inn side of John's building. A common-room, with south-facing, picture windows, allowed access to the entry porch and the stairs leading to the second floor guest rooms. Washrooms and showers occupied rooms to the back of the common-room. The lounge area itself was furnished with comfortable chairs, re-upholstered in thick, local cloth, set facing a forty-five-centimetre T.V. vid-player and stereo on the west wall. A large, masonry hearth occupied the centre of the north wall. Eddie heard his heels strike the room's hardwood floor and watched as three of his troops shifted to look at him.

"This place keeps getting better and better," he observed.

"John reads too many old books. He wants to turn this place into the Hilton," complained Meb.

"Why not?"

"No reason. I'm just old, that's all. Change has its place, but sometimes it seems to be happening in all the wrong places. I asked John to help pay for Carla's education. He said he needed more panels for the inn. What could be more important than getting a real healer into this town?"

"You really love her." Eddie stepped onto the town's main street.

"You know how I feel about my daughter. She could have been something special! She threw it all away to marry that farmer. Carla's even smarter than Susan. She's my last chance to pass on what I've built here. If she doesn't become a healer, this town won't be any better off than Guelph, with that idiot Trina and her silly pills."

"I hear you. When will the ratification meeting be held?"

"For something this important, tomorrow. I'm betting that John's getting Billy and his friends to spread the word already."

"In that case, I have some shopping to do." Eddie crossed the street to the general store.

Chapter Thirteen

The Depths

BRAD WATCHED CARLA insert the needle and start an I.V. drip.

"Good, very good." He rested his hand on her shoulder.

"I think I have the hang of it now." Carla brushed her cheek against his hand.

Brad smiled wearily. "Then I can get moving. You can do them as much good as I can at the moment. Remember, large bore, lactated ringers and D5W, full flow for anyone who comes in with the symptoms."

Brad looked around. Twenty-five cots held patients. He tried not to think of how many lay in the impromptu morgue.

"I wish you weren't going," said Carla.

"Believe me, so do I! But who else would know what to look for? Of course that's assuming I know what to look for."

"I believe in you." Carla turned back to her patients.

Brad left the clinic. Standing beside his van, he filled his lungs, allowing the cool, night air to wash the stench from his nostrils.

"Ready, Tinker?" Ingram emerged from the van.

"As I'll ever be." Brad followed the younger man to a pair of riding horses, tethered across the street. "Remind me to thank the livery master for the mounts." Brad checked that his saddle bag contained the contagion suits and flashlights.

"Too late. Mr. and Mrs. Takaroho were some of the first to die."

"Shit!"

They mounted and rode towards the biohazard facility, arriving to find the area around its opening lit with torches. A figure wrapped in blankets sat in front of the hatch.

"Wendell, what are you doing here?" Ingram sounded surprised.

The blanket-shrouded man shook himself awake and stared sleepily at the mounted men. "I didn't want no one else going in and getting sick, so I decided to guard the entrance. Yacky would have done it, if he was here."

"Go home, Wendell, get some sleep." Brad dismounted.

"What are you doing?"

"We're going to see if we can find out something about this disease."

Wendell stared at the tinker in disbelief. "You can't go in there! You'll die, just like Yacky."

"It's okay, Wendell, we have these." Ingram dismounted and pulled out his biohazard suit.

"What's that?"

"It keeps the germs out." Ingram kicked off his shoes and began pulling on the suit. "See, it completely covers me."

Wendell looked dubious. "Okay, I'll let you in, but no one without one of those suits is getting past me."

Brad checked the seals on Ingram's suit then unfolded his own. Setting an armload of sprits-bottles on the ground, he stepped into the bright-orange outfit. The cloth was coarse where it touched his skin. His movements seemed awkward and sluggish as he pushed against the resistance of the heavy material. The suit gripped him tightly in places and in others hung in loose folds.

"Never could wear off the rack." Brad tugged at the neckline then hoisted an air tank up and slung the straps over his shoulders.

"This is the worst part," he observed.

"What?" asked Ingram

"I hate small spaces... This suit is like a... Well, it reminds me of the time-out room, Mrs. Donnelly, my grade five teacher, used. She was not a nice lady!"

"You going to manage, Tinker?"

"I forced myself not to mind a scuba-diving mask. I'll do this. I just don't like it."

Brad double-checked the seals on each suit before closing the hood over his head. The face shield hampered his peripheral vision, and he felt icy tendrils close around his stomach.

Steady, Brad. That bitch, Donnelly, only wins if you let the scars stop you. Up yours Donnelly, you can stuff your bloody secrets! he thought. Swallowing hard, he nodded at Ingram. "I'm ready. Let's go." Even to himself his voice sounded odd, as if it were being filtered through a tunnel. "Wendell, would you lead our horses a safe distance away?"

"If it will help." Taking the reins, the younger man walked to the field's edge.

"Good man, that." Brad picked up a pair of high-powered flashlights and led the way into the facility.

The steps opened onto a large office about four metres below the surface. The flashlight beams revealed a circular desk with a computer on it. Sliding glass doors opened off the main room, and the walls were a light cream.

"It's like someone cleaned it yesterday," observed Ingram.

"Air-tight seals. Until that hatch was opened, nothing got in or out of here for over a century." Brad moved to examine the computer. "A Prowstar I.C.S. I've only ever seen one of these in a museum. Sometime about 2035. Just a bit before chip technology topped out. This place must have been sealed long before the collapse."

"Damn hot in these suits." Ingram began opening desk drawers.

"Let's not talk about being in these suits, shall we?" Brad examined the end tables that flanked the couches against the walls.

"Here it is, an old Time magazine. 2036. Allow two years for the doctor's office effect." Brad fell silent when he noticed he was alone then screamed, "Ingram!"

"Tinker, over here," called Ingram from a hallway branching

off the entrance office.

Forcing himself to move cautiously, Brad joined the younger man at an open doorway. The flashlight revealed several screens and a complex monitoring board. Stepping back, Brad read a plaque on the door. "Security office." The uneasiness in his stomach lessened as he occupied his mind with the work.

"We'll collect the CD recordings from here before we leave. This type of facility they'd have to be perma-burns. Maybe they'll help us figure out what happened." Brad continued down the corridor. A set of elevator doors appeared to his right then a room labelled "Decontamination Level One," with a set of showers and what looked like banks of lights. They passed several offices and a few examination rooms before coming to a door at the end of the hall labelled "Emergency Exit." A bead of concrete spilled out around the ruptured pressure seal surrounding the door.

Ingram stepped forward, depressed the bar opener and pushed, but the door was jammed.

"Give it up," said Brad. "I'll wager the entire shaft is full of cement. They probably filled it when the base was decommissioned. If we were to dig up top, we'd find the place this used to come out as a solid sheet of concrete."

Ingram stepped back from the door. "Tinker, what exactly are we looking for?"

"My friend. If I knew, I'd tell you. Maybe you already found it in that recording room, and we just don't know it."

They returned to the entry office and started down another passage which led to a room labelled Maintenance. Brad opened it then fell silent.

"What is it?" demanded Ingram.

"If we live through this, we're going to be rich." They walked down an aisle flanked with racks of tools. A row of high-pressure cylinders stood at the back of the room. In front of the tanks were two low, rectangular devices.

Brad moved to the closest tank and checked a gauge built into it.

"What is it?" Ingram poked around on the shelves.

"Gas for these fuel-cell generators. Probably hydrogen, maybe methane. Gauges say the tanks are half full. The valves have held up pretty well."

"This base was on grid power, wasn't it?"

"Yes."

"Why'd they have something like that then?"

"These were emergency backups. They were just a safety precaution. As much for show as anything else."

"Start one up, so we can see what we're doing."

"Probably won't work. The connecter points to the inverter are likely corroded." Brad grasped the valve on a cylinder that connected to a high-pressure hose and tugged. It didn't budge. Bracing his foot, he heaved at it. It let go, sending him staggering into a set of shelves.

"*Oh shit!* Tinker, did you get a tear?"

Brad scrambled away from the shelf and inspected his suit. Sweat dripped into his eyes, and he shook his head to clear them.

"I'm clear." Brad took deep breaths.

"Tinker, look!" Ingram indicated a light above the inverter. It had come on shedding a clear illumination over the machine.

Brad smiled, he could hear the gas hissing into the fuel cell. "Must be a D.C. direct feed to make start up easier. We'll have to kick in the inverter to get the base running."

"What do we do?"

Brad moved to the inverter, which sat at the end of the fuel cell, and pressed its activation button. Nothing happened. Cautiously he undid the wing nuts holding down the device's cover plate and looked inside. "It's what I figured. The connections between the inverter and the fuel cell are corroded to shit. The ones that connect it to the step up transformer aren't much better."

Ingram looked over Brad's shoulder. The connecters were green and fuzzy. "Give it up, Tinker, you won't get that thing working without stripping it down and rebuilding it."

"Probably. We'll pull the connectors and haul them out with us. We might be able to clean them up. Maybe if we come back, we can get this brute started. How's your air?"

"About a quarter tank."

"I'm the same. Think you can pull the connecters and haul them out of here while I scavenge the recording room?"

"Not a problem." Ingram picked up a pair of pliers from the

shelf and turned to his work.

Brad closed the valve leading from the pressure cylinders to the fuel cell. The light above the unit faded to darkness as he left the maintenance room. The facility was silent except for the echo of his footfalls, and the reflections from his flashlight made eerie shadows dance over the walls.

"Wonderful! It's not bad enough I'm stuck in a faceplate, now I get to walk around a set from a horror movie," he muttered.

Entering the recording room, he gathered the CDs into a bag. Several protruded from the recorders. These he set to one side until the rest were dealt with; then he placed them on the top of his pile.

"*Tinker*," called Ingram.

"*Coming*." Brad hefted the bag and returned to the main office. Ingram waited in front of the stairs, holding a sack.

"Can we go?"

"Let's get out of here." Brad fought to keep a waver out of his voice. When they emerged, the torches still burnt giving them light to see by.

"Now what?"

"Now we disinfect." Brad lifted one of the bottles he had lain on the ground then, taking Ingram's sack, dumped the connectors onto the dirt before spritzing liquid all over them. Next he started on the CDs. Following his example, Ingram took another bottle and started on Brad's back. Minutes later they were finishing each other's suits.

"Is this enough?" asked Ingram.

"No, but without a proper facility, it's the best we can do."

Removing the suits, both men revelled in the feel of cool air as it touched their skin. Brad rested while his heart slowed to its normal rhythm.

"That place must have been something in its day," said Ingram.

"A top notch facility. That's what scares me. I think Yackaharo only brought one bug out of there. There could be literally thousands of types of viruses and bacteria in that place."

"And we went into it!" Ingram looked horrified.

"I told you it might be dangerous. I need to know what they

were working on. For one thing, I have to find out if they were making cures or sicknesses."

"I read a book about that once. A crazy person made a super bug that killed most of the women. I thought it was only fiction."

Brad shrugged. "Governments played around with germ warfare. Made some pretty deadly stuff. Most facilities were looking for cures though. People travelled so much it was common for bases to spring up around major airports."

As they spoke, they folded their suits and walked to the edge of the field to collect their horses. Wendell lay wrapped in his blankets, fast asleep.

"Should we wake him?" Brad undid his mount's tether.

"No. It's probably the first time he's slept since Yacky took ill. Poor bugger. His parents turned against him when he married Yacky. All they had were each other. His sister's a good sort, but she's busy with her own kids."

"Sad." Brad led his mount back to the facility's entrance and began stowing his gear in the saddle bags. "I'll need you to review these CDs tonight. Watch for anything that will tell us why the facility was abandoned, or what to look for. I'll write down a list of words to listen for. Anything containing those words, set aside; I'll watch it later."

"Will do, Tinker. About my mum, you haven't mentioned her, is she?"

"No. I should have told you as soon as I saw you. She's still alive, though I don't know why. She's one of the ones with swollen lymph nodes."

"Let's go. The sooner we're back at your wagon, the sooner I can start watching those CDs." Hurling himself into the saddle, Ingram took off at a gallop. Brad paused, staring into the pit-like entrance of the facility.

"You know, don't you? It's somewhere inside you," he growled, before following Ingram at a gentler pace.

Chapter Fourteen

Panic

DAN AWOKE, STRETCHED, and felt the warm body beside him. Rolling over, he saw the back of a head of golden hair. Sleepily his hands traced the slender form, pausing to fondle her breasts.

"That's nice. I'm so glad I accepted Dinah's dinner invitation. Normally my sister's an awful cook, but dessert made up for it," stated a soft, soprano voice.

"That it did, me Susie." Dan started kissing the back of her neck and shoulders.

A bell tolled, and running feet could be heard passing the old station wagon.

"The disaster bell!" gasped the woman.

"The what?"

"The disaster bell. It's on the top of the inn. They only ring it when it's something that threatens the whole town."

Dan gritted his teeth, guessing what the bell announced. Pulling away from Susan, he scrambled after his clothes.

"Where's my shoe?" she demanded.

Dan tried to pull on his pants and found something lodged in the leg. "In my trousers. Can you see my shirt anywhere?"

"Hold on, it's jammed under the pillow. Whose bra is this?"

"Bra?"

"Under the edge of your mattress."

"It must be yours."

"Not likely!" Susan held the D cup up to her B cup sized breasts and quirked an eyebrow.

"Have you seen my... oh, never mind," said Dan, as he realized his socks were still on his feet.

The confusion persisted for several minutes before Dan opened the door, and they stepped onto the broken pavement.

"Before we go, Susan, last night was grand." Dan took her hands and squeezed them.

"Better than usual." Susan winked then they sprinted toward the bell.

By the time they arrived a crowd had gathered in front of the inn. The babble of their voices filled the air.

"Shut up, you lot," bellowed Frank, the innkeeper, from an upstairs window.

The crowd slowly quieted.

"That's better. Now listen up, we have a problem. Jack the baker from Gridtown saw somethin' you need to hear about."

Jack stepped to the window; the clean cloth of his tunic contrasting with the grease-stained apron Frank wore.

"Listen, folks. I was walking over to Eden Mills this morning. Heard there was some pick up work for the taking. Got as far as the twenty-nine and saw a whole troop of soldiers flying the Novo Gaian flag. They were all decked out in camouflage and packing rifles. They yelled at me to stop. Wouldn't let me pass. Said the area was quarantined. I ran back here as quick as I could."

"Quarantined? Quarantined for what? We ain't got no sickness 'ere?" demanded a fat, dirty man with greasy, brown hair.

"Don't know, Ken, all they'd tell me was it was a quarantine."

"It's another Argyle. They don't like that we trade with Gridtown. They're gonna kill us all," screamed a scrawny woman with grey hair.

"'Ey probably got them Guelphers with that 'ere tank of 'eirs in on it," yelled a male voice from the crowd.

The crowd erupted into a babble of sound as the news was

discussed then Ward's voice split the air. "We need to get 'em first. We'll show 'em sun 'umpers that they can't push Arkellians around. Everyone fetch youse guns."

"Now wait just a minute there, me friends!" yelled Dan, his voice barely piercing the din. The chatter continued. Filling his lungs Dan roared "*Hey!*"

Silence fell as the single word reached them all.

"That's a bit better, now. Afore we go running off half-cocked, I think we should be checking this here story. Why don't we send a couple of folk up the street to ask about this here plague? Find out where it's suppose to be. What it's supposed to do."

"Shut up, candle man. You're not part of this town," snapped Amanda, the child slaver.

"Now that be true, but I am a traveller, and travellers know a thing or two about plague. Remember the coughing sickness of one-oh-two. You don't want to be bringing something like that into town, now do you?"

"He's right, we should check this out. Ward, you start getting the folk organized, just in case. I'll take Blair and the candler up to the twenty-nine and see what we can see. If we're not back by this evening, you know this is a crock of shit, and you should get ready to attack the Novo Gaian bastards."

"Even if it is a plague, seems pretty cocky of Novo Gaia to enforce a quarantine in the Dark Lands." Jack spoke loud enough to be heard, but not so loud that it couldn't be taken as a comment to the men in the room with him.

"Fetch your wagon, Candler. The rest of you, go clean your guns," ordered Frank.

The crowd began to disperse.

"This is awful. I don't know what's worse. Novo Gaian troops or a plague," said Susan as she walked beside Dan.

"The plague. I've heard a lot of rubbish about Novo Gaia. I'll tell you, love, that's all it is. The only time they'll kill is if someone kills one of their own," replied Dan.

"But everyone says—"

"It's rubbish! Gridtowners don't like the competition, that's all. No, lass. Don't worry about those troops unless these damn fools start taking pot shots at them. Worry about the plague. Keep clear of other folk, and wash everything you put in your mouth."

"You seem to know a lot about it?"

"I'm a candler. Soap is one of the best ways of stopping a plague. Me trade has done more to keep folk healthy than almost any other. Clean is healthy. It's a bit of an advertisement, but a true one."

They walked past Dan's wagon and continued onto the visitors' field, where his gelding grazed on the sparse grass.

"Be careful, Dan. I'd like a repeat of last night's entertainment, so don't go getting sick or killed." Susan ran her fingers through his hair.

"With a thought as sweet as that to keep me safe, how could I even think of catching a bug?" Dan kissed her goodbye and she left him to his work. Collecting his horse Dan returned to his wagon and hitched the animal.

Entering the ancient vehicle, he pulled the radio from beneath the seat and turned it on.

"Corporal Timothy to base, come in. Over... Corporal Timothy to base. Over."

"We read you, Corporal," replied an unfamiliar voice.

"Get the Major, I have news. Over."

"I'll pass it on to him. Over."

"Not to be insulting you, but how can I know who you are, if you take my meaning? I'll talk to the Major or the doctor. At least I know their voices. Over."

"One minute. Over."

Silence descended.

"All right, Dan, what is it? Over," demanded Eddie's voice.

"That fellow who reached your checkpoint; he's got the townsfolk all stirred up. Came back implying that you were lying about the plague. I'm coming out with the innkeep and his lackey to talk with your guards on the twenty-nine. Over."

"I have no report of anyone reaching our checkpoint from Arkell. Over."

"I can't be speaking to your reports, but he sure as spit stirred the anthill here. They think you're planning another Argyle. Folk are cleaning their guns. If I don't bring back the innkeep, they're gonna go after your team. Over."

"Understood. Good work. Any signs of the disease? Over."

"Not yet, but sure as apples, if it's here, after this morning's little gathering, it's everywhere the folk live. Over."

"Understood. Anything more to report? Over."

"Haven't I reported enough already? Over."

"That you have, Dan. Over and out."

"Over and out."

With a sigh Dan hid the radio under his seat and moved to the driver's position.

Minutes later he was guiding his wagon along the battered thirty-seven roadway toward the twenty-nine. Frank and Blair sat beside him on his wagon's front seat.

"Tell me, Candler. You have much to do with Novo Gaians?" asked Frank.

"A bit," evaded Dan.

"Good old Blair here's a fine example of their work. Aren't you, me lad?"

Blair scowled at Frank and rubbed the T brand.

"Heard a tinker caught you stealing," said Dan.

"Bastard's so rich, couldn't spare a few watts to recharge my lantern. Said I could work it off but wanted way too much work for just a few watts. Fingered 'e wouldn't be so 'ot without all 'is panels and stuff. Bastard caught me. 'urt like fuckin' 'ell."

"Well, laddie, that's a sad one to be sure." Dan managed to keep the sarcasm out of his voice.

"Tinker was a sissy to let it go with a whipping and a black Tee. Last time I caught old Blair here stealin', I saw to it he wouldn't go lifting anyone else's credit bag. Just can't get the hang of cutting a purse-string one handed, can you, lad?" remarked Frank.

"There, up ahead. I think I see them," said Dan. A moment later he reined his horse to a stop by a field phone. Thirty metres away stood a tent surrounded by troops.

"Come no closer. The field phone is there for your convenience. Press the green button and it will activate," stated a voice over a loud speaker.

The three men climbed from the wagon and moved to stand around an intercom box.

Frank slammed his hand down on the green button. "What the

fuck right do you have to stop us?" he demanded.

"This area is quarantined due to plague," replied Eddie's voice.

"Who the fuck do you think you are? You have no right tellin' honest Dark Lands folk where to go and what to do!" growled Frank.

"I am Major Edward Baily, Novo Gaian militia. Eden Mills does not want to be infected. They asked us to keep them safe. That gives us the right," observed Eddie.

"Like shit! No one's sick in Arkell. If there's a plague where the fuck is it?"

"The plague is centred in northeast Guelph. Arkell is part of the safety zone."

"*Guelph.* 'Ow come we ain't 'eared nothin' about it?" demanded Blair.

"It started only a few days ago. Our tinker radioed it in. He's working on a cure as we speak."

"Youse can't force us to stay in a plague zone. We ain't sick." Blair waved his hook in the air.

"Anyone trying to penetrate the quarantine zone will be shot. My advice is go home, stay clean and stay away from Guelph. If your town isn't infected, we'll know in a week or two then we can close in the quarantine. If it is, and we let you out, it could kill other towns."

"This is fuckin' ridiculous. We ain't sick!" yelled Frank, an edge of panic in his voice.

"When you prove it, we'll let you out," explained Eddie.

"Gentlemen. We won't be getting any further here. Maybe we should be going back to town and sending out your healer, so they know what to look for," advised Dan.

"We ain't got no healer, always used the witch Meb from Eden Mills. Shit, I fuckin' hate this. We'll see about you pulling this shit, sun humper." Frank stomped back to the wagon. The return trip passed in empty fuming. When they reached the town, Frank led them into the inn.

"I don't like those fuckin' tree 'uggers tellin' me what to do," snapped Blair.

"Shut up, asshole!" Frank sat heavily in one of the chairs. A skinny girl of maybe fourteen, with short, dark hair, wearing a brown, homespun dress came to the table.

"Whiskey, all the way around." Frank slapped her butt before she left.

"New girl?" Dan had an edge in his voice.

"Bought her from Amanda last month. All broken in and ready. Give her a year or two; I'll show that bitch Nancy what it means to leave my place. You want a tumble?"

"Not for me, bucko. Like them a little older and a lot cheaper," countered Dan.

"I," opened Blair. A look from Frank silenced him.

"Way I see it we only got one thing to do. We got to send someone to check the farms from here to Guelph. Just keep asking folk if they heard of this plague. If you don't hear nothing, Candler, you just keep going into town. If you hear about it, you turn around and come straight back and tell us," said Frank.

"Me?" Dan swallowed hard.

"Sure. If they figure we got the plague here, there's only one way it could of got here. You, candle man. You got to figure, if I see it others will."

"I'll go," agreed Dan.

"I thought you might. Now if only I could get my hands on Major Kiss My Ass. I'd teach him how to brown tongue it, the pushy SOB."

Chapter Fifteen

Discipline

"You moronic, asinine, *slug-brained simpletons! What the shorting hell did you think you were doing?*" bellowed Eddie. A man and a woman barely past their teens stood across a table from him, cringing with each word. They both wore the Novo Gaian uniform, their single stripes marking them as privates. The man had a swollen lip that lent his soft, boyish features an absurd quality. His short, brown hair was matted with a mixture of blood and mead.

"Sir. We were having a discussion, and it became over-animated, sir," he replied.

Eddie closed his eyes then opened them to scan the others who occupied the inn's common-room. A young man wearing a corporal's stripes stood nervously in the corner. John sat at a table, holding a bag of ice to his eye. Meb and Nick sat with him, watching the proceedings. Other worthies from the town sat at nearby tables

"And you, Miss McDowl, do you feel your discussion became 'over-animated'?"

The woman reached to touch her black eye, which was beginning to swell shut, thought better of it and returned to parade rest.

"Yes, sir, I'm sorry sir."

Eddie drew his good hand down his face. "What were you fighting about?"

The privates glanced at each other. The young man replied "The movie, sir. We disagreed about the realism of the ballistics."

"You were fighting about the realism, of the ballistics, in a Schwarzenegger film? I don't even want to know!" Eddie spoke with quiet menace. His face reddened a deeper shade, and he gritted his teeth. His hand clutched the clay tankard in front of him as if he were going to crush it. He took a sip then a long swallow. When he spoke again, it was with chilling mildness.

"John, could you tell me what happened?"

"Sure. I was playin' the movie in the viewin' room. A special morning screenin' for the troops who worked through the night. I was bringin' up another round when I heard a commotion. I rushed up the stairs, and there's these two bustin' up my place. I've had all kinds of folk here, all kinds. There's been a scrap or two in the common-room, but never in the viewin' or music rooms. That just isn't done. I rushed up to try and stop them, and this fist comes out of nowhere. Pow! Right in my eye. I staggered back then I saw that chap there." John waved at the corporal in the corner. "He picked up a bottle from his table and came up behind the other one. Wham, right over his head. Waste of good mead, not to mention a good bottle. Stopped the fight cold. After that, he came over to see if I was all right."

"Thank you, John." Eddie turned to the defendants. "First, you should know the only reason you're not in the bloody, town stocks is John's a friend of mine. The town council has agreed to allow me to punish you. You fools have jeopardised this entire operation. Let alone embarrassed Novo Gaia!

"Master Sing, are you still the woodwright for this village?"

"Yes, Major, I am," replied a short, wiry Caucasian with black hair and brown eyes. He was seated at one of the tables watching the proceedings.

"I wish to commission a replacement table. Price is no object. Please consult with John to see what he'd like. John, I'd appreciate it if you didn't think about what you're replacing. Choose the table and chair you've always dreamed of having. Our good privates will be picking up the bill! Your salaries will be docked for the total price of the damages you caused. Be bloody thankful you didn't damage any of the electronics. Furthermore, you're both pulling double guard shifts at your stations. Better pack your field tents and ration packs. You won't have time to come back to town to eat or sleep. You will also make a public apology to John and the town of Eden Mills. Finally, when this mission is over, you will clean and perform a full maintenance inspection of John's methane composter. This will include shovelling, transporting and spreading the sludge from the unit at the tanners' wood. Now get your field packs and get to your stations. Oh, yes. Don't take a horse. Run!" Eddie glared at the privates, who turned on their heels and marched from the room.

"Corporal Harrison," he snapped.

"Yes, sir," said the man who had been waiting in the corner.

"Why did you enter the brawl?"

"Sir. The innkeeper had been injured. I felt it important to stop the fight before more damage was done."

"So you broke a bottle over Private Gordon's head."

"It seemed... expedient... sir."

Eddie joined the snicker that spread through the room.

"What do you do back home, son?" The red slowly drained from Eddie's face.

"I'm studying to join the police, sir."

"And well you should. Your methods might be questioned, but your motives were correct, corporal. I'm recommending you for a third stripe."

"Thank you, sir," said the young man.

"John, you satisfied with this?"

"As councillor representing the makers, I say it's fair for what they did. As the victim, I feel the compensation is more than adequate. I hate cleaning that composter."

"How about the rest of the council?" Eddie eyed Meb and Nick.

"Speaking for the farmers, I'd say it's a far sight worse than a day in the stocks. And those who remember me as a boy, will tell you I should know," said Nick.

"As representative for the scholars, I'd say it's adequate," agreed Meb.

"I thank you for your tolerance in this." Eddie rose to his feet then called out. "Next round is on me."

The pleased murmur that passed through the room almost drowned out the few disgruntled voices.

"You may buy them for an hour, Eddie, but there's a lot of talk about that fight going around." John moved to the Major's side.

"Do you think they'll overturn your decision to support me?"

"They can't do much about you staying at the inn. Eden Mills is open to travellers. As long as you pay your tab, that's all you are. If I were you, I'd worry about using the visitors' field and that official sanction."

"You change your mind?"

"No, but I am worried about how your troops will behave."

"Those two are young and stupid, nothing more."

"Starting a fight in the common-room is no big deal, but to put the television at risk? Don't they know how precious that thing is?"

"No, they don't. They probably had TVs in their homes growing up."

"Just like before the collapse. You bright landers are so lucky."

"Maybe, but their TVs were powered just like yours. It's only a matter of time before folks hereabouts have systems of their own."

"Maybe. I'm not looking forward to it. It will cost me a pack of business."

"You'll make it up in other ways. Trust me. I've seen this happen before." Slapping John on the shoulder, Eddie slipped from the inn and started towards the visitors' field.

"*Major.*" Lieutenant Newicky ran towards him.

"Yes?"

"I present myself for discipline. Private McDowl was under my command." Barbara stood at attention.

"Barb, drop the shit! I've had enough for one day. You were at the roadblock. There's no way you could have done a damn thing. If you really want to help me, stop asking to be punished, and figure out a way to deal with this PR. mess."

"Bad?" Barb fell into step beside him.

"The town may not ratify our official sanction. If that happens, we're on the moral low ground when it comes to enforcing this quarantine." They walked towards the visitors' field.

"Would we pull out if that happens?"

"Not a chance. With the death rate Brad's reporting, we can't let this thing spread. Containing it could cost us years of bridge building. Most folk out here don't trust us. They're used to being cheated by Gridtowners, and they've heard all the horror stories about tinkers and Novo Gaians. It took me years to convince this town we kept our word. Longer for them to believe we actually had a vision that included them as partners, not slaves."

"And all that is threatened because two twits can't behave themselves. If they were a tumour, I'd cut them out."

"You medical in the real world?"

"Fourth-year, Dark Lands Healers' Certificate. I was doing a clinical placement when I got called up. Actually, I think Dr. Frankel requested me. I was going to do a tour as a junior with his biohazard team."

"Could be. I let the computer pick the names. If he wanted you, all he had to do was ask. I'm beginning to respect him a bit more. Francis said no team, but here he is with a built-in assistant. Medical on the scene is good for this kind of... That's it!" Eddie stopped dead in his tracks.

"What?"

Eddie started running for the visitors' field, his empty, shirtsleeve flapping. A third truck had joined the first two, this one connected to a large trailer, marked with the biohazard symbol. Reaching the back of the trailer, Eddie pulled open the door. A slender, Negro man with powerful looking hands and harsh features sat at a computer console examining data. A screen to his right traced out six sets of vital signs. He turned in his chair to look at Eddie.

"Good. I wanted to speak to you. Your man has to do that autopsy. I can't do any good without those samples."

"Dr. Frankel, you're wrong. You can do a clinic. A full Novo Gaian clinic. Free for all." Eddie's voice oozed relief.

"What?" asked the doctor and Barb in unison, from opposite sides of the trailer's door.

"I need to win the townsfolk back on side before this afternoon's meeting. Meb's good, so's Brad, but they can't compete with your little bag of miracles."

"I'm here to chart a plague, not wipe sniffly noses." Dr. Frankel stood and brushed the creases out of his cream-coloured, hemp clothing.

"I need this, doctor. We need to be able to stay in this field and have local support. Or would you rather take a turn on KP with the rest of us when we get our asses thrown out of here?"

Frankel clenched his fist then looked past Eddie to Barb. "I'll need her help. And yours. You can do the initial screening. I will not have my time wasted with hypochondriacs."

"Fine. Lieutenant, get some of the troops from the inn, and have them spread the word. Free medical clinic with a real doctor, starting in one hour. Make sure they know to stress 'free' and 'a real doctor'. I'll help our good physician set up."

The doctor scowled at Eddie then moved to a nearby cupboard and started preparing his gear.

Two hours later Eddie stood to one side in the medical trailer while Dr. Frankel examined Colleen McPherson.

"Well, Miss. The tinker's treatment seems to be working fine for your venereal disease. I want to give you a follow up shot to be sure."

"I don't have much to pay, doctor," explained Colleen.

"Pay? This is hardly cosmetic."

"We're not in Novo Gaia," observed Eddie.

"Oh yes. Well, for today, don't worry about it." The doctor pushed the needle home. "Take one of these tablets each morning for the next two weeks."

"What are they?" she asked.

"Normal flora pills. The drug kills the good bacteria in your bowel. This will see to it that healthy varieties are there to restore the balance."

"Oh," remarked Colleen.

"Remember to attend the town meeting. We'll do another clinic if we're allowed to stay." Eddie helped Colleen climbed from the table and escorted her to the door.

"Edward, I'm glad you suggested this clinic. It is surprising. Do you know I had to look up two of the parasitic infections? Usually I just don't bother with the database. Are the people here incredibly sickly, or is this normal for the Dark Lands?" Dr. Frankel started putting his examination room back to rights.

"This is a healthy lot. More water stills per capita than most areas and more vaccinations."

"Astounding. And you tinkers deal with this using only the med kits in your vans? I will have to do a paper on diseases of the Dark Lands."

"Hope you get the funding. I've got to go. The town meeting is starting in a few minutes, and I have to be there."

"Oh yes of course." The doctor waved Eddie away. "Send in the next patient as you leave."

Eddie left the trailer and glanced towards his tinker van. Barb sat at the end of a line of people with Eddie's medical gear. Turning to a small group beside the medical trailer, he nodded. A man whose face was covered by a scarlet rash climbed the steps into the trailer. Smiling Eddie moved to Barb's side.

"How's his lordship?" she asked.

"Bubbling over. He thinks the maladies are 'fascinating'."

"The McPherson woman?"

"Just a cyst. He did a needle biopsy."

"Good."

"I'm off to the town meeting. Keep up the good work, and sell the idea that we'll do another clinic if the town lets us stay," Eddie whispered into her ear before he left.

The weather had turned cool, and a breeze kicked up dust, but that wasn't what made Eddie shiver as he turned the bend in the road. A crowd had gathered in the street before him. Nearly two hundred adults filled the small island created by the river and the millstream.

"Tinker!" called Nick from the front of the inn. A heavy, wooden table had been set on the street to form a podium. Nick, John and Meb stood upon it.

Eddie pushed through the crowd to the table and joined them. "Good turn out."

"Too good. I don't like this. A crowd can become a mob too easily," replied Meb.

"The sooner started the sooner finished." John's face reflected concern.

"People!" hollered Nick. The babble of voices continued.

"*People!*" repeated Nick to no avail.

Eddie held up his hand to still Nick's third wail. "John, perhaps the speaker we set up for the harvest festival."

"Right. Back in a flash." John disappeared into his inn. Minutes later he'd hauled a large pre-collapse speaker onto the curb. "Now, Billy!" he shouted.

Eddie, Meb and Nick clapped their hands over their ears as a crescendo of sound bombarded the crowd. Silence followed.

"Good people of Eden Mills, I declare this town ratification meeting in session," called John, mounting the impromptu stage.

"The order of business is..." he continued.

"We's all knows the bloody order of business. Wes 'ave to say whether or not wes wants those Novo Gaian thugs 'ere, stealing our women and smashin' up our town," yelled Greg Thomson. A murmur of assent came from scattered members of the crowd.

"We will have order here," snapped John.

"Youse shut up! 'oo the 'ell youse think youse is anyway?" hollered a filthy man in tattered clothes. He stood in a corner by himself, while the townsfolk crowded away from him.

"*That's enough of that.* John represents the merchants, chosen by their vote. Same as I speak for the farmers and Meb for the scholars. You voted us in; you can vote us out. But you can't say we don't have the right to speak." Nick pulled a nightstick from a loop on his belt and swung it against the palm of his free hand.

"Then speak sense. These Novo Gaians don't 'ave any business 'ere. I say send 'em packin'. Theys just wants to take our town. Kill the men and rape the women, 'at's what 'ere up to. I's knows what they's like. Damn tinker made me Emily so's she ain't a woman no more. Taking us for our 'ard earned credits, for 'eir phoney stills and silly panels," snarled Greg.

"The stills do real good, you stupid man! Cancer is down for every family that has one. Birth defects are dropping too," objected Meb.

"Everyone knows it's sin as makes a body ill, and the sins of the mother as make a child deformed. That's what the preacher man said last fall," snapped Greg.

"I say get rid of them and bring Carla back 'ere. 'ow can you support this, Meb? She's your granddaughter. Leaving 'er in Guelph with a plague there," hollered Michelle.

"If 'ere is a plague," blurted the thug.

"There is a plague, let there be no doubt of that. If we remove the quarantine, it will spread. People in Guelph are dying," called Eddie.

"Youse lies, Tinker," screamed Greg. The crowd gasped and fell silent watching for Eddie's reaction.

After a charged moment a deep, resonant voice split the still air.

"I have never liked the tinker Eddie. I like Major Baily even less. He has always struck me as arrogant and high handed. But I'll tell you one thing. If he said it was going to rain cabbages, I'd put baskets in my field to catch them. Novo Gaians have never lied to us. If they say there is a plague in Guelph, there is a plague in Guelph," said Mr. James.

"Wes all know youse a tinker lover," snapped Greg.

"I enjoy electricity and not having the smell of my cows in my nostrils, if that is what you mean."

"I think Mr. James has a point. The tinkers have never lied to us," said Nick.

"Wes all know whats youse think. Youse little wife still pining after tinker dick. Not man enough youse-self to keep her satisfied," snarled Greg.

"How are your children, Thomson? Tommy's arm any better? How about Jeremy's leg? Oh, have you decided if it's Catharine or Carl for the youngest, that lived? Probably better to call it Terry and be done with it," retorted Nick.

"'Ey're mine, not some tinker's brood."

"Jared is my son! If you want to say different, name the time and place." Nick swung his nightstick suggestively. "This is ridiculous! We're here to ratify or dispel the official request we've made of the Novo Gaian militia to maintain the quarantine. We also must decide whether or not we should let them use the visitors' field. We are not here to rehash all the old lies about the tinkers and their people."

"Hear, hear," called Vicky, Nick's wife, from the front row. She held their child and looked up at Nick with glowing eyes.

"I's says send 'em packin'!" shouted Greg.

"No, we can't. They've set up a clinic, a real clinic, and they're treating everyone, free! Who knows what cures a real Novo Gaian doctor could give us. Besides, a plague is a very dangerous thing. We have to help them," spoke Colleen McPherson.

"Thank you, Colleen," said Eddie.

"What guarantee do we 'ave that youse troops won't smash up our town, Tinker?" demanded a fat man, wearing a miller's apron.

Eddie nodded at the man. "Fair question. I severely disciplined the troops involved in the brawl. Truth is, I can't promise my lot will behave perfectly. No one can promise the actions of another. What I can promise is, I will severely punish anyone who steps out of line and see to it that full restitution is made to any town person they injure."

"I can tell you, he's not making that up. The table I'm making for John to replace that old slab and plank they broke is a thing of beauty. Haven't had call for so fine a piece since I did my master's work," remarked Mr. Sung into the crowd.

"No one came out worse from that brawl than I did, but I'm more than satisfied with how Eddie handled it," added John.

"Course youse is, with youse fancy panels, TVs, radios. Still 'ave to shutdown youse back rooms around Christmas though, don't youse!" yelled Greg.

"Look, the question is simple. Do you trust me and my troops enough to believe we're operating with your best interest at heart? Before you decide that, let me point one thing out. We'll leave if we're told to. If we meant you harm, would that be the case?" Eddie's posture was open and his voice was full of wounded altruism.

"That, I think, is enough. All those in favour of assisting the Novo Gaian militia, raise your hands and say aye," said John.

A forest of hands raised and ayes echoed from the crowd.

"Against?" he asked. Eleven hands lifted from the crowd.

They formed a small knot of dirty, rough-looking men and their wives in one corner.

"By overwhelming majority, the town of Eden Mills supports the council's decisions," called Nick.

"Youse will regret this. Marks my words. When youse wakes with a tinker's knife at youse throat, youse will regret this," snarled Greg, who led his group away.

"He could be trouble," said Meb.

"For another day. May I buy the lady a drink?" asked Eddie.

"Wouldn't be the first." Meb smiled at him; then her eyes stared in the direction of Guelph and worry filled her face.

Chapter Sixteen

Yesterday's Heroes

BRAD LEANED AGAINST the wall and closed his eyes. The sound of laboured breathing filled his ears. The inside of his eyelids felt grainy, and a grey pall seemed to fill him. Opening his mouth, he popped a pill into it.

"How long do you think you can keep using those?" Carla moved to his side drying her hands on a piece of rag.

"Until I find a cure, or fall ill myself."

Carla stared at him, concern in her blue eyes. "We need to open another room for the bodies. The first one's full."

"Use the one with that big table in it. How's Rose?" Brad opened his eyes and pushed away from the wall.

"Still alive. She's lasted longer than most. Her father's beside her. He won't leave."

"He's useful. Don't worry about it."

The door opened. Both of them turned to look at it, dread written on their faces.

"Tinker, I watched those CDs. I think I have something for you," called Ingram from the doorway.

"On my way," replied Brad. "Is Trina here?"

"Yes, she arrived about an hour ago," said Carla.

"Tell her we'll be in my wagon, if she needs us. I want you with me. The more eyes the better."

"Go on. I'll join you."

Brad shuffled to his wagon. Pausing, he looked at the late-morning sun. Puffy, white clouds drifted across the blue sky, and a band of heavier cloud stood out on the horizon.

"It's all set up, Tinker," remarked Ingram from the wagon's back door.

Inhaling deeply, Brad entered and took a seat at the table. A minute later Carla joined him slipping into the spot beside him.

"These were some of the first ones I looked at. Most of the stuff is just people mixing gunk in test tubes. I set it up to show the interesting bits." Dark circles stood out under Ingram's eyes, and he looked pale.

"Good. Show us what you found." Brad felt the warmth of Carla's body beside him. It only served to make him sleepier.

Ingram pressed the play button. Images of people running down hallways filled the screen. Red lights flashed and sirens blared then deathly silence. A sweaty man with tanned skin and large, brown eyes stared into the camera. His bald scalp reflected the overhead lights. As he spoke, he waved a computer CD in front of him.

"His will be done. His will be done. 'And I saw a pale horse and a pale rider upon it, and the name of the horse was pestilence, and the name of the rider was death.'

"I leave this message to all who follow. This place of Satan's work is now the instrument of the Lord. Let loose the plagues to scour the earth. Only the righteous will be spared. Too long have the corrupt struggled against the judgment of Almighty God. Now let loose the plagues upon man. Armageddon must come. His will be done!" The man coughed up blood, which fell to stain his overalls.

"He goes on like that for nearly an hour. Do you want to watch it all?" asked Ingram.

"Not really. Is there something you think might be useful?" replied Brad.

Ingram popped the CD and inserted another.

The image of a man with chiselled features and brown hair

greying at the temples filled the screen.

"If you are watching this, you are fools," spoke the long dead man in serious tones. "This facility was sealed in July of the year twenty-thirty-nine to prevent the spread of contagious disease. I can only guess at why you have entered it, but you must not leave.

"I don't know how he got past the screening procedures. One of our maintenance techs was mentally unstable. He rigged the computer to send false signals to the monitors. He thawed all the storage freezers over the long weekend, when we were running minimal staff. No one caught it until Monday. By then the pathogens were active. When we tried to restart the refrigeration units, the computer popped the magnetic seals on the doors.

"That bastard planned this a long time. He'd set micro charges on the gaskets and manual lock downs."

The image on the screen lifted what looked like a piece of chewing gum with a pin in it.

"Our maintenance chief was demolitions in the army. He said this one was a dud. Plastique and a short-range radio detonator. We figure he made a false tooth out of the stuff and smuggled it past security. Tricky bastard!

"He as much as killed everyone on level three to five with these when he blew out the contagion seals. He must have been pushing the blasted things into the cracks around the gaskets for weeks. That wasn't good enough for the prick!"

The doctor seemed to nod off, shook his head then continued.

"Sorry. Narcotics for the pain. I'm getting fuzzy. Fuzzy wuzzy was… *No!* I will do this with dignity.

"Where was I? Yes, his coup de grace. After setting off the bombs he locked himself in the level-five, pipe room. Before we could get him out, he'd cross-linked the exhaust and intake air systems. Our own ventilation system spread the pathogens. He'd replaced the HEPA filters with paper dummies over the weekend.

"I wish to give a special commendation to Ricardo DesRoches, our chief maintenance tech. He stopped the contamination from reaching level one and the outside world. When the computer refused to shutdown ventilation, he jammed the system with a wrench. Then filled the pipes with expanding foam.

"All our technology. A monkey wrench and crack insulation save the day. Ha."

The image grimaced in pain and drooped.

"All the lower level research teams have been exposed. We have chosen to isolate ourselves in the facility, so we do not risk spreading the contagions. My team voted unanimously to do this. I have never been prouder to serve with any group of men and women." The man's voice cracked, and he seemed on the edge of tears, but he pulled himself together. "You must isolate yourself, and call in help to reseal the facility. We have done our best to—" The man's image coughed; his head dipped out of the camera's angle. Behind him was a room crowded with bodies. Some writhed in pain, others lay perfectly still. The man's face reappeared and he continued.

"I am the last one who's ambulatory. We did our best to disinfect the facility. The seals protecting level one are only jury-rigged. Something may have leaked by them. Ricardo managed to close off level three. We have moved all the organic matter, including ourselves, to that level. I have rigged tanks of chlorine gas to a timer and connected them to the base's security distribution system. They will open twenty-four-hours from now."

The image's eyes drooped and his speech slurred.

"The gas should sterilize all the levels, but there is no way I can be sure it will work. Complete records of disease vectors in this facility have been transmitted to the Ministry of Public Health in Ottawa."

The man fell back. Blood stains covered his shirt, and open sores puckered the skin of his throat and hands. Gritting his teeth, he staggered to his feet and moved back to the camera.

"You are not safe. I pray our efforts will prove successful, but you must not spread these plagues. Think of your friends and families. You must not leave this place!"

Stumbling, the man moved to a chair set by a desk in the camera's field of view.

"I am Dr. Reginald Butinay, Assistant Director of the Guelph Contagious Disease Research Facility. This has been my final log entry."

The CD continued to spin, recording the progress of a dozen unknown diseases as they defeated a lone healer's last strength.

"That's the last thing he said of any use. Later on he starts hallucinating. He believes he's picnicking with his wife and daughter. I think he died happy." Ingram stopped the machine.

"Those poor people," said Carla.

Brad stared at the table, a prayer for the dead running through his mind.

"They didn't die in vain," he said when he finished.

"What?" asked Ingram.

"Think about it. They had hundreds of diseases down there. Only one seems to have penetrated to the top layer.

"The chlorine must have killed off almost all the bugs. At least we can hope."

"Does this help us at all?" asked Carla.

"Maybe. Go back to the clinic and take another set of vitals. Ingram, reset those CDs to the place you started them. I need to call base."

Moving to the front of the van, Brad picked up his mic and started talking.

"Tinker, tinker, tinker. Update, update, update. Over."

"We have you, Tinker. Awaiting Ident," replied an unfamiliar voice.

Brad sighed and started his call. "B one R two A one D three L zero Y two I zero R five V one I zero N seven G PC."

"You are incorrect, Lieutenant. Restate L Y. Over."

"Shit!" Brad rubbed his eyes, looked at his dash then pressed the mic button. "L zero Y three. Sorry about that."

"Restate is correct, lieutenant. Home call sign is CO. MA. E one D two W one A four R zero D three J zero B five A one I zero L seven Y PC. Over."

"Within range. Over."

"What is your update? Over."

"We recovered perma-burn Vid CDs from the facility. I wish to radio-modem pertinent sections to you. Please prepare to receive. Over."

"Preparing. Over."

Pulling a coil of wire from what had once been the van's

ashtray, Brad connected one end to a jack on his radio and the other to his laptop. Using a shorter length of cable, he joined the laptop to the video player.

"Okay, Ingram, this is how it works. The computer will convert the video image to a signal my short wave can transmit. At the base they have a unit that will turn it back into a video image and record it. I need you to play the CDs and watch my computer's screen. That number in the corner represents how much of the video is still in the computer's memory. When the first CD is finished, be sure it's empty before you start the second one. This can't transmit real time, so things get backed up."

"Sure thing, Tinker," said Ingram as Brad left the van.

"I really hate medicine," muttered Brad as he moved back into the clinic.

Carla knelt by a cot at the far end of the room, sponging down a patient.

"What happened?" asked Brad.

"Couldn't keep that soup down no more," explained Trina, moving to his side. "The movies tell you anything?"

"A bit. It was the last words of a courageous man and a complete nut case. The nut case kept ranting about a pale man and a pale horse."

"Was he a preacher man? My mother, she use to read the bible to us each Sunday, and that's from prophecies, I think."

"Not a preacher, as far as I know. Maybe a fanatic." Shrugging, Brad moved to the side of the patient that Carla was cleaning.

"One of the ones without swollen lymph nodes," she observed.

"You noticed that too. I wonder if it's the result of the body fighting back. The ones with the swelling do seem to last longer. Although, I'm not sure that's a mercy." Brad sniffed and pulled his mint gel from his pocket. Opening it, he stared into the empty container then put it away.

Kneeling, he examined the patient. It was a child of maybe ten with sweat-matted, black hair and sunken, almond-shaped, brown eyes. The pudgy cheeks were the last softness in the face.

"Carla, I have something to ask you. No is a fair answer, because it's so bloody dangerous, but I just don't see that I have a choice."

"What?"

"I may need your help with an autopsy."

Chapter Seventeen

Desperate People

"So you've heard of sickness in Guelph?" Dan yelled to the burly man standing five metres away from him. The man held a rifle, but its muzzle was pointed at the ground. His wife, a plump woman in her middle years, stood beside him.

"You have the right of that, Candler. Heard about it three days back. Lost me parents to the cough. Not takin' chances with the rest of me family," hollered the man in reply. The house behind him had obviously been scrubbed, and buckets of soapy water sat on the ground in front of him.

"Any idea how far it's spread?"

"Not a one. All I know is I ain't taking chances. That's all I need to know. Just got a still put in to keep me family healthy. I'll not undo the good with carelessness now."

A slender girl in her late teens stepped through the house's doorway. She waved at Dan and blew him a kiss behind her parent's back. Dan smiled.

"I'll be heading back then. Seems I've found what I was sent to find," Dan hollered.

"Sorry about the welcome, but I ain't taking any chances," replied the man.

Dan waved as he climbed into his wagon. Clucking he started the horse toward Arkell.

"Well that's done it. I hope no one's stirred up trouble while I was off doing this fool's trek," he muttered.

The road was deserted until he reached the first official houses of the town, where he found a crude barricade of piled bricks and garbage blocking the road.

"'Old it 'ere," snapped Ward. He had an ancient rifle in his hand. The barricade hid his body from the chest down.

Steady. He don't necessarily know about me and Dinah, thought Dan as he forced himself to reply in a friendly voice. "Ward, me lad, it's me, Dan the candler. Frank sent me to check the plague story, and I found out it's true enough." Dan stepped from his wagon, so that the other man could see him.

"Youse seen sickins?"

"No, got as far as the McDonald place; they'd heard about it."

Ward pointed his rifle at Dan's chest.

"Don't get me wrong. I didn't come within five metres of the McDonalds. Shouted myself near hoarse talking to them."

"Youse sure youse ain't been close to any sickins?"

"Swear it on me craft and me mother."

"Youse can pass." Ward motioned to a place where a cart blocked a gap in the barricade.

Three men stood up behind the crude barrier and pulled the cart aside. As Dan drove through the gap he could see gun barrels protruding through upper story windows.

Reining to a stop, he waited while Ward came to lean at his window.

"Any sign of the Novo Gaians?" demanded Ward.

"Not a one. I'm thinking they were telling us the truth about this here plague."

"Maybe, but I's don't trust the McDonalds, 'ey're tinker lovers. 'Eard old man McDonald bought one of 'em phoney stills." With this he spat.

"Maybe, but why would they lie?"

"To keep us off guard. I'll tell youse. I's said fer years this town needs a proper militia. Wanted to start 'em drillin' when 'em

Guelphers rolled threw in 'at tank of 'eirs, but no one listens to crazy Ward. A few marches and some target practice is too much for 'em to bother with. Well, when 'em tree 'uggers attack we'll see who's crazy. Way I sees it; this whole plague is just a cover. Tree 'uggers and 'em Guelphers within 'eir toy are out to take us down."

"Ward, I mean Colonel?" said a man with greasy hair, dressed in filthy homespun, carrying a shotgun.

"Yeah lieutenant?"

"Shouldn't we's be closing the gate?"

"SHIT! Close it youse asshole, close it afore somethin' gets past. Gotta watch for spies. Them Novo Gaians is a tricky bunch."

Bloody fools. One AV or an air strike; they wouldn't stand a chance, thought Dan as he started his horse moving.

Minutes later he was tying up in front of the inn. The sounds of loud argument could be heard coming from inside.

"I say we sneak around them. Even if there is plague, we have to get away," shouted Amanda's voice. A chorus of agreement followed.

"Don't be a fuckin' asshole. The sun humpers might be jerks, but they have the same techs as the Gridders. I did a stint in the Regs afore I was thrown into the Dark. There's things that make night brighter than day and others that can spot a rabbit running twenty klicks away. There ain't no sneaking past that," snapped Frank's voice.

Steeling himself, Dan entered the inn. The filthy common-room was crowded, and the stench of tobacco filled the air. A single lantern glowed by the bar, where Frank stood facing the room. A billy club sat on the bar beside him.

"Candler," he called, noticing Dan. "Get your ass up here, and tell us what you found."

Dan moved to the bar. He could feel every eye in the place follow him and sense the tension in the room.

"To be starting, I think you're all being a wee bit foolish clumping up like this here. I went as far as the McDonald place. They've heard of the plague. They're being smart about it. No one coming close, and they're washing everything down."

“If they didn’t let you close how’d you find out about the plague?” demanded Jack Horner.

“We yelled to each other. Not a person here who wouldn’t tell you, I got a voice as carries.”

Several people in the group nodded in agreement.

“McDonalds don’t prove nothing. Youse see any sickins?” shouted Ken. Other voices were added in support of his demand.

“If’n I had, I wouldn’t be here now, would I? I was sent out to ask after this here plague; that’s what I did. You got a problem with how I did it, you take it up with Frank here.”

Frank, who had been standing behind the candler, picked up his billy club and slammed it onto the bar. The crowd silenced.

“It’s plague. What we gonna do? We’ll all die,” cried Nancy. She had traded her bodice for a simple, homespun dress and sat in the back corner of the room.

“Shut up, ‘oore,” snapped Blair, who sat in a chair close to the door.

“We have to get away. There’s no sickness in Arkell yet. We gotta escape before it comes here,” said Amanda. She was sitting in the middle of the room with a girl and boy of maybe twelve. Both of them wore suggestive, leather clothing.

“Shut up, everyone,” hollered Frank.

“I think the best thing any of us can be doing is going home. Keeping our distance from other folk and cleaning everything,” said Dan.

“So we use more soap, Candler?” snapped Jack.

“To kill the germs,” said Dan.

“Maybe you’re right, and maybe you’re wrong, Candler, but we’s all spent so much time together, don’t seem much point in separatin’ us now. If one of us has it, we all do. If none of us has it, we’re all safe,” remarked Frank.

“One thing I wonder is why they think this here plague from Guelph might be here? How would they know about comings and goings round here? Where’d you come from, Candler?” Jack’s grin was predatory.

Dan stared at the crowd. Fists clenched as he became the focus of their fear and rage.

“Well, now. It’s true enough, I was in Guelph afore I came

this way, but I swear, weren't no one with worse than a flu when I was there."

"It's your fault," screamed Amanda. A mutter ran through the crowd.

"Shut up youse nasty bitch," snapped Dinah. She had been sitting quietly at a table in the corner of the room.

"Why should I? It's all his fault. He brought plague among us!"

"Ain't no one taken sick yet," said Frank.

"*It's his fault!*" Amanda launched herself toward Dan. The rest of the room was preparing to follow, but Dinah leapt from her chair, tackling the younger woman. They fell to the ground kicking and scratching, while obscenities flew back and forth. The folk in the inn gathered around the fight, shouting encouragement and placing bets.

"This way, Candler." Frank pulled Dan behind the bar. A section of the floor opened to reveal a ladder descending to an unfinished basement. Grabbing a lantern, Frank led the way down. "That was too fuckin' close. Good thing for you I learned sometimes it's better to run when the brawl starts."

"Thanks, but shouldn't you be breaking up the fight afore someone gets hurt?" said Dan.

"Hell, no! Nothin' like a good catfight for business. 'Sides, Dinah's wanted a go at Amanda ever since she caught Ward with one of her fancy girls. Now come on, there's a door into the back. Better keep down for a bit. Let folk have a chance to cool off and think things through. One thing we got a good supply of here is rope, if you get what I'm sayin'."

"That I do." Dan followed the innkeep up a short flight of stairs and through a door into what had once been the backyard. Weeds choked the for by for metre patch of soil.

"Now go. I've three coppers on Dinah, and I want to collect. For all Amanda's a bitch, she can't take a punch worth shit."

"Thank you again." Dan started across the backyards of the empty houses.

Evening was spreading over the town when he returned to collect his wagon. The horse stood forlornly at the tie and nickered accusatorially when it saw him.

"Candler," called a stuffed-nosed voice from around the building's edge.

Dan drew his gun and moved toward the voice. Amanda appeared out of the shadows. Her eyes were blackened, and her nose was swollen to twice its regular size.

"What is it?" demanded Dan, stepping away.

"Shuu. The town meeting was full of idiots. None of them are willing to cross the Novo Gaians. You know more about them than you tell. I can see that. Help me; I'll make it worth your while."

"Help you? You tried to kill me earlier!"

"Quiet. I wasn't thinking. There's some here who have more sense than to wait around for plague to get us. We need to know. Is what Frank said true about them seeing things?"

"You bet your ass it is."

"He's lying," whispered a voice from the deeper shadows.

"Craft's honour. I've seen things that would do what Frank said."

"But they wouldn't have them on an operation like this. It will be easy to sneak past them," said the voice.

"Horner, is that you?" demanded Dan. No reply came, but a dark image slipped away between the buildings.

Amanda studied Dan then whispered. "Tell anyone about this; you're a dead man. I can afford the best the Dark Lands has to offer. Remember that." She followed the shadow into the night.

"Damn fools!" Dan returned to his wagon and untied his horse. He had barely reached the privacy of the visitors' field when he activated his radio.

Chapter Eighteen

Perimeter Guard

PRIVATE REUBEN HENRIES bit into his ration-bar, wincing when he brushed it against his swollen lip. He and his partner were crouched behind a small rise of land that afforded a view of the surrounding fields.

"It's all her fault, you know. I could be back at the inn eating decent food, but she had to be right," he griped.

"Reu, you could have let it go. Way I see it, you're lucky you're not in the stocks being pelted with clods of dirt by naughty children." Corporal Bob Harrison scanned their surroundings using night-vision goggles.

"Yeah, well. I still owe you for smashing a bottle over my head. I can't believe the major wants to promote you for that."

"I protected the town's TV. You've got to read more, Reu. That thing's worth a year's pay out here."

"Scout three-seven-two, do you copy?" sounded the radio Bob wore clipped to his belt.

"Three-seven-two, we read you. Over," replied Bob.

"Just got word. We're expecting an attempt to break quarantine in your sector. Numbers unknown. We're preparing reinforcements. Over."

"Understood. Over."

"Reset frequency after this transmission. Over and out."

"Resetting. Over and out."

"Shit! That's all we need," griped Reuben.

"Yup. Today's the fourth, isn't it?" asked Bob.

Reuben checked his watch "For another two hours."

Bob reset the frequency on his radio then pulled down his night-vision goggles.

"I'm getting something." Reuben looked up from the sound equipment in front of him. The device consisted of a lunch-box-sized case, with a microphone on a telescoping pole rising from its top. Reuben wore a set of earphones jacked into its side.

"Where?"

"Southwest."

Turning his gaze, Bob examined the ground.

"I don't see anything."

"I'm picking up a lot of noise."

"Shifting to infrared." Bob touched a button on his goggles then swore softly. "Got them. They're hugging the ground, hiding in the grass. I can only see their rising body heat. There's at least twenty of them, maybe more."

"Shit, what do we do?"

"Maintain the quarantine." Bob depressed the button on his radio and spoke. "Three-seven-two to base. Do you copy?"

"Base to three-seven-two. We copy. Over."

"Read approximately twenty targets our sector, requesting back up. Over."

"On its way. Over and out."

"Over and out."

"Bob, I've never shot someone before. If it comes to that, I don't think I can."

"You'll do what you have to, Reu. We both will. Let's try scaring them off first. Maybe we can stall them until the reinforcements arrive."

Filling his lungs, Bob hollered into the night. "We know you're out there. Return to your homes. Any attempt to break quarantine will be met with deadly force."

The sound of rustling filled Reuben's ears; then the directional mic began picking up whispered voices.

"'ey fuckin' know were 'ere. What the fuck do we do now?"

"Shut up, Blair. Jack, can they really see us?" asked a woman's voice. A moment passed before the woman's voice demanded. "Jack, where's Jack?"

"He crawled away to the woods, Miss Amanda," said a child's voice.

"Fine fuckin' time for 'im to take a God damn leak," snapped Blair.

"They have children with them," exclaimed Reuben.

"Shit. Maybe they won't charge," replied Bob.

"We can't go back. The plague will get us," spoke a new female voice on the mic. The sound of other voices whispering in unison cluttered the air.

"Nancy's fuckin' right, for once. I say we charge 'em. They can't know where we are. Probably 'eard us moving, but no way they can know where we are," snapped Blair.

"'Ave the brats charge 'em. They'll draw the fire while we crawl close enough to take 'em out," snapped a new male voice.

"Those kids cost me a fortune. I need 'em to start over," countered Amanda. The voices had risen above whispers.

"Keep 'em and die of the God damn plague then, bitch," replied the male voice.

"Waldo's right. Get those brats up front. Tell 'em to charge the bastards. No way 'em fuckin' sun humpers can see well enough to know they're brats afore we're in range."

"All right. I'll still have my credits, I guess. Children, get up front, and when I tell you, stand up and start running."

"Bob, remember what I said about not being able to shoot someone? I've changed my mind. They're having the kids charge us, so they can sneak into firing range," whispered Reuben. Reaching to his right, he picked up his rifle and checked the night scope. It cast the shadowy world into clear shades of green.

Crawling to the edge of the rise, he looked over the field separating him from his quarry. Like sparks leaping from a fire, a series of small images came into view and charged them.

"I hate this." Bob nestled the butt of his rifle against his shoulder took careful aim at a point in front of the children and fired. The bullet kicked up a cloud of dust as the sound echoed off the surrounding hills.

"Shit!" Reuben fired another warning shot.

"This is corporal Harrison. Children, I want you to walk to your right. There is a road over there. When you reach it, sit down and wait. Someone will be by soon with food and tents."

"Don't listen to him. Novo Gaians eat children, you all know that," called Amanda's voice.

"Children, I promise you, you'll be safe. We only want to keep people from travelling for a little while. Go to the road. We don't want to hurt you," yelled Bob.

"He's lying. All Novo Gaians are liars," hollered Amanda from the darkness.

"What should we do?" wailed a little girl.

A small figure started walking toward the road.

"Get back with the others, Monique," snapped Amanda.

"No! The tinker was nice to me. You lied about him. I think you're lying about these Novo Gaians too."

"Get back there right now! Do as you're told, or I'll punish you," screamed the hysterical voice from the darkness.

"I promise that every child who goes to the road will be given a safe place to live until they grow up. You can go to school and won't have to work until you're grown ups," hollered Bob.

A murmur passed among the children and several moved to follow Monique.

"No you don't, brats," roared a man's voice. Reuben watched through his night scope as a green-hued figure rose from the grass and pointed the barrel of a gun at the children. Rue's finger tightened on the trigger. The stock recoiled into his shoulder. He felt almost unreal as the scene unfolded before him. Time seemed to slow and every detail sharpened. His mind traced the path of the bullet as it sped toward the figure. A cry of surprise and agony shattered the night, as the green image pirouetted in the view of his scope. The target crumpled to the ground. The pounding of Reu's own heart filled his ears. The screams of children as they stampeded to the road echoed through the night.

"They shot Roger," cried a disembodied voice from the field. Hazy, green figures leapt to their feet and charged the Novo Gaian position. Muzzle flashes lit the night as the running figures fired blind.

"I shot him," said Rue.

"Snap out of it!" commanded Bob as he took aim and dropped one of the running figures. Reu forced his attention to the present and fired. By the time the fifth figure had fallen the charge was over, and the Arkellians had dropped back into the grass.

"Shit!" said Rue.

"Double shit! This isn't over. Get your ears back on. I'm radioing in," said Bob.

"Three-seven-two to base, do you copy? Over."

"We copy three-seven-two. Over."

"We are under fire. Repeat, we are under fire. Deadly force had been applied. We need those reinforcements now. Over."

"Understood. E.T.A. for reinforcements fifteen minutes. Over."

"Suggest they approach from the southeast. That will bracket the enemy on two sides. Over."

"Understood. Over."

"Over and out."

"Over and out."

"They're planning something." Reu listened intently to his equipment.

"They can fuckin' see us," snapped Blair's voice.

"My children, all gone for nothing. Do you know how much they cost me?" demanded Amanda.

"We gotta go back. They can see us. We don't got the children to shield us no more," whined Nancy's voice.

"She's right. Half the men with us are dead. I'm going back," snarled Amanda.

"Sure and 'ave 'em sun 'umpers shoot you in the back. I say we split up. They can't get us all," snapped Blair.

"The fuck they can't. It's like Frank said, they've got eyes like a cat's," spoke a new male voice. It had a waver of fear in it.

"Cowards. Do as youse wants. I ain't going back to die in no plague pit. 'O's with me, 'uddle close."

"Asshole," snapped Amanda; then there was the sound of rustling grass.

"I'm with you, Blair. So's Zack," spoke a new male voice.

"Just great. Me and the good fairies against a pair of bloody sun 'umpers armed to the fuckin' teeth. Well any 'elp's better 'an no 'elp. Osric, go left, Zack, 'ead right. Keep quiet and low. I'll go up the middle. When youse got a shot, take the bastards out."

"They're coming. Three of them. They've split up. The leaders coming up the middle, and the others to either side," said Reuben.

"Got them. I can track their body heat. We have to take them out. They'll be close enough to shoot effectively before the reinforcements arrive."

"Right, how?"

"Split up. You take the one to the left. I'll get the one to the right. Since the one in the middle wants our position so much, we'll let him have it." Saying this, Bob pulled a black wafer about the size of his palm from his pant-leg pocket. Pressing a button on its side, he slit the turf with his knife and shoved it into the hole.

"I'm on it." Reuben pulled his sound equipment from their watch station and crawled into the night.

Minutes passed as Reuben moved through the tall, field grass. He dropped the sound equipment as soon as he was a safe distance from the mound and now moved almost silently. A rustle to his right made him point his rifle, but it soon passed.

Damn rabbits, he thought. The darkness closed around him once more. An explosion shook the night, sending a rumble through the earth. A flash of light cast the field into stark relief.

"Jesus!" snapped a voice in front of him.

A head lifted above the grass. Still silent, Reu drew a bead and fired. The skull shattered, sending a spray of blood and brains out in a cone behind it; then the figure fell to the ground.

"Persephone forgive me," muttered Reu. He then crept toward where he knew Bob must be.

Bob lay in the grass near the mound that had been their refuge. After what seemed an eternity, a glint like the moon reflecting off metal appeared over the ridge. A figure crawled into the area and paused. Bob was close enough to see the figure's left hand was missing. A metal hook took its place. Swallowing, Bob stared at the black control in his hand. His chest was tight and his mouth dry. With a sad resolve, he closed his eyes and pressed the button. The roar of the explosion numbed his ears, and the flash of light penetrated his eyelids. When he opened them, the world was dancing shadows. There was the sound of a rifle being fired.

"*Zack! Blair!*" cried a distraught male voice.

No reply came.

"*Oh shit! Listen, I surrender. Just don't kill me,*" hollered the voice.

"Stand up and throw your gun away." Bob was glad that his voice remained level despite his rising gorge.

Maybe five metres away a man rose to his feet. He was tall and dressed in grass stained homespun. His lean frame shook with fear.

"Go back to Arkell. Tell them that we will maintain the quarantine. Leave your weapon behind. Now start walking," ordered Bob.

Osric moved slowly away from the scene of the battle until the sound of approaching horses drove him into a terrified run.

"Station three-seven-two, report," demanded a voice from the radio.

"We're here. We won. You're late for the party. Over." Bob spoke into the mic. His body started to tremble with the release of stress, as his mind tried to cope with the fact that he had killed.

Chapter Nineteen

Autopsy

"Using the information you sent us, we were able to uncover some of the facility's records. They are, however, incomplete. Over."

"Great, Dr. Frankel. Do they give you any clue as to what I'm dealing with here? Over," demanded Brad.

"Not yet. I'm afraid you'll have to perform the autopsy. If you follow the procedures I told you, and are careful, you shouldn't have any problems. Over."

"Wonderful. Over and out."

"Over and out."

Brad sat back in the driver's seat of his van and closed his eyes. His hands trembled; he forced them to steady.

"Too many uppers, old boy. You're starting to react," he muttered to himself.

Opening his eyes, he looked at his battery gauge then at the cloud darkened sky and sighed.

"What did he say?" Carla pulled open the passenger side door.

"They've found some of the records, but they're not much help. Have you set up that back room like I asked you?"

"Yes. That's why I came out. Things have slowed down a bit, and Vance Ragon just died. If you want fresh samples, now's the time to get them."

"Okay. We'd better suit up. I've been waiting on the data search, hoping it would mean the autopsy was unnecessary. I guess my excuses are all used up."

Brad followed Carla into the clinic. Thirty cots lined its walls and, despite the open windows, the stench was worse than when they had first arrived.

"You really cutting up young Vance?" Trina left a patient's side to challenge Brad. Her sweat-soaked dress now bore stains of less savoury origin.

"The doctor needs samples from a patient's organs to figure out what we're dealing with."

"The doctor really wants this? I mean, I've heard about you tinkers and your sick experiments."

Brad sighed and stared at Trina. The dark circles beneath his eyes seemed to deepen as this latest rumour surfaced.

"The doctor needs the samples to search for a cure, nothing more," he explained.

"Then I guess it's all right. If the doctor says he wants it. I just can't see why it's taking so long. Gridtown doctors treat you immediately. Old Emma Fishman told me that the doctors in Gridtown even do surgery in their offices."

"If you know what you're treating and how to treat it, that's easy. We don't." Brad pushed past Trina and moved to the contagion suits laid out on a table by the door to the impromptu morgue.

"I hate these things," he muttered. After checking the gauge on the pressure cylinder he began pulling on the outfit. "I recharged the cylinders with the compressor in my van. They're only half full, but it will have to do."

"Right." Carla began donning the second suit.

"Remember, just pass me the instruments, and be careful with any sharp edges. If we haven't already got this thing, a wound during an autopsy is a sure way to catch it." He started toward the door.

"Brad, your helmet's not closed," warned Carla.

"So it isn't. Thanks." Brad pulled the hood over his head. The stuffiness he knew was an illusion enveloped him. He swallowed in a dry mouth. "The sooner started the sooner finished," he whispered to himself and stepped through the door.

The back room was long and narrow. Years before it had served as a receiving and storage area for the products sold in the store. Now its walls were lined four deep with cots, each containing the remains of a plague victim. Long-dead, fluorescent lights dangled from the ceiling. A row of windows along the roofline of the back wall admitted a twilight illumination.

"I want to be sick every time I come in here," remarked Carla.

"Be thankful we're on bottled air," returned Brad.

"I am. I never would have thought it, but I can't put a name to most of the corpses."

"They don't mind. Why should you?"

"They're people. They should be remembered."

"They *were* people! Now they're meat! Keep thinking that, Carla. We can't worry about the dead, until we've done all we can for the living."

As they spoke, they walked up the narrow corridor between the cots and came to the door of a walk-in freezer. The scratched paint on the metal was dulled by age, but the rusted chromed door mechanism still worked. Brad grasped the handle, pulled it open and stepped in.

An ancient dinner-cart with cracked coasters sat by a formica and chrome table in the room's centre. A corpse lay on the table, its shrunken features seeming to mock their efforts. Several mason jars sat on the dinner cart's lower shelf. Brad's spotlight was taped to a broom handle supported over the corpse. The walls of filthy, scratched sheet metal seemed to crowd in around them.

Brad stared at the window crudely mounted in the back wall. A patch of sky could be seen beyond it. He focussed on the sky and felt his anxiety fade.

"Did you run an extension cord in here?" he asked.

"Of course. I know enough to supply your tools with electricity," said Carla, impatience in her voice.

"Sorry, didn't mean to treat you like a no brain. Guess I'm

too used to dealing with folk who think electricity's magic. Pass me the laser scalpel." Brad felt the familiar weight of the tool in his gloved hand. Clumsily he rotated it, so the cutting beam sat just below the corpse's throat. "Don't tell anyone how I hack this job. Autopsies are for doctors, not tinkers, and I'm not trying for neatness. Set her to full."

Checking that his gloves were clear, Brad depressed the button on the scalpel. The skin split, sending curls of smoke into the air, as he carved an oval reaching from neck to groin.

"Pass me the hand saw," he said. A second later the grating of steel against bone filled the room.

"What a mess!" said Carla.

"I warned you. I've only sat in on a few autopsies, and we don't study thoracic surgery at the academy. It's too advanced. Pass me the broom from the corner." Forcing the broom handle through the cut over the ribs, he pushed down on it. There was a ripping sound then the copse's chest hinged up. Pushing with the broom Brad forced the flap of flesh and ribs to the side, where it hung by strips of connective tissue.

"Taweret!" swore Carla.

"Gods of my fathers!" agreed Brad.

"Use the video camera; make sure its mic is on. I thought my mum was nuts for wanting videos of the Dark Lands. Guess she had a premonition or something."

Carla lifted a palm-sized camcorder from the cart.

"It's hard to get the focus with these gloves on." She directed the lens toward the cadaver's open chest.

"Hard to do a damn thing with these suits on! We don't have much choice. Let's go."

"Got it in focus."

"Good, okay Doc. The body fluids have thickened to a gel-like consistency. There is minimal pooling of blood. The organs all show the effects of acute dehydration."

"Is that thing below the ribs to the body's left the liver?" asked Carla.

"Yes. It's as shrivelled as the rest."

"What are those yellowy white splodges?"

"I'll have to ask Trina, but I'm betting this chap liked his ale a bit too much. Pass me a pair of forceps and a regular scalpel. Then get a jar ready. The sooner this is started, the sooner it's done."

He grasped the liver with the forceps and began cutting a section away.

Minutes later Brad stared into the body cavity and inventoried the work he'd done. "All that's left are the kidneys, I think."

Carla stood behind the dinner cart, tightening the lid on one of the mason jars. "Did you want a brain sample?"

"Shit! I don't, but the medicos do. We'll take that next then do the kidneys last. Pass me the laser scalpel."

Moving to the body's head Brad sliced away the scalp, peeling it back to reveal the skull beneath. Congealed blood formed a tracery of lines over the gleaming bone.

"Dremmel," he ordered.

Carla passed him the tool. A masonry cutter was already in its chuck. Throwing the switch, Brad began slicing at the skull.

The freezer's door jerked open, and a muscular woman rushed in and dove onto Brad's back. The impact drove his chest against the corpse's scull, trapping the spinning dremmel blade between them.

"You can't cut him up. He can't be dead," bawled the woman. Carla grabbed her and, with a heave, threw her into the corner of the room. The intruder's blonde hair hung down over her face, and her shoulders began to shake.

Brad pushed away from the table and began tearing at his bio-suit as he moved to the door.

Trina ran into the room almost bumping into him. "I'm sorry. She came looking for Vance; when I told her he was dead she still wanted to see him. When I said you were taking samples she went crazy. I couldn't stop her."

"What have you done?" sobbed the woman. Her hands twisted in the blue homespun materiel of her dress.

"We took samples to try and discover what the sickness is. Now get out of here before you catch it. This place is full of whatever's causing it," snapped Carla.

"No, No, it can't be, not my Vance. Not before I get to say I'm sorry," sobbed the intruder.

"Leanne here was Vance's wife. Sometimes, if you get what I

mean?" explained Trina.

"I don't care if she's a handmaiden to a Goddess. Get her out of here," snapped Carla.

"Brad, what are you doing?" demanded Carla, as he pulled off his headgear and undid the bio-suit's top seals.

Brad stared at her through the doorway. "Let the murdering bitch stay. She's already killed me. I may as well have an escort to the summer land." He dropped the material of his suit around his waist and pulled off his shirt.

"No!" gasped Carla, staring at the small, bloody cut on his chest.

"My Vance," sobbed Leanne.

"Get out, or wallow in his guts, so there's no chance you won't be infected!" Brad pulled the cap off a spitze bottle of disinfectant and dumped it over his wound hissing with pain as the cleanser burnt on his exposed tissues.

"He has to be properly buried," objected Leanne.

"He has to be burnt with the rest. With this whole place. And with me. If my parents can't have a grave to visit, why should you? Get out now!" snapped Brad.

Still whimpering, Leanne allowed Trina to lead her from the room.

"Wait a minute. Take this. Both of you get naked and spritz yourselves! Your clothes will have to be burnt." Brad held out a bottle of disinfectant.

"I won't str..." Trina began, but one look at the rage in Brad's face silenced her. Taking the bottle, she moved away from the tinker.

Brad returned his attention to his wound encouraging its bleeding.

"She was grief stricken," observed Carla, carefully.

"And I'm almost certainly infected. Maybe I should be sweet and compassionate, but I happen to be enjoying this life. I resent having some hysterical twit endanger it." He took a deep breath to steady himself before continuing. "I'll get the repair tape then we can finish this. Now I have even more reason to find a cure."

Minutes later Brad, in his patched isolation suit, cut through the rest of the skull and took his final samples.

"What now?"

"Now we disinfect the outside of each jar and put them in a saddle bag. Ingram will drop them off with one of the quarantine squads. They'll get them to the doctor."

"Right. Brad, don't get sick. I think I may have plans for you later."

Brad stared dully at Carla. While her body dented the contagion suit in all the right places, he felt too numb to respond. Sighing, he dipped the first of the jars into the disinfectant.

Chapter Twenty

Lynching

"DAN. DAN," WHISPERED the insistent voice from outside the wagon.

"Hummm," murmured Dan.

"Wake up," ordered the voice.

"What? Who?" Dan sat up in bed and knuckled sleep from his eyes. Reaching over, he popped the latch on the driver's side, back door and opened it a crack. So fast that it sent him sprawling, Susan pushed into the van closing the door behind her.

"Susan, not that I'm objecting to your company, love, but do you think it's wise to join me with all that's going on?"

"Keep your voice down."

Dan stared about the cluttered interior of his wagon, collecting his thoughts, then crawled to the front seat and turned on his CD player. The long-dead voice of Frank Sinatra filled the station wagon.

"That should cover our voices. Now, what is it, girl?"

"It's Gorgy, Felicia's boy. They live in the house next to mine. He's sick. I'm afraid what folk might do if they find out. We need your help to get him out of town. If it is the plague, that would keep folk safe. If it ain't, I don't trust folk round here to see the difference."

"Hold on now. Starters, what's the symptoms?"

"Stuffy head, fever, he says he aches all over."

"No vomiting or diarrhea?"

"None."

"Than it's not the plague."

"Thank God. How'd you know what the plague's like?"

"I was one of the ones that went to see the Novo Gaians, now wasn't I?"

"Yeah, you're right. Will you help us? Felicia's my best friend, and since Verge got gored by a bull, Gorgy's all she's got."

"Relax, lass, I'll help. How could any man be saying no to a woman as fetching as yourself?" Dan kissed her and began running his hand along her spine.

"Now, Dan! We can do that later. I'm worried about how long Felicia can keep Gorgy's illness secret. He's coughing so loud you can hear him out the window."

"Then later, me love. Now to save the child. We'll need a place to ourselves." Dan paused as he ran through possibilities in his mind. "Got it. There's a farmhouse tucked back in the woods, just south on the thirty-seven. Tinkers red-T'd it because the land's an aquifer recharge zone. Place's more than a bit run down, but it should do well enough."

"Thank you, Dan. You're a good man."

"Try and prove it to you later, love. For now, let's see to the lad." Dan searched the tangle of sheets and blankets in his van, finally uncovering his clothes.

"Dan. Why is there a girdle shoved into the corner here?"

Dan paused in his dressing. "Well, love, it's for my back, you see. It goes out sometimes, and it helps hold everything together while it heals."

Susan looked from the corset's thin waist to Dan's more ample midriff and shook her head.

"Candler," demanded a voice from outside the wagon.

Susan turned a wide-eyed stare toward Dan, who quickly lifted the blankets on his mattress and motioned for her to get under them. Pulling the blanket up so it completely covered Susan, Dan crawled over the station wagon's front seat and opened the door.

"Frank? What can I do for you on this fine day?" he asked, noting the enraged expression on the other man's face.

"Damn sun humpers killed a bunch of folk as were tryin' to slip past them. All hell's breakin' loose. Ward's talkin' about leadin' the folk against the tree huggen' bastards. We're meetin' at the inn. I want you there."

"How do you stand on attacking the Novo Gaians?"

"Fuck! I know what those bastards can do. Ward's an asshole to think he stands a chance. Sides, them as got killed were all doin' what I told them not to. Ask me, they deserved what they got. Other folk won't see it though. I need you to back me up about what them sun humpers got goin' for them. No use me running a bar, if there's no one left to pay for the drinks. I got to keep these assholes alive."

"Be right there. Just have to see to me horse first."

"Hurry up. Meetin's due to start in ten minutes. Those as survived the escape attempt are fit to stir up trouble."

"Got ya." Dan grabbed his boots as Frank turned and walked away. A minute later he pulled back the cover hiding Susan.

"You heard?" he asked.

"Yes. What's going to happen now?"

"That's up to the townsfolk. The Novo Gaians just want to stop us from spreading the plague. They won't come marching in over something like this. If they're attacked, though, they're likely to burn Arkell to the ground."

"Oh Gods! What can we do?"

"You, lass, can fetch your friend and her lad then hitch me horse. As soon as I'm finished with this lot at the inn, I'm getting you out of here."

"Because of the Novo Gaians?"

"Because of the townsfolk. I always knew there were those in Arkell who were a few watts short of a charge, but this thing's bringing them out of the trees."

"Thank you, Dan." Susan kissed him and slipped out the door.

No sooner was he alone than Dan pulled his radio from under his seat.

"Corporal Timothy to base, come in base. Over."

"We read you, Corporal. Over," said the radioman's voice.

"Trouble. Big trouble. Seem's some of those as tried to slip past you last night made it back. They're trying to stir things up. There are those as would like to come at you with all guns blazing. It looks like the townsfolk might just give them the okay. Over."

"Understood. Is there anything we can do to help quiet things? Over."

"They don't know what they're up against. Maybe if you showed them? Over."

"I'll pass it along. Over and out."

"Over and out."

Returning the radio to its hiding place, Dan slipped from his wagon and started for the inn.

As he walked, a light drizzle began to fall from the grey sky, making the dirty hamlet even drearier. Arriving at the inn, he found people crowded under the eaves.

"*Candler,*" called Ken, who stood in the doorway, his ample girth providing an effective barrier to those who would enter.

Dan moved to stand in front of him.

"Frank said to let youse through soon as youse got 'ere," said Ken, stepping aside. Dan noticed that the man's normally greasy, brown hair now formed a rich fall of chestnut. One sniff told him why.

"Keeping clean, good way to stay healthy," observed Dan, as he entered the inn.

"Damn wife won't let me in the 'ouse lessen I take a bath. Says youse told Susan somethin' about soap stoppin' plague."

"It helps."

"Wish youse kept youse fuckin' mouth shut. Bathin' this much can't be good for a body."

With a shake of his head Dan entered the inn. The common-room was jammed with people. Frank, Nancy, Amanda, Osric and Ward stood by the bar. Dan moved to join them. Amanda scowled at him as he approached. Her clothes were torn and grass stained, while her face had been hastily washed. Twigs and shoots of grass were caught in her usually immaculate hair.

"Good, you're here," said Frank.

"That I am." Dan scanned the faces in the crowd. Jack Horner, dressed in a clean tunic and showing signs of a recent bath, sat in the front row.

"Quiet, you lot," bellowed Frank. "Now there's things we got to be talkin' about. First seems a bunch of you assholes decided not to listen yesterday and tried to sneak past the sun humpers. Them as survived came back to tell us about it."

Amanda sniffed and began speaking in a sad voice.

"We were trying to get away from the plague, that's all. Those Novo Gaian devils came out of nowhere and started shooting at us. They didn't even warn us. There must have been a hundred of them, with eyes like cats. They killed everyone. We only got away because Blair, Zack and Osric here protected our retreat."

"'ey killed Blair. Blew 'im into a thousand pieces. I didn't see what 'appened to Zack, but 'ey must 'ave got 'im. 'e wouldn't leave me less 'ey did," added Osric.

A murmur ran through the crowd.

"I say we's attack. We gotta show 'em tree huggers theys can't go killin' our folk and get away with it," snapped Ward.

"They took my children, all my dear little children," cried Amanda.

The murmur in the crowd grew to a roar.

"Kill the bastards. They can't do that to our folk," cried a voice from the back of the room.

"Kill, kill, kill," Jack Horner began chanting. Soon the entire room had joined him.

Frank and Dan tried to shout over the noise, to no avail. Finally Dan pulled his gun and looked at Frank. Frank nodded and pointed to a section of floor behind the bar. The shot echoed in the room with painful intensity, shattering the momentum of the chant.

"That's better," yelled Frank. "Now let's talk sense. We can't fight the Novo Gaians; they've got too much tech. All they want is for us to sit tight and wait until they're sure there's no sickness here. I say we do it."

"What about Blair, Zack and the others?" demanded Amanda.

"What about them? Blair was an asshole. Sun humpers did us a favour, ask me."

"Don't listen to 'im. Only a matter of time afore 'em tree

'uggers hit us. Youse 'eard Amanda, took a 'undred of 'em to stop one group of us. Tree 'uggers ain't up to no kind of fight," yelled Ward.

"Listen, I've seen what they can do. Novo Gaians have bombs, like before the collapse, and jets. They want Arkell gone; it's gone. Nothing any of you could do about it," interjected Dan.

"Yeah well, where are they then? All I've seen is one small aeroplane. I say that's all they have," snapped Jack Horner. He still stood in the front row, but now he wore a smug expression.

"I say we get 'em," screamed Ward. Jack started the chant of "Kill" again and the room quickly joined in.

"We're fucked!" hollered Frank.

"We're all going to die," cried Nancy.

"We..." began Dan. A roar from outside silenced him. Everyone rushed to the street. Above them circled the ultralight, while down the street the shattered remains of the corner house blazed. As they watched, the pilot tossed an object, about the size and shape of a football, at another corner house. The explosion roared down the street.

"Shoot it down," ordered Ward. Pulling an ancient revolver from his belt holster, he fired at the aircraft. The plane dipped first one direction then another, waggling its wings as it flew. Ward emptied his gun. As he reloaded, the plane roared down the length of the street. The townspeople felt impacts against their skin and screamed. Red blossomed on their tunics and dresses. They turned to run but were too crowded to escape. Dan huddled against the wall, not believing his eyes, until a slug slammed into the back of a woman close to him. Red flew in all directions, and sticky paint splashed against his face. The plane completed its strafing run and flew out of sight.

"I'm hit. I'm going to die," wailed Amanda.

"Quiet," shouted Dan. Slowly the screams subsided. "Do you see what I've been trying to tell you? That was a warning. If the Novo Gaians had wanted us dead, we'd all be dead. You don't have the tech to fight them."

"The candler's right," added Frank. He was mopping paint off his face. His left eye was already swelling shut.

"'ey could 'ave killed us all," remarked Osric.

"How do you know they haven't? Just like a Novo Gaian to use a slow poison, make us suffer," yelled Jack.

"Horner, don't be an ass. Kill them quick, so they can't strike back. That's always the tinker way, and tinkers are sun humpers," snapped Frank.

Jack quieted and shrank into the crowd.

"What should we do?" cried Nancy.

"Go home, avoid other folk and stay clean," snapped Dan.

"Later for that, Candler. Now we've fires to put a stop to, afore they spread. Ward, put those soldiers of yours to good use for a change. Start haulin' buckets up from the well; douse the house on the north corner. Ken, grab the rest of the folk and start on the other one. Candler, come with me," ordered Frank.

Dan followed Frank into the inn.

"Maybe I should help with the fires," said Dan.

"Shit all need for that. Those were concussion blasts, and the buildin's were empty. Couple of little fires, probably burn themselves out without us, but it keeps those assholes busy."

Frank led the way upstairs to a small, private room containing a bed and a chair. Motioning for Dan to sit, he closed the door behind them. "Now talk, Candler. You know too much about what's happenin' and the sun humpers seem to know just when to do somethin' and what to watch for. I ain't no ignorant asshole like these Dark Landers. I served three stints in the Regs. We was told to watch for sun humper spies."

"Now, Frank, I don't know what you're talking about," lied Dan.

"Candler, I don't give a fuck who you work for. Just help me keep these assholes from gettin' themselves killed. Took me too long to become big in this burg for me to lose it 'cause these jerks can't tell their asses from a hole in the ground. You got a radio link with the sun humpers, don'tcha?"

Dan looked at the man before him. Despite the roughness and dirt, he could see the self-serving cunning in his eyes. Decision hardened in Dan, but his hand still slipped to his holster.

"Yes."

"Knew it. So this plague is real an all?"

"Yes. Deadly as anything the medicos have ever seen. Spreads like fire too."

"Shit. I'd hoped it was a lie then I'd of offed you and ended all this shit, but it ain't. Anythin' else I should know?"

"Not from the Novo Gaians. I think there may be a Gridder spy here, stirring up trouble."

"Horner. I've wondered, but he's a slimy one. Sides, why would the Gridders want to do us in? We're good for trade."

"First, to make Novo Gaia look bad. Imagine the stories that would spread if the troops here did wipe you out."

"Yeah, bad as what they say about Argyle. What's the other reasons?"

"Most of this town's second or third generation out from the Grid. They don't long to get back to the Bright Lands the same as new exiles. My guess is they want to kill you off. Make room for new folk kicked out of Gridtowns. Newbies will pay more for charges and stuff, 'cause they're not used to living without the wattage."

"That don't make sense. There's plenty of land for the Newbies."

"Aye, but it's further from the roads. The further the Gridders have to travel to trade, the more it costs."

"Makes sense. I'd do it, if I were them."

"You would, wouldn't you?" observed Dan with a shudder.

"You got something against capitalism?"

"I have something against extremes. There's another reason they want to do you in. This section of the Dark is getting pretty settled. Folk have good lives. The shareholders have to keep the Dark looking bad, or their workers might leave to find a better life."

"That I can believe. I remember the shows back home. Hell of a surprise when I hit the Dark and wasn't killed the first day."

"Look, I have things to take care of."

"Go, but get back here as soon as you can. I don't think old Jack's run out of tricks yet."

Chapter Twenty-one

Samples

"So, Janet, you've gotten as far as Brucedale on your route. That's impressive. Over." Eddie leaned back in the front seat of his tinker wagon and closed his eyes as he carefully chose his words.

"Yes. How's Brad doing? We took some classes together. He seemed like a nice guy. Over." Replied a woman's voice from the radio.

"He's having it rough. He's alone in there, and the Minister won't send in a biohazard team. He's even ordered me not to divulge information to the press. Over."

"Can he do that? Over."

"With my commission activated, in a crisis, he can force me to keep quiet for five years after this is over. The operation is classed as national security. That means what he's up to won't be public until it's old news.

"He's so attached to his political career, he's forcing others to behave like cowards, but I'm not allowed to discuss specifics. I can't even <u>tape</u> our conversations and give them to the press. He's also ordered scramble used on everything but short distance communication. Over."

"Bummer, I'd love to help. I bet you can't even tell the press the de-scrambler code to use? Over."

"Nope. It's a pity you couldn't make it to my place last winter. Remember when I invited you for February 15? Could have been a wild night. Over."

"Sorry, two-fifteen would have been a scramble for me. Over."

"Yes. Understanding is a tinker trait. Well, I'd better sign off. I have to contact his lordship. By the by, I'm planning a party, for after everyone gets off their route for the winter. It will be on November the thirteenth. Radio me if you think you can make it? Over."

"I'll tell you now. With bells on and a wiggle in my step. Over and out."

"Over and out."

"Finished your 'social call'?" Barb sat beside Eddie.

"Yup, Janet and I are old friends. She was one year behind me in the academy."

"Old school ties. You going to call the Minister of Dark land's affairs now?"

"I have to. The purse on this operation just grew substantially." Eddie reached forward and set the frequency on his radio to one, one, one, three, depressed the mic button and spoke.

"Call in, Call in, Call in, Militia, Militia, Militia. Over."

"We read you, Militia, standing by for ident."

"C O, M A, E one, D zero, W four, A five, R zero, D five, J zero, B five, A one, I zero, L seven, Y, PC. Over."

"You are within range. The Minister is standing by. Putting scramble into effect. Over."

Eddie pressed a button on the laptop attached to his radio and waited.

"Major, what's the problem? Over," demanded the minister's voice.

"Francis, we're going over budget on this one. A bunch of Arkellians tried to break quarantine. They were using child slaves as a shield. My man had to offer the kids homes in Novo Gaia to get them away from the adults. Over."

"He did what? He had no authority to do that! We cannot

honour the rantings of some idiot. I want him court-martialled for this. Over."

"It was either that or shoot a group of children. Over."

"I will not have my Ministry funding the wholesale immigration of Dark Landers. Over."

"An officer of the Novo Gaian militia made a promise to Dark Land's citizens. We are honour bound to uphold it. Over."

"Eddie, don't be naive. Hush up the witnesses. Lose the kids. This operation is already costing us a fortune. Just the fuel requirement has set back our reserves by six months. Over."

"So the next town that joins us gets its primary industry in September instead of March. This mission is important! Over."

"Major, I will not authorize those children's entry into Novo Gaia. Do you have any idea of the cost of raising and educating a child? Besides, foster parents tend not to want kids that have been used the way those children probably have. This topic is closed. Over."

"In that case, I renew my request that a biohazard team be sent into Guelph. Brad is not qualified to deal with this situation. He's doing his best, but it's too much to ask. Over."

"I said it before. I will not be known as the Minister that sent Novo Gaian citizens into a plague zone. Over."

"Dr. Frankle's team have volunteered. All they need from you is transport and equipment support. Over."

"What part of no don't you understand, Eddie? If it works, that's great, the idiot masses call me a hero for a day and forget by the next election. If one of them dies, I'm to blame. No way! Over."

"Yes, sir! Over."

"Has your man uncovered the location of that accursed tank? Over."

"He's been busy, he is dealing with a plague, *alone*! Over."

"Tell him to remember where his loyalties lie. The Minister of Defence has been nagging me. She wants that machine. The Minister of the Environment is having nightmares about a containment breach. Over."

"Even if he finds it, what's he supposed to do, steal it? Over."

"I expect him to do his duty. Honestly Eddie, you know as

well as I the danger that machine represents. That cooling and containment system is over a hundred-years-old. With the rad exposure the metal in it will be as brittle as glass. We can contain a plague. No one can contain a major rad leak. Over."

"So is Brad authorized to spend the marks he needs to persuade the Guelphers to part with their toy? Over."

"Tell him to do what he likes. It will be the Ministry of Defence that pays for it, not mine. On that note, remember to lose those kids and watch the bottom line. My ministry has spent quite enough already on this! Over and out."

"Over and out."

Eddie released the mic button.

"What a gutless twit," remarked Barb.

"What goes around comes around. Old school ties. Gotta love them." Eddie, smiled to himself. "We should get back to something important. Brad will be sending those autopsy samples along soon. I want to be there when they arrive. You should go back to your station. Reuben and Bob will be starting their shift, and they shouldn't be alone."

"You can say that again. Reuben is a total wreck. Bob seems to be handling it better."

"Police training. They hope they'll never have to pull the trigger, and most of them don't, but it's always in the back of their minds. He was braced for it psychologically."

"I hope they're okay."

"So do I. That's what I consider the 'too high a price' for this mission."

Opening his wagon's door, Eddie slipped out into the drizzle and began untying the reins of a bay mare.

"It's good of the local horse breeder to let us use his steeds." Barb untied the pinto gelding she had taken a shine to.

"Good of him?" Eddie snorted "Ben's getting a panel and two battery packs for their use. That man never gave anything away."

"Still, we do put the horses at risk."

"That's why we're not allowed to use any of his precious, first-string mounts. Still in all, I have to agree, they're good, solid horses. He treats his animals well."

"Major, lieutenant," called a chubby, Asian man in his early twenties, dressed in the khakis of the Novo Gaian militia.

"What is it, corporal?" asked Eddie as the soldier approached.

"Corporal Timothy just radioed in. The demonstration with the paint pellets worked. The Arkellians are scared. The town leader, Frank, has figured out that Dan's a spy. Dan says he trusts this Frank, at least as long as they want the same things."

"Thank you, Ackley. Too bad about Frank finding out. Dan's probably right about him though. Even a snake tries not to bite the hand that feeds it."

"Should we try and get him out of there?" asked Barb.

"No, we can't break quarantine, and he's too useful where he is. Ackley, keep your ears on. I want someone manning the radio at all times, and I mean all times. You don't take a leak unless someone is filling your duty. Barb, before you go, I want you to arrange for Ackley to get a ten-minute break each hour. Better yet, grab someone from the inn; have them fill Reuben's shift. Pair Reuben with Ackley. That should give him a chance to think things through."

"Yes, sir." Barb mounted and rode toward the inn.

"Well?" asked Eddie.

"Sir?" replied Ackley.

"Is someone manning the radio?"

"Oh. Sorry, sir." Ackley sprinted to the truck that served as the radio room.

"Now maybe I can get where I'm going and out of this bloody rain." Eddie mounted and headed for the highway-seven blockade.

Half an hour later he brought his horse to a stop in front of the tent that formed the base for unit seven-one. It sat to one side of the broken, asphalt strip that was the road. A small windmill and solar panel array stood on the highway, with a wire running from them to the tent. A tarp supported on poles stood to one side, creating a sheltered space over the horse tie.

"Edward, I must protest. My driver refused to bring my lab here. He even refused to unhitch the truck section and transport me. I had to ride here on a horse, in the rain!" snapped Dr. Frankel, who came to the tent flap as Eddie loosened his horse's girth strap and walked the few steps from the horse tie to the shelter.

"If you hadn't noticed, the trucks use chemical fuels. They're not for joy riding." Eddie pushed past the doctor. Inside the tent was about nine metres square, with a table in the centre, on which was pinned a contour map of the area. A large, deacon's bench against its back canvas served as cot, seating and battery pack holder.

"I do not consider the prompt and efficient analysis of these samples to be 'a joy ride'," countered Frankel.

Eddie shrugged out of his leather rain-slick and hung it on a pole by the entrance before turning to the tent's other occupant.

"Any messages, sergeant?" he asked of the large-busted, black-haired woman sitting on a stool in the corner by the radio.

"None since you told us to expect the courier, sir."

"Okay. Who's doing the retrieval?"

"That is another matter. I should be the one to meet the courier. Those samples have to be handled delicately. If one of the jars break, it..." griped Frankel.

"Doctor, you are too important to be put at unnecessary risk. After the bottles have been disinfected, you can have them. Now, Sergeant, who's doing the retrieval? I need to know, so I can add the hazard bonus to their pay voucher."

"It's private Veronica McDowl. The one who got in the brawl."

"That's a surprise."

"She wanted to make up for the trouble she caused. Besides, I think she needs the money to pay for the table."

"Well then, Sergeant, all that's left is to wait. You play poker?"

A glint entered the sergeant's eye as she pulled a deck from her uniform's pocket, expertly shuffled it, and then, with feigned innocence, said, "I'm not very good."

An hour later Eddie looked at the doctor's expression of intense concentration and demanded, "Are you in or out?"

"I am thinking."

"Would you like a calculator? It might help you work out the odds," asked the sergeant. Of the three piles of marks on the table, hers was the largest, followed by Eddie's.

The tent flap pulled back, revealing Private McDowl. "Sirs, Sergeant, I see someone coming. He fits the description. A mounted dark-skinned man with a saddle bag carrying a red flag."

"That's that. Anyone mind if we dump the pot in the mission end party fund?" asked Eddie.

"Not me," agreed the sergeant.

"As you wish," grumbled Frankel, laying a full house, fives over twos on the table.

A moment later the field phone at the communications' stand came to life.

"Hello, hello, this is Ingram. Brad, the tinker, said I should come here. Hello, can anyone hear me?"

Eddie moved to the communications' rig. "We hear you, Ingram. Do you have the samples with you?"

"In my saddle bag."

"How is the disease progressing? Can you tell me if it's zoonotic?" demanded Dr Frankel.

"What, is it what?" replied the voice on the intercom.

Dr. Frankel looked impatiently at the tent's roof.

"Never mind." Eddie shot Frankel a quelling look. "I want you to carry the bottles up the street. About fifteen strides from where you are there's a tank with a lid on it. It's full of disinfectant. Put all the bottles into it. Keep your saddle bag, we have our own."

"Okay. Leave the bottles in the pot. Should I put the lid back on?"

"Yes, and wash the disinfectant off your skin as soon as you can." Eddie hung up the phone. "Here goes."

Grabbing his coat, he led the small group out of the tent onto the road. The drizzle had strengthened into a steady rain. They watched as a bedraggled figure left the shelter of the canopy over the field phone and walked towards them. It paused by the barrel and began transferring the contents of a saddle bag into the disinfectant. A minute later the man replaced the barrel's lid, waved and returned to the horse tethered by the communications' tent. With a final backward glance he rode away.

"Should I get the samples now?" Private McDowl had a quaver in her voice.

"Let us be thorough. Allow them to soak for ten minutes.

As long as your man sealed the jars properly, it won't hurt the samples," said Dr. Frankel.

"You're the expert." Eddie started to pace.

"I must say, I can see why my driver was reluctant to come here. These roads are in horrible repair," commented Frankel.

"Disrepair is more like it. Asphalt reclamation is a major industry in the Dark Lands."

"Really?"

"Both our crowd and the Gridders buy reclaimed asphalt to supplement the by products of our plasma garbage incinerators for use in road maintenance. Reclaimed materials make up most of the Dark Lands non-agricultural exports."

"I remember my father working a road digging crew when I was little," remarked the sergeant.

"You from the Dark?" asked Eddie.

"Sunnyside. I was ten when we joined Novo Gaia."

"I did my apprentice year on your route, just before you were incorporated. Let's see, what was her name? Martha, Martha Widebottom. Do you know her?"

"She's my aunt."

"Hurumm. This is all quite fascinating, but I believe ten minutes have passed," interrupted Frankel.

"Of course." Eddie motioned for Private McDowl to collect the samples.

Taking a deep breath, McDowl walked down the street with a sample case the size of a large toolbox. Eddie watched as she lifted the barrel's lid and extracted the bottles. With meticulous care, she placed the samples into the padded carrying case then sealed the lid. Through his binoculars Eddie could see her hands shaking; then the last jar was in place. Closing the box, she pulled the cord that flooded it with a sterilising gas, before lifting the container and starting towards the station. Thunder roared and a lightning flash blinded everyone. Eddie heard a cry and tried to peer through the dots that danced in front of his eyes. When they cleared, he could see Private McDowl kneeling on the road, staring at her hands.

"She must have tripped!" Frankel started towards her.

"Wait! She dropped the box. The seal might have broken,"

warned Eddie.

"She's hurt. I took an oath!" Frankel kept walking. Coming to the private's side, he knelt and examined her. Helping her to her feet, he waved her toward the field tent and moved to examine the containment case. A minute later, he picked it up and followed her.

"The seal is intact. These things are made to take a beating," he called as he approached the field camp.

"That's good. We should get back to your lab before the sun sets," suggested Eddie.

"As soon as I have dressed Miss McDowl's wounds. They are superficial, really just abrasions, but it is best to avoid infection."

"I can bandage myself, sir," objected the private.

"Nonsense. It will only take a moment. Edward, if you would be so kind as to take the case to my lab for me. I trust your horsemanship more than my own." Frankel glanced at the tethered horses. "Awful creatures!"

"Yes, doctor." Eddie smiled tolerantly then taking the case moved to his mount.

Chapter Twenty-two

Hope In The Darkness

BRAD DIPPED THE cloth into the water bucket and stroked it over the feverish form on the cot. The dry skin seemed to swallow the water. His head ached, and his eyes felt dry and grainy. Focussing on his watch, he muttered, "Two hours before another pill."

"You should get some sleep, Tinker." Trina moved to his side.

"No use trying. I have so much residual amphetamine in my system, I'd only lie there awake. How are we doing?"

"Four more deaths, six more who can't keep down the soup and eight new arrivals. We need more I. V. solution."

"I radioed it in. They'll drop it in the morning. Have Mark pick it up. Where is he anyway?"

"He went with Ingram to fetch more water. I have to admit, he loves his little girl. He soaked her down to keep her cool before he left."

"Smart man, he..."

The electric light in the room's centre dimmed.

"Better break out some candles. I don't like using them because of the smoke, but my batteries are about clapped out."

"I'll get them. It's still raining outside. Do you think you'll have enough to keep your radio working? It's the only link we have with the doctor."

"That's why I'll shutdown everything in the clinic as soon as my tests are done."

"I wish the town council wasn't so close with where they hide the tank. They wouldn't even tell me, and I'm sure it could power everything we need. I know for a fact it has a radio."

"To be honest, I hope it's far away from here. Atomic systems are as dangerous as this plague, especially old ones." Brad closed his eyes and rubbed the back of his neck.

Trina looked indignant. "No ones died from us having our tank, and it means no one is likely to try and raid us! It gives Guelph security."

"No one's died yet. Do you have anyone who knows what to do if something goes wrong with it?"

Trina stared at the floor. "We found some books; the drivers are reading them."

"Wonderful, look one disaster at a time, okay? Could you please get those candles?"

"Of course." Trina left.

Brad moved to the table in the room's centre and opened his incubator. Agar plates sat in rows on the wire shelves. Preparing the microscope slides took only minutes. The light below his microscope glowed dully when he turned it on. He began checking the slides against his computer files.

"Still not a damn thing," he muttered, as slide after slide passed before him. The light below his eye weakened, and his computer screen dulled until he couldn't see it.

"Shit!" He unplugged the lantern. The room fell into pitch black, but his computer screen brightened to legibility. Working by the screen's glow, he finished off the slides before unplugging the remaining electrical units.

The room around him was completely black, and the sounds of the dying assailed him. Trina appeared, carrying a pair of candles. They stood twenty-five centimetres tall and were shaped like fairytale towers. The light they cast gave the room a shadowy, macabre quality.

"Seems a pity to use these, but needs must as the devil drives," she remarked.

"For the summer fair?" Brad eyed the candles wearily.

"Yes. You've never been to our summer fair, have you?" Trina placed the candles on the table.

"No. Guelph is either a spring stop or a fall stop on my route."

"You should come, it's so nice. Cattle traders from miles around, singers, merchants. This year the wandering Stratford players are supposed to come. Though I guess there won't be many who'll want to visit us after word of this gets around." Trina indicated the room with a sweep of her hand.

"You'll do better next year."

Trina shrugged. "Did your, oh what did you call them? *Micras-cip* smears, show anything?"

"Microscope. No. I checked every tissue type and found zip. Whatever this is, it's not a bacterium, though I should talk to... what was his name, the chap we autopsied?"

"Vance."

"Right. I should talk to his wife. He had something that she probably has as well."

"I told that slut she'd get the clap," snapped Trina. Brad looked at her. The candlelight had softened her features, but she still had a lean, vicious cast.

"We better start wetting them down again." said Brad.

"I can't see to work."

"Here's my backup flashlight. When you turn the crank it operates a small generator that charges its batteries." Brad pulled the light from his belt and passed it to Trina.

"What are you going to do?"

"Take a shower, while the water in my tank's still warm, and change into fresh clothes. I think I'll burn the ones I'm wearing."

Leaving the clinic, he stared at the black sky and listened to the steady spin of his windmill.

"At least I have some watts flowing in," he muttered. Moving to the back of the wagon, he assembled his shower unit and let the water fall over him. By the time he finished, morning's first light was lighting the clouds. Dripping, he opening the door of his van and paused, staring. Carla lay naked across his bed. Her breasts rose and fell with the rhythm of her breathing. Brad swallowed as his manhood made itself known.

Reaching into the van he pulled a towel and his spare set of clothes out then closed the door. The rain had stopped, but the sky was still menacing and grey.

"Tinker," spoke a quiet voice as he dressed.

Brad turned to face the voice then looked down. A child of maybe seven stood on the street, holding a basket. Her blonde hair was braided close to her head, and she wore a simple, grey, homespun dress.

"What is it?" he asked.

"I need youse help. My mom said I had to stay away from youse, 'cause of the plague, but Percival's so sick. Will youse help him?"

"Who's Percival?" A chill of dread at facing yet another victim passed up Brad's spine.

The child held out the basket, and he pulled back the covering. Inside was a short-haired, grey cat with white feet.

"You risked catching the plague for a cat?" snapped Brad; then another more frightening thought struck him.

"Please, Tinker. I love him. He's only a year old. We got him his shots last year, like youse said, but he still got sick. Youse gotta help him."

Brad laid a hand on the small, furry body. He felt the slow rise and fall of the rib cage then placed a finger by the animal's ear. It was feverish.

"This is important. Has your cat had diarrhea?"

"No, Tinker, sir. He hasn't used his box in days."

Brad exhaled a breath he hadn't known he'd been holding.

"Not a case of zoonosis. Good!"

"Tinker, can youse help him? It's all I have, but I'll pay it," pleaded the child. She fished a cracked, circuit-board out of the basket and held it out to Brad. He stared at the offering, barely worth a tenth part of a copper mark then at the child and the cat.

"I can't spend much time, but I'll do what I can. I'm going to give Percival a broad-spectrum antibiotic and inject some fluid under his skin. Bring him back here at sunset, and I'll do the same thing. I'll give you some pills then. I want you to mash them up in his food, twice a day. Force him to eat if you have to. Add water to some mashed up meat until it's sloppy, like lumpy gravy, and pour it down his throat, just make sure he eats."

"Thank youse, Tinker." Tears glistening in the child's blue eyes.

Two minutes later Brad watched her walk away carrying the basket and its precious cargo. He thumbed the cracked circuit board, with its salvageable electrical components, and smiled.

"All that's going on, and you find time to treat a little girl's cat. Softy." Carla stepped out of the van.

"You heard."

"You're not exactly a quiet person."

"It's just, well. I've seen so much death and grief the last few days. Maybe what I did for the cat won't work, but maybe it will and..."

"And if it does, you've had at least one victory." Carla placed her hand against Brad's cheek. "I'd better go relieve Trina."

Sighing, Brad tossed the circuit board into his van and followed her back into the stench of the clinic.

The morning's routine dragged on: wetting patients, changing I.V.s, spooning barley soup into reluctant mouths.

Brad sat beside a patient taking a blood pressure when Mark hollered.

"Tinker. Help!"

Brad leapt to his feet and ran to Rose's bedside. The child convulsed wildly as sweat poured off her, and her father tried to hold her in place.

"*Carla, Trina!*" Brad grabbed the arm with the I.V. in it, bracing it against the side of the cot.

"Auhh, auhh, auhh!" Rose screamed in incoherent agony.

"Brad, what...?" Carla reached the cot and secured a flailing leg.

"No, let her bounce. Mark, brace her arm so she doesn't dislodge the I.V. Carla, in my drug box there's a green bottle labelled sodium phenobarbital. Grab it and a syringe."

"On it," said Carla.

"What is it, Tinker?" demanded Mark, while he braced his daughter's arm.

"I don't know. None of the others have gone into convulsions." Brad grasped the child's head and listened for breathing. A moment later he locked his lips over hers and exhaled, forcing air into the lungs.

"Got it." Carla ran up behind them. Brad moved away from the child and grabbed the needle and bottle. In seconds he was plunging the needle home in Rose's buttock. Extracting the syringe, he returned to her head and once more filled her lungs with air.

"She's not stopping," snapped Mark.

"The drug takes time to work."

Minutes passed as Rose thrashed on the cot, and Brad continued to breathe for her. Slowly the motions became less violent, until they stopped. Brad moved back and watched his patient's chest rise and fall in a slow, steady rhythm.

"Is she all right?" asked Carla.

"I don't know." Brad squatted back on his heels. "The convulsions are new. I'd better report this to Dr. Frankel. Oh shit, my batteries. They went flat. Has the sun broken through the cloud?"

"Not as I saw when I went out," replied Mark.

"Shit! Call in will have to wait. Carla, I'll be outside if you need me." Brad walked to his wagon.

"Brad, I delivered those samples like you asked. They had me put everything in a barrel of disinfectant before they'd even get close. Are things really that bad?" asked Ingram, who waited by the van.

"Yes." Brad scanned the cloudy sky. "I need to try and breathe some life into my batteries. Can you give me a hand?"

"You got it, Tinker. Is my Mum...?"

"She's still hanging on, though I don't know how." Brad lifted his van's hood, revealing the battery pack beneath. "I'm too damn thorough. Not a speck of corrosion. Sometimes if you clean the joins of a battery pack, the lowered resistance will give you a watt or two."

"Neat. Wish I was a Bright Lander. Electricity's useful stuff."

"I like it. Not much for it, with only the windmill for charging, it'll be an hour or two before I can call in."

"Anything I can do?"

"Not unless you can speed up the wind, or make the sun shine. Or... Damn, I'm a fool. Ingram, the inn has a panel and battery set."

"And no one's staying there right now, it should be full."

"Right. okay, disconnect one of the inn's batteries and clip it onto my system. Positive to positive and negative to negative. When the sun starts shining again you can return it."

"Sure thing, Tinker." Ingram grabbed Brad's toolbox and walked to the inn. Brad lay his head on his car seat and closed his eyes. He felt hot, and his pulse pounded in his ears. The dryness in his mouth was nothing compared to the grey fatigue in his body, but the pills would not let him sleep. It felt good to lie with his eyes closed, so he stayed there until Ingram knocked on his van's window.

"I've done the hook-up, Tinker."

"Good man." Brad quickly checked the battery connection before re-entering the van and activating his radio. The call in took only moments. His report and the request for more anticonvulsant drugs followed; then he signed off.

"Ingram, when this is all over, assuming we're still alive, you should take applied electronics at the Basic Skills Academy. I'll recommend you, if you like."

"Wish I could afford it, Tinker."

"Get a loan from the Novo Gaian Dark Lands Fund. I'm sure they'd help you."

"Can't borrow money. My Mum won't allow it, and I don't like owing anybody."

"Well, the offer's there to sponsor you, if you want it. You've got a knack for electrical things, and I know there are enough units in this region to keep you busy."

"Brad, come quick. Another one's going into convulsions!" yelled Carla from the clinic's door. Brad grabbed a pocket mask and sprinted into the building.

That evening Brad rubbed at his sore shoulders and let his eyes droop shut.

"What a day! Why are these ones going into convulsions?" Carla's lips were chapped from applying mouth to mask AR.

"I don't know. The only thing I can tell you is they're all ones who had swollen lymph nodes," observed Brad.

"Tinker, there's someone here to see you," called Ingram from the doorway.

"Who in the names of all the Gods would want me now?"

"She says her name's Elisabeth. A little blonde girl."

"Oh yes." Brad followed Ingram to the van. The sun was setting in a partially cloudy sky.

"Tinker, Tinker, Percival's feeling much better," squealed Elisabeth. The basket she held in her hand was still covered. Brad took it and pulled back the towel. The grey tom lay there, its chest moving in a steady rhythm. When Brad touched it, it lifted its head and turned weary eyes towards him. Gently he stroked over the small, furry body and was rewarded with a tired purr.

"See, I told you he was feeling better," exclaimed the child.

Brad smiled and moved to his wagon, returning with a syringe in one hand and a bottle of pills in the other.

"Remember what I said about making him eat and take his medicine?"

"Yes, sir."

Brad pushed the needle home, drawing a faint hiss from his patient. Recovering the basket, he passed it to the child. "Now go home and stay there."

"I will, Tinker. Thank you, thank you," cried Elisabeth as she walked away.

"Bad bugs seventy plus, us, one cat," observed Ingram.

"Sometimes you take your victories where you can get them." Brad slumped against the van.

"Tinker, come quick. I need you to look at Rose. I think she must be just about done. She's breathing shallow, and she ain't passing nothin'!" called Mark from the clinic's door.

"On my way!" Brad ran to Rose's bedside.

"I was sleepin' by her. When I woke up she was different. Quiet like. Oh my Rosie, my little Rosie. I want you to know, Tinker. I know you did all you could."

Brad placed his hand on the child's brow, checked her records then yelled, "Carla, fetch my thermometer!"

A minute passed as Brad probed Rose's small, dehydrated

body.

"What is it?" asked Carla.

Brad snatched his thermometer from her hand and, placing it in the child's ear, depressed its read button. A second later he sat back on his heels, staring at the liquid crystal display."

"What is it Brad?" demanded Carla.

"Thirty-seven point two. Her temperature's thirty-seven point two!" he shouted.

"What are you saying, man?" demanded Mark.

"Her temperature's normal. You said she hasn't passed anything in about half an hour?"

"Yes. I thought she had nothing left to pass."

"Mark, I can't be sure, so don't get your hopes up. The next few hours will tell, but I think Rose's fever might have broken."

"Don't tell me a lie, Tinker. I couldn't live with that."

"No lie, Mark. Rose is badly dehydrated, but there are others here who are just as bad and still alive. The next few hours will tell."

"You mean she might live?"

"I don't know how or why, but I think she's rallying."

"Sweet Mary bless you, Tinker!" Mark bowed his head in prayer over his child.

"Do you really think there's hope?" asked Carla when they were out of earshot.

"I'm not sure, but this is the first good sign I've seen. Rose was the first case we saw with the swollen lymph nodes, wasn't she? I just pray this pans out."

"Me too."

"Bad bugs seventy-eight, us two. Not great, but a start."

"Two?" Carla looked confused.

"The cat lived!"

Chapter Twenty-three

Escape

"Quiet, lad," ordered Dan. The seven-year-old boy lying on Dan's bed struggled not to cough.

"Thank you again, Candler," said the raven-haired woman sitting on the mattress beside the child.

"Thank me when we're past the blockade, lass," replied Dan. His eyes traced her Rubenesque form in his rear view mirror.

"I will," remarked Susan, who sat beside him. "How are you going to get past the blockade? Ward is being a complete ass."

"I know how to get by our boy Ward, love. Don't you worry your pretty self about that. Felicia, you better pull the covers over Gorgy now."

Felicia pulled the blanket over her child's head and stared forward. Grubby, tract houses flanked the street to where it ended in an impromptu barrier fronted by a company of armed men. Dan reined his horse to a stop in front of the barricade.

"Candler, what youse doin' 'ere? No one in or out." Ward moved to the station wagon's window.

"Aw, Ward my friend, can I have a word?" Dan opened his door a crack.

Ward eyed him suspiciously then motioned for him to exit.

Susan watched Dan lead Ward away from the wagon. Ward glanced towards her, leered then slapped Dan on the back and started to laugh. Dan's lips moved as his hand pumped back and forth; they both laughed. Smiling, Dan returned to the wagon. Ward motioned for the barricade to be pulled back. A cough exploded from the rear of the wagon, and Susan stared wide-eyed at the men around them. Dan's hand flashed to his stereo. The sound of a seductive sax solo blared from the speakers. Snapping his reins, he drove the wagon through the gate. After about thirty metres he turned down the music.

"How'd you make him let us through?" asked Felicia.

"I have my ways," replied Dan.

"Tell us," ordered Susan, a suspicious glint in her eye.

"Well, it had to be something Ward would believe, you see."

"You told him you were going to bed me, didn't you?" snapped Susan.

"No! Ward would never have let us leave the town for that. Don't be silly. A little roll in the hay's nice, but nothing extraordinary enough to get that lug to change his mind about anything. Even with a woman a fetching as yourself."

"Then what did you tell him?"

"I told him I was going to bed both of you, in that pretty, little meadow down the road with the brook running through it. Said Felicia here wanted to be out of town, so Gorgy wouldn't get wind of it."

"*You what?*" spat the women in unison.

"It had to be something he'd believe and something rare enough that he'd let us out of town for it. Two women at once is a fantasy most men share. I figured he wouldn't piss on my parade."

"We have to live in that town!" snapped Susan.

"I asked him to be discreet."

"Ward's the biggest gossip in the village. Everyone will have heard by evening," said Felicia.

An explosion of coughing riveted her attention on her son. She smoothed back his sweat-soaked, blond locks and gazed into his deep-blue eyes. The lad's small, muscular body trembled with chills, despite his pajamas.

"It's all right, Gorgy. We're past the blockade," soothed Felicia.

"Dan, couldn't you think of anything better?" demanded Susan.

"Not on the spur of the moment, love. I don't see why you're in such a flap?"

"Every man in town is going to be after us to take them on. We'll not get a moment's peace." Susan trembled with repressed anger.

Dan shrugged. "Sorry, love, it's the best I could do. Ward seems to like me. When I tossed in the line, 'eat drink and be merry, for tomorrow we may die,' he just couldn't say no."

Susan sighed and rubbed her eyes wearily. "Maybe I can move to Eden Mills?"

It took nearly an hour for them to reach the depressed stretch of dirt that marked where a long-absent, asphalt lane had cut into the trees. Reining his horse to a stop, Dan stepped out of the wagon.

"We'll have to walk from here. I'll not risk old Samson on this uneven ground." Upon Dan speaking his name the big gelding turned its head and nickered.

"How far is the farmhouse?" Felicia exited through the wagon's back door.

"Twenty metres or so, but it's all grown in around it. Wouldn't know it was there at all if you weren't shown."

"And who showed you where it was?" A smirk came to Susan's face.

"Well, umm. It was a lass who grew up near here. She thought it might be good if I had a place to hole up round these parts. In case of emergency, you understand."

"Uh-huh!" Susan folded the woman's stocking she'd found under her seat and laid it on the dash.

"I'll carry the lad, if you two bring the blankets. It will take a couple of trips." Dan reached into his wagon, picked up the child and started through the underbrush. Soon a battered house, on a foundation long since shattered by tree roots, came into view. Painted on its front door was a lurid red T.

"It's red Teed. The tinkers will kill us all, if we go in there!" exclaimed Felicia.

"What are you talking about, woman?" Dan elbowed the door open and stepped into the entry hall. The floorboards, under the vinyl tiles, creaked ominously.

"It's red Teed. Everyone knows the tinkers kill you if you go in a red Teed building," objected Felicia.

"That's a new one on me, girl. It's also bull crap. All a red T means is no Novo Gaian trained craftsman or merchant will do anything to help maintain the property. It's how they're trying to get folk to stay off delicate regions, like aquifer recharge zones. Now who told you different?"

"It was Jack, Jack Horner. We stepped out together for a while before I got tired of his taking ways."

"I'm beginning to get a wee bit fed up with that man." Dan laid Gorgy on the floor, and Felicia began making a nest of blankets around the child.

"Where should I put this?" Susan was carrying a large picnic basket of supplies.

"Right here, love. I don't like the way this floor sounds. I think it best not to trust it more than we have."

Nodding, Susan set the basket on the floor and left to get another load from the wagon.

Hours later Dan reined his horse around and started towards town.

"Won't Ward be suspicious if we get back so soon? I mean, after all, two women! I would think you'd like to savour the experience?" asked Susan from the passenger seat.

"Aye. We'll have to find a way to fill some time, me sweet. 'Sides, night's coming on, and I want to get off the road. I was thinking that meadow I mentioned. It's off the main way, and it's where they're expecting me rig to be, if they send someone to check. Still wish you'd stayed with Felicia. Just don't feel right 'bout taking you back to town."

"I can take care of myself, and Arkell's my home."

"Least ways I can keep you safe tonight, me love." Dan reached over, grasped Susan's hand and brought her wrist to his lips. His teeth lightly scraped the soft skin on its underside, and a shudder ran through her.

"Daniel Timothy, you're not fair." She moved to press her

body against his. The horse continued along the road without direction, its slow, steady hoof beats making time as its driver was otherwise engaged.

The next morning, after hitching his horse, Dan clucked; the patient animal reluctantly moved away from the meadow's rich grazing. The sign that marked it as the Chretian Memorial Park was almost obscured by the vines that had grown up around it.

"You're right, Dan, that is a lovely place," remarked Susan.

"Aye. Set aside when some old bigwig kicked it, but it kept it green. The tinkers said not to build on it 'cause it kept the silt out of the stream. Closest bit of green that's not a farmer's field to Arkell."

"How will you explain that Felicia isn't with us when we get back?"

"Some folk like to sleep in." Dan indicated the bed behind them. The blankets were mused, and running up its centre was a human sized lump. "Seems your friend doesn't have your endurance."

Susan rolled her eyes. "That will never work! Ward's a fool, but he's not that stupid."

"Bets? Playing soldier's got him so addled he can't see straight. When I talked to him he was ranting about the Guelphers' tank and how it could take out the Novo Gains. Bloody fool doesn't know a thing about anti-tank guns. 'sides, he'll accept my story 'cause to say it wasn't so would be to say I'm not much of a man. It's a man thing. You don't go questioning another man's prowess, 'less you want to take him on."

"But he has the townsfolk?"

"No lass, for a thing like that it's one on one. And for all Ward's a big bruiser, he has manure for brains. He won't even check. Trust me."

Dan drove his wagon up to the barricade and stepped out.

"Youse can't come in," ordered a tall, lean man with a scar under his eye. He was standing on the other side of the pile of brick and rubble.

"Now don't be foolish. I got's to be getting back to the inn, to see what's up. Frank will want to talk to me."

"Ward left orders, no one comes in."

"He let me out and said I could come back as long as I stayed clear of sickins."

"He said no one comes in until he gets back."

"Well then send someone to fetch him. I'll not stand here all day while he sits in the inn over a dram."

Just then the sound of shots firing split the air.

"What in Odin's name is going on?" demanded Dan.

"It's the McFays. Theys got plague and kept it secret. Folk are taking care of it." The tall man turned to look in the direction the gunfire was coming from.

"Damn it all, let me in!"

"No, I..."

The tall man turned back to find himself staring down the barrel of Dan's gun. The hammer inched back a hair as he watched.

"If anyone shoots, you're meat. I can't miss at this range! Now open that damn gate. Ward promised I'd be let back in, and by all the Gods I want in, *now*!"

The tall man swallowed and motioned for the wagon blocking the gateway to be pulled clear.

"Susan, drive me wagon through."

Grasping the reins, Susan gave them a shake, and Samson moved forward.

"You walk with me." Dan kept his gun trained on the tall man. They moved towards the opening in the barricade. Dan passed through and grabbed his hostage, placing the barrel of the gun against the back of his head.

"Remember, anyone shoots, I pull the trigger." Dan moved to his wagon and forced the tall man to take a seat. Climbing in behind him he closed the door. "Susan, get us to the McFays."

Snapping the reins, Susan brought the horse to a trot, and the wagon lurched ahead. They bounced uncomfortably along on the rutted and potholed road but soon drew to a halt at a rye field reclaimed from the housing on the far side of town. People formed a loose ring about the dilapidated house in the field's centre, screaming and firing guns into the air.

"Candler," yelled Ward, when he noticed the wagon.

"Ward. Tell this asshole I'm allowed to be in town," snapped Dan.

"Captain, why 'ave youse left youse post?" demanded Ward, noticing the tall man.

"He. I mean—"

"Get back to it. Candler and 'is friends are allowed to return to town."

The tall man breathed a sigh of relief as Dan holstered his gun and stepped from the wagon.

"Susan, return my rig to the visitors' field, would you, love? I better do what I can here."

"Okay. Be careful." Susan reined the horse around and started away from the mob.

"Now Ward. What in Odin's name is going on?" demanded Dan.

"'Em McFays got the plague. That brat of their's been coughin' so loud some 'eard it on the street. We mean to get 'em afore it spreads."

"No, Ward. A cough could be a lot of things. Could just be a cold, or the flu. Ain't necessarily the plague."

"No! It's the plague, and we's not takin' chances."

The crowd roared as a man appeared in one of the house's upper windows. He waved and motioned for the crowd to silence, but the roaring continued. A volley of rifle fire tore into the side of the house, and the man vanished.

"What does Frank think about this?" demanded Dan.

"Frank doesn't rule this town," snapped Jack Horner, who stepped from the crowd toward Dan and Ward.

"You! And what do you think of this?"

"Them as have the plague must die afore they can spread it," said Jack.

"Yeah," agreed Ward.

"If it's plague, you're exposing everyone here, you fool." Dan glared at Jack.

Ward looked confused and turned to Jack.

"No chance of that. We're not getting close enough to catch a thing," snarled Jack.

"What you got planned?" Dan felt cold dread creeping up his spine.

"Look for yourself, Candler," sneered Jack, who pointed at

the house. A group of men ran forward with molotov cocktails. Flaming rags protruded from the bottles' necks, making arcs of flame as they were thrown towards the house. The sound of a gun firing echoed above the roar of the crowd. One of the men fell. The bottles shattered, and the alcohol burst into flame.

More shots rang out; another man fell as he ran towards the growing inferno. The crowd fired back. Bullets flew into the house. From where Dan stood he could see that several missed their marks, striking members of the crowd opposite the shooters. The house itself started to burn, as more molotov cocktails were thrown towards it. People began tossing garbage on the flames. Smoke rose up in a greasy pillar. Shots continued to fly in all directions.

"Ward, by all the Goddesses, stop this!" begged Dan.

Ward looked on. The front door of the burning structure flew open, and a woman carrying a child ran out. Their clothes smoldered and smoked. Rifles fired and they fell. People savagely pelted the bodies with wood. The wood soon caught sending another pillar of smoke into the sky. Dan turned away and started toward the inn.

"No stomach for it, Candler? Can't handle doing what has to be done?" Jack called after him.

Dan could still see smoke rising when he reached the inn. He stepped into the empty common-room and called, "Frank?"

"Quiet, Candler," replied the innkeep, as he rose from behind the bar. A lump stood out on his forehead.

"What in Odin's name?"

"Those assholes heard that McFay girl coughin' and figured it had to be the plague. That son of a bitch Horner said they should burn them out afore it spread. I told them no, but they were hell bent on burnin' out the McFays. When I told them I wouldn't supply the alcohol or bottles to do it, they jumped me. I only just finished countin' me bones. They done the job?"

"Yes." Dan moved to the bar and grabbing the first bottle he saw drew a long swallow from it. The liquor burned on its way down, making him think of what he'd just witnessed.

"Fuck. You will pay for that?" said Frank.

Dan nodded and took another swallow before speaking. "I

want Horner. Five minutes alone and that son of a bitch will be out of our hair for good."

"Can't say as I'd stop you." Frank took a long pull at a bottle. "We gotta get out there and cool those assholes down. Way they're actin', the whole town could burn and they'd hardly notice."

Dan followed Frank back to the burning house. The crowd still circled it, roaring wildly each time a timber snapped, sending a shower of sparks skyward. The wounded had been hauled from the field and sat with their loved ones to one side. The dead were missing entirely, carried away by their families, or thrown to the hungry flames.

"Shit," swore Frank, as he watched the scene.

"Listen up!" hollered Ward, who stood on an empty hay cart just outside the ring of townsfolk. The people either didn't hear or they ignored him. Jack stood by the foot of the cart.

Ward looked towards Jack, who passed him a rifle and nodded.

Ward pointed the rifle skyward and emptied its clip. The crowd turned to gaze at the source of the noise.

"Listen up. We gotta get rid of this 'ere plague. We gotta go to Guelph and burn it out. Jack tells me they got all the sickins in that old town 'all of 'eir's. I says we end this once and for all," Ward shouted.

"*No!*" screamed Frank, who sprinted to the hay cart and, throwing Jack to the ground, mounted it. Dan followed, but the alcohol blurred his reflexes, and he tripped on an uneven piece of ground.

"Listen, you assholes. We can't go attackin' Guelph. We gotta keep away from there. That's where the plague is. You go, you'll catch it and die."

"We already 'ave the plague 'ere. We just burnt it out," snapped Ward, and the crowd cheered.

"*You don't know if it were the plague or not!*" Dan had regained his feet and was slowly approaching.

"Don't listen to him. He's why the plague's here in the first place. He brought it from Guelph," snapped Jack.

"Then why don't I have it?" demanded Dan.

The crowd stared at the four men by the hay cart.

"You're a carrier. Plague rat. *Plague Rat!*" screamed Jack, pointing towards Dan. The crowd picked up the chant. Dan began backing away. Clods of dirt flew in his direction. He sprinted toward the abandoned houses at the field's edge, the crowd in hot pursuit. Lead flew wildly in the air as he dove through the doorway of a corner house marked with a red T. In seconds he was in the basement then out a smashed rear window. The sound of the mob filled the air. Sprinting from hiding place to hiding place, he made his way through the dilapidated suburb. The pursuit petered out. Sweat-soaked and exhausted, Dan crept to his wagon in the visitors' field. Samson picked among the sparse grass on the far side of the yard. Slipping into the wagon, Dan searched the night to be sure he was alone before turning on his transmitter. With his free hand he pulled a nondescript backpack out from under the seat as he spoke.

"Base, this is Daniel Timothy. Over."

"Corporal Timothy, we read you. Over."

"Base. It all just hit the fan. Over."

Chapter Twenty-four

Uneasy The Head

"I BELIEVE THOSE are our enemy." Dr. Frankel, waved towards twin images on the electron microscope's screen.

"Are you sure?" Eddie stood in the back of the portable lab. The isolation booth at the far end of the trailer glowed with dim, internal light, while the rest of the unit was in darkness.

"Of course not! Nothing is ever absolute, but I have run my findings through the database. This viral group should not present with the symptomatology we are seeing. The oddest part is they are twinned viruses."

"What?"

"They require each other to survive. A very strange example of symbiosis. The first virus is highly infectious, insinuating itself into the lining of the bowel, but it lies dormant until the second virus attaches itself to the infected cell. After that, they both begin to reproduce causing the symptoms.

"That is why I sent for you. We might be dealing with a new mutation. You have to allow my team and me to examine this illness first hand. Even putting aside the suffering we might prevent, the scientific significance of finding a twinned virulent strain of virus is enormous."

"The Minister will not allow you entry."

"The Minister is an ass! I'm sorry I voted for him."

"He does prove that no system is perfect. Modem what you've found to your team in Powassan. Maybe they can find something."

Dr. Frankel rubbed the back of his neck as he stared at the screen. The dark circles under his eyes advertised the sleepless effort that had isolated the virus. "And maybe pigs will fly. I will do it, Edward, but it is ridiculous to expect them to succeed without even samples of the virus."

"What do you think about the convulsions?"

"I haven't had time to give them much thought. Could just be a response to the fever and dehydration. Your man's observation that patients react to the illness in two distinct patterns seems astute. I wish I were with those patients. I can only do so much with second-hand accounts."

"Doc, if it were up to me your whole team would have been in there from the start."

"I must return to my work. I will begin by trying known antiviral agents, and if they fail, I'll become creative."

Eddie stepped from the back of the lab into the noon sunlight. The cool, spring air invigorated him as he walked to the radio truck. Ackley sat in the passenger seat, his head thrown back and his mouth hanging open. Reuben sat behind the wheel, staring across the field.

"How's the watch?" Eddie leaned in through the window.

"Quiet, sir," replied Reuben.

"I've been meaning to tell you, you did good work in the field the other day."

"I wish I thought so, sir. I never even shot a deer before. My ratings all came from paint-pellet training."

"It might help if you think about all the lives you saved." Eddie rested against the truck's door.

"The kids, that was Bob."

"Not the kids. So far, this plague is 100 percent fatal. If one infected person had gotten past quarantine and reached a population centre, it would have. Not could have! Would have, spread. I ran a computer projection. If it gets past us, in six months it will be all over old Ontario. A year after that, it will have followed the trade routes across North America and be established in the rest of the world.

"You may feel bad about what you did. I'd worry about anyone who didn't, but remember you also saved millions of lives that night."

"I wish it felt that way."

"So do I, lad. You'll be pleased to know I'm giving you a hazard bonus. It should cover the price of the table you broke."

Reuben nodded sadly. "Thank you, sir."

Eddie stepped away from the truck and said, "Think about what I said. You saved a lot of lives." He headed to the inn.

Minutes latter Eddie sat with Meb in the inn's common room.

"So the doctor has isolated the virus. That's a step in the right direction." Meb sipped her strawberry tea.

"Yes, though it's not of much immediate help. It doesn't show up in our database. We have no idea how to treat it." Eddie fidgeted with the remains of his sandwich. Sitting back in his chair, he examined the room. A few people sat at the other tables. A rough man with features aged by wind and sun, dressed in patched cotton, sat close to the central hearth. He pulled a pipe from his pocket and began filling it. The sound of a theatrical cough came from the bar, and John pointed to a sign on the back wall. It depicted a smoldering pipe with a red slash through it. The rough man put his pipe away and sipped at his ale.

"One of the best things John ever did, banning the weed in his inn," remarked Meb.

"Did he lose much business?"

"For a month or two then all the folk who wouldn't come because of the stench started coming and he did better. Helps folk get the message that the weed is bad for them. You should have seen the Gridtown traders when their tobacco sales dropped. It's no wonder they hate tinkers. You keep cutting their exports."

Eddie smiled. "One does what one can."

"How did the doctor find the virus?"

"We had Brad do an autopsy and send samples out."

A chair grated on the floor as the rough man rushed from the room.

"Wonder what his problem is?" John moved to stand beside Eddie and Meb.

"No idea. He's one of Greg Thomson's hands, isn't he?" asked Meb.

"Aye. He paid his tab up front, or I'd tackle him. You can't trust that lot with credit." John refilled their cups as he spoke.

Eddie smiled then Reuben burst into the room.

"Sir, there's a problem in Arkell. Dan is on the radio, I think you should speak to him," explained the younger man.

Minutes later Eddie sat in the radio truck with Meb leaning against the door.

"That's the right of it, Major. They mean to attack Guelph. Frank's dead against it, but they're crazy. I barely got away with my life. They've already killed a family 'cause the child had a cold. Over."

"Dan, is there anything you can do to stop them? Even slowing them down would help. Over."

"Not much. They bloody near killed me. That bastard Horner labelled me as a plague rat. Over."

"Shit, damned ignorant self-serving sons of bitches!" swore Eddie; then he depressed the mic button. "Dan, delay them. You are authorized for full guerrilla action. Over."

"Sir, it's been a long time since training, sir, but I'll do what I can. Over."

"We'll try and help all we can. Over."

"I'll need it. Over and out."

"Over and out."

"They must be mad, going into a plague zone to burn it out. That's the stupidest thing I've ever heard." Meb stood by the truck.

"They're panicked and being manipulated by someone with an agenda. Brad suspected this Horner character. If I get proof positive that this is Gridtown playing games with Dark Land lives, I swear I'll choke the heads of the shareholder families myself," growled Eddie

"What are you going to do?"

"Delay those fools as long as we can."

"Are you going to warn Brad?"

"Not just yet. He has his hands full, and I haven't counted out Dan yet. That candler's proved himself to be one hell of an agent. Besides, if worse comes to worst, I'll send troops in to deal with the invaders."

Meb cocked her head to one side. "How many spies do you Novo Gaians have?"

Eddie smiled before replying. "All depends what you want to call a spy. Look, Meb, thanks for lunch, but I have to get back to work."

"Why won't you answer my question?" Meb fixed him with a piercing gaze.

"What question?" Eddie smiled and a glint came to his eye.

Meb glared at Eddie for a moment longer then shaking her head walked away from the radio truck.

Since I'm here anyway I may as well sort out the snafu at the highway twenty-four base. With all the big messes in this operation you'd think I could be spared the day to day crap of command, but no, somebody always has to be an idiot, thought Eddie as he changed the radio's transmission frequency.

Hours later Ackley knocked on Eddie's wagon's door and called, "Major."

Eddie looked up from his supper, "What is it?"

"Lieutenant Irving just called in. He thinks they might have a survivor. He said the patient named Rose, that's pre-adult three, is back to a normal body temperature and seems to be retaining fluids. He also said he has several others whose temperatures are dropping."

"Have you informed Dr. Frankel?"

"No, sir. I came straight to you."

"Get the doctor. He'll want to talk to Brad. And send someone to fetch Meb. The town council should be kept up to date. I'll be along in a moment."

"Yes, sir." Ackley sprinted away.

Minutes later Eddie and Meb stood around the outside of the radio truck in the evening chill.

"So every case where the fever is breaking had swollen lymph nodes and went into convulsions? Over," asked Dr Frankel, who sat in the truck's cab.

"Yes. I know it's a long shot, but I want to try giving sodium phenobarbital to some of the patients without swollen lymph nodes to see what happens. Over."

"As you say, Bradly, it is unlikely to do any good, but it can hardly make matters worse. Try it and tell me the results as soon as possible. In the meantime, continue supportive care. I suggest you watch for the swollen lymph nodes; concentrate your efforts on those patients. Inform me immediately when Pre-Adult three is recovered enough to give blood. I would like to try a serum treatment. Also, watch for secondary infections. It would be best if you kept the newly recovered isolated from the population at large. They still may be infectious. Over."

The radio went silent; then Brad replied, sadness clear in his voice.

"Understood. To correct you, doctor, PA three is named Rose, a sweet, little girl with a father who loves her more than the world. Over and out."

"Understood, Bradly. I hope, 'Rose,' is feeling better soon. Over and out."

"Doctor?" asked Eddie.

"What? Oh yes, you wish my thoughts. Frankly, I have none but the obvious. Some patients have a natural resistance. With proper supportive care they can survive. I will return to my lab and continue my examinations."

Dr. Frankel climbed from the truck and walked to his laboratory trailer with no further words.

"Friendly, isn't he? Well good news is a welcome change. Did Brad say anything about Carla?" asked Meb of Reuben, who was sitting in the truck's passenger seat.

"Are you Meb?" he replied.

"Yes."

"He said to let you know she's fine, and her teacher can be proud of her."

Meb rubbed her hands together and released her breath.

"Go on. I've a thousand details to look after," suggested Eddie, as he walked towards his tinker wagon.

Full night had fallen and Eddie was preparing for bed when

he heard a knock.

"Come," he called. No one entered, but the knock repeated.

"Damn it! Come in, it's not locked."

The door creaked open to reveal a boy in his early teens. His brow sloped sharply back, and he supported his right side with a crutch. His right leg was a wasted, mangled thing that hung below his cut off trouser leg. His buck teeth were brown with stains and decay, and his lips hung slackly open.

"What is it?" Eddie tried not to stare at the boy.

"Me Maw. She said I's should fetch youse." The boy's dull, brown eyes looked up with a vacant cow-like quality.

"Who's your mother?"

"Maw."

Eddie silently counted to five. "Who's your father?"

"Paw."

"What's your name?"

The youth brightened and said "I'ma Jeremy."

"What's your last name?"

"Thomson. I'ma Jeremy Thomson. My Maw, she said I's should fetch youse."

"Did she say why?"

The youth stared blankly at Eddie, who rolled his eyes and stepped from the wagon. "I can walk to your mother's from here. Would you like to ride my horse? I'll lead it by the reins.

"No! No! Horses hurt." Jeremy shook his head.

"All right then, I'll ride."

The youth nodded vigorously and stood waiting for Eddie to mount. Eddie left the child who hobbled after him.

"Damn you Thomson, you have a lot of suffering to answer for." Eddie was soon turning up the lane to the Thomson house. The smell of manure assailed him. He tethered his mount and moved towards the sheltered candle by the door. A child, dressed in leggings and tunic, played on the porch with a set of pebbles. It paused as Eddie drew near.

"Hello," said the child.

"Hello. What's your name?" Eddie stooped to the child's eye level.

"My Maw calls me Cathy, my Paw calls me Carl. I can count

to twenty. Would youse like to see?"

Eddie smiled. The child's large, brown eyes had a doe-like quality that lent an engaging air to an otherwise plain face. "Go ahead."

"One, two, three," the child counted and with each number moved a pebble from one pile to another.

"That's good. I came to see your mother. Can you take me to her?"

"She's upstairs in 'er bedroom. Since the tinker came and took the baby out of 'er, she's been tired and needed lots of sleep. I bring 'er water when she wants it, 'cause I can climb stairs and have two good arms."

"You're very good, yes. Can you take me to your mother now?"

Cathy grinned up at Eddie, her wide-lipped mouth parting slightly to show strong looking teeth. She led the way into the house. A minute later Eddie stood in Emily Thomson's bedroom.

"Maw. There's a man here to see youse," announced Cathy.

"Eddie, I's sorry I's can'ts get up. I's still sore from the tinker's 'ealin'.

"We have a doctor with us. I could ask him to stop in."

"No. I'ma 'ealin' up right well. Tween youse and me, I think that tinker man did a fine job."

"Then what can I do for you?"

Emily motioned for Eddie to sit on the chair by her bed. It creaked ominously as he settled himself.

"I 'member youse from when youse was tinker from 'ere 'bouts. Though Greg won't 'mit it, youse always played folks fair. I's got a trade for youse."

"I'm not here as a tinker right now." Eddie's voice was soft.

Emily motioned him close. "I's knows somit youse wants to know."

"What?"

"Not so's fast. First I's wants me trade."

"What do you want?" Eddie examined the dirty walls and battered surroundings.

"I's want my's little girl to be a normal. I's 'ad fifteen children and only five as lived. Of 'em, only one is close to being 'ealthy.

Others is all twisted up, and most is dim. I's love 'em, but taint no way they'll ever live normal like. My Cathy though. She's a different. She's almost perfect, 'septing she got a boy's set as well, if youse take what I's means. I's 'eard about youse Bright Landers. I's seen it when Greg bought a battery T.V. one year from a Gridtown trader. Youse can cut 'em off and twist 'em round so's a boy becomes a girl. Cathy's already half way there, alls youse 'ave to do, is cut 'em off."

"It's complex surgery, and expensive."

Emily gripped Eddie's arm. "I's got what youse needs to 'ear. Tell me true, tinker's honour, that youse fix me Cathy, and I's tell youse. Gotta be fast, afore Greg gets back. He 'ates youse and would beat me for talkin' to tinker kind, specially when 'es been drinking."

"If what you tell me is as valuable as you say, I'll have the doctor examine Cathy. Whether making her a boy or girl is better is up to him, but if it's possible, we'll fix the problem."

"Tinker's honour?"

"I swear by my family and my craft." Eddie placed his hand over his heart.

Emily gazed at the room's single alcohol lamp as if mustering her courage then she spoke.

"It's Greg. Our 'and told 'im youse got plague in that there trailer of youse. 'E and a bunch of other folks mean to burn it out afore it gets out. They mean to get their guns and put youse down. Greg, 'e's angry 'bout me not being a woman no more. 'E wants to show youse tinker folk 'e's still a man. I 'eard 'em talking. They's mean to fix youse when Greg's brother from Acton gets 'ere with 'is group."

Eddie sighed from the bottom of his lungs and said "Shit! At least that gives me a day to prepare. Mrs. Thomson, thank you. For what it's worth, you're more a woman now then you have ever been. Standing up for the sake of your child makes that so. When this is over, I'll see to it that Cathy is 'fixed'."

Eddie rushed from the house. Cathy was again on the front porch playing with a tattered doll. Mounting, Eddie galloped to his base. Minutes later he sat with an impromptu war council around the table in his van.

"Okay Barb, we can move two out of the twenty-nine blockade without affecting it too badly. I'll borrow another couple from the seven." Eddie peered at a map of Eden Mills.

"I think you're overreacting. Greg Thomson and his crowd are hotheads, but they won't ignore the council's decision," observed Nick, who sat at the table across from Eddie.

"He might be right. I've been listing to the rumours. They mostly involve the recovery," agreed Barb, who sat to Eddie's left wearing a wraparound robe.

"Maybe, but I believe my source. Nick, this is as much a challenge to the Eden Mill's council as it is to me. Do you think you could let us have a couple of deputies?"

Nick stroked the stubble on his chin as he thought. "Well, you know we don't really have police. As the council member in charge of domestic order, I'm technically sheriff, but normally I only deal with an occasional brawl. Besides, a lot of folk are busy with late planting. I'll find you a couple of men, though.

"That brings us up to ten as a standing force at the main base, plus the off-duties in the inn. Will that be enough?" asked Barb.

"It will have to be. The virus is safely contained in the lab, but if those idiots breach the trailer and let it out, this whole quarantine will have been for nothing."

"I still don't believe that Greg will disregard the council's orders. Let alone bring in folk from Acton to cause trouble." Nick rubbed his big hands together. "I think I'll join you here, if that's all right? If something does happen, I want to know who's part of it. Maybe have a few new sets of stocks built."

"Good. Now I'd better call Brad. With having to defend the base camp, I can't afford the personnel to stop the Guelph invasion. Damn, I hate this."

Chapter Twenty-five

Hope

"TELL ME THIS is a sick joke. No one can be that stupid! Over." Brad sat in his van with his eyes closed. His hand jerked, slamming the mic into his forehead.

"No joke. That fellow you thought was a Gridtown spy has manipulated them. We're keeping an eye open for them and trying to slow them down, but we can't do much. Over," replied Eddie's voice.

Brad felt a chill run up his spine and shook involuntarily.

"Eddie. I need help in here! It's too much for one man. I'm beginning to have amphetamine reaction. I don't know how much longer I can keep going. Over."

"Get some sleep. Let yourself detox. Over."

"When? Every time I turn around there're more victims coming in. Over!"

"Understood. Look, it might get ugly in there. Maybe you should get the town leaders to mobilize their tank. Just showing it off might be enough to scare off the attackers. Over."

"No can do. Half the town council is in the clinic. The other half won't leave their homes for fear of the plague. No one else knows where the shorting tank is. Besides, until that reactor is striped out, I wouldn't trust it in battle. One solid blow might be enough to compromise containment after all these years. Over."

"I hear you. If we can't stop the Arkellians, I want you clear before they attack. Over."

"Forget it. The people here need me, and now that it seems I can save some of them, I'll be damned before I leave. Over."

"Brad, you're a tinker born. Your grandfather will be proud when he hears about this. Over and out."

"Over and out."

"Bad news?" asked Ingram from outside the van.

"A bunch of idiots from Arkell are headed this way. They have some stupid idea that if they burn down the clinic they can stop the plague. More bloody likely they'll get themselves infected."

"Ground out! I have to tell the council. We have to defend ourselves."

"Good luck getting close to any of them. At least wait until morning. I'll try to come up with something clever. Maybe..."

"Brad, you should come and see this!" called Carla from the clinic's door.

"When will it end?" Brad slid from his van. "What is it this time? A new symptom?" He entered the sick room then stood stock still.

"Tinker, look at her," breathed Mark as tears trickled down his cheeks.

Rose sat up on her cot, sipping from a tankard and looking around.

"Rose," breathed Brad.

"Yes, Tinker?" asked the child.

Brad clamped his teeth shut and ran outside, but the sound of his triumphant whoop still woke several patients.

Minutes later he returned, and the smile on his face buried many of the fatigue lines.

"I radioed the doctor about Rose." Brad moved to the child's side. "How do you feel?"

"I'm hungry, Tinker. Daddy tells me I was very sick and you helped me."

Brad smiled and looked at the others in the room. "We all helped you. Trina, could you make up some broth? Any type should do. We should start Rose off slow."

"Brad, over here. I need you." Carla had moved to the side of another patient.

Brad rushed over. The desiccated figure lay still. He pushed dirty, black hair away from the corpse's sunken, brown eyes.

"She's gone." He examined the chart. "No swelling, no convulsions, but we did try sodium phenobarbital. A few more like this and we'll stop administering it to anyone who isn't convulsed."

"It was worth a try." Carla patted his arm.

"Yeah." Brad stroked his hand over his face as fatigue once more etched deep lines around his eyes.

Hours later Brad sat at the central table staring into his computer.

"Tinker," called a weak voice.

Brad moved to the dehydrated man's side. "You should rest."

"I need to know. Bernice, my wife. Is she...?" The man's head with its dirty, dark-brown hair fell back to the cot. Brad stared into his brown eyes and saw the pain there.

Brad checked his chart for a name.

"I don't know, Oscar. You'll have to ask Trina when she gets back." Brad took Oscar's pulse at his wrist and noticed a tank tattooed on his upper arm.

"Will I live?"

"You had the convulsions and swelling. I think you will. A few hours ago you were unconscious; now you're talking. Your fever's broken."

"One of the lucky ones?" Oscar's voice held bitter sarcasm.

Brad patted the man's shoulder. "I noticed your tattoo."

Oscar took a deep breath and let it out. "All the Guelph heavy-armoured division got them. Division, five guys who got the job because we could read well enough to get through the manual. Figured the tank would keep us safe and this hits us. What's the point?" Oscar closed his eyes on tears they were still too dry to shed.

"I know. I need to know what kind of shape your tank is in. What it uses for a power source?"

"No way, Tinker. The town council would have my hide if I

told you anything. Everyone knows Bright Landers steal weapons so they can keep the dark down."

"That's not the reason. If that tank's nuclear and it loses containment—"

"We was careful." Oscar turned his back on Brad.

Sighing Brad returned to his desk where Carla waited.

"He's the fifth to regain consciousness. All had the convulsions and swelling. We lost three more. I don't think the sodium phenobarbital does any good." Carla leaned heavily against the table.

"Discontinue the drug except when indicated." Brad stared wearily into his computer.

"What's that?" Carla indicated the collection of lines and figures on the screen.

"Between you and me, a catapult."

"A what?"

"I haven't spread it around, but the Arkellians are planning to attack us. Someone convinced them that if they burn down the clinic they'll stop the plague." Brad slumped into his seat.

"No!" Carla shook her head in disbelief.

"Yes."

"That's insane. Why design a catapult?"

"They're afraid of the plague. We toss a few bodies their way, it just might scare them off."

"Brad, that's crazy." Carla gripped his shoulder.

"You don't think it will work?" Brad forced an exhausted smile to his lips.

"It would work, but there's no way we'll get it built in time. Besides, isn't the point to limit the plague's spread?"

"Shorting." Brad folded his arms on the table and rested his head on them. "I'm not thinking straight. I just wish I knew what to do."

A slender, black woman on a nearby cot wailed and began to thrash.

Brad rushed to her side and gripped her arm, holding it so the I.V. remained steady. His hands trembled and jerked, releasing his grip.

"Brad," snapped Carla, as the I.V. needle shifted.

"*Shit!*" Brad tried to will his hands steady and grasp the arm.

"Mark, grab her arm," ordered Carla.

The big farmer pushed Brad to one side and grasped the flailing limb.

"Brad!" Carla held out a syringe. Brad struggled to control the trembling and weakness in his hands but couldn't.

"Do it. Into the buttocks, intramuscular. Check for air bubbles and clear them first," he ordered.

Carla drove the needle home before putting a pocket mask on the woman and starting mouth to mask AR. The convulsions eased, and the patient resumed breathing. With a monumental effort Brad stilled the trembling in his limbs and checked the I.V. The needle had torn the skin. Bandaging the wound, he started a fresh I.V. at the patient's ankle.

"What in Taweret's name just happened?" demanded Carla.

"Amphetamine reaction. I couldn't control it," explained Brad.

"That's it! Go to your wagon and get some sleep."

"But—"

"*Now!* You've become a hazard to the patients and yourself. No one could ask half of what you've already done. Trina and I can handle the I.V.s and anticonvulsants. We've watched you do it enough. Now go."

"I—"

"Mark. If Brad doesn't go to his wagon immediately, carry him there!" Carla's voice was so like Meb's that Brad almost looked for the old herbalist.

"I'll go. You're right. I'm no good here, if I become a patient myself."

Dragging his feet, he made his way to the van.

"Brad. You okay?" asked Ingram, who was checking the fuel in the alcohol torches at the clinic's door.

"I need sleep, but I won't get any. I know amphetamines; the residual will keep me awake for hours.

"Shorting. Why not take something to help you nod off?"

"Drug interaction. Never know what will happen when you mix your meds. Oh well, I'll lie there awake. It will rest my eyes at least."

"How's my Mum?"

"Better. She just went through the convulsions. I figure another day; she'll be up and talking."

"Thank you, Tinker."

"Don't thank me. All we're doing in there is keeping them alive long enough for their bodies to find a cure. And we're not always succeeding." Brad looked at the silver flecked sky. "About three hours until sunrise."

Brad entered his wagon and collapsed onto the unmade bed. Thoughts chased each other around in his head, making sleep impossible. Several more fits of trembling racked his body. Finally he sat on the edge of his bed listening to his heart race.

"I thought I told you to get some sleep?" Carla stepped into the wagon from its back.

"I'm too drugged out."

Carla moved to sit beside him and took his hand. "You need sleep. Let your body refresh itself."

"You're right, I'm so tired."

"You need something to relax you that won't react with the drugs you've been using. Hmmm. Things are pretty quiet in the clinic right now. I can stay and keep you company. Maybe talking will help you stress down."

"I'd like that. I've wanted to tell you. I'm sorry I got you into this."

"You got me...? Brad, don't be silly! I wanted to go with you. The chance to become a healer. I'd have given anything for that. I don't think Michelle ever appreciated how important healing is to me."

"Probably not. People with a calling are a mystery to those who don't have one. My Mom can't understand why I didn't get a nice job as an engineer at one of the factories. My Granddad, he understands me."

"Meb's like that with me. At least about healing. I wish she understood other things."

"Like you liking girls?"

Carla shrugged. "That's the one. She's always been after me to step out with some of the boys from town."

"I just think she wants you to explore all your options." Brad closed his eyes and lay back on the bed. "How'd you and Michelle meet anyway?"

"We grew up together. She lived down the street. I guess that's how it happened. I was thirteen, Michelle was fourteen, she was sleeping over. We were laying in my bed talking about boys and things. Pretty normal stuff. We both wondered what it would be like. Somehow we started kissing. One thing led to another, and we became lovers." Carla blushed.

"So you've never even kissed a man?"

"No. I wonder sometimes though. I mean, I like the view, and I've met some men who excite me."

"Grab life, Carla. Try everything at least once. If you like it, go back for more. Life's a smorgasbord. All you can eat for a silver mark."

Carla smiled and lay her hand on Brad's thigh. She brought her face close to his, and her lips parted. Brad found he was kissing her before he realised what was happening.

"Carla, you..." He began, but she lay her finger to his lips.

"I want to. I want to be with you. I know you're tired. You don't have to prove anything about men to me. I just want to be with you. Bradly Irving, tinker, person extraordinaire." She stroked his cheek then standing pulled her dress off.

She stood naked before him, her firm, young flesh flushed with passion's first tinting. Brad inhaled as his manhood rose to answer despite his exhaustion. He reached out and, taking her hand, drew her into his arms. Their lips met and he caressed her. His kisses strayed to her neck as she undid his trousers. She smiled as this new experience filled her. The firmness of his body contrasted with what she had known. Brad flowed into her as their passion built. His hands were firm but gentle, touching her in a way both familiar and new. Finally, together they peaked and, crying with exultation, wrapped about each other. For a moment, two becoming one.

In the languor that followed Carla stroked the hair away from Brad's eyes.

"Maybe grandmother knew what she was talking about. I enjoyed that."

"I'll do better when I'm rested." Brad released an enormous

yawn.

Carla kissed his chest. “I’d like that as well. A person needs ample data to form a hypothesis.”

They both smiled. Brad reached a hand up to stroke her cheek. “You are so beautiful.” His face clouded with sadness.

“What’s wrong?”

“I just pray I never see your beautiful, blue eyes staring up at me from one of those cots, like— like—?”

Brad shot up in bed and grabbed Carla by the arms.

“Carla, think. Have any of the patients had blue eyes?”

“What? Of course there was... No. I can’t think of any. Why?”

Brad trembled with excitement. “And Mark’s eyes are blue.”

“Yes. What is it?” Carla looked confused.

“Gods of my fathers, that’s it! It’s a purity virus.” Brad leapt from the bed and started pulling on his trousers.

“A what?” asked Carla, consternation in her features.

“A purity virus. I remember them from my high school history class. Back in the twentieth and twenty-first centuries there were groups of morons who thought their race was superior to all others. Mostly by virtue of the fact that they were members of it. At first they weren’t that dangerous. A lynching here, some political oppression there. Then came the Human Genome Project. They mapped human DNA. Wonderful for medicine, but the power to cure is the power to kill. These hate groups used the map to tailor diseases that would only attack other races.”

Carla sat up in bed her breasts covered by a sheet. “And you think that’s what we have here?”

“It all fits. We’ve all commented on how the disease seems to degrade the victims before killing them. Rose’s recovery, her father’s of European descent. The fact we haven’t been infected. I want to find out the heritage of the parents and grandparents of everyone who recovered. I’ll lay odds there’s a European in each one.”

“Who’d want to kill everyone with brown eyes?” demanded Carla as she pulled on her dress.

“Brown eyes are just one marker. That probably means that Negro, Asian or Amerindians were the target race.

"I have to radio this in. Carla, love, start that survey for me, would you? Find out as much as you can about the dead as well. I need to know their racial mix."

"On it, and, Brad."

"Hmm."

"When you finish on the radio, get some sleep. I still need your help for my research later." Carla stepped from the back of the wagon into a new day's light.

Chapter Twenty-six

Parade Of Fools

DAN AWOKE AND stared through a hole in the roof of the house he had hidden in. The brightest stars were just being swallowed by the approaching day.

"Dan, me lad, you're in it deep this time," he muttered and stood. The decrepit house seemed haunted, and the morning air held a chill. Moving to a broken window, he peeked out onto the street in front of the inn. People were gathering, most armed. While he watched, eight rough, dirty men rode up on plough horses. Ward was among them. Horner followed them, mounted on a light, riding horse with expensive tack.

"Right! We take Guelph and burn that 'all of 'eirs. That will stop the plague but good. Might even find that old tank. We get that taint no one gonna be pushing us around," called Ward from his saddle.

"You're a bunch of fools," snapped Frank, from the upstairs window of the inn.

"We's done listenin' to youse. All's youse do is talk. Youse'll let this 'ere plague take the lot of us afore youse move youse ass," hollered Ward. He looked to Horner, who nodded with approval.

"Don't listen to this asshole. I'll give a free round to any of you who's sense enough to stay put," called Frank. Several of the men gathered on the street murmured amongst them selves. One took a step towards the inn's door. A shot rang out and the man fell. Ward's mount shied at the noise of his pistol, but, with a yank on the bit, he brought it under control.

"I won't be 'aving any traitors," he snapped. The other men on the street stared at the corpse. People continued to arrive.

"Wish we'd found that filthy plague rat," observed Horner, as Ward surveyed his troops.

"I left folk to look after 'im, if'n 'e comes back. 'is wagon and that 'orse of 'is are gone. Probably off spreadin' 'is sickness. I's says good riddance," remarked Ward.

"Susan, lass, I thank you from me heart for hiding me gear," muttered Dan.

The sun crested the rooftops. Bellowing orders, Ward brought his motley crew into columns, placed his cavalry in the front and started them marching down the road to Guelph.

Activating his radio, Dan spoke.

"Corporal Timothy to base, come in base. Over."

"We read you, corporal. Over."

"They're on the move. Thirty foot and twelve horse. Over."

"We read you. What's their equipment like? Over."

"Rifles, pistols. Damn fools ain't thought about food though, or water. Only saw a few folk with skins, and I ain't sure about what was in them. Over."

"Stay as close as you can to them. Try and slow them down. Over."

"I'm not the most popular fellow hereabouts. Over."

"Understood. I'll do what I can. Over and out."

"Over and out." agreed Dan. "Well Timothy, it looks like it's up to you. My luck, another week I'd have been in the Mills and out of this." Dan quickly stuffed his radio into the satchel he carried and descended to the building's basement. The battered interior showed the dirt of years, and water had damaged many of the walls. Trash cluttered the floor.

"Perfect," he whispered. Collecting a pile of paper and splintered wood, he pulled a lighter from his pocket and kindled it. He watched the flame long enough to be sure it would spread then slipped out the back door. Sneaking around the house, he checked the street before sprinting to the inn.

"Candler, you crazy?" demanded Frank, when Dan slipped through the door into the common-room. Grabbing Dan's elbow, the larger man dragged him to one of the upstairs rooms.

"They're lookin' for you. Ward's got a bunch of assholes with orders to shoot you on sight."

"I figured as much. Look, the place across the street is about to catch fire. Send someone to fetch back Ward's lot to help fight it. Tell him the whole town will be going up if he don't help."

"Candler, what you done?" demanded Frank.

"We need to slow down Ward's lot. This should cost them at least the morning, probably the day. Offer a round to any who help fight the fire."

"And who'll pay for it?"

"Novo Gaian militia."

"Well then, I'll offer 'em two. Get the lot of 'em pie-eyed, long as I'm paid."

"Do that. The drunker they are the more hung over they'll be tomorrow."

Frank moved to the room's window and looked out. "I see smoke comin' out of that place. Best I be sendin' someone to fetch back Ward's assholes."

"I also need help getting out of town."

"You leaving?"

"I need to follow the troops when they go. It's not as if I can join them."

"Aye, Candler. There's still some with sense enough to follow me. I'll get you out. Wait here 'till I come for you."

Frank left and Dan stood peeking through the window at the burning house. Smoke poured through its open windows and flames could be seen through the doorway. The image made him think of the McFays. "If it weren't for the innocents, I'd let the lot of them drop dead," he muttered.

Frank's working girl appeared on the street and ran after the group of armed men. A minute later Frank appeared in the doorway with Ken in tow.

"I got to be here when Ward gets back, else everythin' goes

to hell. Ken here will get you clear of town. He's an idiot, but he knows enough not to follow Ward when I tell him not to."

Ken glared at Frank and grunted. "Come on, Candler, we better go 'afore others arrive."

"Right you are, Ken me lad, and thank you."

Ken snorted and led the way down the stairs and out the back door.

"Ward took most of 'is folk with 'im so's only the main street's guarded. Youse can slip over 'is barricade most other places now."

"Good. I really need to get out of town, if what I'm..."

A shot sent a cloud of shattered brick from the house beside them into the air.

"Shit!" Dan threw himself to the ground and scrambled for cover.

"I's got 'im," hollered Mike, the tall man who'd been manning the barricade.

"Mike, put that damn thin' down. I's 'ere," shouted Ken.

"Youse 'elping that plague rat. Ward says any who's 'elps the plague rat's a traitor and should be shot," snapped Mike.

"Maybe you should help fight the fire," hollered Dan, who had found a sheltered place behind the remains of a crumbling deck.

"Not a chance, Candler. My orders to do youse in, so's youse can'ts plague rat no more."

"Candler, I's out of 'ere," said Ken. He put his hands in the air and stood.

"Get down," snapped Dan, but it was too late. A shot rang out, and the big man fell.

"Those as are with the plague rat got the plague. Jack tells me so. Dun did Ken a favour endin' it sooner stead of later," said Mike.

"All I want is to leave town. Why put more blood on your hands," pleaded Dan.

"Shut up, Plague Rat. Youse ain't spreading youse sickness no further."

Dan heard the crunch of leather soles on broken brick and turned his gaze to a place where the wall on the house next door had collapsed, spreading rubble over the backyard. The muzzle of a rifle could be seen projecting past a tree trunk.

Drawing his pistol, Dan crawled along the house's back wall, coming to a basement window. He kicked in the glass then slipped into a small, gloomy room. The room opened onto what once must have been a rec room. The walls all showed wear, and mould had formed along their base. He moved towards the stairs, but before he could reach them a pair of ankles appeared.

Dan gripped his gun and took aim as the legs descended, revealing calves then the tattered hem of a robe. Slowly more of the person became apparent. Finally he stared down the barrel of a revolver aimed at his chest. It took him a moment to take in the substantial cleavage behind the revolver then move his eyes to the angular face and short, brown hair above that.

"Dan?" asked the astonished woman.

"Maryloo," replied Dan.

"What in the lady's name?" she demanded.

"It's Mike, he's trying to kill me. He's already shot Ken."

"I heard shots. They woke me up. Come on, I'll hide you."

Dan followed the woman to the house's main floor, where she pushed him into a closet and closed its door. The sound of someone pounding at the front door echoed through the house then Maryloo's husky alto.

"Mike, what the hell's going on? I heard shots!"

"'at 'ere plague rat of a candler 'es round 'ere. Youse basement window's kicked in. 'E must of dun it."

"Damn it. I heard him do it, but when I checked weren't no one there. I figure he must have done it to throw you off. You better get after him. Don't want no plague rats round here. I got little Audrey to think of."

"Don't worry, I'll get 'im," replied Mike then the door slammed. A moment later Maryloo opened the closet.

"Glad to be rid of him. I was afraid he'd want to search the house."

"I appreciate it, lass."

"Couldn't very well let the man who made Audrey possible get shot by the likes of that fool."

"Where are the little lass and Jacob?"

"They were off visiting his mother in Aberfoyle when this

whole plague thing started."

"Than you're all alone here," remarked Dan with a smile.

"What are you suggesting, Candler?"

"I was just thinking that Audrey might like a little brother."

"Wonderful idea, Candler. Shall I fetch the shot glass and eye dropper? It will be just like last time."

Dan sighed and shook his head. "Your Jacob's a lucky man, lass, a lucky man. I'll have to take you up on your offer later. I better be getting out of town while the getting's good."

Maryloo led the way to the backdoor. After checking that the coast was clear, she motioned Dan through. He slipped between houses until he reached the pile of rubble that served as the town barricade. A moment later, he was over it and moving through the streets on the other side.

"Now to get myself positioned for tomorrow," he muttered, as he slipped into an abandoned house on the road to Guelph.

Settling in an upstairs room with a view of the main road, he called in.

"Corporal Timothy to base, come in. Over."

"This is base, we read you. Over."

"Tell the Major he's picking up a bar tab. Over."

After reporting in, Dan pulled a ration bar from his pack and settled for the night.

He awoke with the dawn and began his preparations. Opening his pack, he pulled out a stained and battered homespun tunic and trews. After dressing in these, he pulled out a scraggly, grey, false beard and moustache. Using a pocket mirror, he glued them to his face and pulled on a battered hat with a wide, floppy brim. A pair of dark, wrap-around sunglasses finished the disguise. His gun, a few ration bars, and his radio were slipped into pockets in the lining of the tunic.

"Always thought I'd be using you to slip a jealous husband, not chase a bunch of fools," Dan remarked to his reflection.

Stowing his gear, he descended the stairs to the first floor and slipped out the door. Affecting a limp, he started along the road to Guelph.

Chapter Twenty-seven

A Drive In The Country

"Bradly, it couldn't possibly be a purist virus. They were destroyed after the international biohazard treaty of 2054. Over."

"Doctor, there hasn't been a single case we've been able to verify that was predominately European ancestry. Of the recoveries, we've been able to check on, all had partial Caucasian ancestry. Maybe some group ignored the treaty. Over."

"You obviously haven't studied twenty-first-century history. At first, some governments did ignore the biohazard treaty. Their leaders were captured and placed in isolation chambers. They were then exposed to a variety of pathogens including their own creations. It was the first time that leaders were made truly accountable for their actions. After the second example, there were no dissenters. Over."

"Doc, it's the only thing that makes sense. Everyone we've treated has brown eyes. Over."

"That hardly means anything. The virus attacks the intestinal wall. The protean markers for eye colour would be dormant in those cells. Though, hmmmm.

"I suppose it could be a companion genetic. Something regularly associated with the target race that in fact has nothing to do with the actual infection.

"Wait a moment... Oh yes, over." Dr. Frankel shuffled through a collection of notes on a clipboard. He paused, staring at a printout listing the details of the Guelph Contagious Research Facility. He dropped the clipboard and depressed his mic button.

"Bradly, my boy. You may well be right! The facility in Guelph was decommissioned in twenty-thirty-nine, before the biohazard treaty! Now if memory serves, the first purist viruses appeared in twenty-twenty-eight. Over."

"So it gives us a place to look. Over."

"Yes! I will begin a hard copy search. The purist diseases were never entered into the database, because it was thought they had been eradicated. I will contact you when I know more. In the meantime, continue assessing the racial background of your patients. I will run a screening of the class 1 MHCs on the samples you sent out. If the virus is racially linked, they would be the most probable means of differentiation. Over."

"The what? Over."

"Simply put, proteins on the cells surface that are inherited from the parents. I do not have time for lectures in genetic structure, Bradly. Continue supportive care and keep me informed. Over and out."

"Over and out."

Dr. Frankel sat staring out the truck's window as dawn spread shadows like skeletal fingers across the field. An icy dread clutched his heart at the thought of this hate child of the past's return. A new voice spoke from the radio, and he slid from his seat to make way for the radio operator. Moving to his lab, he activated his computer. A few keystrokes followed; then he began to read.

An hour later Eddie and Barb stood in the lab as Dr. Frankel spoke.

"The purist viruses were man-made, with all the inherent dangers that implies. They are genetically unstable, with high rates of mutation. Although it appears that European decent offers an immunity to the one we face, this might not last. We cannot let this spread. As well, I have no way of telling if the immunity is a true immunity, or if those not affected are carriers."

"Do you know which virus it is we're dealing with?" asked

Eddie.

"Not yet. My team in Powassan is searching for a match. The Gridtown team in Ottawa are doing the same, but even if we identify the virus, it will do us little good."

"Why?" asked Barb.

"Our ancestors feared that some individuals might recreate the viruses, so all records were destroyed, along with the diseases. If we are lucky, we may get a picture to match with what I have isolated, but I doubt it."

"So this does us exactly no good," commented Eddie.

"There is the possibility that a file search will turn up some useful information." Dr. Frankel stared at the toes of his dress shoes and sighed.

Rising, Eddie gripped the doctor's shoulder, which brought a startled glare from the man. "Get some sleep. You're no good to us if you drive yourself into the ground. Besides, I want you alert for tonight."

"And what, pray tell, is going to happen tonight?"

"I'm expecting an attack. Some idiots have the idea that the samples in your lab are placing them at risk, so they're going to try and burn it out."

"No! That is asinine! The samples are safely compartmentalized. If they burn my lab, they could be released!"

"I know, doctor. That's why we're going to stop them," soothed Barb.

"Stop them! How?"

"We've set up a force to counter the attack."

"Armed conflict!" Frankel looked horrified.

"If needs be. Oh yes. I'm going to bring you a patient in a little bit. The price of our forewarning is that you do gender assignment surgery. I think she's primarily female, but it's hard to say."

"What? Oh yes, bring the unfortunate individual along. I'll do an assessment." Frankel absently stroked his chin.

Eddie left the lab with Barb hot on his heels.

"What do we do now?" she asked.

"Same as we have been. I'll try talking to the Minister again, but it probably won't do any good. Are our people in place? I want everything ready for this evening."

"They're all set."

"Good. I'm going to fetch the Thomson child. I think the doctor needs something to keep him busy, so he doesn't have to think about the attack."

Eddie mounted his horse and was soon riding up the lane to the Thomson house. The boy with the crippled leg let him in and he climbed the stairs to the master bedroom. Mrs. Thomson lay in bed her face sporting fresh bruises. Cathy was huddled in the corner of the room.

"What happened?" demanded Eddie, rushing to the bedside.

"Tinker. 'e was about 'ittin' on Cathy for being what she is; I's told 'im to stop. 'e 'it me for bein' uppity. Said I's no wife o' 'is and that I's was out soon as I's could walk. 'es all riled 'bout this 'ere raid and youse tinker folk bein' 'ere."

"I have to get you out of here."

"No. Greg's a good man. 'e just got a bit o' temper. 'e don't mean it. Youse take Cathy to that doctor now 'ear. Maybe if 'e 'as a child as is normal like, 'e be 'appy."

Eddie shook his head and moved to the child's side. She whimpered. When he lifted her face he could see that one of her eyes was swollen shut.

"Come on, sweetheart. I'm going to take you to see the doctor," soothed Eddie.

"Mawwwww," wailed the little girl.

"Youse goes with the tinker man." Emily lay back on her bed, as if that order had drained the last of her strength.

Eddie carried Cathy from the house and placed her on his horse.

"You ever ride a horse before?" he asked.

Cathy stared back over her shoulder and snuffled.

By the time they reached the portable lab Cathy had stopped crying and looked around from the back of the mount inquisitively.

"How many 'orses does it take to pull those big wagons?" She waved towards the tractor-trailers.

"We use a machine that's as strong as three-hundred horses." Eddie held her hand as he escorted her into the lab.

Dr. Frankel was tidying up his workspace and locking

everything away in its travel position.

"Dr. Frankel, this is Cathy," said Eddie.

The doctor turned to face his young patient. "Hello, Catharine. What happened to your eye, child?"

Cathy buried her face against Eddie's leg.

Eddie mouthed the word "abuse."

A shadow of rage clouded Frankel's eyes. The emotion was quickly replaced by professional detachment.

"Let's check you over, shall we?" suggested the doctor. He gently lifted Cathy onto his examination table. A half hour later he led Eddie out of the lab.

"Edward, it is good you brought this one to me now. We must take immediate action."

"What? For a gender assignment?"

"Those testicles are becoming cancerous. I do not believe the cancer has had a chance to spread, but if action is not soon taken, it will. Under these primitive conditions, that means death for the child."

"What can you do?"

"Since the child is a hermaphrodite, I suggest castration. The ultrasound shows the female reproductive organs as complete. Hormonally, she may or may not produce adequate estrogen to pass through puberty, but that is something to be dealt with on a later date, as is the removal of the superfluous appendage."

Something in the doctor's tone caused Eddie to shift his hand so it covered his groin. "Her mother did want a daughter."

"Good! I will anaesthetize the child and begin immediately. The operation shouldn't take more than half an hour. Could you send Barbara in? I wish to coach her on postoperative procedures.

"Of course."

Eddie walked to his wagon. Pulling open the door he found Barb shifting markers on the map.

"The Doc wants you. If you need me, I'll be at the village school. I'm going to go talk to Billy, find out what's happening on the rumour mill."

Barb looked up from her work. "Billy, the kid from the inn? Wouldn't his father know more?"

"John's the councillor. People won't tell him certain things.

Billy's just a kid. I learned when this was my route that if you want to know what's going on in this town, you ask Billy. That kid has ears on him and he's smart."

"Should I get him for you?"

"No, you get to the Doc."

Ten minutes later Eddie leaned his back against the school. This building stood across the street from the mill and in its time had gone from hotel to home, and in its latest incarnation housed the teacher on the top floor, while using what had been the lobby as a classroom. A half dozen thin-film solar panels lay on its metal roof. When Eddie glanced through the window he saw an ancient computer in the corner of the room.

The building's door opened, and a portly man with a bald head and ruddy complexion stepped out.

"Major Baily, pleasure to see you. I was going to ask if you could give a lecture. I wanted to get that Brad fellow while he was in town, but I never got round to it."

"Glad to, Yancy. You still focussing on the R.R.K,s?"

"Reading, arithmetic and keyboards. Why don't you come in? I'm quite proud of my students. Bright class."

"Sorry, I'm working. I need a word with Billy."

"That scamp." Yancy smiled tolerantly. "Lad has a gift for math, especially addition."

Eddie snorted. "You've been playing cards with your students again, haven't you?"

The teacher shrugged. "Man needs some recreation. Beside, it teaches them math."

"Yancy, you have to learn. Gambling's what got you into the Dark in the first place."

"Yes, Yes. I'll send the little bugger out. It's almost recess anyway."

Yancy disappeared into the classroom; a minute later Billy stepped through the door.

"Hello, Tink, I mean Major," said the lad.

"Hello Billy. I need to talk with you."

Billy smiled and, with an oddly adult sweep of his hand, indicated that they should walk together. They started up the road that led to Meb's house.

"I need to know what people are saying about the plague and my troops."

"I don't know much. You should ask my dad."

"I need to know the things they won't tell your dad."

Billy stooped, picked up a stone and threw it into the river, which paralleled the road. It landed with a plop. "Is it true you're making your troops clean our methane composter?"

Eddie smiled. "Yes. It's part of their punishment for getting into that fight."

"Thank you. Dad always makes me help him with that and it stinks. Old man McPherson was tellin' some folk that he thinks this plague is just a bunch of silliness. That you Bright Landers are making too much of it, but as long as you keep spendin' marks like you have been, he ain't gonna complain."

"How many people do you think feel like that?"

"Maybe a dozen. Then there's Mr. James. He's been saying that the plague's running rampant, and we should bless the lot of you for keeping us safe from it. He says that it's swallowed up Guelph whole, and they're dropping like flies. Is that true?"

"No, but it is pretty bad. Some folk are getting better though."

"Michelle says folks are getting better 'cause Carla's found a plant that heals them, and she don't need to go to school in Novo Gaia 'cause she already knows more than the doctors there."

"Anything else?"

Billy paused looking at the river. "I heard some men whispering, but I didn't want to get too close 'cause Mr. Thomson was with them. He's real nasty. He hit me last year. Nic put him in the stocks for three days for that. Paw wanted to sap and feather him. Paw made him apologize to me before he'd let him back in the inn. Anyway, the men were real angry and kept mentioning that trailer of yours. One of them said something about Acton and you getting yours."

"That's interesting. Here." Eddie held out a copper mark. Billy took the chip and flipped it across his knuckles with practised ease, before slipping it into his pocket.

"Thank you, Major. Any time you want me to fill you in on what folk are saying, you just drop by."

Eddie smiled before starting back to town.

He was in the inn, relaxing over a tankard of ale, when the ground shook.

"Great Beaver! What's going on?" Looking up he watched in disbelief as the Med lab crept past. He ran to the door, but the townsfolk crowded around it blocking his exit.

Finally he forced his way out, only to see Barb galloping towards him from the visitors' field. She reined to a halt in front of him.

"What is going on?" he demanded.

"It's Dr. Frankel. He hijacked the truck."

"What? Why? Does he even know how to drive it?"

"He left a letter. He pinned it on the inside of the blanket he wrapped Cathy in. He had me move her to your van after the surgery. The next thing I knew the whole lab was pulling out."

Barb held out the letter, which Eddie grabbed. It was labelled in a spidery script with his name. He opened it. Inside it was computer printed, except for the final signature, which was an illegible scribble.

"What does it say?" John joined them in front of the inn.

Eddie read it aloud.

To the attention of Major Edward Bailey,

Sir. I find I can no longer tolerate the cowardice of the Minister's order. I have sworn an oath to do no harm, but obviously the presence of my lab and the necessary samples is inciting an armed conflict. As this conflict can only cause harm to those involved, I am removing its cause. I will establish my lab in the Guelph area, where it can do the most good. I will practice full quarantine procedures. I hereby state that this action is completely of my own volition, and no others bear any responsibility.

I apologize to those who my actions may inconvenience.

Yours truly

Wingate Frankel, MD.

"Shit, we have to get after him." the letter shook in Eddie's hand.

"We'll never catch him." Barb looked at the truck as it moved past a rise in the road and out of sight.

"We have to try. Look at him, he's moving like a snail. Shit! He doesn't know how to change gears. He's going to drive the whole way in first. If he crashes that thing, we're shorted for sure!" Eddie ran towards the visitors' field where his horse was tethered.

Minutes later hoof beats thundered in his ears as his mount galloped along the ancient road connecting Eden Mills to highway seven. The corner appeared before him. He could hear Barb following close behind. They reached highway seven almost together. The lab lumbered along the road.

"We're gaining on him!" hollered Barb.

"We can beat him if he stays in first, especially on these roads!" Eddie yelled in reply.

They drove their mounts forward, but despite their urging the horses began to slow.

"The horses have had it!" shouted Barb.

"Just a little further!"

A minute later Eddie pulled even with the trailer. Its black expanse stretched between him and the cab. He road along the trailer's length until he heard the sound of grinding gears.

"Shit!" Eddie pushed his mount into a last sprint. Pulling alongside the cab he grabbed the entry bar. The truck lurched and sped up. Desperately he kicked out of his stirrups as he was yanked from his horse's back.

"Stop, doctor, stop! I'm losing my grip!" screamed Eddie as the truck continued to move forward.

Dr. Frankel glanced over his shoulder. A panicked expression spread over his face when he saw Eddie's feet kicking below the running board. The truck jumped as a tire descended into a pothole. Eddie slipped down on the pole, so the toes of his boots scraped along the ground.

The air brakes hissed as Eddie slipped lower on the bar. The truck lurched in and out of potholes and slewed to the right. Only the slow speed they were travelling stopped it from rolling. It came to a shuddering halt thirty feet in front of the highway-seven, guard-unit's windmill. The turbine engine squealed then wound down to silence.

The driver's door flew open, and the doctor hurtled onto the road.

"Edward, are you injured?" he demanded.

Eddie stood, using the mounting bar for support. He stared at the toes of his boots where the leather was scuffed through, revealing the metal toe guards beneath.

"You crazy son of a bitch! You're just bloody lucky I wear safety boots, or my toes would be two klicks back. What in the name of the great spirit did you think you were doing?"

At that point Barb rode up, leading Eddie's winded mount.

"I could not allow my presence to cost human lives. I had no choice but to remove my laboratory from the area of contention."

"Frankel!" Eddie began, but words failed him, so he stood red-faced, staring at the doctor.

"Dr. Frankel, I think what the Major is trying to say is you misunderstood us. Greg Thomson and his group are using your lab's presence as an excuse to attack. If it wasn't your lab, they'd find some other excuse."

Eddie raised his hand, silencing Barb. "Doctor, if you ever pull a stunt like this again, I swear, I will beat you senseless. Your lab is being returned to the field, where I will see that the cab is disconnected. Just be thankful you didn't roll the damn trailer, spilling viral samples all over the road. These trucks aren't toys!

"Barb, you're to escort the doctor back to town. I'll wait here for a transport tech to drive the trailer back. I want you each to walk a horse. Those mounts have done quite enough for one day. And, doctor."

"Yes, Edward?"

"Barb will show you how to rub down my horse. I want a thorough job. The animal deserves it. When all that's done you can help feed and water them."

"I'm a doctor, not a stable hand!" objected Frankel, before a fiery glance from Eddie caused him to change gears. "I guess kindness to all living things is what Hippocrates intended."

"Come on, doctor, we'd better go." Barb passed him a set of reins and started for town.

Eddie stared into the patchy, blue sky and sighed before climbing into the truck's cab to radio for a driver.

Back at base he was sitting at his table eating a supper that John had delivered to his wagon when someone knocked on his door.

"Come," he ordered between bites.

"Excuse me, Major, I have a message for you from Corporal Timothy. He's delayed the Arkellians at least a day and escaped the town. He said that he thinks they'll still march tomorrow, and he can't do much more," said Ackley.

"Understood. Tell him good luck, and send the doctor in here. I was saving the good news so I could blend out the bad." Eddie wiped his lips with a cloth napkin. Sliding from behind his table, he moved to the radio in the front of his van.

"Main base to Lieutenant Irving, come in, Brad. Over."

"I'll talk to him when I'm dressed. Waiting is something Eddie should learn how to do. How are the patients?"

"Ten recoveries, fifteen deaths and thirty new arrivals. The bad news is, some of the new ones are from central Guelph," answered Carla.

"Shit! That's bad, but not unexpected." Brad swung from his bed and reached for his trousers as Ingram stepped away from the door.

"Who's Tabby?" Carla wore a sly smile.

"Aw. A friend from the academy, Tabitha Divasky. She does an aquatic tinker route on Lake Superior. Actually, I wish she was here right now."

"Oh?" Carla had a dangerous tone in her voice.

"She's the best medical tinker I've ever met. Worked as an E.R. nurse before she decided to go back to school and become a tinker."

"And she's just a friend?"

"Well, umm." Brad blushed.

Carla laughed and kissed him before she left. Moving to his radio, he dressed as the call idents were exchanged.

"Bit slow picking up, weren't you, Brad? Over," said Eddie's voice.

"Short your briefs. I was sleeping. I crashed just before my last call in, and am still pretty fried. Over."

"Well then, I have good news and bad news. Over."

"At least there is good this time. Broccoli before dessert. What's the bad? Over."

"You can expect a visit from the Arkellians sometime tomorrow. Over."

"Is there anything you can do to slow them down? People are recovering. All I need is time. Over."

"We'll bomb the bridge when they reach it, but that will only slow them a bit. Maybe a couple of hours. Over."

"I'll try to do something here. What's the good news? Over."

The voice on the radio changed to that of Dr. Frankel.

"You were correct regarding the nature of the virus. It is a purist disease, developed in 2031. The Gridtown team turned up a picture of the twin viruses in an old medical text. The electron

Chapter Twenty-eight

Discoveries

Carla knelt by Brad's sleeping form, staring at him.

"It seems a shame. He needs to catch up with his sleep," she commented.

"The radio said it was important." Ingram stood in the van's doorway.

"Why didn't you wake him?"

"After... Well, I heard the two of you earlier, and, well. I think he'd like it better if you did. I know I would."

Carla blushed and gently shook Brad.

"Tabby, hmmmmm," he murmured.

Carla flushed then dug him in the ribs.

"What? What?" Brad sat up in bed.

"Who's Tabby?" Carla glared at him.

Brad's eyes darted nervously about his van.

"That doesn't matter right now. There's a call on the radio. It's Major Baily, and he'll speak only to you," said Ingram.

"What does he want?" Brad rubbed sleep out of his eyes.

"How should I know? I was taking a nap, on the front seat, when the radio started yapping. You should tell your friend that I can be trusted. He wouldn't tell me anything."

microscope photos match to within point zero two percent. Over."

"That's great! What's it called? How do I treat it? Over."

"It is called Asiatic Dehydrant Fever. A.D.F. From its name it is safe to assume that it was targeted against the Asiatic race. We don't have any more information than that. Over."

"I have people in the clinic who don't look Asian. Over."

"Yes. I assumed you would. If you examine their heritage, you will find an Asian individual. Over."

"So we have a name. Any chance you'll find something more? Over."

"The teams are continuing to search, but the destruction of records on the purists viruses was very thorough. I do not believe they will find any more pertinent information. Over."

Brad leaned back in his seat and closed his eyes, allowing the radio to sit silent.

"Do we know if there was a cure? Over," he asked.

"The text was very basic and only used the image to illustrate classic features of man-made viruses. It said little about the disease itself. Over."

Brad sat silently, allowing his mind to run over the problem.

"Brad, are you still there? Over," demanded Eddie's voice.

"Just thinking. You have no useful records on this thing. Doc, what are the chances of you discovering something independently? Over."

"Given time and resources, I am confident a cure can be found. Over."

"How much time? Over."

The tone of the doctor's voice spoke more eloquently than words.

"With a large enough budget, ten, maybe fifteen years. Our forefathers may have had a cure, but we have to re-invent the wheel. Over."

"Great. Keep me posted. Over and out."

"Over and out."

Brad stepped into the evening light and looked at the clinic. Mark sat on the front step, a small figure wrapped in blankets beside him.

“Hello, Tinker,” called the farmer. Dark circles stood out under his eyes, but a smile split his face from ear to ear.

“Hello, Mark, Rose.” Brad nodded first to the man then his daughter. “What’s up?”

“I wanted some fresh air. It smells real bad in there,” explained Rose.

“We’ll see about sending you home soon. How do you feel?”

“Good.”

“Good doesn’t say it, Tinker. Me Rose passed water ‘bout an hour ago, normal and fine as you please,” interrupted Mark.

“Paw!” A blush colouring Rose’s cheeks.

“That’s good to know. Kidney damage was one of my big worries.”

“What damage?” Rose’s soft, Asian features took on a quizzical expression.

“Kidneys clean your blood and make pee. I need to talk to both of you. Mentioning blood reminded me. I want to take some of Rose’s blood. Sometimes, if someone recovers from an illness, their blood contains a cure that can help others with that same illness.”

“Now, Tinker, I’m grateful and all, don’t get me wrong. No way Rose would have made it exceptin’ you cared for her, but I won’t have her put at risk.”

“There isn’t that much risk. I’ll only take a small amount.”

Mark stared at Brad, a calculating expression on his face.

“Rosie, what you think?”

“Will it hurt?” Rose looked nervous.

“A prick, like with the I.V.” Brad smiled reassuringly.

“Okay.” Rose put on a brave face.

“We’ll do it, but I want somet for it. I’ve been thinkin’. The smell and such in there ain’t good for a body.” Mark’s face was thoughtful.

“I know, but we can’t spread people around and still treat them effectively.”

“Too true, Tinker. What I’m thinkin’ is, there’s the inn over there, all empty like. I have a friend or two willing to help out with those as are on the mend. How ‘bouts you start movin’ those as don’t need I.V.s no more over there. My friends and I can see to keepin' them fed and such. You could still check up on them by walkin' cross the street."

Brad smiled and nodded. "Mark, you're a genius. Get Rose settled. I'll be by later to..."

Trina careened through the clinic's door, skidding to a stop when she saw Brad. "Tinker, you better come."

Brad followed her back into the clinic. Carla knelt beside Oscar whose body was racked by a coughing spasm. As Brad approached he hacked up a yellow glob of mucus, which fell to the floor.

"What is this?" demanded Brad.

"He's rehydrated, but now he's coughing and spitting up mucus. He's also complaining of chills," explained Carla.

"Shit, what now?" Brad examined Oscar.

"Let me go, Tinker. Let me be with my Bernice and our boys," breathed Oscar who then fell into a coughing fit.

"Too many people have died already for me to do that. Hang on, if only so someone remembers your family."

Oscar scowled but didn't argue.

Brad turned to Carla and Trina. "Is he the only case like this?"

"None of the others have started coughing," said Trina.

Brad pinched the man's skin, noting its returning elasticity, and inserted his thermometer.

"Temperature's normal." Sitting back on his heels he fell into desperate thought.

"I'm getting him a blanket." Carla was moving towards the stack of blankets as she spoke.

"Might as well." Brad stood and stared at the man. "The last thing we need is a new twist on this. You said he was recovering then started coughing and complaining of chills."

"Yes." Carla returned and covered Oscar. The shivering lessened.

"Maybe you should talk to the doctor?" said Trina.

"I will after I've had a chance to watch this for a bit. For now, Mark had an idea about moving the patients who were on the mend to the inn. Carla, I want you to grab Ingram, and help Mark get set up. Take everyone who's ambulatory. I think they're past this, whatever it is. That should give us some cot space."

"I have to speak to you about that," said Trina.

Brad turned to the scrawny woman. "What?"

"The cots. We only have a dozen or so left. We'll have to start reusing the ones that the dead are on."

"They're filthy!" Bad shuddered with revulsion. "No, if we have to we'll make beds of blankets on the floor, but I won't lay patients in other people's shit."

"I think they'd be more comfortable on the cots." Trina looked ready to argue. Brad turned away from her.

"Shorting! And I thought things were getting better." He moved to the central table and booted up his laptop.

"What are you looking for?" Trina followed him.

"I want to try and make a serum from the blood of folk who recover."

"Do you know how?"

"No. I'm going to read up on it."

"I don't see how that will work. Only doctors can make medicines. They're special people." Trina smirked as if she'd scored some kind of a point.

Brad stared wearily at Trina and pushed his chair back. The skinny woman looked at him with smug self-satisfaction. Brad rubbed his tired eyes.

"Trina, what is a doctor?"

Trina's features shifted to puzzlement. "They're healers who know everything. They know all the cures and are special people."

"Trina, a doctor is anyone who's completed a doctorate. It means you've studied in university for eight years and done two theses or equivalents. There are doctors of physics, chemistry, just about anything you can name. Medical doctors are just people who have studied for a long time. They don't know everything, and they can make mistakes. They aren't magical. Shorting, if it makes you feel better, I'm a doctor."

"You're just a tinker," snapped Trina, annoyed shock in her voice.

"And what is a tinker? I am a doctor of applied general technologies. Every "tinker" is. Truth, I'm working on a second doctorate, in engineering then I'll have two. Two..."

"Well, I hardly..."

Brad's raised hand halted Trina's reply. He closed his eyes and cleared his mind allowing his thoughts to sift quietly across his awareness.

"Two," he whispered. "I'm an idiot! The doctor told me to watch for secondary infections. Useless Brad. You're a bloody useless dolt!"

Trina took a step back. "What are you talking about?"

"Two diseases. A secondary infection. That's what's making that man cough. Frankel warned me to be on the lookout for them. Fetch me the pills you and Carla sorted a few days back."

"But my pills don't work against viruses."

"No, but they might work against the secondary infection."

Trina shook her head and left to fetch her pills while Brad moved to Oscar's side.

"I need to get some mucus from the back of your throat," he explained, as he prepared a cotton swab.

Oscar's rugged features were a mask of woe. "Just let me die! I don't want to live without them."

"I need to figure out how to treat you in case I have to treat others. Are you willing to sacrifice other people's lives?"

Oscar coughed then opened his mouth wide.

"Thank you." Brad collected his sample.

"Tinker." Oscar's voice was a whisper and Brad leaned close to hear him.

"What?"

"How bad would it be if... How dangerous is our tank. Could it be causing this?"

Brad's face became grim. "It's not the cause, but if it's nuclear and the containment broke, the radiation poisoning would make this look like a case of the sniffles."

Oscar fell into another coughing fit as Brad moved away. Minutes later Brad pushed a syringe into Oscar's I.V. injecting a blue-tinted fluid.

"What's that?" Carla moved to Brad's side.

"Tetracycline. I think he's got a secondary infection."

"Of course. Ground out! I should have seen that. I've read

about them."

"You have a right to miss it. I've been educated, and the doctor warned me, and I almost dropped the ball. We're wearing down, all of us. Did you get Rose settled?"

"In the big, private room in the attic. Mark insisted." Carla smiled indulgently.

"He's earned the right. How about the others?"

"Settled in the other rooms. One of Mark's friends has sparked up the stove and is heating water. Everyone wants to bathe."

"Can't say I blame them. I'm going to make a culture from this swab. You can bet, if he's caught a secondary, others have. I want to know what I'm up against. I won't save them from A.D.F. to have them die of a bloody cold." Brad moved to his workstation with Carla in tow.

"A.D.F.?"

"The name of the disease we're fighting."

"I have the pills." Trina returned carrying a variety of wooden bowls on a tray.

"Good. I'll find out which one to use now."

Much later Brad sat reading a computer file, oblivious to the macabre shadows the overhead lamp sent through the clinic. The sound of laboured breathing became nothing but a backdrop for his concentration. A half-eaten sandwich sat on a plate by his right hand.

"You could have taken that outside." Carla was scrubbing her hands in a bucket on the table.

"Wanted to keep an eye on the cultures. The sooner they're ready, the sooner I can tailor the antibiotics to the secondary. How's Ingram's Mum?"

"Happier since I sponged her down. I think she'll be able to go to the inn in the morning."

"Good. You should tell him."

"I will, when he wakes up. Right now he's stretched across the front seat of your van, snoring."

"Aw, a consummation devoutly to be wished." Brad leaned back in his chair.

"What?" Carla looked confused.

"From Hamlet. Great movie, once you get past the language.

Where's Trina?"

"A patient vomited on her; she went to rinse herself off." Carla took a seat and rested her head on the table.

"I hate medicine!"

"How's Oscar?" Carla spoke without raising her head.

"He's responding to the tetracycline, so it is bacterial." Brad reached out and tentatively stroked her hair.

"That's nice. You have nice hands."

Brad smiled for a moment the horror around him forgotten then he returned to the present. "Can you keep an eye on my culture? I'm going to see Rose and take some blood. I want to try a serum treatment." Brad slowly stood.

"Do you think it will work?"

The conversation was ended by the cry of a patient going into convulsions. Brad and Carla raced to the woman's side.

Half an hour later Brad opened a door, which creaked on its hinges. The attic room beyond had a roof that sloped up from one metre on all sides to level out at over two in the middle. Rose lay in a double bed pushed against the far wall. The light of stars and moon entered through a skylight.

"Who?" asked the child in a sleepy voice.

"It's the Tinker." Brad moved to her side and sat on a stool.

"Tinker?" The child stared at him blearily and clutched a ragged doll closer to her.

"I need to take some blood, Rose."

"Okay."

Holding a rechargeable flashlight in his teeth, Brad secured Rose's arm, placed the tourniquet and inserted the needle. She whimpered then lay still. He released the tourniquet and let the red fluid dribble into the collection bag. Moments later he was slipping from the room.

"How was she, Tinker?" Mark stood on the landing in front of the stairs to the inn's second floor.

"Hardly woke up. I'd guess that in a day or two you'll be taking her home."

"And glad of it. I saw she had a proper bath. I love my little one, but the smell of her..." Mark grimaced.

"I hardly notice after being in the clinic so much."

"Just as well Lee Lee ran off with that cooper. From what I've been hearing, she'd of been a goner for sure."

"Probably." Brad descended the stairs and returned to the clinic, where he found Carla dragging a cot towards the side room that was now serving as the morgue.

"Let me help with that." Brad picked up the bottom of the cot. It was light despite its gruesome burden.

"She was eight-years-old." Carla's voice was harsh.

"Go get some sleep."

"I'm okay."

Brad looked at her in the half-light of his lantern. Fatigue had etched deep lines in her face, and a trick of the light flecked her hair with grey.

Still pretty, he thought. *How many years ahead am I seeing? Thirty, forty?* He nodded and followed her into the morgue. Bodies lay everywhere.

"We're almost out of space in here. How many have died?" Brad scanned the lines of cots.

"Last I checked, nearly two-hundred. How many people live in this part of Guelph?"

"About a thousand."

"This will destroy them. I mean the survivors." Carla shivered as she surveyed the dead.

"It will be a long time before they get over it. The more who die the worse it will be. Come on, let's get out of here. I have a serum to make."

Carla followed him from the room. "Wouldn't it be better to send the blood to the doctor?"

"I'm going to send Ingram out with the dawn, but I want to try something. We were lucky, Rose's blood is O neg."

"So?" Carla shrugged.

"Universal donor. Anyone can, in theory, accept her blood."

"Neat. Why is it important? Artificials work better, and these people don't have blood loss."

"Tinkers and Dark Land healers are taught about blood groups, so if we run short on artificials we can still transfuse. I'm taking half the blood I drew from Rose and injecting a group of patients. Two with partial European backgrounds. Two without. One of each will be in the advanced stages of the disease."

"Human guinea pigs." Carla looked indignant.

Brad shrugged. "Got a better idea?"

"No."

In minutes the work was done.

"Now all there is to do is wait." Brad started towards the clinic door. "Wake me if you need me and try to be gentle. My ribs are still bruised."

Carla shot him a tired smile before returning to her work.

Chapter Twenty-nine

What's That Sonny

THE SOUND OF HORSES alerted Dan to his quarry's approach. Deepening his limp, he leaned on a wooden staff he'd found on the roadside. When the horses were almost on top of him, he turned to look at them.

Ward and five other men slouched painfully in their saddles, wincing with each hoof fall. Nineteen men and women followed them, looking grey and unsteady. Most of them squinted painfully against the morning light.

"'ear now. What's this?" Dan affected an old man's voice.

Ward raised his hand, and the motley crew came to a stop.

"Youse a sickin, old-timer?" he demanded, his hand slipping to his pistol.

"What? Speak up, onny. Can't go whispering if'n youse 'spect folk to 'ear," shouted Dan. A smile, which his false whiskers hid, touched his lips as Ward winced.

"A sickin. Youse got plague?" asked Ward louder.

"What's?"

"'Ave youse got plague?" Ward buried his head in his hands.

"Plague. No's, I's ain't got no's plague. I's was tryin' to get to Little Lake, down old three five. Bunch of Gridtown bullies stopped me. Been lookin' for some folk as would 'elp me out. Got me daughter in Little Lake; ain't got nowhere else I's can go."

"We's off to deal with 'is 'ere plague. We's mean to burn it out," said Ward in a loud voice.

"'ell nows 'at makes sense. Supposin' someone gets in youse way?"

"We'll deal with 'em," said Osric, who sat on a horse behind Ward.

"What's?" Dan cupped a hand to where his ear was concealed by the bush of his false beard.

"We won'ts let any folk stop us," hollered Ward, who then grimaced in pain.

"What's about 'at 'ere tank of 'eirs?"

"Figure ey're too sick to use it. Figure we can take it. 'at 'ill stop 'em Guelphers throwing 'ier weight around. Then Arkell can step up; take charge here abouts. Not even 'em Bright Landers could stop us. Only needs right man in charge to do it." Ward's face practically glowed with self-aggrandising avarice.

"What's?" Dan squinted up at Ward.

Ward grimaced again before replying. "Don't matter, we's won't be letin' anythin' stop us."

"Good to 'ear. 'bout time folk did somit. Mind's I joins youse, was a crack shot in me younger days. Once brought down a pheasant from a 'undred paces, 'ad not but a pistol. Course I was younger, but I still reckons I could..."

"Get to the back, old-timer. Anything, so's long as youse stop shoutin'," ordered Ward.

Dan limped to the rear of the infantry and took a place beside a girl barely past her teens. The green cast to her skin, and the pained squint on her face spoke to her previous night's activities.

"'ody lass, gonna be a fight," shouted Dan.

The girl glared at him and replied, "Probably."

"I can tells youse, I's lookin' forward to this. 'aven't 'add a good fight since we's raided 'espeler years ago. Lot of belly wounds that time. Lot of sharp sticks. Youse ever seen a sharp stick stuck in a belly? Ugly that, blood and guts oozing out. Member one guy we hooked 'im and he ran. Left his guts strung out behind him, near thirty strides, just draggin' there like."

The girl's cheeks bulged. She raced to the side of the street, where she fell to her knees retching. The column moved on. When she staggered to her feet, she watched them, shook her head and started back toward Arkell, cradling her stomach as she walked.

One, thought Dan as he moved up between a pair of men who were sharing a wine skin and laughing.

Half an hour later Dan smiled and thought *five*, as the latest in a string of his travelling companions staggered towards Arkell. A buzzing sound filled the air, and the troop around him were watching the sky. A wind blew from the north; Dan concentrated his gaze in that direction. The ultralight appeared low over a field of crops. It raced toward them as the Arkellian force began firing at it. A ball fell from the plane. The ultralight shot into the air, away from the ground fire, as the ball bounced across the field.

Dan dove for the ditch beside the road and buried his head in his hands. The ball jarred to a stop and exploded, filling the air with yellow droplets. Dan held his breath and closed his eyes. When he was forced to breathe, he inhaled and gagged. A stench like the urine of a hundred large cats filled the air.

The sound of horses neighing and clopping was everywhere. Dan rolled from the ditch, just in time to avoid a panicked steed running over him. Looking up, he saw the six horses rearing, heedless of their riders' commands. One of the foot men raced to grab a horse's bit, but a hoof smashed into his shoulder. The crack of splintered bone added to the confusion and he fell. Ward wrestled himself free of his mount and leapt to the ground. Mad with fear, the horse galloped off. Two others followed it, carrying their riders with them. One of the mounted men fell from his saddle, landing on the broken asphalt head first. His mount bolted through the infantry ranks scattering them.

Osric pulled tight on his horse's reins, driving the bit into the animal's lips. The horse bucked, throwing him over its head. Osric tucked when he hit the ground, managing to roll with the impact. His horse bolted, and the final mount followed it, dragging its hapless rider by the stirrup until the leather gave out.

"Bloody 'ell! What the fuck was 'at?" swore Ward.

"Were somet like cat piss. Makes 'orses afear somit awful,"

said Dan, starting toward the man who'd been dragged.

"Fuck! We's lost the 'orses," said Ward.

Osric stumbled to his feet. "I's gonna hurt tomorrow." He joined the group around the man who'd been thrown.

"We's got to take Sam back to town. 'is shoulder's all broke up," said a young man, who knelt beside the fellow who'd tried to grab the horse's bit.

"We's can'ts lose no more troops," objected Ward.

"This ones still a breathing, but 'e won't be walking for a time. Think 'is leg's been pulled clear out of its socket."

Ward rubbed his temples and tried to think.

"We's better be making up stretchers for 'em as are wounded," said Dan.

"We 'ave to go on," said Ward.

"I's takin' Sam back. Wilma won't ever forgive me, if'n he dies," said a blond-haired, burly man.

"'at's treachery." Ward's hand inched toward his gun. The sound of a hammer being cocked behind him gave him pause.

"Send the injured 'ome, lad. 'ats what a good general does," said Dan.

An hour later only eight men stood by Ward as they watched the rest of the troop leave with the wounded.

"'at's it then. We don't stand a chance less we get more men," said Osric.

"We's got to burn out 'at plague. Show 'em tree huggers we's Dark Landers can take care of ourselves," snapped Ward.

"Just wondering. Which one of you chaps is this Jack I been 'earing 'bout? Others said 'e was a smart one. Maybe 'e could think up somit?" said Dan.

"Yeah. Where is Horner? This 'ole thing was 'is idea," demanded Ward.

"He went into the bushes, long ways back. Ain't seen him since," replied a small, bearded man, wearing a Stetson and black western-style clothing.

"Comes to think of it, 'e was all after us to do the McFays," said Osric.

"McFays needed doing. They's 'ad plague," objected Ward.

"Maybe, but I knew Howard right well. I think I'm gonna find me Jack and have a word or three with him. Who's with me?" said the small, bearded man.

"We are, Tex." Two of the remaining men moved to his side.

"What about Guelph?" demanded Ward.

"The tree huggers keep saying we should keep clear. I figure it's about time we listened. Come on, boys, let's find us a rattler to fry." Tex led the two men back along the road.

"We's can't do it with only us five," said Osric.

"We'll sneak in quiet like and burn out 'at 'all. 'Ey won't even knows we's 'ere. Or better, we's find 'at tank. Then we can blow up the 'all on our way out of town."

Ward started walking along the road. Reluctantly the other men fell in behind him. An hour later the bridge spanning the Eramosa came into view. Dan slipped into the underbrush and allowed the others to move away before activating his radio.

"Corporal Timothy to base, come in base. Do you read? Over."

"We read you, Corporal. What is your status? Over."

"They're a persistent lot, I'll give them that. Four still active. They're almost at the bridge."

"Understood. Over and out."

"Over and out."

Dan stayed huddled in the bushes watching as the Arkellians moved on. Minutes later the buzz of the ultralight filled the air. The Arkellians searched the skies. Dan saw the small aircraft skimming the surface of the river, a hundred strides from the closest Arkellian. The men ran toward the bridge, but before they could get close the plane dropped a torpedo-shaped object and climbed into the air. The object struck the bridge. A thunderous roar split the air as asphalt and stone flew in all directions. The smoke cleared revealing a pile of rubble where the bridge had been.

Dan kept his distance as the four figures stood at the edge of the river. The sound of raised voices reached him, and finally two of them walked off. Before they had travelled three metres there was the sound of gunshots. Twin explosions of red flew from the retreating figures. Dan shifted his focus in time to see Ward holstering his pistol.

Aw, Dinah me sweet, you're young to be a widow, but this has gone too far, thought Dan as he crept through the bushes at the roadside, drawing ever closer to his target. Before long he could hear the other men's voices.

"We's can still burn 'em out and get 'at tank. I's in command. I's the colonel, and don'ts youse forget it."

"Alls I said is, I don't think you needed to shoot 'em."

"Fuck youse, they was traitors. Gonna sell out to 'em damn tree 'uggers. We burn out this 'ere plague, we'll be 'eros. They'll make us councillors, put up statues. Youse'll see."

Dan took careful aim at the figure seven metres from him and pulled the trigger. The bullet sped towards its target. Ward's chest opened, spraying Osric with gore. Dan watched his foe pivot in place. The dying man's arm jerked, trying to raise his pistol, but his body was too injured to obey. He fell to the ground, spasmed twice then lay still. Osric screamed and sprinted back along the road to Arkell. Dan looked at the thirty-eight revolver in his hand and slid out the empty casing.

"I hate guns!" he said. Reloading the weapon, he returned it to his pocket and pulled out his radio.

"The invasion from Arkell is off. You owe me a bullet. Over," he spoke.

"Sorry about the bullet. Eddie told me to give you some good news when you called in. If there are no signs of plague, we'll be closing in the quarantine tomorrow. Over," said the disembodied voice on the speaker.

"A little late. I'm going hunting. If it weren't for Horner, none of this would have happened. Over and out."

Chapter Thirty

Fools In All Sizes

Barb slid into the foxhole and adjusted her night vision goggles.

"Quiet." Nick lay in the bottom of the pit, an ancient semi-automatic rifle clutched across his chest.

"Waiting for it is always the worst part," commented Barb.

"You've never shot someone, have you?"

"No, have you?"

"Once. Happened a couple years back. Bunch of exiles from the Niagara Grid Region started demanding tolls for using the roads. I had to form a posse and deal with them before they choked the life out of this town. Managed to take most of them alive, but the leader kept shooting at us. I had no choice. I'm pretty good from hunting. I still remember his face. That's the worst part."

"I'm sorry."

"Man shouldn't suffer lessen he throws the first punch, but you do. Least I do. Still, most folks from the gang settled hereabouts. Most of them good folk. Hell, Albert, the skinny chap I deputized for this, was one of them."

Nick fell silent as Barb continued to scan her surroundings. The night deepened, and the sound of crickets filled the air. Stars shone down from the inky sky, occasionally obscured by scuttling clouds.

"Two o'clock on the other side of the road," snapped Barb.

Nick crawled to the foxhole's rim and stared into the night.

"I can't see anything."

"They're there. I think three of them... Arrgh." Barb stifled a scream and scrambled with her night-vision goggles. A flare shot skywards, bathing the visitors' field in a radiance as bright as noon.

"What the hell?" swore Nick.

"Day-flare. They're designed to light battlefields. Thomson's group must have had one. I can't see anything but spots."

"Shit!" Nick began firing. "They're charging."

"Damn. Hold them back, I'm beginning to see a bit again."

"Hurry up."

Eddie sat in his wagon examining his battle plans, when light poured in through the window.

"Shorting!" He clamped his eyes shut and buried them in the crux of his good elbow. The sound of gunfire echoed over the field.

"It's started." Drawing his pistol, he leapt from his wagon and threw himself to the ground. The sound of shooting grew as the flare continued to light the area.

"Major, they're coming in from the south," cried Bob Harrison's voice.

"*Units attacking from the north!*" Screamed out the radio in his van.

"Bastards are smarter than I thought." Pulling a radio from a pouch on his belt, Eddie spoke into it.

"Reserves, deploy reinforcement sweep pattern. Start north to east. Sleeping beauty manoeuvre on my command." Eddie began crawling towards the portable lab.

"I got one." Nick dropped down in the foxhole and fumbled with his rifle's clip. Barb popped up on the rim of the crater and squeezed off a shot.

"You able to see again?" demanded Nick.

"Only shadows." Barb fired off another round.

"Save your ammo." Nick crested the mound beside her and fired.

"This is unit three. We're pinned down. Francine can't see a bloody thing. Help us, they're charging, I can't keep them down," screamed the radio on Barb's belt.

"Shit, shit, shit!" swore Barb as Nick dropped into the hole beside her, and she popped up to fire. Now the shadows were more distinct. She saw movement at the edge of one of the spots dancing in front of her. Three shots later a scream rent the air.

Bob lay flat in the grass. His vision was still blurry, but luck had been with him. He'd pulled off his goggles, to wipe sweat from around his eyes, just before the flare went off. He now crouched behind the corner of the visitor's barn, his goggles hanging around his neck, and listened to the sound of stealthy movement.

"We's got us some tree huggers now. Teach 'em right for stickin' 'ere noses in 'ere they don't belong." The voice was harsh and came from just behind the fence surrounding the visitor field. Bob pointed his rifle in the general direction. Moments later a large figure, dressed in black, appeared. Bob held his breath as the figure started over the fence. Two other figures followed it. Bob squeezed the trigger. The first figure dropped. A volley of fire flew in his general direction, peppering the barn. He hit the dirt and crawled toward his attackers.

"I can't see anything. I'm blind. I'm blind," cried Francine. The blackout on her face almost blended with the ebony of her skin, while her khakis hugged her small, muscular form.

"Steady, girl," said Albert. His dark, homespun clothing was stained with the blood that poured from a wound on his pale scalp. Grabbing his partner's gun, he rose above the foxhole's rim and started firing at the approaching group.

"About six of them, as I can count." Albert dropped back to the bottom of the pit and grabbed the rifle Francine had reloaded for him.

He lifted his head above the foxhole's rim, but something fell to the ground behind him. He glanced at the green object, about the size of his fist. There was a roar he never heard.

"Ground out! Those sons of bitches have grenades!" Eddie depressed the talk button on his portable radio for the last part.

"Sir, shouldn't we go help them?" Reuben lay beside Eddie under the lab trailer.

"Negative. I underestimated their commander once. I won't again. Their main goal is the trailer. They'll go for it. Now be quiet."

"Bastard got Duke," spoke a gruff voice. Bob hid behind the fuselage of the plane, its folded wings blocking his enemy's view.

"We got to get 'em," spoke the other man.

"We's got to stick to the plan. Break through and start settin' fires. Burn 'em out. Give me the hootch."

"I ain't got the hootch. Youse was suppose to bring the hootch."

"Nos, youse was."

"Nos, youse was."

"Shit, don't matter. This here thing flies on fancy hootch. Me da' told me 'bout 'em. Alls we's got to do is find the fuel tank."

Silently Bob crept to the end of the wing, took aim and fired. One of the attackers fell to the ground. The other lifted his gun. Before anything more could happen, a shot rang out from the direction of the fence and the man fell. A Novo Gaian militia man gave Bob the thumbs up and motioned for him to stay put.

Barb fired again, keeping her opponents pinned behind a fallen log but accomplishing little more. The sound of the explosion still echoed in her ears.

"Trade off," she barked.

Nick took her place as she dropped down to reload.

"Something's up." Nick motioned to a rustling in the bushes behind their opponents.

"About time." Barb joined him in looking over the hole's edge. A voice barked, "Drop your weapons and stand up." A shot echoed, and a shower of bark kicked off the log.

"That was your only warning. Drop your weapons, now!" menaced the voice. The figures behind the log slowly rose into view. Soldiers, Barb recognised as being from the Victoria Road and Highway Six blockades, grabbed the men who'd attacked them. Pulling handcuffs and leg irons from their packs, the soldiers chained the Dark Landers to the trees.

"Stay put until we call you," ordered the new arrivals' leader; then they were gone.

"Shouldn't we—" began Nick.

"No, we shouldn't, but you'd better put this on." Barb passed him a gas mask.

Eddie lay watching and waiting as the battle unfolded. The Eden Mills and Acton rebels had his troops pinned down to the northeast, and on the field's northwest corner they had pushed in past the silent foxhole. The troops manning the radio truck had left their post and were crouched behind the second large transport, fighting a rear guard. Something by the gate caught his eye. The flare was beginning to burn out, its light growing tricky, but he was sure he saw movement. The gate swung open; a troop of men rushed through it, pulling a small wagon piled with fuel. They charged toward the lab. Eddie depressed the button on his radio and said, "Mark." There was a roaring sound as the Novo Gaians and their allies scrambled to pull on gas masks. A cloud swept in from the south, like a thick fog. Eddie whiffed a honey-sweet fragrance as he struggled one-handed to get his mask into place. His head was beginning to swim when Reuben knocked his hand to the side and secured the mask for him.

"Hope none of them have a heart problem, or the gas might do them in." Reuben watched the attacking forces fall to the ground.

"Thanks for the help, lad, and as far as that goes, I don't give a shit! I don't like killing, but sometimes..."

Minutes later Eddie scrambled from under the trailer. His troops were sweeping the area. Moving to the back of the lab, he pounded on the door.

"Is it over?" demanded Frankel, his gas mask making him look and sound like an aardvark with inflamed adenoids.

"I think so."

"I must treat the wounded."

"Our side first, doctor."

"Triage is not about sides, Edward. I will require Barbara's help." Frankel picked up a bag he had prepared and strode into the field.

"I heard him." Barb approached with Nick. She left to follow the doctor.

"I never would of thought it. Greg is a fool, but to disobey a ratified council decision... Where is he?" Nick's voice held rage.

"On the ground behind you," said Eddie.

"Can you check him over? If he's not about to die, I want him in the stocks before he wakes up."

"Major," interrupted Bob Harrison.

"Yes." Eddie turned to the younger man.

"Lieutenant Newicky ordered me to check on everyone and report to you."

"And?"

"Three of our people are wounded. The doctor is with them. Francine and Albert, well. All I found were pieces, sir. I... There were three feet showing. I..." Bob looked pale.

"Understood. Damn, why did it have to come to this? A simple medical quarantine." Eddie shook his head.

"It's more 'en that. Gridtown traders have been threatening that if we don't stop trading with you, they'll stop trading with us. Some folk want to close out you Novo Gaians. I recognize these faces. Practically all of them voted to ban Novo Gaians when the issue came up. They were voted down four to one. I guess they didn't take it too well," observed Nick.

Eddie moved to Greg's side and took the sleeping farmer's pulse. After doing a quick body check he turned to Nick.

"He's okay. Won't wake up for at least half an hour."

"Good. I'll put him where he belongs and if you could check a few of the others. We have six sets of stocks in town. I'd like 'em filled." Nick threw Greg roughly over his shoulder.

"I'll send them along with your deputies. We'll need a place for the rest of them." Eddie moved to the next unconscious figure.

"Choose any red T'ed place you like. Look I'm sorry about your troops. This should never have happened."

"Wasn't your fault."

Nick grunted and walked towards town carrying Greg.

Hours later Eddie was sleeping in his trailer when a knock sounded.

"Who is it?" he asked wearily.

"Sir. Lieutenant Irving's on the radio. He wants to talk to you and the doctor."

"Brad, damn it, this had better be good," growled Eddie as he pulled on his robe and boots.

Chapter Thirty-one

Lost Scrolls

BRAD HALF-AWOKE when the warm body slipped in beside him.

"Go back to sleep," whispered Carla.

Rolling onto his side, he wrapped her in his arms and felt her press against him. Desire warred with exhaustion and lost.

"Well, if this isn't a pretty picture. All that's going on and all you two can think about is having it off. Honestly!" intruded Trina's voice.

"What?" Brad shook his head to try and clear the fog. He was surprised to find Carla beside him.

"You would know what, if you hadn't been busy here. Those patients Carla told me to watch are doing something strange."

"Oh really?" Carla shamelessly stretched.

Trina's face reddened and she snapped, "You should come and see for yourself." She then stalked off.

"That woman runs off to do this and that all the time. Now she complains because I got some sleep!" griped Carla.

"More because of where you got it. Not that I object. Pity we have to rush off." Brad pulled her close and kissed her before grabbing his pants.

"We'll have other chances." Carla picked her rumpled dress

off the floor.

Brad stepped from the wagon into the late-morning sunshine and rushed to the clinic. Ignoring the pleading of patients, he moved to the four he'd inoculated.

"'lo, Tinker. I's don't knows what youse gave me, but I's feeling better from it. I's really is," remarked the burly man that Brad privately thought of as quarter target, initial infection.

Picking up the man's chart, Brad scanned it then checked the name before replying.

"Glad to hear that, Ted. I want to run some tests, if that's okay?"

"Way's I's sees it youse saved my bacon. Youse does what tests youse like."

Brad turned to Trina and asked, "No convulsions and only mild swelling of the lymph nodes?"

"Yes. You wouldn't have to ask, if you weren't busy doing other things."

Moving to the patient who was half Asian that had been in the advanced stages, Brad examined her. The child opened her large, brown eyes and whispered in a raspy voice through her cracked lips.

"Thirsty."

"Still no convulsions. Good. Carla, get Sabrina here a glass of water, and refresh her I.V. This one's almost out."

Moving to the patients without strong European genetics Brad's face collapsed.

"Standard disease progression. It didn't even slow it down."

"So the little girl's blood only helps some of them?" said Trina.

"Yup. A serum introduces antibodies from a person who has already beaten the disease. It helps kill the pathogen in the person injected. Why it isn't working for these people, I don't know."

"Brad," called Carla, who knelt by Sabrina's cot. Brad moved toward her, but she took him aside.

"She's asking after her parents."

"And?"

"They both died. Her father went full cycle. Her mother didn't survive the convulsions."

"Shit! Don't tell her anything until she's stronger. Does she need a sedative?"

"No. She's out again. At least the serum will save the ones like her mother."

"At least. Speaking of despair, how's Oscar?"

"He went to the inn while you were sleeping. Couldn't stand the smell here anymore. I just hope there aren't too many like him. He just kept muttering about how he should have died too." Brad squeezed Carla's arm before leaving the clinic. Leaning against his wagon he allowed the fresh air to wash the smell of sickness from his nose as he thought. He was jerked out of his musings when Ingram reined a small wagon to a stop in front of the clinic. The back of the cart was piled with parcels.

"More supplies? Good, we need them."

"Yeah. Picked them up when I took those bottles of blood you left for me to the checkpoint on the seven. Folk there said they'd take them to the doctor."

"Good. How's your Mum?"

"Pure wattage, Tinker, pure wattage. She moved to the inn this morning, had a bath and is reading stories to the kids."

"Good. I'd better call in. It seems like the serum is partially effective. We got lucky."

"Is it true folks built this sickness?"

"Yes."

"Stupid. Folk shouldn't play with life. No good comes of it."

"Don't know about that. Same research that built this bug allows folk to regrow arms and legs. Shorting, my granddad has a new heart grown in a tank. Without it he'd be dead. Half the alcohol fuel we use in Novo Gaia comes from a man-made bug. It eats cellulose and pisses ethanol. It's not the knowing that's the problem, it's what you do with it."

"Maybe, Tinker. I still can't forgive the assholes who built this one."

"Neither can I, but they're all long dead, so there isn't much we can do about it. I have to radio in. Once you've dropped off the Meds can you fetch some water from the still?"

"Sure thing."

Brad moved to his wagon and climbed in behind the radio.

"Lieutenant Irving to base, come in base. Over." He spoke into the mic.

"Base to Lieutenant Irving, we read you. Ready to receive Ident. Over."

"Fetch Eddie and the Doc while we do this silliness. Over." Brad traded identification codes with the base radio.

"Okay. Brad, what's so important you got me out of bed? Over," spoke Eddie's voice.

"Still in bed? It's noon. Over," observed Brad.

"Bit of trouble here last night. Greg Thomson's in the stocks. Thought you'd like to know. Over."

Brad smiled then depressed the mic button. "Tried giving some of the folk here whole blood from a recovered patient. Those with partial European ancestry recovered in less then ten hours. No effect on more or less full Asian test subjects. I can't figure that one. Over."

The doctor's voice issued from the speaker.

"Bradly, that was rather poor procedure. Still, it is hopeful. I am isolating the plasma and preparing a serum. I have hopes of making a vaccination that should be at least partially effective.

"I think I may understand why your serum did not work on the full Asians. The viruses were designed so they do not show up well against Asian MHC antigens. In simple terms, the antibodies can't 'see' the virus. I have doubts that a simple vaccine can be made that would do these people any good.

"The serum I am making should be ready tomorrow, or the next day. Over."

"Reinventing the wheel. Good work, Brad. Over," remarked Eddie.

"I just wish we knew what our ancestors knew about this. Over."

"Unfortunately the data searches have found nothing new. All that research is gone, along with the diseases it was meant to combat. Over," said Dr. Frankel.

Brad sat up with a gasp. "This bug survived. Not all records were destroyed. The base, it was decommissioned in twenty-thirty-nine. Over."

"Yes. You are right. The research they were doing could be

invaluable. You must download those records to me immediately. Over," replied the doctor. Before Brad could speak, Eddie intruded.

"Hate to piddle on your parade, but by now those hard drives will be degraded. Not to mention the fact that base is built to run on A.C. Your inverter couldn't handle more than a computer or two. Over."

"Shorting! Wait a moment... Back-ups. They must have done back-ups and archives. Bear with me, Eddie. Perma-burn CD archives were standard for sensitive material back then. If I can find them, we can probably get to within a few months of where their research was. Over."

"If you can find them. You'd still have to load them and sort the data. That could take years, with only one or two computers working on it. Over."

"How about a whole facility's mainframe? The base's fuel cell generators are still there and there's fuel. Over."

"Do you think you can get a generator going? They are old. Over."

"The inverter and transformer may pose a problem, but if they burn out after an hour or two, it may be enough. I have to try. Now that we have a name for this bug, a global search command should find its particulars. I can download them to cube and get the Doc up to speed. Over."

"Go to it, Brad, and Gods bless. Over."

"I need some things from you. If you could find me a copy of the base's blueprints, it will speed this up. I also need extra air tanks for the suits and a high-pressure compressor. One of the portable models that scuba divers use should do it. Over."

"Tanks are a go, but I don't know about the compressor. Over," said Eddie.

"How does the Doc keep his suits tanks charged? Over."

"I regret to inform you that the compressor in my lab is built-in. We will simply have to send you full tanks. Over."

"Great. Get all you have to the seven checkpoint. Ingram and I will be by to pick them up. Over and out."

"You got it. Over and out."

Brad leaned back on his seat, working through the things he

would need. Minutes later Ingram appeared from down the road driving a wagon full of water buckets. One of Brad's horses was pulling it.

Brad left his van and moved to intercept him.

"What they say, Tinker?" asked Ingram.

"They think they'll have a partially effective serum by tomorrow." Brad moved to the horse's head and stoked the big animal's black coat.

"She's a beauty. Wish I had one like her."

"They're a good team. I need your help. I have to go back into the base and try to get that generator on line."

"Tinker, you slipped a cog or something? You said yourself there could be thousands of different bugs in that place. So far only one's got out. I don't think we should be playing around."

"I know. Believe me, I know. But there may be a cure in their records. I need someone who can read to help me search."

"My Mum never figured she'd be gettin' me into this when she taught me to my letters. Right, I'm with you, but only 'cause no one should have to suffer liken my Mum did."

"Great. I'll tell Carla while you take in the water. Then we have to pick up a few things."

Hours later, Brad pored over blueprints while Ingram drove back from the seven pick-up point. A dozen air cylinders crowded the back of the wagon.

"You see what you're lookin' for?" Ingram tried to make sense of the blueprints.

"I'm working it out. Level three is off limits, obviously. No way I'm stepping into that abattoir. Level seven was their morgue, so the disks won't be there. I think the offices on level two will be our best bet."

"Why'd they put the offices on level two and a lab on level one?"

Brad shrugged. "PR. The first level lab was a showpiece. Probably didn't work on anything worse than a nasty cold. Meant local big wigs could go down into it and snap their suspenders. The real labs were from levels three to six."

"I hope you're right about level two. I get the creeps just thinking about going down in that place."

"It won't be so bad, if I can get the generator going."

Ingram reined the horses to a stop by the field containing the facility. A tent now stood by the entrance, and Wendell sat by a small fire in front of it.

"He's still at it." Brad sounded surprised.

"Good thing, too. Since word got out 'bout this place, three folks with more greed than brains tried to get in. Wendell and a buddy of mine have been spelling each other on guard."

"People are crazy. Why would anyone want to go down there knowing about the plague?"

Ingram snorted. "You're a Bright Lander all right. Each one of those video units is worth a year's wages out here."

"Sorry, easy to forget a thing like that." Climbing from the wagon, Brad began hauling the air cylinders to the facility's entrance.

"Wendell. Glad to see you're on the job," greeted Brad.

"Tinker. Folk tell me you got a cure as you're only given to those as 'ill pay. Some say you're letting any who won't die. Like my Yacky." Wendell eyed Brad suspiciously.

"That's crap!" snapped Brad, his face reddening.

"Told you, Wendy. This here tinker's a good one. Some live 'cause they have a Mum or Dad who was white as snow. Folks who are pure white can't catch this at all," explained Ingram.

"Truth, Tinker?" demanded Wendell.

"Truth."

Wendell gave a decisive nod and helped Brad lower the cylinder to the ground.

"You going back in?" Wendell looked fearfully at the facility's entrance.

"I have to try and find out what they knew about the sickness. Try and find a cure." Brad started laying out his contagion suit.

Wendell stared at the tinker's obviously Caucasian appearance.

"You're a good one, Tinker. Sorry 'bout what I said."

Brad nodded. "Rumours are like poison. It's better to bring it up than let it lie."

Oscar sat on the edge of a cot in a small upstairs room of the inn staring out the window at the impromptu clinic.

“Feeling a bit better since your bath?” Mark spoke with a forced heartiness.

“I don’t stink.” Oscar turned to face Mark. “Do you trust the Novo Gaians?”

Mark pursed his lips. “Now that’s a tricky one. I’m about trusting Brad. The rest of ‘em. Well, folk is folk. Look at some of the stunts our town council’s pulled. I figure Novo Gaia’s about the same. Good and bad. Brad ain’t done us wrong on this plague, if that’s what you’re getting at.”

Oscar sighed. “Hard to know who to trust sometimes. Brad was asking after our tank.”

“I always said we should burry that thing deep and leave it alone. It’s blooming dangerous, and we don’t know what we’re doing with it.”

“So you don’t think we should give it to the Novo Gaians?”

“We could, they’d probably pay a handsome mark for it, but I don’t be liking war. Bury the old killing machines deep and forget ‘em, that’s what I say. Like this here bug. Folks built it. Things like that should just stay buried in the past where they belong.”

Oscar nodded and turned back to the window. “You ever wonder if anything you did mattered? If you made a difference? Counted?”

“Sure-in everyone wonders about that sooner or later.” Mark patted the other man’s shoulder.

“How’d you get through it?”

Mark smiled. “Me Rosey. She keeps me sticking around to see the type of woman she’ll become.”

Oscar berried his face in his hands and sobs shook his chest.

Chapter Thirty-two

Priorities

DAN TUGGED AT the fake beard, pulling a bit more of it off his face. His skin, where the beard had separated, was rough and red from the glue. He'd changed into his regular travelling clothes and retrieved his pack.

"Bloody disguise! Odin never had these problems." Kneeling at the roadside he examined a faint trail leading into a wheat field reclaimed from the urban sprawl.

"Looking for something?" demanded a voice from behind the hedge flanking the road.

Dan stood and found himself staring down the barrel of a shotgun. "Steady on. I don't mean no harm."

"I'll judge that, Candler, and it seems the old-timer as well."

Dan's focus shifted from the gun to the man holding it.

"Tex. I... Look, let me explain."

"Nice bit of work you did on Ward's boys."

Tex lowered his gun barrel until it pointed to the ground.

"Not that I'm complaining but..."

"I know right from wrong. Grew up in the Timmins province of Novo Gaia. Got caught doing a B and E, and was banished for a five-year stretch about a dozen years back. Learned my lesson, but never chose to go home. Got a wife and kids in the Dark. Tagged along with Ward to keep an eye on him. Glad you stepped in before I had to. I wouldn't have been as gentle."

"I was none too gentle. Ward's dead." Dan paused, only then noticing the bloodstained shirt wrapped around the smaller man's leg. Tex propped himself up with an impromptu cane. "What happened?"

"Caught up with Horner. Bastard's an eel. He shot Reid dead, caught me in the leg, and Marco ran off. When I heard you coming, I figured it was him coming to finish the job. I hid."

"Good man. How far behind him do you figure I am?"

"Close, I know that much."

"How bad are you?"

"Figure I'm for it. Bandages hide it, but I'm bleeding like no one's business. Who you figure Horner really is?" Tex carefully lowered himself to the ground.

"Gridtown spy. Tinker spotted him when he passed through. With all that's happened, I figure he got the right of it." Dan rushed to help the smaller man.

"You're gonna get him then. Tell Colleen, my wife, I love her."

"I can't leave you like this, Tex, not with a wife and kids waiting on you back home. Sides, there'll be other days for Horner."

"What you gonna do; take me home so I can die in my bed? Ain't no way I'm gonna live in the Dark with a wound like this."

"They're closing in the quarantine. The militia has a doctor with them."

"Shit. If I'm not a lucky son of a bitch. Thanks. I'm looking forward to seeing forty."

Kneeling in front of Tex, Dan hoisted him onto his back. The small man groaned with pain. Dan started walking toward Arkell.

Half an hour later Dan strode up to a well-maintained, twenty-second-century house and pounded on the door. A slender, red-haired woman glanced through the door's window and wrenched it open.

"Tex! What have they done to you?" demanded the woman.

"Mam, we should get him to bed." Dan was sweating and his legs felt wobbly under the load.

"You're the candler. What did you do to him?!" The woman's hands bunched into fists and her face went red.

"He saved me, Colly. He found me and brought me home." Tex rolled his head so he could look at his wife.

"He's not as light as he looks," remarked Dan.

"What? Oh, this way." Colly led Dan into a clean, if battered, living room. There was a couch draped in homespun cloth that Dan lowered Tex onto. Rising, his eyes automatically fell to the woman. Her hair was pulled back and tied into a bun, while her gaunt body and bony face gave her an awkward, bird-like quality.

Lovely green eyes. I wonder what she'd be like? thought Dan, who then turned his attention back to Tex.

"Cold," said Tex.

"I'll get a blanket," offered Colly. The homespun fabric of her dress nearly swept the floor as she left the room.

"Where, doctor?" breathed Tex.

"They'll be here in the morning. We have to keep you going 'till then."

"Thirsty."

"Hang on, Tex. Just one night. Hang on."

Tex's wife returned with the blankets.

"What happened?" she demanded, as soon as her husband was covered.

"Horner shot him and left him for dead."

"What can we do?" Colly wrung her hands.

"We have to keep him alive until morning. The Novo Gaians are closing in the quarantine. Their doctor can look after him."

Dismay filled her face. "But he. I mean, well..."

"He was banished for a crime, but he served his sentence. He could have gone back years ago. They'll treat him."

Colly knelt by her husband and took his hand in hers, kissing it. "Don't you be leaving me!"

Dan slipped from the house into the twilight and pulled his radio from his pack.

"Corporal Timothy to base, come in base. Over."

"We read you, Corporal. Over."

"Tell the Major I've a wounded man here who needs help. Ask him to close in the quarantine now. Over."

A few minutes passed before Eddie's voice issued from the speaker.

"Major Baily to Corporal Timothy. Over."

"Got you, major. Over."

"We can't close in until morning. Arkell's been enough trouble. I won't run the risk of an ambush in the dark. Over."

"I've a wounded man here. Says he's a Novo Gaian citizen. Over."

"Wish I could help you. I'll send a healer along at first light, and have the Doc set up for surgery, but I won't risk my troops on a night deployment. Over."

Dan gritted his teeth and counted to ten before depressing the talk button.

"I'll meet the healer on the road and guide her in. Over and out."

"Over and out," returned the Major's voice.

"Ain't that just a bit of loveliness." Dan re-entered the house and began collecting candles against the long night ahead.

Barb yawned as she listened to the truck's turbine whir to life. The first glimmers of false dawn were making themselves apparent. Opening the flap on her saddle bag, she reviewed its contents before mounting.

"Listen up," she snapped to the nine Novo Gaian militia standing by horses behind her. "The truck will follow us in. Our task is to establish base points where we can deploy our equipment. Once we're in place your sergeants will be in charge. I have a medical to deal with. The Watson Road team is to off-load your gear ASAP. Don't worry about set up until the rig has left. The Arkell road company will ride ahead of the truck to establish a presence. Team one is to set up on the banks of the Eramosa, where we blew out the bridge. Team two, take the corner of Arkell and Victoria. Stay clear of the locals until I can ascertain the town's mood.

"Reuben, Bob, you're to stay with the truck as guards. Any questions?"

The silence was deafening. Barb scanned the faces of the troop. They all showed a vague regret that she felt in her own breast.

You were right, Nick, she thought then said aloud, "Move out."

She pushed her horse to a slow trot and led her troops through the town. At first the truck kept pace with them, but as the roads got worse it began to fall behind. By the time they reached the barricade of piled rubble at the outskirts of Arkell, the truck was out of sight.

"'Alt! Who be youse?" demanded a wiry man dressed in a loose pair of jeans and a T-shirt sizes too big for him.

"They're all right. They're the ones I was telling you about." Dan appeared from behind the barricade. Frank rose to his feet beside the candler.

"What is this?" demanded Barb.

"I'm Corporal Daniel Timothy. I told the Major I'd meet you. This here is Frank, the closest thing this town has to a leader."

"The moron is Ritchie. Figured he could get back with me by helpin' out," observed Frank.

"We need to pass, and a truck is following us," explained Barb.

"We'll take the healer to Tex, and your troops can clear a way for your truck. Won't no one bother you now, or they'll answer to me," said Frank

"Is it safe?" Barb stared at Dan.

"Aye, safe enough. I got to the tavern last night and spread the word about Horner, our own little Gridtown spy. Folk came round right sharp after that."

"After I busted a head or two of the ones that were still for lynching the plague rat, Candler. Don't you forget that," interrupted Frank.

Dan grimaced. "How could I?"

"Fine. Troop, clear a way for the truck then continue. I'll see to the injured man," ordered Barb.

"She's the healer. Shit on a stick, worth getin' shot for a bit of that, aye, Candler?" observed Frank.

Dan looked to the sky then started toward Tex's house.

Barb looked up from her patient into Colly's eyes.

"If I'd been here sooner, it would have been better. The bullet missed the artery, or he'd be dead already."

Reaching into her saddle bag, Barb pulled out a bag of pink liquid and a tourniquet. Wrapping the tourniquet around Tex's arm, she waited for a vein to rise.

"Can you help him, lass?" Dan stood behind Colleen, gently holding her shoulders.

"I'm trying. He's lost a lot of blood. I'm going to start him on artificials with a coagulant mix."

"What?" Colly looked confused.

"This pink stuff is artificial blood, with a chemical added that helps blood clot." Barb pushed an I.V. needle into her patient's vein and hung the plastic bag. Releasing the tourniquet she set the flow to full

"Will he make it?" asked Dan.

"I think the femur got chipped, and he's lost a lot of muscle tissue. I'm sorry, his chances are maybe fifty-fifty. Even if he lives, he might lose the leg." Barb pulled the flap of a second saddle bag open.

"No! My poor Tex." Colly knelt by her husband and took his hand in her own.

"Corporal, help me get these on him." Barb held up what looked like a pair of bulky canvas trousers with velcro straps on the legs.

"And what in Odin's name are those?" Dan moved to her side.

"M.A.S.T. trousers. They squeeze the blood out of the legs so it can get pumped through the rest of the body." Barb broke the velcro seals on the pant legs and spread them out on the floor. "I need you to lift his buttocks off the couch, so I can get these under him."

Moving to Tex, Dan slipped his arm under the small of Tex's back and lifted. Barb spread the M.A.S.T. trousers then Dan lowered him into place. Minutes later she had finished sealing the velcro seams around Tex's legs.

"Good, now to blow them up." She produced a foot pump from her bag. Shortly she eased Colly to the side and took a blood pressure.

"Ninety over sixty, that's a damn sight better than sixty-five over twenty." She took his pulse. "Still fast, but it's getting firmer."

"He gonna make it?" Colly's voice was pleading.

"He's looking a lot better."

"Thank you." Colly took Tex's hand and kissed it as she stared into his pale face.

Barb joined Dan, who stood in the corner.

"I want that bastard Horner." Dan's voice was ice and his fists clenched.

"Heard he was trouble," remarked Barb.

"He caused all this."

"Let it go. He's long gone by now."

"Yeah, off to drink champagne with his Gridtown friends no doubt."

"Maybe, but stewing won't help." Barb touched his arm in a calming way.

Dan started at the touch and a smile came to his lips. His posture straightened and he took a steadying breath as his eyes traced over Beth's figure. "Aye. You're right. Intelligent and beautiful. With all that was about, I never did properly introduce myself. I'm Daniel Timothy, candler, soap maker extraordinaire." Catching Barb's hand, he swept it up and kissed it.

"Corporal Timothy," began Barb.

Dan interrupted her. "My friends call me Dan."

"I'm sure they do. Actually, you remind me of my father. He's about your age and worked as a wandering cooper in his youth. Maybe you've met him, Rupert Newicky."

Dan looked at her with a pained expression and released her hand. "Can't say as I've had the pleasure."

"And I doubt you ever will." Barb smirked.

Dan coughed into his hand, glanced about the room then spoke.

"What's the latest from Guelph? I took a bit of a shine to that tinker chap. I'd like to know how's he's doing."

Chapter Thirty-three

Darkness, Light, and a Spinning Disk

"Okay. I've ungucked the junction clips between the inverter and the fuel cell and put the connects back in place. How's it going on your end?" Brad pushed away from the generator. Filth crusted the hands of his suit.

"Finished hooking up the transformer," replied Ingram.

"Let's put the cover plates back and try it." When the last wing nut was tightened Brad looked around him. The flashlights gave the room a crypt-like appearance. He almost expected to see coffins on the tool shelves. His hand moved to scratch his nose but was stopped by the faceplate of his visor. His breathing caught at the reminder, but he forced his stomach to unclench.

"Okay, Tinker, I'm all set."

"Don't expect this to be pretty. Might not even work. Stand back."

Ingram stepped away from the generator as Brad opened the valve on the feed hose. The D.C. light came on. A second later he depressed the inverter's start button.

The transformer hummed and Brad released the button. A horrible screeching sound issued from the back of the inverter.

"What the fuck is that?" shouted Ingram.

Brad scrambled around to the back of the device. “Shit! It’s the cooling fan! Corrosion must have gotten into its armature sleeves!”

“We’re screwed!” yelled Ingram.

“Don’t give up so easily!” Brad searched the shelves, finding a can of spray lubricant he applied it to the screeching fan. The noise lessened but didn’t disappear.

“We did it,” bellowed Ingram.

“Yup,” agreed Brad. Then the start up light died, and the transformer silenced.

“Shit! What happened?”

“Let me think. We have fuel. I disconnected the feed pipe, so it’s drawing oxygen from the room. Exhaust. They must have buried the exhaust port. The pressure built up and stopped the fuel from passing through the plates.”

Moving to one side of the fuel cell, Brad undid the bolts on a pipe that led into the wall. A mix of hot water and steam shot into the room followed by the start up light flashing back to life.

“Try the inverter now.”

Ingram pressed the button. The transformer hummed as white clouds of steam billowed from the open exhaust port.

“Wattage!” Brad moved to a breaker box and started throwing switches. The overhead lights flickered and flashed. Of ten ceiling lights in the room, two came to life.

“Could be brighter,” observed Ingram.

“Better than I feared. Come on, let’s get to a terminal.”

Brad led the way to the computer sitting on the reception area’s desk and turned it on. The unit hummed, checked its resident memory then came up blank.

“What happened?” asked Ingram.

“System’s degraded. The whole thing’s blanked. We have to go down and find the perma-burn back-ups. How’s your air?”

“About a quarter tank.”

“We’ll swap tanks before we start.” Brad moved to the pressure cylinders they’d left in the lobby and grabbed a bottle of disinfectant that lay beside them.

“You sure that shit will kill whatever’s on the join?”

“This shit will melt the gasket after a couple of days.” Brad spritzed the join of the pressure cylinder and dropped the one he was wearing beside it. "Watch me and remember to hold your breath while you change over."

Brad closed the valve on the cylinder he was breathing from and disconnected the regulator. Spritzing the tank link clamp, he connected it to the fresh tank and opened the flow.

"Shit! That stuff stinks," he griped as soon as he inhaled.

"Will it hurt us?" Ingram stared at the replacement cylinders like a nest of snakes.

"In the time we'll be breathing it, maybe irritate our throats a bit."

"Okay. Here goes." Ingram pulled a tank to himself.

Brad watched Ingram change over his tank then they moved to the elevator.

"Will it work?" asked Ingram.

Brad pressed the call button, which lit up. A moment later the door slid open, revealing a large chamber.

"Yes." Brad paused staring into the elevator and remarked, "It's a nice big one, good!"

"I thought we might be shorted with no computer and all." Ingram led the way into the chamber.

"Must have been set to operate as a default. Probably a safety precaution." Brad hesitantly followed the younger man.

"Good thing it was." Ingram pressed the button for the second floor.

A moment later, the door opened, and Brad stared into bedlam. The floor was littered with broken glass and bits of metal. Occasionally data disks poked out of the rubble. The few operational fluorescent tubes cast a twilight over the scene. The walls were scrawled with graffiti and doors opened at about three meter intervals.

"Ground out!" Brad felt his heart sink.

"What'd they do to this place?" Ingram scanned the destruction.

"They told us in the tape, remember? We have moved all organic materials to level three. They ransacked the other levels to remove anything that might have hosted the bugs. That's not the worst of it though. Look there." Turning on his flashlight, Brad directed the beam to a furry body.

"A dead rat. So?" Ingram shrugged.

"This base was sealed. If rats have gotten in..."

"Zoroaster, protect us!"

"We need the records from this place, not just for today but for what might come later." Brad stepped gingerly into the hall and stared down at the rat. It lay with its back arched, and blood crusted its fur in several places.

"What killed it?" Ingram nudged the rat with the toe of his boot.

"I'd rather not find out. Start bringing down the air tanks. I'll try to get the computer up and running."

"Right." Ingram returned to the elevator.

Brad moved to the closest door and peered into a cluttered office. The overhead lights were dead, but a lamp with a naked incandescent bulb sat on the table. He turned it on, filling the room with dim light. A computer sat on the desk against the wall, with a vinyl and chrome office chair in front of it.

Brad activated the system. The wall screen flickered and fought its way to life.

"Okay, Brad, keep busy, don't think about small offices," he muttered to himself. "Big open sky. The park near grandad's place. Yeah, that's the ticket."

Pulling a CD from the pouch he'd worn over his shoulder, he inserted it in the machine. A press of a button later the system scanned the disk then loaded the operating system it contained. The computer beeped as it contacted the mainframe passing on the data; then the screen lit up with menu options.

"Good, now all I have to do is find the right disk to boot." Brad took the first disk he saw from the pile on the desk. It was out of its container and had no discernible label. Inserting it into the machine, he found that the data was degraded. Grabbing another disk he tried it. This one was a perma-burn. He started loading files.

Ingram laid another stack of disks on the table and said, "I need a fresh air tank."

Brad glanced at his pressure gauge. "Me too. I want to try to get a couple more systems running. Speed this up."

"We can't keep up with the four you have running as it is."

"You're probably right."

"Find anything?"

"There's enough shit here to keep a data search team happy for years, but nothing on our bug so far. I have the computer scanning for A.D.F. as it goes along. I've..."

The computer chirped. Brad turned his full attention to the screen.

'A.D.F.' headed a set of seven files. Brad loaded the first file and scanned the index. "Contagion vectors, vaccine, treatment. It's all here. Gods of my fathers, it's all here!"

"Take the disk, and let's get out of here," said Ingram.

Brad inserted a data cube and marked the files for download. A minute later he placed the cube in his pouch and said, "Let's go." Reaching the elevator, he pressed the call button.

"Insert pass card and enter security code," spoke an inflectionless, female voice.

"What the fuck?" demanded Ingram.

Brad pressed the button again.

"Insert pass card and enter security code," repeated the voice.

"No, damn it! No! We're trapped. One of those disks must have been the security protocols. We're locked in."

"Tinker, do something."

"I- I- I," Brad started glancing around the hallway. "We're locked in. There's no way out. We're trapped. We can't get out. We're—"

"*Tinker*, Brad! Pull yourself together." Ingram grabbed Brad by the shoulders and shook him.

"I'm... I'm." Brad took a deep breath. "I'm all right. Well not all right. It's just being trapped in a small space with no way out and." Brad's voice held a panicked edge and his body trembled.

"*Brad... Tinker.*" Ingram shook Brad once more.

The combination of the title and the shaking pierced Brad's growing panic.

"Ptah and Hephaestus! You're right. You're right. I need to think. It's computer driven."

"I think we should start new air tanks while you figure this out."

"Right." Brad took another deep breath. "Ingram, thanks. Look when we get out of here."

"I hate spiders. Won't either of us go spreading it around, okay."

Minutes later Brad scanned the wall around the call button, for the first time noticing the slot and keypad above it.

"We have to find a card that will fit into that," he said, jabbing a trembling finger toward the slot.

"Great just great." Ingram began rummaging through the junk in the hallway. Brad raced back to the functioning computer and tried to access the programs in the mainframe.

'Enter password for access to main data storage,' appeared on the screen.

"Ptah help me. It's been a long time since the academy hacking 101," he muttered and typed in 'God.'

'Non-valid password. Try again or quit system,' appeared on the screen.

'King,' typed Brad.

'Non-valid password. Try again or quit system. Security has been informed of multiple failure.'

"I found a card," said Ingram from the doorway.

"Good. Let's try it." Brad stood and took the card. "Must have belonged to a department director. It's labelled Master Card."

Brad pressed the elevator button and inserted the card.

"Invalid card. Invalid card. Security alert. Security alert. Security personnel to level two for security protocols violation."

"Lot of good that did us," snapped Ingram.

"Ingram, I don't need to be reminded of the obvious right now. Anyway, we're not beat yet." Brad fought to keep a waver from his voice.

Returning to the computer he pulled a data cube labelled 'hacker's friend' from his pouch and loaded it into the operating system.

"What the hell is that?" Ingram walked up and stared into the computer screen.

"Standard issue. It's a computer busting kit. Every tinker

carries one. Tell it what you want to do and it does it."

"How's that work?"

"The assumption is anything a tinker comes across is pre-collapse, so it contains the best, current ice-cutter programs."

"It cuts ice?"

"That's what computer types call breaking security. Don't ask me why. I took enough computer operation to get by and no more."

"That's great, just great. What do you do during the winter, play tiddlywinks?" Ingram's voice was shrill.

"I finished my Masters in engineering last winter. That answer your question?" The screen blinked several times as the system fought against the program. Sound blared from speakers in the room. Brad clamped his hands against the sides of his helmet.

"Level one security protocols. Computer integrity has been breached," boomed a voice over the ear-splitting background whine. Clouds of white gas spewed out of nozzles on the floor.

Gritting his teeth, Brad grabbed a stapler from the junk on the desk and drove it into the wall speaker. It sparked and the volume diminished. Slamming closed the door reduced the whine to a tolerable level.

"My ears are bleeding," bellowed Ingram.

"Ultrasonics. If it wasn't for our suits baffling the noise, we'd be unconscious!"

"What's this friggen fog?"

"Knockout gas. I don't know what they were working on here, but their security is nuts!"

"Do something!"

Turning to the computer, Brad popped his cube and purged the program. The noise ceased.

"Computer integrity restored," spoke the voice.

"We better start new air tanks while I try and figure a way out of this."

"We're screwed, aren't we?"

Brad bit down on his own fear and moved to the mist-shrouded silhouette across the room. He placed his faceplate against Ingram's, so he could see the younger man's face. "I haven't found a damn cure just to lie here and die! Ingram, you have to stay with me here because I don't trust myself. The room is so small, and—"

Ingram pulled himself together then said, "No, don't go there, Tinker. You be the brain. I'll keep it together. Now get us out of here."

Brad nodded then opening the door to the hall stumbled through the smoke and felt something catch on his leg. "Shit! Shine your flashlight on my calf."

Ingram obeyed. Brad stared at where a jagged piece of metal had split the surface layer of the suit. Closing his eyes, he tried to still the trembling in his limbs.

"Tinker?"

"It's okay. I only split the outer layer. Pass me the disinfectant and repair tape."

Brad spritzed then taped the split. Feeling like a blind man he started toward the elevator. Minutes later he bumped against the air cylinders piled on the floor.

"So now what? Do we just wait here until we run out of air?" asked Ingram, after they had switched to new tanks.

"No, we try and force the elevator doors, pop the maintenance hatch, and climb up the shaft."

"Tinker, I'll melt first. It's getting hot in here."

"It's these damn suits, that's all." Brad pulled a steel table leg from the rubble on the floor and moved to the elevator.

"At least the smoke is clearing."

"Ventilation system. It's spreading it throughout the facility." Brad jammed the chair leg into place and pulled against it. The door parted slightly. "Help me."

Ingram added his muscle to the bar, and the door pushed further into the wall.

"Security breach. Initiating protocol A 5."

Brad jerked as the shock passed through his gloves and up his arms. Ingram gasped and stiffened. Brad's spasms tore him away from the bar, throwing him against the wall. He slipped to the floor. The elevator doors slammed shut. The current died. Ingram crumpled into a heap.

Chapter Thirty-four

Law

"That's enough!" shouted Nick from the tabletop in front of the inn. Meb and John stood to either side of him. The prisoners knelt in the street, chained hand and foot. The rest of the townsfolk formed a tightly packed mob, blocking either end of the street, held in check by a mix of Nick's deputies and off-duty militia. Eddie stood beside the table watching the crowd.

"Let 'em go," screamed a voice from the crowd.

"Kill the lot of 'em," screamed another.

"Quiet!" bellowed Nick. All fell silent.

"We are faced with a problem," opened Meb. She was dressed in a black dress.

"Youse was gonna let these tree 'uggers gives us all plague," barked Greg Thomson, from where he knelt in the street.

"That is ridiculous," countered John.

"That's not the charge anyway. These folk are accused of ignoring a ratified council decision. They also killed Albert Paterson and Francine DeAngilo, the lass from the Novo Gaian militia," spoke Nick.

"Do you deny this?" demanded Meb.

"Youse got no right actin' so 'igh and mighty. Youse sold out to 'em tree 'uggin' bastards," snarled a burly unkept man who pulled futilely against his chains.

"Tell 'em, Borus," called a voice from the crowd.

"Sold out? Is there plague here? Haven't the Novo Gaians done fair by us and kept the plague from spreadin' out of Guelph? Is there a merchant or tradesman who doesn't like the marks they've been throwin' around?" asked John. A general murmur of agreement went through the crowd.

"Youse waits. They'll make us another Argyle. Some of their folk died. We's all knows what that means!" snarled Borus.

"Tells 'em little bro," added Greg.

The crowd fell silent; all eyes turned to Eddie.

"We didn't start the killing. We won't continue it. The town of Eden Mills claims the right to punish the offenders. We support the council's decision," hollered Eddie.

"'e lies," snapped Greg. Eddie looked at the chained man with contempt.

"There is a question to be answered. Do you deny the charges?" demanded Meb.

"Why's shouldn't we?" called a voice from the back of the prisoners.

"We'll give you a break. Tell us who threw the grenade, and those who led this 'rebellion' and you'll only spend a couple weeks in the stocks," stated Nick.

Eddie glanced at the three on the pedestal, his mouth falling open in shock. He was about to speak when he felt the eyes of the townsfolk on him and stopped himself.

The prisoners glanced warily amongst themselves.

"They tryin' to split us up. Don't lets 'em," called Borus.

"Borus's right. They's all be in with 'em sun 'umpers," called Greg.

"I was with 'em. It was Borus as threw the grenade. Seen it with me own eyes, I did," spoke a pale, slender man in the middle of the group.

Nick nodded to a deputy, who escorted the man to the stocks set up along the roadside.

"Was all Thomson's idea. 'e told us as 'em tree 'uggers was after killin' us, so they could steal our land," complained another voice. Over the next five minutes all but five of the prisoners confessed, naming Greg and Borus as the ringleaders.

"Youse got no right. They's lyin'. I's ain't done nothin'," spat Greg toward the table where the council stood.

"I's a Actonite. Youse can't touch me," growled Boris.

The other three in the street glared belligerently at the town leaders.

"We have every right. The townsfolk voted us in and agreed with our decision. You ignored that," observed Nick.

"String 'em up. They killed me Albert," hollered a plump, dark-haired woman with a baby in her arms. She pushed to the front of the crowd and glared at the men in the street. Tears streaked her cheeks. "Weren't even enough left of 'im to bury proper," she added; then she fell back into the arms of a woman who held her while she wept.

"No, Tinker, youse can'ts kill me Greg," wailed Emily Thomson. She sat on a wooden stool, bundled in blankets. The healing bruises on her face stood in contrast to her pale skin.

"The council will discuss this and return shortly," said Meb. She stepped from the table and entered the inn. John and Nick followed. Eddie brought up the rear.

"What in a shorted circuit are you thinking of? Those bastards killed one of my people, and all you give them is two weeks in the stocks," snapped Eddie, when the door closed behind him.

"Major, you agreed to let us handle this. We will. We now know who actually instigated the rebellion, and who threw the bomb. The rest doesn't matter. Now you are welcome to stay, but don't interfere again," snapped Meb. Fire crackled in her eyes. Eddie looked to John.

"This is for Eden Mills to deal with. We may be tinker friendly, and we did welcome you here, but there are limits. Our own folk have died. Maybe, probably, with the plague it would have been worse. We don't deny that, but don't forget, you're a guest here!" John sat heavily into a chair at one of the common-room's tables.

"He's right. Our town has suffered more from this than you know. Albert is dead, and while your woman died, he's our main concern," stated Nick.

Eddie fell into a chair at the table and stared from face to face.

"We should decide on Borus first. What are we going to do with him? He is from Acton," said John.

"Don't matter. He did his crime here. We punish him here. I say string him up," said Nick.

"That won't bring back Albert. Besides, if we start killing the rebels for their attack, don't we have to kill the deputies and militia for the rebels they killed?" Meb drummed her fingers on the table.

Eddie gasped but bit down hard on his words. Three sets of hostile eyes turned to him.

"Now maybe you see. It's not just the folk the rebels killed to us. The rebels were our townsfolk too. We lost all those you killed and all they killed," explained Meb, her features softening.

"I don't want any more death from this," added John.

Eddie stared at the table as the others discussed what to do with Borus. After a long time he tentatively raised his hand.

"Yes?" Meb's voice was flat.

"I have an offer for you. I can have him transported to and detained in the C Zone."

"The C Zone. That's worse than a death sentence!" exclaimed John with a shudder.

"All I've heard is rumours 'bout that place. Tell me true, what's it like?" Nick shifted forward in his chair.

"It's the coastal region of Lake Ontario. Our ancestors polluted it so badly it's pure poison. When the nuclear plants went up, they added radiation to the mix. You can live there for years, if you don't eat anything grown there, or drink the water. Novo Gaia and the Gridtowns both use it as a kind of prison. We put special collars on our worst violent offenders. If they get farther than ten kilometres from the lake, the collars buzz; at twelve they explode. Borus would be right at home with his own kind of people."

"Eddie, it's called the C Zone because if you go there you die of cancer," observed Meb.

"Not necessarily. We sell the convicts food and clean water in exchange for them salvaging the old cities and growing non-edible crops. A man can build a life for himself there, but he can never leave. The criminals there are legally dead."

"I'd rather do that then hang him," said Nick.

"We can't. It's just a slow death sentence. You know Borus's type. He'll drink the water and eat whatever he finds," objected Meb. She drummed her fingers on the tabletop.

"What else can we do, Meb? You won't go for hanging, and he needs more than a few weeks in the stocks for what he did." Nick's voice held strained tolerance.

"I suppose you want to send Greg there as well?" Meb looked at Eddie.

"It's your decision. I'm just offering the services of the Novo Gaian justice department. If you're asking me, I'd be willing to let Greg Thomson go with a black T and a promise from the local merchants that they won't trade with him."

"That's soft, Tinker," remarked John.

"Greg's as good as dead. Skin cancer's a miserable way to go. Brad spotted it and told me," explained Meb.

"They'll say we're playing favourites, being soft on our own people. I say whatever we give those who didn't 'fess up we give Greg as well," observed Nick.

"I agree, and I have something to add as well," said Meb, a cruel gleam in her eye.

"About Borus, I think we should C Zone him," said Nick.

"And me," agreed John.

"I reserve judgement," remarked Meb.

"Meb," started Eddie.

John raised his hand, saying, "By majority decision the motion is carried."

Eddie sighed.

"That leaves the three who wouldn't talk, and Meb's addition."

"Twenty lashes in public, three weeks in the stocks, when they can take it; then they must see to Albert's widow and child's needs for the rest of their days," said Nick.

"Agreed," spoke John.

"Yes," added Meb.

"Satisfied, Major?" demanded Nick.

"What I think doesn't matter, but it seems just enough for some. Now Meb, what do you have in mind for Greg?"

Minutes later, the three councillors and Eddie rose from the table and stepped outside. One of Eddie's troops passed him a bottle of black fluid and his laser scalpel. The crowd had stayed to watch the show. Milly stood at a table in front of the inn's far entrance, selling pastries and cider, while several small children played throwing pebbles at the people in the stocks. The unjudged prisoners had been pushed close to the base of the stand.

"Gonna be a hangin'," cried a voice from the crowd.

"Whoop 'em first," called another.

"Let 'em go, they's townsfolk, these outsiders ain't got no claim," called yet another.

"They came for a show," said John sadly.

"Folk is folk, most of those as rebelled weren't too popular." Nick then called for silence.

The crowd slowly grew still as the party-like atmosphere slowed in preparation for the grand finale.

"Borus Thomson, you have been judged guilty of murder," spoke John. A cheer went up from the crowd.

"The Novo Gaians have intervened on your behalf, offering an alternative to hanging. You will be banished to the C Zone for the rest of your life."

The collective gasp of the crowd nearly drowned out Borus's roar. He leapt to his feet, straining against the shackles. A gesture from Nick brought two of his deputies forward, and the man was hauled off.

"Make 'em dance on a rope. I ain't missed a day's plantin' to watch 'im carted off," called a voice from the crowd.

"We better give them something before this gets out of hand," whispered John to Nick.

"Set up the whipping posts. For the raiders who wouldn't help set things to rights, twenty lashes, three weeks in the stocks and the care of Mrs. Paterson and her child," Nick called to the crowd. The only woman not to confess was stripped to the waist and tied to the hitching frame in front of the inn. A large bullwhip was brought from the general store.

An hour later the last of the whippings were done and the convicts carried away by friends and relatives.

"Now, Greg Thomson, you who organized this raid must face

our judgment," said Meb.

"He's gonna swing," came the cry from the festive crowd.

"Youse got no right. I's done what 'ad to be done," snarled Greg.

"You accomplished nothing except killing innocent people," countered Meb.

"Youse was sellin' out to 'em tree 'umpers."

"If you mean we accepted their protection and good faith, yes we did. The fact that you will not hang is proof we haven't sold out," remarked John.

Nick stepped from the table, grabbed Greg's head and forced it around so the crowd could see his brow.

Eddie stepped up and activated his laser scalpel, setting the beam to its broadest.

"Burn 'im, Tinker. Burn 'im good," screamed a voice from the crowd. A chant spread through the populace. "T, T, T, T."

Greg's scream split the air as Eddie's laser scorched the T into his brow. A cheer rose. Eddie poured fluid from a bottle into his hand and rubbed it into the wound, staining it permanently black, and drawing another agonized screech from Greg. Thomson fell to his knees whimpering.

"It is the council's decision that all merchants in this town will respect the Black T. None will trade with Greg Thomson in any way. As well, one week from today, he will present himself for twenty lashes. A week after that he will stand three weeks in the stocks. Meb," said John.

Meb stepped from the dais. "We of the council feel that Black Ting isn't enough for your crimes. So we are adding this. All you own is taken from you: your cattle, your house, your lands and all other properties. This will extend to the very clothes on your back. You own nothing and may own nothing."

A gasp rose from the crowd; then Meb continued.

"All these items are now the sole property of Emily Thomson. She may give you access at her whim."

"And to see this is so, I'll be dropping by regular like. If I see one new bruise on Emily, you're out of town dressed in sap and feathers and singing soprano!" added Nick.

"Youse can'ts. 'ats me daddy's farm," gasped Greg.

“The council has spoken. Do any in the town challenge our decision?” demanded John.

“I’s wants to see a rope dance,” called a voice from the crowd.

“Hasn’t there been enough death?” Meb walked back into the tavern. The other councillors and Eddie followed her as the crowd broke into small groups and muttered about the decision.

Chapter Thirty-five

Shafted

"Brreep, brreep, brreep." The sound smashed into Brad's throbbing head like a sledgehammer.

"What in Ptah's name was I drinking?" he muttered then opened his eyes. A dim light shone from an emergency unit over the elevator door, leaving the rest of the hall in darkness.

"Brreep, brreep, brreep," continued the noise. Brad reached to rub his eyes, but his hand struck his faceplate.

"Oh shit!" He swallowed in a dry throat then noticed that his stomach was settled. "Just like the scuba mask, do something often enough, you get used to it. Either that or I just feel too bloody wretched to be bothered being afraid." He tried to grasp the gauge on his tank and heard a cracking sound as pain shot through his hands.

"What?" Shuffling into the light, he stared at the palms of his suit. The rubber had melted and hardened.

"Brreep, Brreep, Brreep," continued the sound.

"I know, damn it. I'm low on air. What to do about it?"

A second beeping started below the source of the light.

"Ingram," called Brad.

"Tinker. Lucky I'm a volunteer. You couldn't pay me enough

to do this."

"How are your hands?"

"They're shorted. What the fuck was that?"

"Security. I had no idea this place was such a fortress, or I'd never have gotten us into this."

"That beeping. I'm almost out of air. You have to change my tank. I can't move my fingers!" Panic tinged Ingram's voice.

"Our gloves are fused. We have to break them open."

"The bugs. They'll get in. We'll die!"

"We need the repair tape."

Brad moved to Ingram's side. With arms still spasming from aftershocks, he pushed back the flap of the younger man's bag. Clamping the repair tape between both hands, he lifted it free.

"Now what? I don't have fingers to get its end," demanded Ingram.

"Find a piece of metal, anything with a thin edge, that you can hold. We'll try and get it under the tape."

"How much time do we have?" Ingram began a blurry-eyed search.

"The beeper sounds at thirty-five kilograms per centimetre. We have a few minutes."

"Found it." Ingram grasped a long sliver of glass between his ruined gloves and held it up. Brad dragged the tape against the glass. On the third attempt the end of the roll bunched up and stuck to the shard.

"Wrap your glove in tape," ordered Brad.

Ingram pushed the palm of his glove up under the roll and began looping the tape crudely around it.

"Good. Now me." Brad braced the roll between his heels and wrapped the glove of his right hand. In less than a minute he pulled hard, sending a ribbon of pain shooting up his arm and snapping the tape.

"Now what? I still can't move my hand," demanded Ingram.

"Now the hard part." Brad slammed the palm of his hand down on a clear section of floor, welcoming the pain, which swept away the last dregs of his fear. He repeated the action. Under the tape the rubber cracked and grated against the burnt skin beneath. Blinking away tears he watched as the crude mitten of tape moved with his fingers.

"Shit. Tinker, I can't."

Brad took a shuddering breath and spoke. "You must, or we're dead."

Grabbing the tape, Brad quickly wrapped his other hand and repeated the procedure. Through the pain he was vaguely aware of Ingram's screams and the ever-present "Brreep, brreep, brreep."

Brad felt his breathing catch. Scrambling in the dim light, he pulled a cylinder to his side and spritzed its connector. The burning in his lungs added to his other agonies as he fumbled with the release on his regulator. In seconds the join was made, and he cracked the valve. Air, barring the acrid disinfectant stench, flooded into his suit. He slumped against the wall.

He became aware of Ingram's warning beep still echoing through the corridor.

"Damn it man, change your tank." Brad moved to the side of the weeping figure.

"Hurts!"

"I know, but move." Brad dragged over a tank and spritzed it with disinfectant.

Ingram struggled gingerly with his valve. Soon the new cylinder was in place.

"This is bad, Tinker."

"Sorry I got you into this."

"Wasn't no gun at my head. Wish we had more light. What happened to the overheads?"

"The generator must have clapped out. Probably the cooling fan seized and the inverter overheated. I'm just glad it ran long enough to recharge the batteries on the emergency lights."

"Too bad it ran long enough to fry us." Ingram grinned.

"You're a genius!" Brad stumbled to his feet.

"Mind telling me why?"

"The generator's dead. No juice, no computer; no computer, no security system."

"No juice, no elevator." Ingram sounded resolved.

"We can pry open the doors now."

"Tinker, in the shape we're in?"

"Got a better idea? We have two tanks left, after that."

"Got you." Ingram rose shakily and helped Brad jam a pry into the elevator's doors. Using their hands was agony, but with a heavy pull they forced the outer doors into the wall.

"One more set and we're in." Brad leaned trembling and spasming against the wall. He began breathing deeply, activating a biofeedback block to the worst of his pain.

When his shaking eased, he pressed the pry into the elevator's inner doors. Ingram joined him and they pulled. The door held for a moment then popped open.

"Now what?" breathed Ingram, as he inspected the palms of his gloves. The repair tape was showing signs of fraying.

"We have to pop the emergency panel on the elevator's ceiling and climb to the upper floor."

"Great! I can barely loop my fingers. How am I supposed to climb?"

"Once we have the panel open, we'll take a break and re-wrap our gloves." Brad activated his flashlight and began searching the rubble in the hall. He returned minutes later with a long shaft of metal with a hooked end. "Here goes."

Clumsy in the bulky, damaged gloves, he swung the metal shaft, hooking the ornamental grill on the elevator's ceiling. He jerked downward. The grill gave way with the sound of cracking plastic, crashing onto his back.

"Tinker?" asked Ingram.

"Remind me to write a testimonial about these damn suits." Brad shuffled off the debris. He stumbled and leaned heavily against the wall.

"You okay?"

"Dizzy. I'll be all right." Brad stared at the palm of his glove. Nothing showed through the tape. Lifting his hand above his shoulder, he felt a warm wetness trickle along his arm. *At least I know the seal's good*, he thought.

"You better sit down."

"In a moment. Give me a hand with this."

Ingram moved to Brad's side, and together they pushed against a hatch in the ceiling. It flopped up and over, landing with a dull 'bong' on the roof above them.

"I can see the doors. They're only about two metres up," said

Ingram, shining his flashlight through the hatch.

"Good." Brad half-stumbled, half-shuffled from the elevator and slumped onto a clear section of floor. Clumsily he checked his pressure gauge.

"About half a tank," remarked Ingram, as he sat.

"Wish these things had a drinking spout. I'm parched."

"I wish they had a fly. I've needed to go for an hour."

"I haven't," Brad said wryly.

Ingram stared at Brad and started to laugh. When his chuckles subsided, he spoke. "The wonderful tinker myth. Wonder what would happen if it got around you wet yourself?"

"If it's good enough for the first American in space, it's good enough for me."

"Who?"

"I'll fill you in later. We need to get something to stand on, so we can get through the hole. Then we have to re-wrap our gloves."

"I saw a stepladder while I was searching for disks. I'll fetch it."

Brad nodded. Whether he slept or not, he wasn't sure, but all too soon, he heard the persistent beep of his air alert. Glancing at the elevator, he saw the stepladder below the hatch. Ingram sat beside him resting his wrists on his knees.

"Now or never." Brad reached for his last full air cylinder.

Ingram nodded and followed the tinker's example.

As soon as the tanks were changed and the gloves re-wrapped Brad scrambled up the stepladder onto the elevator's roof. He turned to help Ingram as he climbed through the hatch then examined the shaft.

"We'll set my flashlight here, pointing up. Turn yours off and clip it to your belt," instructed Brad.

"Sure. We should pull the ladder up. It would reach the bottom of the door."

"Wish we could, but look at its base. It's too wide to fit through the hatch. We've got to use the hard way. Up the emergency brake track." Brad moved to the narrow slot along the wall and placed his foot against a crossbar. Taking a deep breath and gritting his teeth, he grabbed a bar and began to climb.

"You okay?" yelled Ingram.

"Shine your light up here. I've found a catch." Brad stood with one foot on the narrow, internal shelf of the door, clinging to the brake track with his right hand.

Ingram shone his light on the door. Grunting, Brad depressed a lever then grabbed at the door edge. With a cry of agony he pulled against it. The hardened fragments of his glove drove into the scorched flesh of his hand. A wave of dizziness struck him as the door gave way. He released it and clung to his perch, regaining his equilibrium. "Climb up the other track and help me here."

Clipping the flashlight to his belt, Ingram scrambled up the other brake track, stopping at the far side of the door.

"Together." Brad grasped the stubborn lever with one hand.

Gasping in pain, the men heaved. The doors slid into the wall, leaving a gap wide enough for them to pass through. Brad was the first to scramble into the hall. An emergency light illuminated the area and another could be seen shining in the lobby. Rolling to one side, he let Ingram follow him onto the floor.

"Come on, we still have to decontaminate before our air runs out."

It was over an hour before they reached Brad's wagon and the final act of their efforts.

"Careful," whimpered Brad as Carla cut away his hacked-off glove. His arms rested on his table and Carla sat across from him.

"Sorry. This stuff is tough." She spoke without taking her eyes off her work.

"I got the wires hooked up like you said, Tinker, and I've slipped in the cube." Mark spoke from the front seat of Brad's wagon. Ingram looked up from where he sat beside Brad. The tattered edges of Ingram's gloves were bloodstained.

"I'll be right there." Brad tried to stand but Carla caught his arm.

"Taweret's nipples you will. I have to get this off you then clean the burns!"

Brad smiled at the commanding tone in Carla's voice before replying. "Work on Ingram while I call in."

Carla gritted her teeth in frustration. "Grandmother was right.

Little boys." she muttered.

Brad moved to the front of the van and sat in the driver's position."Okay, press the mic button."

Mark complied and Brad began to speak.

"Tinker to field base. Field base, this is Lieutenant Irving. I have a priority message, come in. Over. Let the button out now, Mark."

"Brad, you're still breathing. What happened to you? Over," demanded Eddie's voice.

"Security was nuts. I have the information, but we need the Doc in here. Over... Mark when I say over let the button out until the other person says it."

"Give security code for ident check. Over."

Brad gritted his teeth but knew it was useless to fight it. "B one R five A five D six L zero Y nine I zero R five V one I zero N seven G PC. Over... Mark I'm done."

"Received and acknowledged. What's going on in there? Who's Mark, and why is he holding your mic? Over."

"My hands are bloody toast. That's why I need the Doc. Are you set to receive ASCII files? Over."

"Set and ready. Begin transmitting at will. Over."

"Mark you can let the button out."

Mark released the mic button like it was a strange magical talisman. "Tinker, I don't be knowing about all these wires and things. I'm just a farmer."

"You're doing great. I want you to take the end of the wire you hooked to my computer and slip it into the little hole on my radio." Brad indicated a jack on the transmitter's face.

Mark complied then stared at the computer he held in his lap.

"Now move the arrow on the screen to the box labelled modem and press the button."

The farmer obeyed. Sweat was standing out on his forehead as he worked with the strange equipment.

"Now point to the line labelled transmit and press the button."

Mark followed instructions and the computer beeped. "What I do wrong?"

"Nothing, it's supposed to do that. Now all we have to do is wait for the files to transmit and sign off."

"OUCH! Watch it, woman!" snapped Ingram. Glancing back, Brad could see that one of Ingram's gloves had been cut away except for the palm. Now Carla was working on peeling back the layers of tape.

"I can knock you out if you want?" offered Brad.

"I can take it."

"Big tough men," commented Carla sarcastically.

"Transmit complete," appeared on the computer screen.

"Tinker, it says it's done. What now?" asked Mark.

"Unplug the jack and press in the mic button." Brad spoke into the mic. "You get all that Eddie? Over."

"Got you. Doc will be like a kid in a candy store. Good work. We'll get that serum to you by morning. Over."

"Good. We need it. Over and out."

"Over and out."

"You better come look at this." Carla was holding the revealed palm of Ingram's hand. Ingram sat on the bench-seat opposite her, trembling and pale. His teeth were clenched.

Brad sat beside him, hissing when his hand bumped the table. He stared at the charred flesh of Ingram's palm.

"I don't know what to do. The plastic has cut him in places. I can hardly see anything for the blood," explained Carla.

"Wash and disinfect the area. It's a light, third degree. I'll talk you through the treatment."

"You first, Tinker," said Ingram.

Brad nodded.

Chapter Thirty-six

Promises

BARB HELD THE suture tray and watched as the needle darted in and out of Tex's wound.

"Notice how the tendon on the rectus femoris has twisted with the damage to the muscle tissue. Clamp." Dr. Frankel stared into the wound. They were in the back of the portable lab, with Tex lying unconscious on the examination table.

The doctor closed the clamp on a small, blood vessel that had started leaking into the surgical field.

"I see it," said Barb.

"In this type of surgery the goal is to return things to their proper positions. So with an injury like this you run a suture thusly, to apply tension at key points, and voila." The doctor's hands worked with a steady confidence, and almost magically the tendon twisted back to its proper position.

"Will he have full function in the leg?"

The doctor was quiet as the work absorbed him; then he answered.

"Probably some stiffness. I'd prescribe physio and massage therapy as follow-ups. I'd also like to confer with an acupuncturist and maybe a rikist. You would know more about those areas than

I."

Barb smiled behind her surgical mask. "I'll teach his wife what she needs to know."

"Good. I've done what I can. He'll live and have at least some use of the limb." The doctor's voice took on a disgusted quality. "I hate guns. As if there aren't enough ways to damage the human body without such foolishness." Tying off a final blood vessel he added, "You may close for me."

Barb glanced from the doctor to the gaping hole in Tex's leg. The muscles had been restructured and the empty space filled with bio-regenerative, gel packing, but the skin was still peeled back.

"I've never closed a wound this large before."

"I'll talk you through it. It will be a good diversion. I've spent so much time perfecting the vaccine, something as straightforward as surgery is a welcome change. Now to begin, you..."

Eddie sat in his van, the mic from his radio in his good hand.

"So Brad's found some files. Are they any use? Over," spoke the radio.

"Who knows? The doctor won't let them out of his sight. You won't forget the date for my sister's birthday party, will you, Janet? I really need an escort for this one. Over."

"You got it. That address was two, three, five Mill Harbour? Over."

"Yup. I'd better sign off and call his lordship, the jerk. Over and out."

"Over and out."

Eddie changed the frequency to 235 megahertz and started his call in.

Dan paced back and forth in front of his wagon, occasionally pausing to affectionately stroke his big gelding's side.

"Will you stop that?" demanded Susan from where she sat in the open back door.

"Sorry, lass. I'm just kicking myself for not doing something about Horner earlier."

"Dan, you did all you could, and a damn sight more than you had to. Though you should have told me you were a Novo Gaian spy."

"I wouldn't exactly call it that now."

"What would you call it then, Corporal? I always liked the thought of a man in uniform."

"I'll have to borrow one then, now won't I."

Susan laughed. "I'd love to see you in one before you go."

Dan turned, looked at her and paused, thinking. His back ached from carrying Tex. He glanced down and saw there was more to his stomach than he remembered.

"Susan, me love, I've been thinking. There are folk enough hereabouts who are keeping themselves clean. Good honest work for a candler, if he was willing to stick around."

Susan placed a finger against Dan's mouth. "Later, when things have quieted down. Now let's see if those old James Bond books I read were more 'en fiction, my spy."

"I don't give a rat's nether regions about the expense. We still need a biohazard team in there. Over," Eddie snarled into his microphone.

"This has cost quite enough as it is. Even supplying equipment to your man in the plague zone is costing a fortune. I want you to start tapering back on the shipments. This whole thing is a political nightmare. I have to find some way to control the spin on that woman you let die. Over," snapped the Minister of Dark Land's affairs.

"We have a responsibility to our fellow living things, Francis. Over."

"Dark Landers. They can't vote for me. Have you dealt with those children yet? Over."

"We have an obligation to keep our word. You were elected to serve the ideals of Novo Gaia, what happened to you? Ground out! You used to be a tinker. Over."

"Reality. The electorate are sheep, everything is appearances, and ideals are for keeping fools in line. Those children are your problem, but they will not set foot on Novo Gaian soil. Over."

"You won't budge on these issues will you? Over."

"Major, if you ask me again I will pull funding for everything but the quarantine and place Colonel Ramses in command. Is that clear? Over."

"As crystal! Over."

"Good. I want you to order your man in Guelph to tell the town leaders that we will cut off aid unless they hand over the tank. If I can bring that blasted machine back to Nova Gaia, it just might justify this debacle. Over."

Eddie's expression reflected shock then shifted to rage. His hand trembled where he clutched the mic. After a long moment he pressed the transmit button.

"Message received. Over and out."

"Over and out."

Eddie sat seething then turned his radio back to the tinker chat frequency and spoke.

"Calling Janet, do you read me? Over."

"I read you, Eddie. Back so soon? Over."

"Wanted to check with you. I haven't watched the news lately. I was wondering if there was anything interesting on? Over."

"Nothing for the last few days. Over."

"Well, maybe tonight it will pick up. Over."

"I'm sure it will. Over and out."

"Over and out."

Eddie rubbed the bridge of his nose and balled his infantile hand into a fist. Tuning in a new frequency, he went through the ident procedures.

"Beth. I need a landline. I want to talk to Dr. Samuel Irving. Over."

"Eddie, you'll never get through. Over."

"Tell the founding minister's secretary it's about his grandson, Brad. Over."

Nearly an hour later Barb moved to Eddie where he sat on the bumper of his van.

"You look stressed," she commented.

"I've been on the radio with that ass Francis, his holy bloody Minister of bloody Dark Land's Affairs."

"That bad?"

"Worse. He wants to cut off aid to Guelph unless they surrender their tank to us."

"That... That. That is so Gridtown. He can't be serious."

"He is. I don't know what he hopes to achieve. Maybe the uneducated can be lied to and cheated, but with the one vote per degree system we use, the balance of power is tipped away from them."

"What are you going to do?"

"Fortunately he didn't phrase it as an order. I don't have to implement requests. That gives me time to fix the bastard's wagon. Brad is getting his biohazard team, and those kids are going to Novo Gaia like they were promised."

"That's not the only thing, is it?"

"You read me too well for someone I've only known a week. I may lose my commission for this. Shorting, I might even be banished. I've broken the essential secrets act."

"That act was never intended to cover up things like the Minister's doing. The other ministers won't press charges. Will they?"

"I hope not. I've only met a couple of the others, but they seemed decent chaps. I'm also worried about Brad. That Carla girl may be a talented amateur, but from the sound of it his hands are pretty badly damaged. He needs a proper doctor, or at least a fully trained healer."

"Not a tinker?"

"You do what you have to, but I never had delusions of grandeur. In the Dark, I'm the best of a bad lot. That's all I ever claimed. I hate it when I can't do anything. That's why I became a tinker. You wade in, do what you can, then bugger off. You don't sit around waiting to see if you made a difference, you're on to the next job."

"You'd make a lousy archer."

"Tell me about it."

That evening Eddie and Barb sat at a table in the front of the inn's viewing room watching the T.V.

"The Dark Lands store. Pre-collapse Technology, collected and maintained by the tinker collective. TV's, stereos, telephones, household appliances. We also carry the finest in Dark Land manufactured goods. Cloth, leather, clothing and much more. So before you buy those expensive Gridtown imports, remember to look through the Dark." As the voice spoke the image passed over shelves filled with assorted goods, their prices plainly showing.

"When'd they shoot that?" asked Barb.

"Last fall, just after the routes were finished," replied Eddie.

"Must have been. The shop in Lakefield was empty by midsummer last year."

"Now for the eleven o'clock news," spoke the T.V. broadcaster, an attractive woman of Amerindian descent, dressed in a well-cut pants suit. A fetish bag hung discreetly from a thong around her neck.

"Today's top story; The Minister of Dark Land Affairs implicated in a cover up regarding Novo Gaian involvement in the mishandling of a Dark Lands medical emergency."

"*Yes!*" Barb leapt to her feet.

"Too late to turn back now," observed Eddie.

The screen filled with the image of Francis pushing past a group of reporters saying "No comment," over and over again.

Eddie started to laugh and Barb looked at him.

"What's so funny?"

"Look at the background. They caught him leaving the Pink Pussy Cat. His wife will kill him."

There was the sound of feet running up the stairs then Ackley appeared, huffing and puffing. Seeing the officers he panted out, "Sir, Ma'am. The Minister is on the radio demanding to speak with you, sir."

"I bet he is." Eddie casually rose and made his way towards the radio truck. "Well, Brad, here's hoping you really are your granddad's favourite."

"This information is truly astounding. It would have taken me years to ascertain this much about the virus." Dr. Frankel sat before the computer screen in his lab.

"Does it give you a cure?" Eddie stood groggily in the doorway, behind him the sun was beginning to rise in a grey sky.

"The researcher who studied this was quite brilliant. Rather primitive and heavy-handed by today's standards, but that is to be expected. My version of a vaccine is nearly identical to hers."

"Doctor, does it tell us anything we don't know?"

"What. Oh yes, much. It confirms my belief that the viruses

were twinned. The first can infect anyone. It interrupts the cell's ability to absorb ions, forcing the cell to pump out water in an attempt to maintain its internal homeostasis. Fortunately this virus sits dormant and cannot reproduce without the intervention of its twin. The twin is bound to the Asian Class 1 MHC markers. In short, it can only enter the cells of persons who have markers associated with the Asian race. When it has done that it activates the first virus, they both divide causing the person to dehydrate to death."

"Why do some infected people recover?"

"That is part of the diabolical brilliance behind these viruses. They have coat proteins that blend into the Asian MHC antigens. In simple terms the immune system of a predominantly Asian individual can't see the virus. The immune systems of those of mixed descent can detect the virus and so, in time, mount a defence. The researchers believed the convulsions were the result of electrolyte imbalances. More a side-effect than a consequence of the virus. Only those of mixed descent would live long enough to suffer them."

"Are other racial types carriers?"

"Only of the first virus and then only for a short time. So long as Bradly takes reasonable hygiene precautions he can leave the quarantine zone at anytime.

"Also, I am reassured by the low possibility of zoonosis. The only animal they were able to infect was a chimpanzee, and that took massive doses.

"If you can overlook the horror of it, this illness is truly a work of art. I doubt we could do better today."

"I'm glad you appreciate it. Is there a cure?"

"Yes, a retrovirus."

"A retrovirus?"

"They took sections of the genetic code governing class 1 MHC antigens and designed a virus that in effect throws a protein jacket over the cells disguising them. The activating virus cannot penetrate the jacket and behaves as if it was in a person of pure European descent. This shuts down the triggering virus long enough that the body can purge the dormant one. Thus the disease is deactivated."

"So we have a cure," breathed Eddie.

"Yes. Normally I would prefer to repeat the test procedures, but given our current situation we can expedite that protocol."

"How long before you have a viable counter-virus?"

"I need Young Eagle from my team. He is our gene splicing expert. With his help, I believe we could recreate the nucleotide sequence in two days, maybe three."

"I'll get you your team come flood or drought, doctor. Get ready to move. You're entering the quarantine zone tomorrow." Eddie pounded his fist on the wall.

"About time!"

"I'm just about to send Brad the serum you made."

"Send him this as well." Dr Frankel passed Eddie a tube of greenish gel.

"What is it?"

"Aloe. I've found it to be an excellent topical for burns. From what you told me, he needs it."

Chapter Thirty-seven

Dawn

"Err!" grunted Brad as Carla peeled the glove's palm from his hand.

"I'm sorry. Everything is stuck together," said Carla.

Brad steadied himself and stared at his palm. Blood seeped from cuts made by the broken rubber, and the skin was red. Small, burst blisters marked where he had gripped the pry bar.

"Mostly bad first degrees with a bit of light second. Wash the area with the antiseptic from my kit then put a dressing on it."

"Will that be enough?" Carla continued to examine the injury.

"It will have to be. The Doc might have something in his bag of tricks. I'll ask him next time I call in." Brad took three deep breaths and focussed his mind, creating a barrier against the pain as Carla readied the disinfectant.

Minutes later she finished bandaging his hands. "That's it then," she said.

"Shit, Tinker. Ain't no way I'll ever listen to those who call Bright Landers soft again." Ingram sat by Brad with his one hand wrapped in a bandage while the other still wore the glove.

Brad lifted his free hand and examined the gauze dressing that surrounded it.

"Your turn now, Ingram." Carla's skin was ashen with stress and sweat had dampened the surgical mask she wore.

"Shit."

"I'll dope you so high you'll be on a first name basis with eagles," offered Brad.

"You better." Ingram laid his hand on the table.

Talking Carla through the injection and preparing Ingram took only moments and soon Carla was pealing away the scorched material of the glove.

"This is a lot easier when the patient's asleep," she observed.

"Easier on the patient too. Watch out. He has some nasty cuts there. I'm lucky the spasms threw me clear. His burns are a lot worse than mine." Brad stared down at Carla's work.

"I not aslee-ee-ep, sleepy, sleepy, sleepy, deepy," mumbled Ingram. He leaned back in the chair and started to snore.

"High as a kite," said Brad.

"Will he heal properly?"

Brad stared into the wound and nodded. "The Doc will have to apply a cell division accelerant, but he should be able to get the dermis to grow in from the sides. Doing it's way over my head, but I've seen it done."

"Good. Ingram doesn't deserve to be crippled for helping us." Carla finished washing the wound before undoing the ties that held the hand in place.

"You can handle the bandaging on your own. I need to crash."

"Go on. When I'm done here I'll tell Trina you trust us so much you're letting us run the clinic on our own. She won't know whether to be flattered that you trust her or annoyed that she has to do more work."

"Sorry to put it on you."

"Don't worry about it. We have more help now. Mark's been spreading the word that only Asians can catch the plague. There's about twenty folk taking shifts now."

"Maybe Guelph is worth the effort after all. Call me if you need me." Brad moved to the front of the van and draped himself along the seat.

"Tinker, I got the stuff," called Mark from outside the wagon.

"Ingram, shut up," growled Brad.

"It's not me, Tinker. What the fuck did you give me? My mouth feels like a bear shit in it," replied Ingram from the bed. Brad shuffled along the front bench seat and scrambled for the door handle but fell back, hissing, when his hand made contact. "Mark, you have to let me out. My hands are useless."

The door opened, revealing a grey, overcast morning.

Mark and two other men were unloading a small wagon drawn by one of Brad's shires. Brad looked at one of the newcomers' faces; recognition jiggled at the back of his mind.

"Excuse me. I know you, don't I?"

"Aye, Tinker, that you do. I's was one of 'em you 'elped. Figure I's can'ts catch same thing twice, so I's 'elping out.

"Were three others felt same as Ehren here. A couple more that says they'll 'elp out when they're a bit stronger," explained Mark.

"Good to have you aboard." Brad followed them into the clinic.

The cots were crowded at the far end of the room, while people lay on blankets in front of the door. Five caregivers moved amongst the patients.

"There you are. I was wondering when you'd bother to come back." Trina approached from the middle of the room.

"We have the serum the doctor made," said Mark.

"I want to try it on everyone. Probably will only help those with a recessive resistance, but it can't hurt." Brad moved to the central table reached for a needle and pulled his hand back, grimacing.

"What happened to you?" Trina looked at his bandaged hands.

"I missed the elevator. You and Carla will have to prepare the shots. I'll talk you through it."

Two hours later the last shot had been given, and Brad sat in his van with Carla holding his radio for him.

"Got good news, great news, and news to warm your heart,

and a warning. Over," said Eddie.

"Carla please press the button for me. Give it to me. I need all the smiles I can get. Oh, before I forget. Thank the Doc for the aloe vera. Don't know if it's doing any good, but damn, it feels nice. Over."

"Will do. Over."

"So what's the news? Over."

"Seems Francis got found out. Somehow a tinker, whose commission wasn't active, got a tape of our transmissions and cracked the code. We'll be doing a full security review when this is over, of course. Over."

"That's great. I hope they fry that over-stuffed pig. Over."

"By the way, your grandfather says hello. Over."

"My. Eddie, I don't play that game. Who's in my family is an accident of birth. I don't use it. I think that's why granddad likes me. Over."

"Sorry, Brad. There's a time and place for everything. You can tell him it was my idea to call him. I'll give him this. He can get things done. Over."

"What are you talking about? Over."

"Two hours after I called him there was an emergency meeting of the section ministers. The necessary secrets act has been deactivated regarding this plague, and review hearings for its wording are scheduled. Over."

"My granddad shouldn't have been bothered. He's a hundred and twenty-two years old. Over."

"I think he enjoyed it. Besides, I needed his clout. When the last surviving founding Minister asks a favour from the government, how can they say no? Over."

"What's the other good news? Over."

"The immunity is a true one. You're not a carrier. Over."

Brad breathed a sigh of relief.

"You thinking of leaving these people now?" asked Carla, misinterpreting his gesture.

"Hardly. It just means when this is all over, I can move on. Settling here with you and raising a herd of blue-eyed rug rats isn't the worst fate I can think of, but it's not what I have planned for my life. Hope you're not hurt."

Carla laughed and kissed him. "So damn sure of yourself."

"Brad, are you still there? Over."

"I hear you, Eddie. What's the great news? Over."

"We have a cure. Those files you sent us had the plans for a retrovirus that gives immunity. Over."

"Gods of my fathers, that is great! When will I get it? Over."

"Doc says two to three days. Over."

"Eddie, people are dying. I need a specific for this thing now! Over."

"Can't speed it up. It will take that long to build the damn thing. Be thankful the science is that advanced. Over."

"Understood. What's the warning? Over."

"Francis is coming down with the biohazard team and news crew. I think he's trying for spin control. Over."

"He never gives up, at least. Over and out."

"Over and out."

"We won!" Carla leaned back in her seat and closed her eyes. Brad watched her, wondering if she'd fallen asleep; then she spoke again.

"Your grandfather is really old. I never thought people lived that long."

"In Novo Gaia he's not that extraordinary. We can slow the aging process."

"How old are you?"

"Thirty-two."

"So when I'm old and grey you'll be middle-aged."

"Not if you go to the academy. As a foreign student you'll have non-voting citizen status. You're too old for the first longevity treatment, but you can get the second. You'll probably see a hundred, if you can afford the third when the time comes."

"You should share this."

"It's expensive. At least we give it to all our citizens. In Gridtowns the average life expectancy is about eighty, unless you're rich."

"And my grandmother's old at sixty."

Brad shrugged. "I'm glad we're getting the biohazard team. With any luck they'll be here tomorrow. Let me out of the truck then you get some sleep."

"I won't argue." Carla opened the door.

Hours later Brad stood at the clinic's door and smiled as another group of patients left the building.

"The doctor's serum is working wonderfully. Nearly half the people are getting better," said Trina.

"It's an improvement." Brad turned to gaze at the patients who still half-filled the room.

A tall, burly woman with wild, red hair, dressed in a filthy, patched dress, burst through the door.

"Tinker, my husband's a sickin. We needs this cure youse got," she snarled.

"We have a treatment that works for some. Bring your husband in and I'll do my best," replied Brad.

"No, youse gotta come. I don't trust youse tinker kind or these low grounders."

"Are you from a Tower Vil?"

"We know 'bout youse cure. Trader from Arkell told us how youse only letting them as can pay have it. Typical Bright Lander, always lining youse pockets. No reason we poor folk should die."

"We're treating everyone. Some people recover because..."

"Jack told us that was the lie you're spreading. A cure's a cure," screamed the Amazon as she pulled a battered, dirty revolver from the sash she wore about her waist.

"Don't be foolish! The tinker is telling the truth," said Trina.

"Shut up, Low Grounder. Tower Vil folk might be poor, but we ain't stupid. We know youse want us all dead, so youse can steal our glass works. Come on, Tinker, we're leaving."

The clinic's door creaked open, and a shaft of light entered the room, dazzling Brad's eyes. The woman turned as Ingram stepped in. Trina leapt grappling the woman's arm. Brad seized the opportunity and rushed his opponent. The Amazon's arm jerked; the sound of a gunshot split the air. Brad's training took over. His foot drove into the woman's solar plexus. She buckled and he chopped down on her wrist with his hand, knocking the gun from her grasp. With an effort he pulled back on his killing blow as it sped towards his enemy's throat.

"Shit!" swore Ingram.

Brad crumpled to his knees, cradling the hand that had delivered the chopping blow.

"Gun," he breathed through clenched teeth.

"Got it." Ingram kicked the weapon away from the woman. "Tinker, look," he added a second later.

Brad turned and stared at the still form of Trina where she lay in the dust.

"Shit! You and you, tie this madwoman up. You get over here and listen to see if Trina's breathing. Ingram, fetch Carla from my wagon. I need her hands." Brad pointed to people who were helping in the clinic as he spoke.

"She's breathing, Tinker," said the small woman who knelt by Trina. Ingram rushed from the room as Brad talked the woman through another simple test.

"Taueret's tits!" Carla entered and rushed to stand by Brad.

"Breathing is fifteen and regular, pulse is eighty. Left pupil is reactive to light, right is sluggish. Patient is unconscious. Write that down then pinch her nipple."

"Brad!"

"For a pain response. It will help us assess the head injury."

Carla scribbled the information onto a scrap of paper along with the time then viciously pinched Trina's nipple.

Trina groaned and tried to knock Carla away with a sweep of her arm.

"Is that good?" asked Carla.

"Good, not great. Take my flashlight and shine it in the wound," ordered Brad.

"I'll get some water to wash it," offered the small woman Brad had drafted.

"Thanks Esta." Carla positioned the light.

"The bullet just grazed her. See how it dug a furrow in the skull, but didn't penetrate. Trina's one damn lucky woman."

"Will she be all right?"

Esta returned with the water. Carla took the dipper from her hand.

"Wash the area clear of blood. I can't see any details."

"Won't that encourage bleeding?"

"Bleeding is the least of our problems."

Carla tipped the ladle out over the wound, and Brad stared at the bone. A tracery of cracks spread out from the groove.

"Brad, I think cerebral spinal fluid is leaking out of her nose," said Carla.

Brad turned his gaze to Trina's face. A straw-coloured liquid dribbled from her nostril.

"Carla, get the oxygen from my wagon and my intubation kit. Esta, can you read?"

"No, Tinker, I never learned."

"Come with me anyway. I need you to hold the bottle."

Brad rose and Carla rushed to his wagon. A minute later they were back beside Trina.

"Okay Carla, you're my hands. If we do this right, she might live long enough for help to get here."

"Live long enough for..."

"She's bleeding into her skull. If it isn't stopped, the pressure will squeeze her brain through the hole her spinal cord comes out of. Now you have to intubate her for me. I'll talk you through it."

Carla wiped the sweat from her brow with her sleeve and listened carefully to Brad's instructions.

Chapter Thirty-eight

Promises

BRAD LEANED OVER Trina, checked her endotracheal tube then spoke quietly.

"Squeeze Carla's hand when I say the day of the week. Monday, Tuesday, Wednesday, Thursday, Friday, Saturday, Sunday."

"She got it wrong," said Carla.

"Where are we? At home, on a picnic, in the town hall, in the clinic, in the tavern." Carla shook her head.

"What's your name? Cathy, Jessy, Trina, Beth, Jorget."

"She got that one right."

"Oriented to person. She's slipping fast. Have you seen any more cranial fluid?"

"A drop or two in her ear. The drugs seemed to help."

"Mannitol and steroids will slow the swelling; so does the O2, but they only delay the inevitable. We need..."

"*Tinker*, you better come 'ave a look at this," called Mark from the doorway. Brad rose then became aware of a deep rumbling sound.

"They've come!" he called and sprinted from the clinic. The street was in bedlam. People leaned out their windows or stood in groups on the sidewalk as the medical trailer rolled into view. Mounted Novo Gaian troops rode in formation around the leviathan. At their head, a one armed man rode a grey gelding.

"It's the bloody cavalry. *Yeah whoo!*" Brad ran to meet them. Drawing level with the one-armed man's stirrup he fell in beside him.

"Eddie, you are a sight for sore eyes. You got that retrovirus made in a hurry."

"Unfortunately, no. I moved up the timetable when you told me about Trina getting shot. She may be an ass, but she's earned our help. The Doc will look at her as soon as we stop. I need to set up the outpost. What's the status on the inn?"

"It's a convalescent hospital."

"I hate sleeping on pavement."

"Pick an empty house. There are more than enough of them."

"It's almost over. You can sit back and coast for the rest of the ride."

"Glad to hear it."

The trailer halted just short of Brad's wagon. Frankel leapt from the cab and moved to Brad.

"Bradly, it is a pleasure to meet you face to face. Edward tells me you have a trauma case that is quite serious," he opened.

"Dr. Frankel?" asked Brad.

The doctor nodded.

"The clinic's this way." Brad led the older man to the town hall's doors. Frankel eyed the building dubiously. Mark held the door as the other men stepped inside.

Frankel gagged and fumbled a pot of mint cream from his pocket. His eyes widened as he scanned the dismal room and its miserable human residents.

"This is where you treated the plague victims? The smell alone," he opened.

"Best available."

Frankel stared at Brad in surprise.

"Do not mistake my words. It is a wonder so many survived with such primitive conditions. Where is the head injury?"

Trina lay on a pile of blankets near the entrance. Picking up the pad that served as her chart, Frankel examined it then started some basic tests. Standing, he turned to Brad.

"I wish to consult with you privately."

"Doc, there isn't a lot of empty space around here."

"Come." Frankel strode towards the doors at the back of the room.

"Doctor, you don't want to..." Brad stopped in mid sentence as the doctor pushed through the door. Frankel stood transfixed, staring at the rows of bodies that filled the room. The stench was overpowering.

"Hippocrates guard me. So many!" breathed Frankel.

"There are three other rooms just like this. You okay?" Brad joined the doctor.

"I will be all right, Bradly. It was the shock that is all. Death is an old opponent. It is simply the scale here."

"Brad," yelled Carla from Trina's position.

Brad and Frankel rushed to her side. Carla shone a flashlight into her patient's eyes. "Right pupil is fixed and non-reactive; left is reactive but sluggish," she explained

"Shit! Doctor, you've got to do something for her," said Brad.

"That is what I wished to speak to you about. She needs an operation to relieve the cerebral pressure."

"No shit, Sherlock. Do it!"

"Sir. I am an outstanding immunologist, a fair general surgeon, but I am not a neurologist. Brain surgery is simply not an area I am proficient in."

Brad stared at Frankel in disbelief then snapped, "Carla fetch my surgical tools and dremmel. I'll do it if he won't."

"This is not a mechanical object that can be repaired if it breaks, this is a human life," objected Frankel.

"Doctor, if we do nothing she's as good as dead. She won't last long enough for someone qualified to arrive."

"She needs surgery that is outside my specialty, but I will do what I can. Have someone fetch the gurney from my lab and bring her there. Hurry, she doesn't have much time."

Frankel strode from the clinic as Brad moved to conscript volunteers.

"*Barbara*," hollered Frankel as he stepped into the dull evening light.

"Doctor," replied Barb, moving to his side.

"Set up for cranial surgery. You are assisting me. I must review the database. I will leave it to you to prepare the instruments."

"I just have to..."

A look from Frankel quelled her objections, and she rushed to the back of the lab.

Carla ran beside the gurney. She sealed her lips over the endotracheal tube and exhaled. Trina's chest rose. She pressed her fingers against the dying woman's neck and felt the flutter of her heart.

"She stopped breathing when we put her on the cart," said Carla, when she reached the back of the lab.

"Got you." Barb slammed the gurney into its locks. She snatched a hose from the wall and connected it to the tube. Setting the controls, she watched Trina's chest rise and fall.

"You Carla?"

"Yes."

"Get in here. We need a grunge nurse, and you're the best available. Try and stay out of the way, and don't touch anything unless you're told to. Clear?"

"Clear."

"Had a bit of trouble last week or so, have you?" said Dan. Brad sat on the clinic's steps with his bandaged hands supported on his knees.

"Could say that."

"Had a chat with Veronica, the lass with the gun. Seems our old friend Jack Horner didn't leave the quarantine zone. He slipped into the Tower Vils in central Guelph and has been about spreading his poison."

Brad stared at the setting sun and sighed. "I'll be going that way when this is done. I'll keep my eyes open for him. From what I've heard he's caused more than his fair share of trouble."

Dan looked sly. "It's about that. You're a lieutenant, and your commission's active isn't it?"

"Yes."

"And no one's told you you weren't 'officially' in charge of the medical aspect of this mission any more, now have they?"

"No. I'm still 'officially' in charge, even though the doctor's here. No one relieved me of the duty."

"Well, I think a bit of a look see, just to find out how bad the plague is in the Tower Vils, might be called for. And if word about a Gridtown spy stirring up trouble, maybe even plague ratting, should get out along the way… Well, rumours do happen now, don't they?"

Brad smiled. "That's a good idea. Maybe we should discuss it with the Major."

"I wouldn't want to do that. The Major's a busy man, and he is very concerned about keeping the peace. Feels too many folk have died of lead poisoning on this trip."

Brad considered for a moment. "What do you think?"

"I think there wouldn't have been much trouble 'cepting good old Jack stirred the hornet's nest. There's some folk as shouldn't be allowed to wander free about the Dark. They's just too much trouble. Sides, we don't need him planting any more ideas about burning out this here clinic like he did in Arkell. All it would take is one desperate person."

"I see what you mean. Very well corporal. I order you to visit the Guelph Tower Vils and chart the plague's progress. Use all your local contacts." Brad winked.

"Thank you, sir." Dan walked towards his horse.

"Inflate the scalp tourniquet," said Frankel. He stood over Trina's still form. The respirator cycled, making a reassuring hiss-click with each forced breath. Barb pressed a button causing a cuff around the patient's head to inflate.

"Young lady, remove the wound dressing and finish shaving the patient's scalp," ordered Frankel. Carla cut away the donut bandage around the wound and ran an electric razor through the last pieces of blood-clumped hair.

"Laser scalpel." With a decisive motion Frankel split the scalp around the bullet crease then peeled it back, exposing the bone.

"I wish Doctor Ishtara were here. The skull has small stress fractures radiating from the crease. I do not know if the core will come out as a single piece. Wipe."

Carla stood back, staring at the revealed skull.

"Wipe!" snapped Frankel.

"Wipe his brow," commanded Barb.

Carla rushed to comply.

"Coring drill," ordered Frankel. Barb passed him the instrument. "Safety glasses." Carla slipped a pair onto his nose. The saw activated with a whine that was soon replaced with a grinding noise as it dug into the bone.

"Irrigate. Wipe!" ordered Frankel. Carla wiped away the sweat as Barb washed the area around the drill. A mix of bone chips and clotted blood flowed down to stain the gurney's sheets. A moment later Frankel resumed cutting.

The stop on the drill came against the skull and he pulled back.

"No good, she has a thick skull. Carla adjust the stop for one more millimetre's depth."

"How?"

"It's the knob on the unit's side."

Carla obeyed and a moment later Frankel completed his cut. He lifted the bone fragment from the hole.

"Check her pupils," he ordered.

"Sluggish and reactive, on both sides. It's better than it was," said Carla.

"Good. The haematoma is in the area of the initial graze." Frankel stared into the wound. The fibrous white dura matter bulged into the hole he had carved.

"Scalpel."

Barb passed him the laser scalpel.

"Bladed scalpel," he revised in a stinging tone. Carla grinned under her mask.

"Now for the hard part." Frankel placed his scalpel against the dura and pushed. Blood spurted from the incision, striking him in the face, dirtying his glasses. Before anything could be said Carla snatched up a large dressing and held it between the doctor and the wound. A moment later the squirt subsided. Trina moved on the gurney.

"Get these damn glasses off me. I can't see a thing," snapped Frankel. Carla whipped the glasses away and started cleaning them.

Frankel continued his incision then, clipping retractors to the cut, pulled the tissue to the side, exposing the pia matter.

"Shine the light in here," he ordered. Carla adjusted the lamp's position. A tracery of bruised and ruptured blood vessels were visible in the usually transparent pia matter.

"Wipe me then fetch the coagulant spray."

Carla wiped sweat from the doctor's face then turned to the cupboards in the lab. "Where is it?"

"Damn it, can't I have one competent nurse? How can I be expected to work like this?" Taking a deep breath, Frankel controlled himself. "Of course you are not a nurse, either of you. It will be in the third cupboard back, in a pink spray bottle."

Carla retrieved the bottle and, after wiping it with disinfectant, placed it in the doctor's gloved hand.

"Under-trained, under-staffed, make-shift equipment," grumbled Frankel, as he sprayed the coagulant mixture onto the surface of his patient's brain. A moment later the blood stopped oozing from the damaged pia matter.

Trina tried to move against her restraints.

"I had better close." Minutes later Dr. Frankel replaced the section of skull he'd removed and secured it with stainless steel screws and plates.

"Will she be all right?" asked Carla.

Frankel folded the scalp back into place and began securing it. "I cannot say. I am not a neurologist. I thank you both, though. The surgery would have been impossible without your help.

Carla and Barb smiled behind their masks.

Chapter Thirty-nine

Victory

CARLA PULLED THE blanket over the face of the plague's latest victim. "How much longer?"

"The gene dogs said anytime now." Brad stared at his hands encased in burn gloves as he cautiously flexed his fingers.

"How are your burns?"

"The accelerant is working. I'll be good as new in a few days."

"Thanks to the Doc."

"If you hadn't done such a good job of the initial treatment the accelerant wouldn't have made a difference."

"He is quite accurate in that. Considering the resources available to you, you both have accomplished something quite extraordinary here," said Frankel. He moved to a patient.

"Is it done?" asked Brad.

Frankel held up a spritz bottle then pushed its nozzle into the patient's nose and depressed the trigger.

"How long for it to take effect?" Carla moved to the patient's side.

"According to the literature, about two hours," replied Frankel as he wiped the bottle's nozzle with disinfectant.

"The cases at the back won't last that long." Brad looked down at the newly treated man as if expecting some miraculous transformation.

"Then we shall take a chance on them, Bradly." Frankel moved to the advanced cases and began applying the cure.

Brad sighed as he tried yet again to accomplish what he had realised was impossible. "Doctor, please call me Brad. Not even my mother calls me Bradly."

Frankle shrugged.

"Brad, you asked me to remind you about the meeting," said Carla.

"Shorting, thanks. I hate politics, even if my grandfather thinks I have a knack for it! Of all the people to put on a shorting planning committee."

"Who is Brad's grandfather?" asked Carla, after he left the room."I am surprised he has not told you. Then again, maybe not. A man such as Bradly would rather be known for his own accomplishments. Samuel Irving is one of maybe twenty men who pulled Novo Gaia from the wreckage of the collapse. National hero best describes his position."

"Oh."

"Yes. Has there been word about how the disease is affecting the rest of Guelph?"

"No. Dan, the candler, hasn't come back yet. He should be back soon, though.

"Good. We will have to be sure all susceptible persons are exposed to the cure. Tell me as soon as you hear from Daniel."

"Sure."

Dan allowed the angry mob to flow by him. He could see Horner running down the broken street and wondered at the man's endurance. A Tower Vil resident tackled Jack.

"Plague rat, plague rat, plague rat," chanted the villagers as Horner was hurled into the hands of two bear-like men. His screams echoed off the dilapidated high-rises of central Guelph. The crowd converged. Fists beat against their hapless victim. His captors slammed him into a corner where two buildings met. Screaming, they pelted him with pieces of broken brick, stone and glass. Horner huddled away, using his arms as shields. Dan walked to his horse.

"Couldn't happen to a nicer chap." Dan rode off to make his report.

Brad stared at the burned-out inverter and shook his head. "Not much to salvage on this one eh, Ingram?"

"You blew it, Tinker. A cut of nothing is still nothing," replied the younger man, who turned to examine the rest of the facility's maintenance room. Cables ran over the floor, supplying lights set on tripods along the aisle. "How much do you think the rest of it's worth?"

"This room or the base?" Brad tried to scratch his nose, but his hand came up against the face panel of his biohazard suit. He was surprised at how little this now bothered him.

"The base."

"Somewhere in the billions of marks. Of course, the expenses of properly decontaminating it will have to come off the top, but at a guess, I'd say the net will be over fifty million."

"That is grossly overestimating it." Francis shifted about uncomfortably in his biohazard suit.

"Don't worry, Minister. The germs won't pick up knives to get you. You'll live long enough to face the electorate." Brad's smile was predatory.

The scowl on the politician's face was blurred by his mask.

"Gentlemen, I believe you should go for decontamination now. If you have assessed the relative value of the base, that is?" spoke a young woman dressed in a suit marked with a full caduceus.

"Yes, doctor, I have seen enough." Francis led the way from the room.

"Pity about having to involve the government. But only Novo Gaia and Gridtowns have the resources to properly decommission this base," remarked Brad.

"So the plan is to empty it out, so there's no reason for folk to dig into it then in fill with rubble from salvaged houses?" Ingram looked around the hallway of the now well lit facility.

"Yup," agreed Brad as they ascended the stairs. A trailer sat in the field by the base. Entering through its back door, they fell silent as disinfectant sprays bombarded them. Finally they removed their suits and stepped out the other side into bright sunshine.

“Far cry from a spritz bottle and a roll of tape.” Ingram shook his head at the disparity.

“The percentages we discussed. They seem rather untoward, considering the expenses my ministry has already undertaken on Guelph’s behalf,” remarked Frances.

“You were the son of a bitch who wouldn’t send in help. I’d tell you to fly a fucking kite, but Brad said the deal’s fair. The town set me up to handle the bargaining ‘cause I’d seen the base close up, back when we didn’t have a nice big trailer to clean up in.” Ingram went red in the face.

“Getting emotional won’t do any good. My ministry must receive a larger portion to make dealing with this base worthwhile. Brad’s—”

“That’s Doctor Irving, or, at the least, lieutenant, to you!” Brad glared at the minister.

Francis seemed ready to comment then thought better of it. “The lieutenant’s estimation is grossly optimistic. This will be at best a break-even task.”

“Bull! Only creative accounting could hide the profit in a cache like this.” Brad’s tone was adamant.

“Need I remind you, your commission is still active. Have a care to the protocols due my position.”

“Yes, Minister. All I meant to say is, I have already cut my traditional percentage from a cache in half. With fifteen each going to the town and the landowner, you’re still the big winner. Though you know, Ingram. I think a reward for those who helped us... Maybe a Novo Gaian scholarship fund. Start off with you, Carla, Trina and Rose, since Mark wouldn’t use it. After that, it could be used to fill in vital skills for the Guelph area. Ten percent of the net should do it. I mean, how could the Novo Gaian council say no? They’re still getting 60 percent; only ten of it goes to the ministry of education.”

“That is completely unacceptable.”

“No, it’s not. I’ll call my grandfather about it. The other ministries will be thrilled to get a cut of the profits.”

Brad and Ingram smiled at each other as Francis glared.

"You're going to use this ploy to force my hand. My ministry should get the profits. Very well, I agree to your terms."

"Good, I'll write it up and..."

"And?"

"Listen!"

The sound of a metallic growl reached them accompanied by a banging sound and distant screams.

"Look!" Ingram pointed a burn-gloved hand towards a cloud of dust rising into the air where the clinic was.

Brad sprinted to the mount tethered at the field's edge and clambered into the saddle. In minutes he turned onto the street where the clinic stood. The building was half collapsed and dust filled the air. As he raced to Eddie's side he saw the butt of a large machine disappear into the dust cloud.

"Oh shit!" Brad practically leapt from his saddle.

"Brad, thank Beaver you're here." Eddie's face was caked with dust and he stood just behind Ackley who half knelt on the ground with a tube like anti-tank gun on his shoulder.

"What happened? And put that damn gun down! If we crack the rad-shielding on that antique it will do more damage than the tank ever will."

The massive form of a tank burst through a section of the clinic's remaining walls sending a shower of debris out in front of it. The armoured vehicle was half as long as a tractor-trailer and its battered, grey armour-plate was scratched and dented with age. Ackley kept the A.T.-gun trained on his target.

"I'm not a complete fool, Brad. The A.T.-gun is just a precaution. That tank came out of no where and slammed into the clinic. Whoever's driving it seems determined to level the place. We're hauling out the patients as fast as we can." As Eddie spoke two dust caked people, with kerchiefs tied over their mouths and noses, emerged from the fast-collapsing building carrying a woman supported on a blanket between them.

"Carla and the Doc?"

"Frankel's okay. Carla's helping get everyone out. The dust's so thick you can't see in there."

Brad watched as the tank turned. Its main gun was snapped off halfway along its length, but secondary guns bristled from it like a porcupines quills. As it moved it dragged to one side. A blast of steam vented through a port by its main turret.

"*Shorting! Get everyone out of here, now!*" Brad watched in horror as the machine once more smashed through the building's wall.

"What is it?" demanded Eddie.

"That steam was the reactor's over-pressure release. The heat dissipaters can't keep up with the core temperature. If that reactor boils dry it will go critical." A section of the building's roof fell in.

"Is there anything you can do?" demanded Eddie.

Brad held up his hands in the burn gloves.

"I know, but none of my other personal have AV training. Is there anyway you can stop that beast before it melts down or blows up?"

"Ground out! Okay Brad, time to think." Brad bit his lower lip. "It looks like a 3A urban suppression unit. I know a trick to open the hatch, if I can get to it. Get me a portable defibrillator from the med trailer and rig a pressure hose. If I get control of that thing, I'll need to drop the core temperature fast."

"On it." Eddie ran to the medical trailer while Brad confiscated a military helmet from a man carrying a victim from the building.

Eddie returned and passed Brad the toolbox sized defibrillator.

"If I'd known I'd be asked to do things this crazy, I would have joined the navy." Brad checked the defibrillator then raced towards where the tank was emerging through another section of the clinic's wall.

The behemoth slowly turned preparing for another pass. The sound of its treads grating on the rubble and its gears grinding was deafening. The tank stopped moving when Brad stood in front of it. The red dot of a laser scope appeared on Brad's chest.

"Don't try and stop me, Tinker." A man's voice blasted from the speaker on the tank's turret. "Damn fools on the council don't want to burn this down. My Bernice, my boys, all my kin gone, and they won't burn it out. I won't let 'em do it. You said we should burn it out, so no one else gets it. It's gotta come down. No more dying cause the town council is cheap. My life's gotta count for something."

"Oscar, is it you in there?" yelled Brad.

"It's me, Tinker. You said the hall should burn when you was done, so I'm gonna burn it."

Brad looked at the battered machine in front of him. It's armour showed a tracery of cracks and there was a mettle plate patching the area over the reactor. "We'll burn it down. We just need to get the rest of the patients out. The building's no good now anyway. You've accomplished your goal."

"I miss my family, Tinker. Why'd you save me if you couldn't save me kin?"

"I tried. Will killing the people in the clinic bring back your family?"

"I heard the doctor talking. The cure came to late for those as are left inside. Better end it fast than make 'em suffer." The tank inched forward.

"Wait, Stop. Some of the cases could go either way. Let them have their chance."

The tank stood still and silent then the speaker came to life. "Five minutes, Tinker then I finish what I started."

"Fine. You need to throttle back your reactor. You're boiling off your coolant. You probably have radiation leaking out already. It could kill you."

"Good then I'll see Bernice and me boys again. You've got four and three quarters minutes left. Don't worry when I'm done this tank will be buried deep like we should have left it. It won't ever hurt anyone again."

"That won't work. The reactor could still melt down. Poison the water, irradiate the air. It could—" There was a loud click signalling that the tank's speaker and pick-up were shutdown.

"Oscar... Oscar... Shorting!" Brad moved to the clinic's main entrance.

"I heard, what now?" Eddie moved to Brad's side.

"I have to get on top of that thing, and I can't do that if he can see me coming. If he buries it, it's just a dirty bomb waiting to go off. Use the time he gave you to get the rest of the patients out and Evac the area. I need to get into position."

"Right, do you need a warm body?"

"No, better I not have to worry about where other people are. Just be sure everyone's out of the clinic when he starts moving again, and don't let anyone back in."

"Consider it done. Good luck."

Brad stepped into the collapsing clinic building. The dust blocked his visibility turning everything into vague shadows. A pair of dark images rushed past him carrying a blob on a blanket. Brad moved deeper into the gloom then called, "Carla."

"Brad," came the reply.

The dust was slowly settling and he saw a dim outline ahead of him. As he scrambled towards the outline it took on definition, becoming Carla.

"You have to get out of here," said Brad as he approached her.

"That maniac ran over the end patients. Squashed them like grapes. I've been pulling the ones at the back forward as fast as I can, but he's gaining. We can't get them out fast enough." Carla's voice held tears.

"We have four minutes. Get out as many as you can in that time. Is the stairway to that old second floor office still intact?" Brad tried to grab a corner of the blanket Carla was dragging to help her and pulled his hand back with a hiss of pain.

"Don't do that! I don't know about the stairs. I can't see any better than you! It should be, he's kept pretty straight lines going through."

"All I needed to know." Brad's foot slipped on a piece of rubble and he lost his balance. Throwing his hand out he grabbed a fallen roof support, which gave way.

"Shit!" yelled Brad as the ceiling above him fell with a metallic shriek. Dust swirled up blocking all vision.

"Brad, you okay?" called Carla before she collapsed into a coughing fit.

Brad tried to move but something pushed down hard against his stomach. "I'm stuck. I'll try and wiggle free." Brad could just make out a ceiling support resting across his midriff. One end of it was lodged against a toppled wood stove; the other sloped to the ground.

"I have to get out of here." Brad wiggled under the roof

support but couldn't find a gap.

"Can you move at all?" demanded Carla.

"Not much, and I think it's slipping down."

"Are you hurt?"

"No, just pinned."

Carla searched the rubble with her eyes. Then moving to a broken roof support, she pulled on it and twisted. With a groan, the bar let go at the weld.

"When I lever this up you crawl out from under it," she ordered.

"It's too heavy," objected Brad.

"Shut up and be ready!" Carla drove the bar home under the fallen ceiling. A snapped section of table served as her fulcrum and she heaved. The ceiling shifted but not enough.

"Could you use a hand?" Mark's voice came out of the dust-shrouded air. Without waiting for an answer he added his weight to the bar. The support strut inched up.

Brad scrambled free. "I'm out. Get the rest of the victims, but be outside before the deadline." Brad stumbled through the rubble until he came to a staircase. Climbing to its top he waited.

Eddie alternated between watching the decrepit tank and his watch. The seconds seemed to drag and the minutes fly. Another jet of steam erupted from the tank. More victims were carried from the building. Then the tank started to move.

Carla and Mark carried a victim on a blanket in the general direction of the exit. The dust cleared as they neared the outside, and the doorway became a bright spot in the gloom. A smashing sound blasted through the half demolished building and the dust swirled up just as they rushed into the light of day.

Brad heard the smashing sound and felt a tremor run through the staircase. He waited. The world filled with the groan of collapsing roof supports and the grinding of gears. A dark shape loomed below and before him. The shape drew closer sending up clouds of chocking dust in its wake then it was beneath him.

Brad leapt landing on the behemoth. He scrambled for a

handhold and managed to catch one of the mounting rails that were placed at intervals along the turret's side. Ignoring the pain he scrambled behind the turret just in time to avoid being hit with a mangled roof support. The tank ground on, there was a smashing sound and it emerged into daylight.

Brad blinked in the bright sunshine and scrambled up to the entry hatch on the turret's top. Placing the paddles of the defibrillator on the hatch he let a jolt go through it scrambling the electronic lock causing it to reset to factory default. He winced as his injured hands objected to holding the panels.

The tank began a slow turn as Brad punched in "0000" and the hatch popped open. He threw himself headfirst into the gunner's compartment scrambled around and pressed the button that closed the hatch behind him. The gunner's station was a small room with vid screens covering its forward wall. Controls for selecting ammunition type angle of shot and types of visual display were built into a chair that dominated the centre of the room. A hatch in the floor lead to the driver's section.

Taking a deep breath Brad pressed the open button in the floor and the hatch slid into the deck plating.

Brad quietly climbed down the ladder into the driver's compartment. It was a little over a meter high and long. At the front two seats sat behind a control console and viewing screens. In the middle, where the hatch let into, there was a foldout cot on each wall, separated by a walkway. The engineering control panels and another seat filled the back of the vehicle.

Brad pulled his gun and duck-walked silently forward. Oscar's attention remained riveted to his screens until Brad was immediately behind him.

Oscar swivelled his chair and leapt at Brad. The two men fell to the floor, and Brad's gun skittered out of his hand.

The tank careened to the side smashing the building in a random ark and slamming Brad against the wall winding him.

"I'm doing the right thing! I gotta do it for Bernice, gotta make a difference! Why are you trying to stop me?" Oscar grasped Brad's throat. Brad felt his brain begin to fizzle and pop as his air was cut off. Mustering his strength he slammed his closed fists against Oscars ears. Both men gasped with pain and Oscar released his grip.

Gasping for air Brad pushed himself clear of the other man then drove his boot heal into Oscar's jaw. Oscar hit the floor and lay unconscious.

"Shorting, that hurt." Brad scrambled into the driver's seat and stopped the tank's random travel through the building. Taking a deep breath he tried to ignore the throbbing in his hands and examined the controls.

"Shit!" Gingerly operating the controls he inched the throttle forward.

Carla watched the broken building that had been the clinic as a large section of its roof collapsed breaking the pattern of straight rows of destruction the tank had previously made.

"I think Brad got in," remarked Eddie.

Mark nodded in agreement.

"He was hurt. His hands haven't healed." Carla shifted uncomfortably from one foot to the other. All around her were people moving people and equipment away from the clinic building.

"Brad was the only one here who knows how to drive that thing." Eddie felt that the justification sounded hollow to himself.

"Brad tain't the type to go down easy. He'll be all right." Mark nervously brushed dust off his clothing.

There was a smashing sound and a section of the front of the building burst out as the tank rolled through and came to a stop in the middle of the street.

Brad turned off the drive system and threw open the intercom switch before racing to the back of the control chamber.

"*Eddie, get that hose here fast. I'm opening the back maintenance hatch. Connect it to the orange nozzle and get the water flowing.*" Brad threw himself into the engineering chair and began throwing switches. Several gauges on the console in front of him were in the red. After a moment a diagram showing a configuration of fuel rods appeared on the engineer's screen. Using a built in mouse Brad started moving the rods apart.

Eddie watched as two of his people rushed up and attached a water hose to the tank. Another pair of officers clambered up the tank's side and through the now open access hatch.

Brad directed the flow of water through the cooling pipes in the core chamber and watched as his gauges crept down into the orange. Two Novo-Gaian troopers dropped into the tank and secured Oscar who was still unconscious. Lifting his sleeve to his brow Brad wiped away a combination of sweat and grit leaving a smeared mess on his face.

"Sir, if the danger is passed, I have been instructed to tell you that Major Baily orders you to decontamination," said Private McDowl.

Carla washed the dust off herself in a horse troth as she waited for Dr. Frankle to finish scanning Brad with a Geiger-counter. Brad stood beside the tank wearing nothing but a towel as water dripped off him. Ingram waited to one side holding a hose at the ready.

"This is overkill. I didn't lose containment," complained Brad.

"It would appear you are clean. You may dress now, if you wish." Frankle smiled.

"About time!" Brad moved into his wagon.

"Is he really all right?" Carla moved to Frankel's side.

"Yes, we were all fortunate that the reactor's containment and shielding remained intact.

Eddie appeared in the inn's doorway smiling. "They've agreed to let us fire bomb the ruin," called Eddie.

"Finally. Why does it always take politicians so long to do what is obviously necessary?" said Frankel.

"How are the patients?" Brad emerged from his wagon pulling a comb through his wet hair.

"Recovering nicely. The viral cure is everything we hoped it would be. It stops the disease progress cold. I believe we can completely eradicate this contagion in little over a week."

Brad smiled and gestured at what was left of the clinic. "I'm glad I got my equipment out of there before this happened. Oh Doc, I hope you don't mind, I restocked from your stores."

"Not at all."

"Look over there." Carla, pointed to where a man with a camera and a female interviewer stood on the street with Francis.

"Carla, Ingram, would you hitch my team for me, please? Eddie, do you see what I see?" Brad pointed to Francis.

Eddie scowled. "Unfortunately."

"Major, my commission has not been officially deactivated. Perhaps we should see to it." Brad winked.

"Figured I'd hold off until you left Guelph. Wanted you to be Johnny-on-the-spot when you moved on to the central Tower Vils. Just in case."

Brad looked towards the interview then back to Eddie.

"Oh, I see." Eddie smiled. "Well, I guess there's no reason I can't deactivate you. After all, both you and Carla are immune. You should get back to your route." Eddie led the way into the house that was serving as Guelph H.Q. A portable file sat on the edge of his desk. He opened it and pulled out a form.

"Here it is. Day, month, year. I'll just write the time in and initial it. Sign on the dotted and you're officially off duty."

Brad smiled and signed. Eddie escorted him from the building and watched him walk towards Francis.

"Due to my prompt mobilization, the plague was contained and lives saved. Furthermore, it was only through the support we gave our field man that the goal of a cure could be realised. Now there are many heroes, but let me..."

Brad's fist slammed into Francis's face, and the politician sprawled on the ground. Brad grimaced and shook his hand as he spoke through the pain of his burns. "Bullshit! You left me and everyone else in the quarantine zone flapping in the breeze. There should have been a full biohazard team here the day I called for it, but you said no."

"Doctor Irving, what is your opinion of how this life threatening situation was handled?" asked the reporter, as Francis shook his head to clear it.

"It wasn't. The top was rotten and forced courageous people to act like cowards."

"I'll have you arrested for this. I'll have you court-martialled. I'll..." screamed Francis, turning red in the face.

"You'll nothing! My commission has been deactivated, and if you hadn't noticed, we're not in Novo Gaia. You want a piece of me, come and get it. Otherwise, shut up, you gutless wonder. You were too involved in getting re-elected to do your job. You screwed me and killed more people that I can count. Coward!" Brad turned and walked to Carla, who was securing his team's tack. The camera followed his every move.

"Good right hook. Next time put a bit more hip in it," suggested Ingram with a smile.

"Glad you liked it. I'll be in the Tower Vils for the next week in case he tries to weasel out of our bargain." Brad moved to Carla's side and took her dusty body in his arms, kissing her passionately. The kiss parted and he spoke.

"You've never seen a Tower Vil, have you?"

"No. What are they like?" Slipping from his arms, she opened the door and slid into his wagon. Brad followed her example.

"You're about to find out."

Epilogue

The Secret Agenda

SUSAN SAT ON the birthing stool, gritting her teeth.

"You're doing fine, me love, just fine." Dan stood behind her supporting her shoulders.

"He's right about that," reassured Meb from where she knelt in front of Susan.

"I got here as soon as I could. What's the problem?" demanded Brad, bursting into the room.

"That stupid boy. I told him to tell you it wasn't an emergency," snapped Meb.

"I just galloped from Aberfoyle to Eden Mills for nothing?" Brad massaged his buttocks and looked around the room. Its plaster walls had been thoroughly scrubbed, and the new wooden bed in its centre was comfortably appointed.

A baby's cry split the air. Meb lay the infant on a blanket while the afterbirth was expelled.

"I wouldn't call it nothing, Tinker. Not everyday Suzie and I have a..." Dan paused to glance at the child then finished "... pretty wee lass added to our family."

"Five fingers, five toes, two eyes, one nose," said Meb as she wiped the infant down. "Well, Brad, don't just stand there. Help

Susan to bed."

With a bemused expression, Brad moved to Susan's side. He and Dan each took an arm and helped her to the bed.

"Thanks, Tinker," she breathed then Meb placed the infant at her breast. Susan lost interest in everything else.

Dan stared at her for a minute then quietly followed Meb and Brad from the room.

"Fine looking daughter. Though I never took you for the settling-down type," said Brad, when they all stood in the hall outside the bedroom door.

"Man gets older, starts thinking about the things he hasn't done. Suzie felt the same. Figured we had to hurry, if it was to be. If you get my drift."

"I hear you. Look, I borrowed a racer to get here, so I don't have your contract with me."

"Not to worry, weren't expecting it. Not that far to the still in the visitors' field, and folk hereabouts know to keep it filled."

"I'm sorry you rushed over. The boy was supposed to say it was a social invitation," explained Meb.

"All I heard was they needed me to help with a birth. Oh yes. I have a letter from Carla for you, Meb, but it's back at my wagon."

"How is she?"

"She's straight A's at the academy, and the Guelph scholarship money is picking up all her fees. Frankel put a word in for her; they're taking her trip with me in lieu of her Dark Lands clinical term."

"And that's all?" Meb grinned.

Brad squirmed a bit then added, "Well, we did share residence last winter."

Meb smiled and Dan slapped Brad on the back.

"Well, that's a bit of good news, but I better be getting back to my Suzie and little Sylvia. Hope you don't mind showing yourselves out."

Brad wasn't sure if the vanishing back even heard his farewell.

"Come on, Tinker, I'll treat you to a meal." Meb led the way from Dan's house.

"Is he all right with a family and all? I mean, money-wise?" Brad stepped onto the street. Twenty-first-century houses lined their way.

"With the money pouring into Guelph there isn't a tradesman for sixty klicks out who can keep up with the demand. Folk have so much work that wages are coming up. Surprised you haven't noticed a change."

"I have. I had to hire space on a transport going to Guelph to carry everything in the radio order I received last winter. Did you hear that Wendell took over the inn?"

"Who?"

"Sorry, it's easy to forget who's who from that time. He was the life-mate of patient number one. I figure with his order, he'll be giving John a run for his money in a year or two. Be good for him to get away from the farm where it happened."

"Did you know they've decided to turn the area where your clinic was into a park?"

"Good use for it."

"Ingram arranged for it, before he went off to the academy. He's going to cost you money, that one."

"I can always push deeper into the Dark."

"Until there's no Dark left."

Brad smiled. "You just guessed the secret Novo Gaian agenda."